The Twentieth Century Fund is a research foundation undertaking timely analyses of economic, political, and social issues. Not-for-profit and nonpartisan, the Fund was founded in 1919 and endowed by Edward A. Filene.

John Brooks

A Twentieth Century Fund Book

T·T

TRUMAN TALLEY BOOKS
E. P. DUTTON
NEW YORK

Published in the United States by
Truman Talley Books • E. P. Dutton,
a division of NAL Penguin Inc.,
2 Park Avenue, New York, N.Y. 10016.

Published simultaneously in Canada by
Fitzhenry and Whiteside Limited, Toronto.

Library of Congress Cataloging-in-Publication Data

Brooks, John, 1920–
The takeover game.
"Truman Talley Books"
"A Twentieth Century Fund Book."
Bibliography: p.
1. Consolidation and merger of corporations—
United States.   I. Title.
HD2746.5.B76   1987   338.8'3'0973   87–5967
ISBN: 0-525-24586-3
W
Designed by Earl Tidwell
1 3 5 7 9 10 8 6 4 2
First Edition

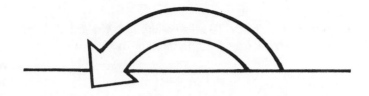

Contents

CONTENTS

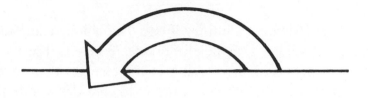

Foreword

It was not so long ago that *Wall Street* connoted both a precise location and a carefully ordered—and regulated—way of doing business in finance. There were clear lines of demarcation between commercial banks and investment banks, between stock brokerages and dealers in securities. The rules of the game for each group were set, and changes, when they took place, were brought about slowly and incrementally. But no longer. In the past few years, the financial business has undergone dramatic change—in technology, in the enforcement of antitrust legislation, in the shedding of regulation, and in the accelerating increase in international capital flows.

The Twentieth Century Fund has a long-standing interest in studying financial markets. When its Trustees and staff discerned the coming of the changes that have now shaken up Wall Street, it began to consider who best could describe and analyze what was beginning to take place in critical sectors. When it came to investment banks, once perhaps the most traditional and hallowed of all financial areas, the Fund quickly realized that there was no one better equipped to write about the transformation than John Brooks, who over the years has earned a well-deserved reputation for his informative and entertaining accounts of the personalities and rituals of the financial community. Some things, as he pointed out, such as man's greed and ingenuity, do not change, except perhaps in extent and magnitude. But in this book, more than in any of his others, Brooks has been faced with chronicling what amounts to a revolution in Wall Street, and has done so in the illuminating fashion that we expect of him.

The Fund is grateful to John Brooks for his masterly explanation of the new world of Wall Street. So, I am confident, will be his readers.

M. J. ROSSANT, Director

The Twentieth Century Fund

February 1987

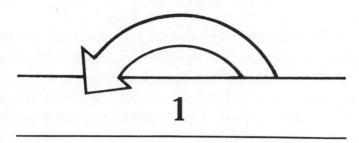

1

The Time
of the Takeovers

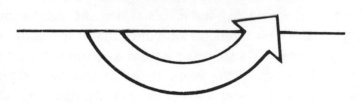

In July 1974, the International Nickel Company of Canada (INCO) announced that it was making, through a subsidiary, a $157 million tender offer to buy all of the common shares of ESB, Inc., a Philadelphia battery maker, for $28 per share. The day following the announcement, ESB announced that its board of directors was opposed to the offer on grounds that the price was too low, and would recommend to its stockholders that they decline to tender their shares.

Over the subsequent weeks, there ensued a series of events that over the years since 1974 has become perhaps painfully familiar: lawsuits and the threat of lawsuits; frantic conferences among the executives, investment bankers, lawyers, and public-relations experts of both companies, some of them lasting far into the night; announcements and paid advertisements from the two sides, each denouncing the other; and wary, tight-lipped conferences between representatives of aggressor and target, in which each tried to persuade the other to his point of view, or to arrive at an accommodation. The outcome of these maneuvers was that INCO proved to be willing to raise the price it would pay for ESB's shares. At last, in mid-August, INCO was able to announce that it had acquired 95 percent of ESB's shares at $41 per share—even though the market price of the stock at the time of the original offer had been below $20—and that the takeover was virtually complete.

The INCO-ESB transaction was covered in relatively small articles on the financial pages of the leading general-interest newspapers of the United States, and generally attracted little interest among laymen, even among those with some knowledge of financial affairs. What makes it of special interest in retrospect is the identity of the investment-banking firm representing INCO. It was Morgan Stanley & Company.

In the world of investment banking, Morgan Stanley was, and for years had been, the glass of fashion and the mold of form. It was the lineal successor in investment banking to the old J. P. Morgan & Company, which had ruled as a more or less benevolent despot over the field at the turn of the century, when investment banking had sometimes come close to controlling the country's economy. Morgan Stanley's lordliness was such that it would participate in a corporate stock or bond underwriting only as manager or co-manager, never as a mere participant; year after year, its managed or co-managed issues amounted to greater sums than those of any rival firm; it enjoyed the status of *traditional,* or customary, banker to General Motors, Exxon, IBM, U.S. Steel, Du Pont, and almost fifty other firms among the Fortune 500; and—although this aspect should not be overemphasized, since Morgan Stanley had always been known even more for professional astuteness than for the social elegance of its principals—as recently as 1965, when the country at large was moving into a period of revolt against tradition and social authority, almost half of its partners were listed in the *Social Register.*

Until INCO-ESB in 1974, Morgan Stanley had never represented the aggressor company in a hostile takeover attempt, and neither had most of its leading competitors. It was not that such takeovers were unknown at the time, although they were comparatively rare. (After all, the dramatic, and ultimately unsuccessful, attempt of Saul P. Steinberg and his Leasco Corporation to take over Chemical Bank through an exchange of securities had been one of the major business events of 1969.) It was, rather, that until 1974 hostile takeovers had been widely regarded in Wall Street as a dirty business, beneath the dignity of the likes of Morgan Stanley. For many decades, the prevailing ethic among the leading investment-banking firms had been gentlemanly cooperation as opposed to competitive confrontation (and that ethic, as much as anything else, had provided the ammunition for the antitrust case

3

against the leading firms that the federal government had brought in 1947). Managing hostile takeovers, among the investment-banking elite, was, in the words of an old Noel Coward song, "seldom if ever done"—a powerful sanction in a business that in 1974 (and still to a degree now) was ruled by custom as much as by law.

As to why Morgan Stanley did it, a whole complex of forces seems to have been at work. The face of investment banking was changing. Securities underwriting—the traditional job of investment bankers, which had accounted for 95 percent of Morgan Stanley's business until the early 1960s—was becoming increasingly competitive and decreasingly profitable. Large-scale trading in already-issued securities, once left by the leading underwriters to lesser firms, had become, in the rising era of the institutional market and the huge block trade, a sine qua non for investment-banking firms; Morgan Stanley, struggling to adapt to the new environment, had begun such trading in 1970. The aggressive young head of the firm's Mergers and Acquisitions Department, Robert F. Greenhill, felt strongly that the time had come to take the next step in modernization by abandoning the old company taboo against hostile takeovers. Recalling the INCO-ESB affair now, Robert H. B. Baldwin, then Morgan Stanley's president and chief operating officer, says,

> We did a lot of mental gymnastics about it. There had been some hostile takeovers in London, and we saw that it was coming, whatever we did. You can't stop water; it will find its level. When the water rises in London, it will soon flood New York. We set ground rules. We decided that we'd never do a hostile take-

4

over for a company that wasn't already a client of ours—and INCO was a client. Moreover, we made it a rule that we would always be careful to advise the aggressor company that "a lot of people are going to be unhappy." And then, we went ahead.

Baldwin insists that the INCO deal was not a watershed either for Morgan Stanley or for the investment-banking business, but others feel otherwise. A Wall Street observer has said that it "changed the whole nature of the business and the whole nature of the firm," and "made aggressive action respectable."[1]

The nature of the business was indeed changing, and in revolutionary ways. Symbolic of that change was a virtual reversal of the public and private style in which investment banking in the 1980s was and is conducted. First of all, the key people involved are a new breed: exceptionally bright and ambitious young men (and women; in 1985 it was estimated that at least one-third of entry-level investment-banking jobs were occupied by women, although there were virtually none at or near the top) willing to work long hours, including overnight when required, rather than the old, trust-inspiring underwriter-gentlemen of proper breeding and schooling, breathing out casual charm and an air of leisure. The old courtesy-before-competition ethic is gone or all but gone: when a member of one investment bank today speaks of another firm as "lacking total greed," that is meant as criticism—a snide implication that the less-than-totally-greedy firm still clings too sentimentally to obsolete ways.

Or consider the advertisements that investment

5

banks now put in newspapers and magazines, as opposed to those they used to. Until quite recently, the sole form of investment-bank ad was the celebrated "tombstone," announcing a new issue of securities and listing the firms managing and participating in its underwriting. Such ads were (and, of course, are—tombstones continue to flourish) of little interest to the layman; and their interest can hardly be increased by the fact that, in conformity with the securities laws, they invariably state either that they are not offers or solicitations to buy the securities, because such offer is made only in the prospectus, or else that the securities have already been sold and the advertisement appears only as a matter of record. On the other hand, tombstone ads are of intense interest to underwriters because, by a tradition that still lives, the placement of the name of each participating firm indicates with exquisite precision its status in the business in relation to the others. At the top, of course, comes the lead underwriter (or underwriters) responsible for managing the issue; below come the members of various successive "brackets," the members of each bracket listed alphabetically. The lines between them are invisible to the layman but well understood by all investment bankers. A position at the left-hand margin is desired and sought after, sometimes even at the expense of more substantive privileges in the syndicate. Some years ago, according to Harvard's Samuel Hayes, "the managing partner of a well-known house fatally shot himself when he learned that his firm was being denied what he considered its rightful bracket position in an important syndicated issue."

Along with these intricate and explicit announcements of hierarchical rank, investment banks now, for the first time ever, aggressively advertise their services to prospective corporate clients. Nor, in doing so, do they always stop short of using Madison Avenue's more baroque manifestations of whimsy. In 1984, First Boston Corporation flooded the major newspapers and magazines with an ad featuring a huge picture of the face of a baby, captioned, "The $40 Billion Baby That the World Hasn't Adopted Yet." (The text beneath explained that the "$40 Billion Baby" was interest-rate swaps.) The ad had been devised by First Boston's newly hired agency, Della Femina, Travisano and Partners, a more or less swinging Madison Avenue shop that, according to its co-founder, had first made the big time by plugging a product called Pretty Feet.

If traditional dignity was out of the window in the new form of investment-bank advertising, so was traditional discretion and restraint. In January 1984, First Boston ran an ad touting its services to corporations defending against threatened or actual takeover attempts. "You Owe Your Shareholders the Best Defense," the ad was headed; and it went on to list twenty-one "strategic devices" that First Boston claimed the competence and the willingness to employ in defense of a threatened client, including "staggered board election," "super majority vote," "blocking preferred," "going private," "self-tender," "stock repurchase," and "poison pill." Among these, as any connoisseur of the takeover game will recognize, are various strategic devices that some have considered abusive or potentially illegal.

In fact, a year later, when First Boston in another ad

7

listed its merger-acquisition-and-divestiture activity during 1984, only two successful takeover defenses were included (and an enormous third one, Phillips Petroleum vs. Mesa Partners, still undecided at the time) out of a total of 135 transactions. So the original ad would appear to have been only moderately successful in attracting clients. But the point here is style. If its advertising may be taken as a measure, investment banking had abruptly reversed the style that it had always held most dear.[2]

Along with the new style went new substance. Before we come to the biggest and most far-reaching new element— the prevalence of multibillion-dollar mergers, both friendly and hostile, and the related frenetic trading of takeover stocks that came to an initial climax in 1986, with the ominous insider-trading scandals involving Dennis B. Levine and Ivan F. Boesky—let us pause to look briefly at recent changes in several other forms of investment-banking activity.

Underwriting. The traditional activity of investment banks has changed its nature in a dramatic way. In the 1960s, the time-honored system—underwriting and distribution of new securities of important companies by large syndicates, their places in the syndicates determined by a well-defined hierarchy—was still in full operation, and such underwriting was still the fountainhead of investment-banking profit; in 1969 it still constituted the second-largest source of gross income, after security commissions, to New York Stock Exchange member firms.

The 1970s brought an avalanche of new conditions:

8

the beginnings of stock-trading deregulation, notably the end of fixed commissions on Stock Exchange trades in 1975; galloping inflation, particularly after the OPEC oil embargo of 1973–74; galloping overhead costs at securities firms; huge increases in the volatility of bond interest rates, culminating in the Federal Reserve Board's October 1979 decision to abandon control of interest rates in favor of stabilizing money-supply growth; increasing international underwriting, largely beyond the reach of what remained of American regulation; and a gradual breakdown of the old hierarchical Wall Street structure under the pressure of increased competition. In particular, interest-rate volatility meant increased risk for bond issues. With interest rates sometimes moving 100 basis points (or 1 percent) in a couple of days, where once three basis points over a like period had been considered a big move, a small error in timing could cost a corporation a huge sum in the price it got for new bonds, sometimes with disastrous consequences. Issuers clamored for the right to put their securities on the market more quickly than they had formerly done, in order to catch the most favorable moment—the "window of opportunity." Late in the decade, a complaisant Securities and Exchange Commission cut down the waiting period from registration to sale of new securities from the long-required twenty days to as little as forty-eight hours in certain cases.

Then in March 1982 came the symbolic, though not necessarily the most important, event in the deregulation of underwriting: the promulgation by the SEC, after a vehement debate in which Wall Street had generally taken a negative stand, of Rule 415, under which qualifying corporations could register a quantity of securities for a period of two years—and then put them on sale piecemeal, with no waiting period, at chosen intervals over the two years. Billions of dollars' worth of bonds or stocks of leading companies could now be released with no notice at all, and sold by the underwriters in a matter of hours or even minutes. Or sold by *one* underwriter: Rule 415 brought to the United States a type of transaction previously known in modern times chiefly in the Eurodollar market: the *bought deal,* in which a single firm buys an entire issue from a corporation and then markets it unassisted, using its own distribution facilities.

Apart from the introduction of the bought deal, the effects of Rule 415 in its first three years were less far-reaching and deleterious than its detractors had predicted. Among those effects were: improvement of the market opportunities available to securities issuers, and reduction of their middleman costs, enabling them to get somewhat better prices for their offerings—the chief effect that had been intended by the new rule's promulgators; a drastic reduction in the size of syndicates, resulting in the freeze-out of smaller broker-dealer firms, many of them based outside New York City; and unprecedentedly furious competition among the handful of New York–based investment-banking giants, resulting in underwriting "spreads" averaging, for bond issues, much less than 1 percent of the new security's price.* Finally—and, in the

*The underwriting *spread* is the difference between the price at which underwriters buy a security from a corporation and that at which they offer it to investors; as such, it represents the underwriters' gross revenue in the transaction.

opinion of some, most critically—because of the speed with which new issues could now be brought to market, Rule 415 appeared to compromise seriously the possibility for the underwriters to comply with the Securities Act of 1933 by exercising "due diligence" in determining the integrity and intrinsic value of the securities being offered. That is, the cost of increased speed and efficiency to the seller seemed to be decreased fairness to the buyer.

Trading. Rule 415 and, particularly, the bought deal tend to transform the underwriting of securities into simple block trading among giants: investment banks on one side, financial institutions such as pension funds on the other. The change is part of a larger trend that has been going on since well before Rule 415. Over the past decade, the investment-banking business has been perfused by a trading, or *transactional,* environment. Previously, investment banks tended to look down on securities trading, and some to avoid it entirely except for price-stabilization activities in the open market during offerings of new securities. Traders were thought of as "gnomes," devoid of cachet; underwriters were the house aristocrats.

But in the 1970s, lower spreads were taking some of the profit out of underwriting, and simultaneously, market volatility was creating new opportunities in trading. The best market for traders is a bull market, the second best a bear market (in which short selling can be profitably employed); the worst is a stable one. In the late seventies and early eighties, with the institutional investors who now dominated the markets strongly oriented to short-term profit, those markets were anything but stable. Trading had now become the biggest single source of revenue to investment banks. One of its offshoots, *risk arbitrage*—investment in stocks on the basis of presumed price rises caused by impending mergers and acquisitions—was now massively practiced at all of the leading firms. (Its second cousin, venture-capital investment by a firm for its own account in promising start-up situations, real-estate ventures, and the like, became the fastest-rising manifestation of investment bankers' reach for the brass ring. The giant First Boston Corporation, which first invested for its own account as recently as 1977, was said in 1984 to have between 10 and 20 percent of its capital committed to venture capital, and a partner in another leading firm told a Harvard Business School professor in the same year that he expected that in ten years *merchant banking*—investment for its own account—would account for one-third of his firm's profits.)

The new trading environment has changed the structure and character of investment banking. It has changed, for example, the character of the leadership. Traditional underwriting men—the sort who ran the firms until recently—have moved their desks to quarters near the trading rooms. Meanwhile, men with backgrounds in trading have moved to the top. In 1983, Lewis L. Glucksman, a trader, became first co-chief executive and then chief executive of Lehman Brothers. (He went out the following year when the company was sold in an atmosphere of extreme internal rancor.) Also in 1983, at First Boston—where once the underwriters' quarters were called "the House of Lords" and the trading desks "the House of

Commons"—Peter T. Buchanan, a trader, was named chief executive.

Even Morgan Stanley, almost exclusively an underwriting firm until less than twenty years ago, in 1984 named as its president Richard B. Fisher, the man who had taken the lead in pushing the firm into trading.[3]

The trading climate has wildly increased the importance of equity capital in the business. Whereas the old underwriting business was based on experience and prestige, block trading and venture investing, not to mention bought deals, call for huge commitments of a banking firm's own money. One now needs a large capital base simply to be in the game. A few firms, led by Goldman Sachs,* First Boston, and Morgan Stanley, accumulated the necessary capital through internal growth and public sale of their stock; the other giants, such as Shearson Lehman Brothers and Salomon Brothers, acquired much of their capital through mergers with firms either inside or outside the investment-banking business. In 1949, only seven of the sixteen leading firms charged by the government with antitrust violations had capital of $5 million or larger; two of them had less than $2 million. As late as 1970, Morgan Stanley had $7.5 million, much of that sum uncertain because it belonged to partners over sixty-

*Actually, Goldman, Sachs & Co. Throughout this book, I have omitted commas in the names of investment-banking firms on the grounds that their relentless use would be an act of pedantry at the expense of readability. For the record, the following frequently mentioned firms use or used one or more commas: Bear, Stearns & Co.; Dillon, Read & Co.; Goldman, Sachs & Co.; Halsey, Stuart & Co.; Kidder, Peabody & Co.; Kohlberg, Kravis, Roberts & Co.; Kuhn, Loeb & Co.; Lee, Higginson & Co.; and—the most eccentrically punctuated of all—Merrill Lynch, Pierce, Fenner & Smith.

five years old. In 1986, Merrill Lynch had $3.1 billion in capital; Salomon Brothers, $2.9 billion; Shearson Lehman, $2.8 billion; Drexel Burnham, $1.8 billion; Goldman Sachs, $1.5 billion; and six other firms $1 billion or more.

One effect of the new capital-intensive, trading-oriented atmosphere was to raise into the rarefied air at the top of the profession certain firms that had never been there before. Salomon Brothers, for example, made it into the so-called *special bracket*—the top five in the management of underwriting syndicates—because of its capital and because, far ahead of the pack, it had brashly specialized in the scorned field of large-scale bond trading and thus acquired superior access to institutional investors. "We weren't a member of the Club of Seventeen that the government sued in 1947," says John H. Gutfreund, chief executive of Salomon, and adds with a wry smile, "although we would have liked to have been." For another example, Merrill Lynch made the special bracket largely as a result of the nonpareil access it had gained to the individual investor over many decades through its huge network of retail brokerage offices. Others of the old Club of Seventeen—among them Kuhn Loeb, White Weld, and Glore Forgan—had disappeared into the maws of merger partners for a variety of reasons, not the least of which was failure to adapt themselves sufficiently to radically new conditions.[4]

New products. Yet another effect of the new conditions has been to bring into being in investment banking a new sort of "creativity." In the ever-more-zealous quest for new sources of profit, teams of young MBAs are set to work dreaming up "new products" that may create new and profitable markets, if sometimes only for a short time before those markets become overrun by competitors. In the late seventies, Robert Dall and Lewis Ranieri of Salomon Brothers conceived the notion of packaging mortgages backed by the U.S. government into securities for sale to the public. The market grew like a mushroom; Goldman Sachs and others quickly planted and reaped their own crops. By late 1984, there were some $270 billion in mortgage-backed securities on the market; for that year, dealings in such securities generated about half of Salomon's pretax income; and Mr. Ranieri—all of thirty-seven years old by that time—told *The New York Times* that he had "more money than I ever knew existed."

In 1982, Salomon and Merrill Lynch adopted the idea of buying Treasury bonds, stripping them of their interest, and then selling the stripped bonds and the interest coupons separately, at appropriate discounts. (The Treasury at first considered the stripping of its bonds to be defacing of government property, but by 1985 it had reversed itself so decisively that it took to issuing stripped bonds itself.) The esoteric advantage of this procedure, especially for pension plans, is that it enables purchasers, because of the discounts offered, to lock in current high interest rates not just on principal, but also on interest itself as it accrues. Salomon called its "product" CATS, for "Certificates of Accrual on Treasury Securities"; Merrill called its version TIGRs, for "Treasury Investment Growth Receipts." Soon others joined the game, and Lazard Frères put the office crossword-puzzle addict to work thinking up catchy acronyms for its products. In October 1984, syndicates headed by Salomon advertised and marketed, with little fanfare, two new issues of its CATS totaling $3.789 billion—more than three times the total of Salomon's enormous equity capital at that time.

Perhaps the most esoteric of vastly successful new products is the interest-rate swap, developed in 1982 in Europe, and intended to help large corporations manage their liabilities—by, for example, borrowing money in one currency and paying the interest in another. First Boston, along with the ever-present Salomon Brothers, was most active among investment banks in 1984 in interest-rate swaps, which were then being used regularly by at least a thousand top U.S. corporations.[5]

Thus there has emerged in investment banking a new figure: the cloistered inventor, counterpart of the research scientist in manufacturing industry (and, indeed, quickly nicknamed the "rocket scientist" by his colleagues). Unlike others in the business, the new-product man needs no social aplomb or marketing skills. Usually (like other inventors at their peak) he is still on the good side of forty or even thirty; he often has a background in mathematics; he sits alone with his computer, seldom consulting texts or colleagues (and often drawing a six-figure salary), trying out new combinations until he hits on one that may bring some investors a small but significant edge, and his firm a vast profit. He needs no capital—only an inventive brain. ("Investment bankers are no *better* than corporate people or commercial bankers," says a partner in a leading firm. "But we're smarter.")*

*By way of refutation of the claim that investment bankers are smarter than corporate people, the chief financial officer of a leading American corporation

The Time of the Takeovers

The very term *new products* to describe investment vehicles has an alarming connotation to a layman. Specifically, it calls to mind Charles E. Mitchell's use of the word *manufacturing* to describe his method of operating his National City Company in the 1920s. ("We have," Mitchell said, "a certain part of an organization—and it amounts to a large force—devoting itself to the manufacture of long-term credits suitable for public distribution, and for the analysis of the production of other manufacturers.") By the mid-eighties, however, the new products of investment banks looked less sinister than merely ingenious, and sometimes economically useful. Often client-driven even though they originated in the heads of investment bankers, they represented adaptation to the needs of corporations and large investors in times of radically new market conditions—for example, wildly fluctuating interest rates and currency-exchange rates. Certainly their proliferation had brought about confusion in the time-honored storefront of the securities business, the local retail brokerage office. Brokers who five years earlier had dealt in stocks, corporate and municipal bonds, and not much else now found themselves pressed by their companies to market a multiplicity of investment vehicles the significance and risks of which they did not begin to grasp. Understandably, they sometimes marketed them to inappropriate customers, and lawsuits ensued. "Very few

offers the following instance: The CFO's company was selling one of its divisions to a foreign buyer, with a top-ranked investment banking firm representing the buyer, and the selling company representing itself. As part of the deal, the American corporation succeeded in *selling*, and actually getting paid for, a $10–$20-million deferred-tax liability that had been plaguing the division it wanted to get rid of—a feat that one would think P. T. Barnum might have admired.

brokers fully understand" many of the new products, said Ira Lee Sorkin, head of the SEC's New York office, in 1984; moreover, he added, "very few regulators do, either." Just as new computers were being pressed upon customers who might find themselves unable to use them, so were new forms of securities.[6]

Do the investment-banking "new products" of the 1980s help or hurt small investors? On balance, the evidence suggests, they help; for example, zero-coupon high-grade bonds provide a safe way of maximizing return on individual retirement plans. According to the theoretical laws of economics, every investment that carries higher interest than others must involve increased risk. Yet stripped bonds, for one example, actually increase interest (provided, of course, that the long-term trend of interest rates is downward) without increasing risk at all. The geniuses of the new investment banking would seem to have found some real boons to investors.

The corporate takeover, and more particularly the hostile takeover, is the most controversial, and quite possibly the most characteristic, activity of the new investment banking.

Investment bankers were deeply involved as corporate advisers in the previous merger waves—the first at the turn of the century, the second in the 1920s, the third in the 1960s—that swept over the American corporate landscape; but seldom if ever before have investment bankers had so much visibility, or reaped such financial rewards, as they have in their roles as advisers to attackers and defenders in the current wave, which may be said, broadly speaking, to have begun with INCO's takeover of ESB in 1974. The typical opening maneuver in the new takeover wave—or, very often, the event that starts a chain of events ending in a takeover—is a cash tender offer to which the directors and managers of the target company react with more or less hostility. Then the offer may be improved upon, either by the original aggressor or by some other company; meanwhile the target company, assisted by its investment bankers, may solicit a bid from yet another company with which it is more content to merge—a *white knight.* Eventually, either a white knight or a hostile aggressor consummates the deal. Or the takeover attempt may be defeated, sometimes by one or another of the sort of defensive maneuvers advertised by First Boston, sometimes through the target company's satisfying the aggressor by buying back his initial stake in its stock at a premium over the market price—the almost-universally-deplored practice known as *greenmail.*

The economic bases of the takeover wave are usually assumed to be two: the underevaluation (or the perceived underevaluation) of the assets of asset-heavy companies by the stock market and the ready availability of credit in gargantuan amounts from commercial banks and other lenders—which are able to get premium interest rates on takeover loans, and which, in the earlier 1980s, had ample reason to be disillusioned with huge loans to other types of borrowers, such as foreign governments and domestic oil entrepreneurs—to finance the efforts of aggressors to get their hands on the undervalued assets at bargain prices. Such bases appear rational, and indeed, on their face, they are. (For a more detailed discussion of takeover motives, see Chapter 8.) But the takeover movement made so many people so rich so quickly that it generated its own momentum, and by the mid-eighties had become emotionally charged and apparently irrational—a sort of Damoclean sword hanging over much of the corporate world. The $9-billion takeover of Conoco by Du Pont in 1981, and the $13.2-billion takeover of Gulf Oil by Standard Oil of California in 1984—each the final outcome of a series of maneuvers involving various smaller public companies or private investors—led both the public and corporate executives to realize that now almost any company, no matter how large or long-established, was vulnerable.

The Gibraltar-like corporate bastions of the past were no longer inviolate. Once a company was put "in play" by an initial bid—even a shakily financed bid by some entrepreneurial upstart—the dynamics of the situation dictated that it would probably end up being taken over by somebody, because the directors and managers of the target, being bound to represent the interest of their stockholders, faced legal and moral difficulties if they refused without explanation an offer well above the market price of the stock. (Meanwhile, the fees paid investment advisers for takeover work, particularly when successful, constituted an enormous incentive to them to initiate and execute such transactions; a Harvard Business School professor calculated that in the $2-billion Texaco-Getty transaction of 1984 one investment banker was paid $126,582 per hour of work.) Peter Drucker, dean of management experts, argued in 1984 that the trustees of pension funds, the Goliaths of institutional investors, had abetted if not created the takeover craze by going along with aggressors in order to avoid the charge of violating their fiduciary responsibilities to their constituents; he added that takeover fear had "traumatized" corporate employees, from senior managers down to the rank and file, and that it was "a main cause of the decline in America's competitive strength in the world economy."[7]

Those conclusions are arguable, and the arguments will be assessed later. For the moment, some ostensibly minor aspects of the takeover wars may show them in an oblique and revealing light. In December 1984, when T. Boone Pickens and his Mesa Petroleum Company of Texas made a takeover run on giant Phillips Petroleum, Phillips brought suit in a Delaware court alleging that about two years earlier Pickens, in concluding an earlier takeover attempt on General American Oil Company, had signed a "standstill agreement" promising not to try to acquire any of various companies, Phillips among them, for five years. However, the written agreement did not mention Phillips by name, and the contention that Phillips had been intended to be included in it was challenged by Pickens. It happened that Joseph G. Fogg III, chief of mergers and acquisitions at Morgan Stanley, who was now representing Phillips in its battle against Pickens, had been Pickens's investment banker in 1983 when the standstill agreement had been signed; and the key question in the Delaware courtroom now came to be, What had Fogg said to Pickens at that time? Phillips, in papers filed with the court, declared that Fogg and the takeover lawyer Joseph H. Flom had explained that the agreement "would operate to bar Mesa from seeking

21

control of Phillips," and that Pickens had "recognized the fact, expressed a lack of concern, and proceeded to execute the agreement." Pickens and Mesa denied that it had happened that way at all. The judge ruled for Pickens, and Mesa's takeover attempt went forward (at least until three days later, when an accommodation was reached between the parties).

Apart from the question of confidentiality raised by the fact that Fogg, now representing Phillips, used as evidence against Pickens a conversation between him and his former client who was now Phillips's antagonist, there remained the curious and disturbing conclusion that, for a moment, the fate of a great company had apparently turned on what an investment banker and a lawyer had said to their client, in private, in the midst of the haste and confusion of a takeover battle many months earlier.

The insouciance of some merger proceedings was illustrated vividly the following month—January 1985—when Occidental Petroleum Company and Diamond Shamrock Corporation almost merged, but didn't. Agreement in principle on terms for a merger of the two companies was reached over the weekend of January 5–6, and announced on the morning of January 7. That same afternoon, after the boards of the two companies had met, the merger was called off. What was startling was the subsequent revelation of how it had almost come about. William Bricker, chairman of Diamond Shamrock, explained that since well before the first of the year, he and the top executives of Occidental had been talking on "an entirely different subject"—some said, although Bricker denied, that it had been the possibility of making a joint bid for

Phillips—when suddenly, on about January 2, they had changed the subject and begun talking about a merger with each other. Out of such casual, almost accidental conversations, it appeared, had almost come a merger that would have involved $3.2 billion.

Finally, consider the case of the highest, although not the winning, bid in the case of Gulf Oil in 1984. A firm called Kohlberg Kravis Roberts & Company was at the time (and still is) a leader in the takeover-related business of *leveraged buyouts*—the "taking private" of public corporations by groups usually including the target company's management, accomplished largely through borrowings to be repaid out of the target company's assets or future cash flow. The Kohlberg firm had been formed in 1976 by a group of refugees from the investment-banking firm of Bear Stearns & Company. In the thick of the Gulf fight, the Kohlberg firm came in with a bid of $87.50 per share for Gulf stock—$7.50 per share more than the bid of the eventual winner, Standard Oil of California, with about half of the sum required, or more than $7.2 billion, to be paid in cash. (A Kohlberg principal said later that his firm had prepared a fee on the deal of "around the $50-million level.") Gulf reportedly rejected the Kohlberg bid partly because it would have taken four to six months to consummate. When eight-year-old Kohlberg Kravis Roberts & Company could command the resources, and the nerve, to submit the highest bid for imperial Gulf Oil, the world of corporate finance was indeed turned upside down.[8]

The colloquial language of mergers and acquisitions—"bear hugs," "two-tier offers," "scorched-earth policies," "shark repellents," "Pac-Man defenses," "crown-jewel options," "poison pills," "greenmail," "golden parachutes," even "in play"—point clearly to the perception of such activity by the participants as being a game. The almost childishly frivolous nomenclature is generally attributed to the fact that the principal players, that is, the investment bankers, are almost all young and therefore not many years from their time on actual playing fields. (Indeed, they had better be young; the merger and acquisition business, as Woody Allen has said of filmmaking, is not for the old or the tired. In the mid-eighties a young woman who had been research assistant to a Harvard Business School professor went to work in mergers and acquisitions at one of the biggest investment-banking firms; finding herself on the job one hundred hours per week, she quit after three months. Such a debilitating schedule hardly suggests the joy traditionally associated with play; but then, neither do the exhausting practice schedules and tension-filled competition to which top athletes in the age of sports professionalism are subjected—and to which some of them, like the teenage tennis star Tracy Austin, eventually succumb.)

It is tempting to think of the American takeover business as a board game, the board being the grid of Manhattan Island, where more than ever before the investment bankers and their lawyers are concentrated. At a certain point in the mid-eighties, at 919 Third Avenue and 299 Park Avenue, respectively, were spotted Joseph Flom and Martin Lipton, the two leading takeover lawyers; westward, at 1251 Avenue of the Americas, sat Eric Gleacher, Fogg's successor as head of M&A at Morgan

Stanley; nearby, at Park Avenue Plaza, were Joseph Perella and Bruce Wasserstein of First Boston; and, in a cluster down at the southern tip of the island, Geoffrey Boisi of Goldman Sachs, Jay Higgins of Salomon, and Kenneth Miller of Merrill Lynch. The mere physical move, by taxi or limousine, of one of these counters to the square of a famous corporation, or to the square occupied by another of their own number, was an important development in the game.

The Dutch philosopher Johan Huizinga, in his famous book *Homo Ludens,* first published in 1944, argues that "a far-reaching contamination of play and serious activity has taken place." "The two spheres are getting mixed," Huizinga goes on to say, with the result that in recognized play—actual sport—"the indispensable qualities of detachment, artlessness, and gladness are . . . lost." The converse of Huizinga's thesis seems to be borne out, since his time, in the surface playfulness of the takeover game. Radical changes in the structure of huge corporations that produce goods, provide jobs, and support communities are surely a serious matter; and if a sportive approach to such activity at least provides a new form of spectator entertainment for the public, it certainly seems to constitute a "contamination" of play and serious activity, and, as far as the participants are concerned, to lack detachment, artlessness, and gladness.[9]

Instant new offerings with reduced public disclosure; massive short-term trading in already-issued securities; a wave of hostile takeovers that, whatever else they do, are virtually certain to increase the debt loads of important companies, and may end in their partial or total dismemberment; a rash of leveraged buyouts, which by definition have a similar effect: these and other characteristics of the new investment banking all point to the presence of a new speculative era in American finance, with greater emphasis on short-term profit and less thought to the day after tomorrow—sowing the wind, and not worrying about reaping the whirlwind.

One cause of the new speculative era may be simple chronology. For all the laws and rules (most of them dating from the 1930s) that are intended to encourage long-term stability of the economy, the American investment climate continues, in conformity with both economic and human laws, to be cyclical, though the cycle lacks a fixed periodicity. Following a boom and bust, burned and frightened investors lie low for a while, and reforms are put in place. Then, gradually at first, inventive, adaptive minds find new paths to quick profit. As the new movement feeds on itself, it accelerates; memories of the last bust fade, greed again takes precedence over fear, and a new era of speculation comes into being. By such a process, the last speculative era—that of the late 1960s, often called "the go-go years"—has been succeeded by a new one. Another cause, surely, is the march of technology. The coming of the video screen providing instant access to price changes, the refinement of the computer, the perfection of the automobile telephone, and other technical advances tend to put the whole national investment community* effectively on one trading floor, and

*Indeed, the whole *world* investment community. The effect of new technology, combined with that of economic booms in many foreign countries and

thus to increase the speed and efficiency of the market; this increased efficiency diminishes the investor's chance for reward, causing professionals to increase the scale of their operations and to seek exotic, original devices to outwit the market for a moment. Finally, the new mood is undeniably part of a larger, worldwide one transcending the boundaries of the investment business: "The whole pace of life is changing," says John Gutfreund of Salomon Brothers, describing investment banking in the mid-eighties. "There's a sense of hyperactivity, of frenzy. It permeates all society, and is constantly and vividly reflected on television and in the newspapers."*

It will, at any rate, be instructive to compare and contrast the go-go years and the 1980s as examples of speculative booms. The contrasts are striking. In the 1960s, a corporation's goal was constant earnings growth,

increased access of Americans to foreign markets because of deregulation, made internationalization of American investment banking one of its major trends in the 1980s. This subject is discussed further in Chapter 10.

*Philosophically and politically, meanwhile, Wall Street's relative disregard of the social impact of its actions in the 1980s was encouraged by the rise of the so-called efficient-markets theory. Largely the product of American academia over the past two decades, the efficient-markets theory comes in several forms of varying strength; in essence, it holds that at any given moment, the market price of a security fully reflects all available information about it. In the 1980s, academic literature purporting to present empirical evidence for the theory proliferated, and it came to be taken seriously in many countries. Broadly speaking, it became the basis of Reagan administration economic policy. Its implication for deregulation is obvious: what can regulation of securities trading achieve but distortions of "natural" prices? The theory is seldom taken seriously on Wall Street, which derives its profit from market inefficiencies—for one example, the case of a company whose stock price does not reflect its known asset value. There is some irony in the fact that American investment banking was generally left free to reap huge profits in the 1980s partly because of a theory refuted by those profits themselves.

leading to a high stock price in relation to earnings; such growth was sometimes obtained in the traditional way, by more efficient production and increased sales, but very often it was obtained in other ways—through accounting trickery, aggressive salesmanship, or making use of an already inflated stock price to buy companies with lower price-to-earnings ratios, thus creating illusory growth. In the 1970s and 1980s, earnings growth and price-to-earnings ratio had become secondary, and sometimes all but ignored. Undervalued assets—takeover bait—were the new name of the game. In the 1960s, investors, both institutional and individual, looked for a long, unbroken series of reported quarterly earnings increases. In the eighties—when such increases might go on for years before being more than marginally reflected in stock price—they looked more often for the asset-rich, price-depressed company that might bring them a 30- or 50-percent profit overnight through a takeover offer.

Underwriting in the sixties was mostly its staid old self, except for a hectic fad for new issues of untried and sometimes barely existent companies, many of them ostensibly devoted to new technology—the so-called garbage market. Such was these stocks' popularity that by issue time they often commanded market prices well above the offering price—only to drop, in two or three years, to virtual worthlessness. Such was their profitability to underwriters that dozens of new investment-banking firms sprang up to distribute them—and, in many cases, to vanish with their collapse. In the eighties, or at least in the first half of the decade, there was no garbage market. Except for a period in 1983, new issues were not a prominent feature of the markets until the unprecedented bull market of 1986.

The contrast is especially visible in the nature of mergers. In the go-go years, companies were taken over almost always with the agreement of the target's managers and directors, through exchanges of stock that, at current prices, increased the value of the holdings of the target company's shareholders. Since the antitrust laws as enforced at the time usually prevented vertical or horizontal mergers within an industry, almost all of the takeovers were *exogenous,* that is, conglomerate mergers. The new elements in the mergers of the 1980s were willingness of the buying company to deal with hostility on the part of the target and the use of borrowed cash, rather than market-inflated securities, as the buyer's currency. Moreover, with antitrust enforcement in an extreme phase of laxity, even the biggest mergers of all, such as the oil mergers of early 1984, could now be intra-industry, bringing into being in the oil patch an era of consolidation like nothing seen in any industry since the end of the last century.

As the chief goal of the mergers of the go-go years was increased earnings per share, the chief goal of the 1980s mergers was acquisition of undervalued assets. As the acquirers of companies in the sixties usually intended to operate them or let them operate themselves, those of the eighties—particularly as the decade wore on—seemed more and more often to be for the purpose of dismantling them in whole or in part for a quick-cash profit.

The characteristic "players" of the two booms were similar in one feature—their bias toward youth—but contrasting in their functions. Those of the go-go years were conglomerate bosses and managers of institutional port-folios, whom the writer "Adam Smith" aptly nicknamed "gunslingers"; those of the eighties were investment bankers, takeover lawyers, corporate raiders, and deal-minded corporate executives. The former two were at least incidentally surrogates for small investors; the latter two, for all their protestations of concern for stockholders, were in a functional sense tending to their own concerns first and those of the stockholders afterward.

Finally, one great similarity exists between the two eras. The "gunslingers" and conglomerators of the 1960s on the one hand, and the traders, new-product inventors, merger-makers, arbitrageurs, and leveraged-buyout artists of the 1980s on the other, were preoccupied with the short term, with profit today or tomorrow rather than in five or ten years. Students of human psychology say that a key mark of maturity is the ability to postpone gratification to achieve larger gratification later; immaturity, in this sense, may be the central feature of all economic bubbles. In due course, the instant gratification of 1969, for investment professionals, small investors, and the national economy, led to the disappointment or disaster of 1973–74. As far as the 1980s boom is concerned, the denouement has not come yet; whether it will end in disappointment and disaster is a question on which the jury is still out.

In the boom-and-bust cycle that still plagues our national economic life, reform follows bust as night follows day. Alas, such reform usually misses the mark. It is directed at the abuses of the past, which are known, and not at the abuses of the future, which are unknown, and which predictably will be different. The reforms of the seventies were directed mainly at the new-issues market. Since the new-issues market as a medium for the fleecing of investors had largely ended even by the time the reforms were put in place, the reforms proved to be largely irrelevant. It is of interest to note that—in marked contrast to the 1930s, when most leaders of the investment community stood adamantly against reform—many of the leading critics of the 1980s boom at its very height were professional practitioners of the abuses they denounced. The leading takeover lawyer Martin Lipton repeatedly and insistently proposed anti-takeover laws that would, by his own account, substantially reduce his own practice. Andrew Sigler, chairman of Champion International Corporation, which in 1984 became the white knight in the $2-billion takeover of St. Regis Corporation (and in the process borrowed more than $1 billion in hardly more than an hour), in 1985 called the disruption of companies by corporate raiders "a horrible wrong" that was "hurting the country [and] the economic system," and became chairman of a task force of the Business Roundtable formed to urge legislation against takeover abuses. And Irwin Jacobs of Minneapolis, known as a master greenmailer, when summoned before a House subcommittee in May 1984, carried the do-as-I-say-not-as-I-do principle to its ultimate point. "Greenmail is not right," Jacobs, by his own later account, told the representatives. "Change the law. But rest assured—if you don't, I guess I'm going under the term of a greenmailer."[10]

Perhaps the most comprehensive public assault on the new investment banking to come from any source up to 1985 came the previous year from Felix G. Rohatyn, senior partner of Lazard Frères & Company, almost certainly the most publicly visible of all investment bankers at that time and an old master of the merger-and-takeover trade. Speaking in 1984 to the American Society of Newspaper Editors, Rohatyn said, "What is happening in the financial markets today bears the same relationship to what happened in the 'go-go years' of the 1960s as Caesar's Palace bears to the local church bingo game. . . . We are turning the financial markets into a huge casino." In that context, it is relevant to recall John Maynard Keynes's remark in *The General Theory of Employment, Interest, and Money:* "When the capital development of a country becomes a by-product of the activities of a casino, the job is likely to be ill-done."[11] One might well add that under the same circumstances the protection of investors from unwarranted risk is likely to be not just ill-done, but rather not done at all.*

Some, like the Nobel laureate Yale economist James Tobin, saw the current tendencies in corporate life and investment banking as part of a larger cyclical trend in

*The question of why financiers themselves should, in the 1980s, be the chief critics of dubious financial practices is an interesting field for social speculation. (As recently as the 1930s, a financier who spoke up for financial reform was apt to be ostracized by his colleagues; now they take such statements in stride.) Is it repentance? Hypocrisy? Or just the pot calling the kettle black? Perhaps it is a response to the new age of publicity, in which reticence has lost respectability and to remain silent is, in the public view, to indict oneself. Confronted with a television mike or a reporter's tape recorder, what *can* a prominent investment man or corporate chief say? That the prospect of widespread publicity nudges him toward high-minded statements may serve to accelerate the process of reform—even though he may not apply the spirit of his public words to his own future professional operations.

American political and social thought: "The undiluted pursuit of personal gain is more accelerated in society, as a result of the conservative ideological revolution."[12] Whatever the cause of these tendencies, how much harm, if any, are they doing to investors and to the economy? And what, if anything, can be done to cure them? A closer investigation of the origins and nature of the new investment banking may show the way to some answers.

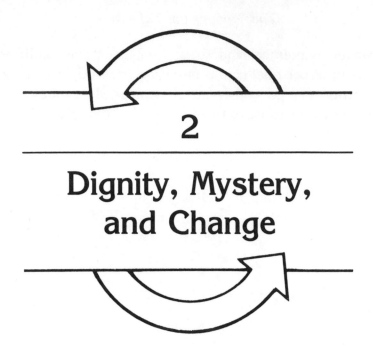

2

Dignity, Mystery, and Change

Writing in 1967, Erwin Miller of the Wharton School of Finance and Commerce of the University of Pennsylvania declared that "in its strict sense, investment banking is that business which has as its function the flotation of new securities, both debt and equity, to the general public (including institutions) for the purpose of acquiring funds for clients that are private firms or public bodies." Miller went on to say that "in essence," investment banking is "intermediation in the public new-issues market for all types of issues."[1]

That is to say, investment banking is, or was, under-

34

writing almost pure and simple. Perhaps Miller might have included advice to clients on a variety of financial matters—corporate investments, mergers, acquisitions, divestitures, and reorganizations, for example—that have always been part of the accepted investment-banking function in this country. With this amendment, Miller's definition was sound enough for 1967, and for United States financial history up to then. Over the past two decades, however, investment-banking firms have taken on so many other activities on such a large scale that, in accordance with the lexicographers' now-accepted practice, we must alter the definition to conform to new usage. Trading in already-issued securities, along with such offshoots as risk arbitrage, is now so important to investment banks that it has become in fact part of investment banking. The development and marketing of "new products," some but not all of them variations on underwriting, are similarly a novel part of investment banking. Capital ventures by investment-banking firms risking their own money—what in London is called *merchant banking*—must be included under the same rubric. In general, for the purposes of this study, investment banking is taken to be whatever large investment banks do—except retail brokerage and other retail services such as insurance and residential real estate, which some firms do and some don't, but which in any case are clearly not investment banking. The traditional clients of investment banks have always been corporations, governments, and a few very rich individuals, never the general public.

Looking back over the story of investment banking in America, then, we find that until recently it is essentially the story of underwriting. (And mostly of a single form of underwriting, that of debt securities. As late as 1912, the first president of the Investment Bankers Association of America said in his inaugural address, "Investment banking . . . broadly speaking, has to do with the organization and distribution of a secured form of credit known as bonds.") Underwriting in America arose around 1800 out of a practice imported from Europe called *loan contracting*. The loan contractor was simply an individual or a firm that bought debt securities wholesale, hoping to sell them for a profit. The first glimmerings of the syndicate system appeared in 1813, when the Treasury raised $16 million through a bond issue to finance the War of 1812. Public subscriptions to the issue being poor, most of it was sold to three individuals—Stephen Girard of Philadelphia, John Jacob Astor of New York, and David Parish, American agent for Baring Brothers of London—who subsequently resold their bonds profitably through business and family connections. Girard, Astor, and Parish were perhaps the wealthiest merchants in America at the time; they were also all foreign-born (in France, Germany, and Britain, respectively). Other early investment bankers were less successful, and the panic of 1837, followed by the depression of the early 1840s, virtually decimated the first wave. Investment banking in the fledgling republic lived in an atmosphere of extreme risk and overhanging disaster—a condition into which some see it now tending to return.[2]

According to Fritz Redlich, the first historian of American investment banking, the industry in the pre–Civil War period remained in a rather immature stage. Its principal activity was raising money for federal and state governments; its key figure was Nicholas Biddle, who, after failing as the nation's first central banker, made his Bank of the United States of Pennsylvania the first full-fledged American investment bank, and the first American bank to put investment banking ahead of commercial banking. (There was no legal separation of the two at the time.) In 1841, Biddle's private bank followed its unlucky competitors into bankruptcy; but meanwhile, new investment banks were appearing, one of them—Drexel & Company, founded in 1838 in Philadelphia by a former Austrian portrait painter, Francis Martin Drexel—bearing a name that still resounds on Wall Street. Around 1850, attention began to shift from government issues to those of the rising new railroad industry; potential customers for securities by this time included savings banks, insurance and trust companies, and a few wealthy individuals. The small individual investor had a short-lived day in the sun during the Civil War, when Jay Cooke & Company of Philadelphia, using a nationwide sales force some 2,500 strong, and a publicity campaign involving the press, posters, handbills, and educational literature, succeeded in peddling several hundred million dollars of war bonds to small investors—to all intents and purposes, the young nation's only specimens of that breed through most of the nineteenth century. (The Cooke firm was to go bankrupt in 1873—one more casualty of an era when the investment-banking business still usually turned out, over the long run, to be an exciting form of financial suicide.)

The end of the Civil War marked the start of investment banking's rise to imperial status in the national economy. The 1860s saw the appearance of many of the great and long-lived German-Jewish firms: J.&W. Seligman in 1862; Kuhn Loeb in 1869; Goldman Sachs in 1869. (Lehman Brothers, in its original form as a cotton broker, dates back to the 1840s.) Key Yankee firms appeared in the same decade—J. S. Morgan & Company, predecessor of Drexel Morgan and of J. P. Morgan, in 1864; and Kidder Peabody of Boston, successor to John E. Thayer & Brother, in 1865. The chief clients of these companies were railroads, and their chief lure for those clients was their access to overseas capital: British in the case of the Yankees, Continental European in that of the German Jews. (The new British and European investors were lured by higher interest rates than were generally available to them in their home markets and by the age-old romantic attraction, going back to the Dutch East and West India companies in the early seventeenth century, of investment overseas.) Syndication became the customary, rather than the occasional, method of underwriting railroad bonds, particularly after the successful sale of a $2-million issue of the Pennsylvania Railroad Company in 1870.

It was at about this time that the investment banks moved rapidly from a passive to an active role—that is, from serving as mere financial intermediaries to intervening in the management of companies. Bankers came to demand the right to choose top corporate executives in exchange for the use of their all-but-exclusive access to scarce capital; by the 1890s, that right was routinely granted. In some cases, companies became in effect the creatures of their bankers: the Pennsylvania of Kuhn Loeb; the Erie and the Chesapeake & Ohio of J. P. Morgan; the Santa Fe of Kidder Peabody. Redlich makes the interesting point that, at least originally, the active role of the bankers came about not as a grab for power but as a measure of protection for themselves and their investors against the ethics and practices of corporations, which were generally several cuts lower than those observed by bankers. Redlich writes, "Control of enterprises by investment bankers, which at a later stage was to become dangerous as an expression of financial power, originally was an act of self-defense on the part of the bankers."[3]

Let us pause for a snapshot of American investment banking during its imperium, which lasted roughly from 1890 until 1913. The business is ruled by six firms: J. P. Morgan & Company, dominated, of course, by the elder J. P. Morgan himself; the First National Bank of New York, dominated by George F. Baker; the National City Bank, dominated by James Stillman; Kuhn Loeb & Company, dominated by Jacob Schiff; and the two leading Boston firms, Kidder Peabody and Lee Higginson. There is a good deal of cross-ownership among them; for example, Kidder, Peabody, Schiff, and the Morgan partner Robert Bacon are stockholders of Stillman's National City Bank. Hardly surprisingly, business relations among them usually emphasize cooperation rather than competition, the matter being treated as one of social etiquette. Apart from an occasional conflict like the Morgan–Kuhn Loeb battle for the Northern Pacific Railroad in 1901, they honor one another's corporate relationships; as Schiff puts the matter, competition in investment banking is considered "not good form." The Jews of Kuhn Loeb are not invited to be members of the Morgan partners' social clubs, but after the Northern Pacific affair they are treated as equals in Wall Street.

Little capital and few partners are needed to play in the game. Kidder Peabody sometimes admits new partners who bring social connections but no capital at all, and rewards them according to their "usefulness to the firm"; Kidder and Kuhn Loeb each maintains a total staff of fewer than fifty people. The methods of syndication used by the various firms are similar but not identical; for example, Morgan does the principal selling for the syndicates it heads, while Kuhn Loeb requires each member of its syndicates to share in the selling. Frequently, members of syndicates make large profits simply by lending their names and assuming some of the risk. Profits of syndicate members ordinarily range from 2.5 to 10 percent of the amount of their participations, and sometimes up to 20 percent. *The New York Times* writes in 1902, "The profits to be divided from underwriting have grown to such an extent that many banks of considerable reputation rely almost entirely on such profits for their income, letting the conventional banking business entirely alone." *The United States Investor* says that underwriting has provided investment bankers with "a pleasant occupation, involving no great risk and entailing the most exaggerated fees."

In short, it has become a cushy, cozy business; no longer do leading firms fail like clockwork each time there is a financial panic. They have learned, instead, to let the client corporations do the failing, and then to profit a second time on the reorganization of the unlucky client, which is at their mercy for new capital. As for disclosure by investment bankers to potential customers of the facts and risks involved in the securities they sell, it hardly exists. The customer is seldom told the syndicate's charge or even the amount of the issuing company's assets. His confidence is expected to reside in the imperial names of Morgan, Kuhn Loeb, or whoever is at the head of the list of underwriters.

In 1900, 95 percent of all investment-banking business was in railroad bonds, but securities of industrial firms, including common stocks, were sharply on the rise. The first great era of consolidations was in full cry—between 1895 and 1904, about one-third of all large American companies disappeared through mergers—and investment bankers were getting richer through fees for arranging and financing those mergers. Two decades later, the social philosopher and economist Thorstein Veblen would put his eccentric but arresting gloss on turn-of-the-century-style American financing: The old-time "captain of industry" was gone; the captaincy had been taken over by "absentee owners,"* principally investment-banking syndicates, who were concerned with "regulating the rate and volume of output in . . . industrial enterprises" in order to maintain their profits. And Veblen went a step further. In doing their regulating while lining their own pockets, he insisted, the "vested interests"—that is, investment bankers—were engaged in nothing less than deliberate, calculated "sabotage" of the industrial process.

*Veblen's term was poorly chosen in regard to investment banks. These institutions, with their comparatively small capital, could not hope to own industry outright. Rather, they controlled it through effective control of investment capital belonging to others.

This last point is, of course, debatable; what is not is that the turn-of-the-century era was a captain's paradise for investment bankers. In style, they went beyond a captain's dignity to a lord's pomp. As a contemporary observer wrote of the atmosphere in a leading banking house,

> There is an air of omniscience as if nothing could ever happen. Doors do not slam, men walk softly upon rugs, voices are never lifted in feverish excitement over profit and loss; no one is permitted even to call off prices from the tape. There is a feeling of space, quite different from that sense of limited margins which pervades a broker's office. Ceilings at a banking house are higher than ceilings anywhere else, and that may account for it, but even before one is conscious of dimensions one gets the feeling of space from the manners of the person in uniform who attends to the noiseless opening and closing of the main portal and asks people what business they have to enter.[4]

The paradise could not last. The reform wave of 1902–12, although it did not end the investment-banking imperium in American economic life, made the first cut into its sway. Especially after the panic of 1907—in which the fact that J. P. Morgan & Company played the role of banker of last resort, and thereby helped end the panic, failed to obscure the fact that Wall Street had been one of the panic's principal causes—the public and its tribunes reacted to restrain the excesses of investment bankers. Beginning soon after 1900, state after state enacted "blue-sky laws" (so named from the then-current expression "blue sky merchants" to

designate securities swindlers) intended to protect investors from unscrupulous dealers. Previously, beginning in
the middle of the nineteenth century, various states had
enacted laws touching on securities, but for the most part
they had been aimed at controlling the capitalization of
issuing companies. By contrast, the blue-sky laws were
aimed at controlling securities dealers. The one enacted by
Kansas in 1911—the first comprehensive system for licensing the securities industry, and, in the opinion of financial
historians, the beginning of modern securities regulation—required registration of most new securities, licensing of dealers and brokers, and a detailed disclosure of the
financial condition of an issuing company. Enforcement
was entrusted to the State Bank Commissioner, and such
were his powers that no new security covered by the law
could be issued without his permit.

In 1914 the newly formed Investment Bankers Association of America conducted a strong campaign against
blue-sky laws, singling out that of Kansas as so drastic
that it virtually prevented most investment bankers from
doing business there. Between 1914 and 1916, many of the
blue-sky laws were voided by federal courts on various
grounds, among them that they interfered with individual
freedom, exceeded the permissible police power of states,
burdened interstate commerce, and violated due process.
However, in 1917 the Supreme Court ruled that comprehensive licensing of securities dealers was constitutionally
permitted. At that time, twenty-seven states had blue-sky
laws; by 1933, every state but Nevada had one, although
they varied wildly as to specific provisions.

Meanwhile, compulsory competitive bidding among

underwriters became, for the first time but not the last, an issue for lively debate among bankers and public officials. The Senate Pujo Committee investigation of 1912 threw a vivid, although distorted, light on the purported New York "money trust," thought to have its headquarters at the Morgan bank; a whole constellation of investment-banking abuses aimed at concentrating money and credit was alleged, among them consolidation of banks and trust companies, interlocking directorates among corporations, and reciprocal arrangements among investment bankers to purchase securities issues for resale. None of the Pujo Committee recommendations was enacted, but they had their effect: investment bankers were forcefully identified to the public as the enemies of economic democracy.

The death in 1913 of the elder Morgan, living symbol of the investment-banking imperium, was one of those coincidental events—like the death of another American quasi emperor, John Kennedy, in 1963—that mark a historical watershed. (Or perhaps not so coincidental: some of Morgan's friends insisted that he had been hounded to his death by the Pujo Committee, at whose hearings his testimony had provided the centerpiece.) In any case, the enactment later that year of the Federal Reserve Act reaffirmed the right of the federal government to regulate the activities of national banks. The following January, Pierpont Morgan's successor, his son J. P., announced that he and his partners would resign from the boards of twenty-seven corporations on which they sat. Before that year was over, Jacob Schiff of Kuhn Loeb had come out strongly in favor of federal supervision of investment-banking activities, and a measure to institute such regulation of railroad securities had passed the House, only to fall in the Senate in the panic attendant on the outbreak of war in Europe.[5]

The imperium of investment banking was over, but not its power. It had been pushed from the throne of the American economy, but it remained in a seat at the throne's right hand. Indeed, in the celebrated antitrust suit of 1947, the government would allege (on shaky evidence, in the opinion of Judge Harold R. Medina) that it had been "in or about 1915"—not earlier—that the leading investment-banking firms had "developed a system" to eliminate competition and monopolize "the cream of the business." World War I gave investment bankers a chance to improve their public image by patriotically selling Liberty Bonds for no commission; but there was enough for-profit business, particularly in foreign loans, to enable the House of Morgan to increase its assets from $228 million at the end of 1914 to $481 million at the end of 1917. Meanwhile, huge profits from war contracting enabled American corporations to market greatly increased amounts of common stock. Between 1914 and 1917 the aggregate sum raised by new corporate bond issues remained almost constant, whereas that raised by new stock more than doubled between 1915 and 1916.

Thus the stage was set for the stock-market boom of the 1920s, and a second day of wine and roses for the investment-banking industry. With the United States becoming for the first time in its history a creditor nation, its economy bounded forward, creating vast amounts of new capital. Again for the first time, the American market for new securities became chiefly domestic. Thriving on it, the old-line investment-banking firms grew rapidly. Their syndicates became larger, their numbers augmented by ambitious new or newly expanded firms like Blyth & Company of San Francisco and Halsey Stuart & Company of Chicago; meanwhile, formerly prominent firms that had remained too dependent on European connections went into eclipse. Up to 1915, there had been only about 250 securities dealers in the United States; in 1929 there were almost 6,500, of which some 3,000 could be classified to one extent or another as investment bankers.

The pendulum of public opinion having swung away from reform toward laissez faire, syndicates in the 1920s operated in most respects much as they had at the height of their turn-of-the-century imperium. Along with some newer players—the securities affiliates of leading commercial banks—the same firms still dominated. Morgan and Kuhn Loeb were the leaders in railroad financing, Lehman Brothers and Goldman Sachs in that of merchandising enterprises. Morgan and Kuhn Loeb were still the unchallenged leaders of their industry as a whole. Issues became far larger than ever before; those of $20 or $25 million were now quite usual. Common stock, with its appeal to the new player in the investment game, the individual of modest means, was gaining rapidly in favor, and stock issues were now being undertaken more and more often even by the firms that had long held the traditional investment bankers' view that common stock was generally too risky for the public. Kidder Peabody, for example, by the end of the decade had raised the common-stock component of all its annual offerings to 25 percent.

Officers and directors of issuing corporations sometimes participated as individuals in their firms' underwritings and collected the appropriate share of commissions—a surviving touch of nineteenth-century practice
that was later spoken of caustically in congressional hearings as "the gravy train." As to disclosure, underwriters
were still under no statutory duty to disclose anything at
all about the quality and safety of the securities they offered for sale, or, indeed, about the state of their own
finances. It was this factor, along with the aura of unhur-
ried ease and beyond-reproach probity that investment
bankers were at pains to project, that led the government
in its subsequent antitrust case to describe the 1920s in
investment banking as "the era of dignity and mystery."
Otto H. Kahn, Schiff's successor at Kuhn Loeb, later
described very graphically what "dignity" meant at his
firm. Kahn said in 1933 that not poaching on the preserves
of other nominally competitive underwriting firms was a
matter of "conscientious scruples." "We [do not] go to
corporations and ask them to do business with us," Kahn
explained. "We hope that we have established a reputation
which is our show window, which attracts customers.
. . . I would not seek to take any client away from anybody." Concerning other firms going after *his* business,
Kahn allowed that it had occasionally happened, and
commented charitably, "I regard them as reputable bankers. I would not have done what they did, but who am I
to sit in judgment upon others? 'Let him who is without
sin cast the [first] stone.'" When competition among
themselves is quite ingenuously regarded by leading suppliers of capital as a "sin," must not the resulting potential

overcharge of *users* of capital, resulting from the absence of competition, be regarded as a virtue? Kahn, a charming and persuasive banker, was not asked that question.[6]

In sum, 1920s investment banking was to some extent a return to the ways of the period of the imperium—but with a difference. The imperium had been based on scarce capital and the consequent absolute dependence of corporations on their bankers to find it for them. Now, with the economy booming and the public at almost all economic levels falling over itself to get into the booming securities markets, capital was in good supply. Corporations knew that they could pick and choose among investment bankers. In conformity with tradition, they seldom felt inclined to do so. The power balance between corporations and their bankers, however, was beginning to tilt in the direction of the corporations.

Toward the end of the decade, as the stock-market bubble moved toward the bursting point, investment bankers tended to relax their own principles. Most conspicuously, in blatant disregard of their cherished principle against subjecting the public to unwonted risk, some of them took to forming highly leveraged investment companies composed largely of stock portfolios, and aggressively marketing the shares of these companies to small investors. By 1929 there were more than 770 such trusts, 265 of them organized in that year alone. Dillon Read & Company, later called the most active investment-banking house in the country at the time, was the first such house to involve itself with investment trusts; the most retrospectively visible one was Goldman Sachs, whose Goldman Sachs Trading Corporation would within a few years bring disaster to its investors and very nearly to the firm itself.

In retrospect, perhaps the most attractive thing about investment banking in the 1920s was its emphasis on good manners (whether or not such conduct represented a conscious effort to protect a cartel). Voices were well modulated; verbal commitments were honored; dress was subdued and elegant, but not *too* elegant. Those young aspirants who came to the industry without such manners had to learn them or fail; thus, as Frederick Lewis Allen noted, Wall Street became a school of manners. A fairly rigid, self-imposed code of conduct served as a surrogate for the government regulation that did not yet exist. Sometimes the code worked to preserve honesty and fairness, but not always, especially at the end of the decade.

A single case may stand as an example of how investment banking's high principles could, in the 1929 climate, be used to serve causes by no means associated with such principles. In January 1929, the House of Morgan bought 1,250,000 shares of common stock of the Alleghany Corporation, a new holding company (similar to an investment trust) set up by the Cleveland railroad and real-estate tycoons and long-term Morgan clients the Van Sweringen brothers. The Morgan partners decided to keep most of the stock for themselves, and to sell about 575,000 shares in a private offering. Even when asked to do so, Morgan had never sold common stock to the public, in conformity with the firm's almost religious belief that it was wrong to subject uninformed investors to so much risk as common stock entailed. In accordance with that principle, it offered the Alleghany stock not to the public but to a select list of individuals who were either friends and relatives of Morgan partners or persons of Wall Street or national influence—all persons of sufficient substance, in the Morgan partners' opinion, to be able to "afford the risk." Among those on the list were John J. Raskob, chairman of the Democratic National Committee; Joseph R. Nutt, treasurer of the Republican National Committee; a former Secretary of War; a future Secretary of the Treasury; and three who qualified on both professional and family grounds— Richard Whitney, acting president of the New York Stock Exchange and brother of the Morgan partner George Whitney; Charles Francis Adams, President-elect Hoover's choice for Secretary of the Navy, as well as J. P. Morgan's son's father-in-law; and the national hero Charles A. Lindbergh, who happened also to be the former Morgan partner Dwight Morrow's son-in-law.

Impeccable as these arrangements were, by the House of Morgan's code, what seemed to compromise both their logic and their probity in the Alleghany case was the market situation in early February 1929, when the offer was made. The offering price was $20 per share, while at that time the new Alleghany shares, not yet issued, were trading in the "when-issued" market at an inflated price of $35 per share. To make an instant profit of $15 on each share he was allotted, a recipient of the stock needed only to sell his shares immediately on the "when-issued" market and then, when they were duly delivered, hand them over to his broker. The "risk" from which the general public was so sedulously protected was entirely theoretical; what the public was being "protected" from was in effect an offer of cash, amounting in all to $8,625,000 for the 575,000 shares, in return for nothing. The recipient of 1,000 shares was being handed $15,000; the recipient of 10,000 shares $150,000; and so on.

Thus, by strictly following the investment-banking code as it existed in its highest form in the twenties, Morgan in practice dispensed patronage to friends, relatives, clients, and others in a position to offer future favors in return. There may be poetic justice in the fact that the scandal created by the Alleghany case, when its circumstances were luridly revealed in Senate hearings in 1933, did much to bring about passage of the regulatory laws under which investment banking has lived ever since. In any case, the two-sided nature of the bankers' old code, and the weakness of self-imposed good manners and rigid principles as a form of self-regulation of investment banking, were never more vividly revealed than in the Alleghany episode—a fitting gravestone for the era of dignity and mystery.[7]

The stock-market crash that began in September 1929; the terrible national Depression that began the following year; the dark days of 1932, when the nation itself was bankrupt in everything but name; the "bank holiday" of March 1933, in the first days of the new Roosevelt administration; the Senate Pecora hearings of 1933–34, when the misdeeds of securities dealers big and small were paraded before ruined investors and the public at large: these well-known events need not be detailed here. It is enough to say that they set the stage for passage of the three laws that restructured American investment banking and established the rules under which, as amended from time to time, it has operated ever since.

The Glass-Steagall Act, also called the Banking Act of 1933, was the most far-reaching. Signed into law on June 16, 1933, to go into effect one year later, it undertook nothing less than to revolutionize investment banking by mandating a nearly complete separation between it and commercial banking, for the principal purpose of preventing commercial banks from jeopardizing their depositors' money by committing it to securities investment. Its most crucial part, Section 16, stated that any Federal Reserve System member or state-chartered bank belonging to the Federal Reserve System "shall not underwrite any issue of securities or stock, other than securities of the United States or any of its states and other political subdivisions." The law further stipulated that partners and officials of securities firms were forbidden to serve as officers or directors of commercial banks belonging to the Federal Reserve System, and empowered the Federal Reserve Board to regulate bank loans serviced by bonds or stocks.

Passed in haste in the crisis atmosphere of 1933, the Glass-Steagall Act—named for Senator Carter Glass of Virginia and Representative Henry B. Steagall of Tennessee—scarcely represented a new idea; rather, it was an idea that had been around a long time but had been kept in abeyance by the power of Veblen's "vested interests." (It is ironic in retrospect to note that the act, in the 1980s so cherished and protected by the Securities Industry Association, was vehemently opposed at the time of its passage by that organization's predecessor, the Investment Bankers Association.) Way back in 1902, the Comptroller of the Currency had ruled that national banks could not underwrite equities, as opposed to bonds, and were limited in their ability to underwrite bonds, until the 1920s, when the rule was gradually relaxed and banks were allowed to maintain "securities affiliates" through which they could deal in bonds to their hearts' content. (Such affiliates were outlawed by Glass-Steagall.) The Pujo Committee of 1912 had criticized the move of commercial banks into under-writing of bonds, and had recommended prohibition of such underwriting to national banks; but Congress had failed to act. The McFadden Act of 1927 had given the Comptroller of the Currency power to allow bank affiliates to underwrite both bonds and stocks. In December 1929, with thousands of banks in bankruptcy and their securities dealings in many cases accused as a principal cause, Presi-dent Hoover himself had suggested to Congress the advis-ability of separating commercial and investment banking; but nothing had immediately come of the proposal. Now at last, suddenly and definitively, the step so long consid-ered and so often avoided had been definitively taken. While such traditional investment-banking firms as Kuhn Loeb and Goldman Sachs were relatively unaffected, the greatest of them all, J. P. Morgan—which had derived much of its unparalleled power from interaction between its deposit-and-loan function and its underwriting func-tion—was neatly cut in half.

With a single stroke, the Securities Act of 1933, which went into effect that July, ended investment banking's era of "dignity and mystery." Called the "truth-in-securities law," it became effective in July 1933; its expressed pur-pose was "to provide full and fair disclosure of the character of securities sold in interstate and foreign commerce and through the mails, and to prevent frauds in the sale thereof." To accomplish this purpose, it required every nonexempt issuer of new securities—that is, most corporate issuers of securities worth $100,000 or more—to file with the government a registration statement providing detailed information about the issuer, the securities, and the underwriters; and subsequently, before the issue went on sale, to provide possible buyers with a prospectus containing nearly all of the information in the registration statement. A period of twenty days after the filing date of the registration statement was required before it could become effective and the securities go on sale. In both the registration statement and the prospectus, issuers and their underwriters were required not to misstate any fact or to withhold any "material" fact. Liability for criminal violation of the act was set at a maximum fine of $5,000 and imprisonment for five years; as to civil liability, damages could be imposed on issuers, corporation directors, and underwriting houses. (At first, the Securities Act made each underwriter in a syndicate liable for the entire amount of the issue; however, after a great outcry against this draconian provision arose from investment bankers, Congress in 1934 amended it to limit liability of each underwriter to his share of the issue.)

Like the Glass-Steagall Act, the Securities Act did not spring newborn from the brows of its creators—in this case, James M. Landis and Benjamin V. Cohen, its principal authors, and Senator Duncan U. Fletcher and Representative Sam Rayburn, its congressional sponsors. Rather, it embodied ideas that had been around since at least 1918, when Carter Glass had supported similar legislation, only to see it dismissed with horror as flagrant government interference in the free economy. Both before and immediately after its passage, the Securities Act was attacked more or less across the board by the securities industry. The liability and damage clause was too onerous, they said; the twenty-day waiting period would put issuers and their investment bankers at the mercy of changing market conditions; overall, the act would drastically reduce the number and size of new issues and thus the flow of new capital into American enterprise. Half a century later, it is interesting to note how wrong in the long run the protesters were, even by their own lights. Apart from the waiting period, which for issues of very large companies was abolished by Rule 415 in 1982, the 1933 Act has stood essentially as it was written, with only fine-tuning changes.

The Securities Exchange Act of 1934 focused on eliminating abuses that had come to flourish in stock-exchange trading in already-issued securities. It prohibited the techniques for manipulating stock prices—wash sales, matched orders, and pools—that had been put gaudily on display in the Pecora hearings; it extended the registration requirements of the Securities Act to include registration of all securities listed on national exchanges, not just newly issued ones; it required issuer corporations of nationally traded securities to file quarterly financial reports, and their officers and directors to report their own transactions in the securities of their firms; and—a provision that would be particularly helpful later in preventing conditions favorable to a repetition of the 1929 crash—it

55

empowered the Federal Reserve Board to control stock-market credit by setting minimum margin requirements for brokers' loans to finance transactions on national stock exchanges.

Crucial as these provisions were for the integrity and relative safety to the investor, none of them bore directly on investment banking. One other section of the 1934 Act did. This was the creation of a Securities and Exchange Commission to administer both the 1934 Act and the Securities Act of the previous year. (Until then, such administration had been in the hands of the Federal Trade Commission.) The new SEC, to consist of five members of whom no more than three could belong to the same political party, was given unusually wide discretionary powers to implement the two interlocking laws for which it had responsibility; over the subsequent years and up to the present, its rules and rulings, periodically changed and augmented, have loomed at least as large in the regulation of Wall Street as the language of the laws themselves. Meanwhile, the SEC, through all its ups and downs of quality and degree of strictness, has become as essential, familiar, and grudgingly accepted a part of investment banking as umpires are of baseball.

In a cultural sense, the coming of the Securities Acts and the SEC marks the greatest of turning points in American investment-banking history. Previously, the restraints had been almost entirely internal. The industry's elaborate, self-imposed codes of conduct, its flaunted gentlemanliness, and its carefully cultivated elitism had served as buffers against external control; the public and the government had been—for the most part successfully—encouraged to accept the principle of noblesse oblige as their guarantee against investment-banking misconduct. Now the industry had a cop instead of a code. The old spirit of autocracy would die slowly and hard. Still, beginning with 1933–34, the relationship between investment banking, its clients, and the investment public was democratic at least in form—eventually it would become so in content—rather than autocratic as before. The new controls, and also the new forms of abuse, were democratic forms, subject to the law rather than only to individual or institutional conscience.[8]

Because of Glass-Steagall, the new game began with some new players and some old ones. Old partnerships like Kuhn Loeb, Lehman Brothers, and Goldman Sachs were little affected, because they had never been heavily engaged in commercial banking. The securities arms of the Chase National Bank and the First National Bank of Boston joined forces to form the new investment-banking firm of First Boston Corporation, which immediately became an industry leader; while those of the National City Bank and Brown Brothers Harriman became Harriman Ripley & Company. When J. P. Morgan and Company chose to stay in commercial banking, a group of partners and staff of that firm and of Drexel & Company, its Philadelphia affiliate, broke away to form the investment-banking firm of Morgan Stanley & Company—a baby with an assured future, like the firstborn son of a duke.

At first the new game was listless, indeed almost actionless. Investment bankers were accused in 1933 and 1934 of conducting a "sit-down strike" to force modification of the Securities Act; but in fact the paralysis of the capital markets in those years was probably a greater cause of the period of inactivity than foot-dragging by the bankers. When the underwriting business finally began to pick up in 1935, it turned out that things hadn't changed so much after all. J. P. Morgan and Kuhn Loeb had been the underwriting leaders of the 1920s; now Morgan Stanley and Kuhn Loeb emerged as the leaders of the 1930s. Morgan Stanley in particular began at the top. Between 1935 and mid-1939, $1.3 billion in top-rated bonds were issued by all firms; Morgan Stanley managed 65 percent of the entire amount, and almost one-fourth of all new bond issues of every quantity. The reasons for this are not obscure. The Morgan name, combined with the previous association of leading corporate executives with the Morgan firm and its underwriting partners, was enough to do the trick. The phenomenon is eloquently illustrated in the process by which Morgan Stanley became the principal investment banker (as it still is) for American Telephone and Telegraph. In 1935, before Morgan Stanley had been finally organized, President Walter S. Gifford of AT&T sought out Harold Stanley, the former Morgan partner with whom he had often dealt when the Morgan firm had been AT&T's regular underwriter, and who was to become president of Morgan Stanley. Gifford asked if it was true that some former Morgan partners and employees, Stanley included, were planning to form an investment-banking firm. Stanley said that it was; whereupon Gifford replied, "That solves my problems," put on his hat, and went home. Thus Morgan Stanley was able to open its doors with the largest corporation in the nation firmly in its stable of clients. Indeed, Morgan Stanley's very first issue, that October, consisted of $43.7 million of AT&T bonds.

Even so, although such a comfortable, tradition-oriented way of doing business played a large part in the investment banking of the thirties, such methods no longer ruled the business entirely. Competition for issues increased, and spreads for the bankers narrowed. The government itself, through its Reconstruction Finance Corporation, emerged as a major competitor with private-sector bankers in financing corporations. "There can be little doubt," a Harriman Ripley partner told a House committee in 1941, "that . . . a great part of the function of what in an economic sense is investment banking is now being conducted by government." At the same time, what with weak corporations and weak capital markets, underwriting risks were greatly increased. After the conspicuous and costly failure of two issues in 1937—convertible bonds of Bethlehem Steel, and convertible preferred stock of Pure Oil—had shaken the entire investment-banking industry, it took to forming huge syndicates, often consisting of fifty or more members, to spread the risk more widely.

The campaign, beginning in 1937, for competitive public bidding among underwriters for new issues, to replace the traditional technique of private negotiation between issuers and their chosen bankers, appeared as a big event in investment banking of the thirties—a species of populist revolt against entrenched privilege. No less a figure than future Supreme Court Justice William O. Douglas, a member of the SEC and soon to become its chairman, said in

March of that year that competitive bidding would put an end to banker domination of industry, excessive underwriting charges, and a host of other evils. Thus encouraged, three prominent financiers—Robert R. Young of the Alleghany Corporation, Cyrus Eaton of Otis & Company of Cleveland, and Harold Stuart of Halsey Stuart & Company of Chicago—launched an all-out campaign to force compulsory competitive bidding on the entire underwriting industry. As Judge Medina would note later, each of these men had personal reasons, entirely separate from populist idealism, for urging competitive bidding; among their motives, the judge noted, appeared to be "revenge for real or fancied wrongs"—particularly such wrongs at the hands of those fierce opponents of competitive bidding and citadels of entrenched privilege, Morgan Stanley and Kuhn Loeb. In any case, the campaign was markedly successful; in 1941 the SEC promulgated Rule U-50, requiring competitive sealed bidding for most new issues of public-utility holding companies and their subsidiaries, and three years later the Interstate Commerce Commission required that railroad bonds, although not railroad stocks, be sold competitively.

But the revolution envisaged by Douglas never materialized. The new rules affected certain firms: Goldman Sachs, for example, went in heavily for sealed bidding in utility issues after U-50, and Halsey Stuart, already an experienced competitive bidder for utilities, gained in importance; while after the ICC ruling Kuhn Loeb, whose business until then had consisted principally of selling railroad bonds, began offering common stock for the first time.

Since Rule U-50 and the 1944 ICC ruling, competitive

bidding for public-utility and railroad bonds issues has been fully assimilated as a permanent feature of the business. Between 1941 and the mid-1960s, well over half of the dollar volume of all corporate bond issues of $2 million or more was handled by competitive bidding—the reason being that the majority of dollar volume of all issues over that period consisted of public-utility and railroad bonds. Meanwhile, though, corporate issuers showed little inclination to use competitive bidding when not required to do so. Almost all stocks and bonds of industrial companies and stocks of utilities and railroads continued to be underwritten in the traditional way, by negotiation. What experience seems to have proved is that, generally speaking, compulsory competitive bidding is simply not very applicable to American investment banking as a whole. With the coming of the SEC's shelf-registration rule in 1982, de facto competitive bidding was urged upon the nation's largest securities issuers, yet many of them, after accepting bids from others, ended up staying with their traditional bankers. Competitive bidding, *the* big reform issue in investment banking of the late thirties, is now hardly an issue at all.

In 1939, at the end of the Great Depression and the beginning of World War II, American investment banking was at a kind of stable low point. More than ever before, it was concentrated in New York City. Struggling to salvage the remnants of dignity and mystery, it was kept ever on the defensive by encroaching government regulation. Looking back longingly at the turn-of-the-century imperium, it was hobbled by slim resources (average capital of the eight largest houses ranged from $16 million for Kuhn

Loeb to $4 million for Blyth & Company), and by the relative absence of young talent, which both the economics and the ethos of the 1930s had tended to steer toward other fields. Investment banking seemed to be an industry with a past but not a future.[9]

A future would materialize, of course, with the coming of the postwar business boom. But meanwhile, during wartime, investment banking was one of the few American businesses that did *not* prosper. The Treasury's insistence that investment houses refrain from issuing securities in competition with government bond drives; the government's direct financing, through the RFC, of something like two-thirds of the vast plant expansion necessary for war production; the fact that the ranks of many of the leading Wall Street firms were temporarily decimated by departures to military service—all of these factors combined to keep private investment banking in the doldrums. Came at last V-E Day and V-J Day, and then—in October 1947, just when the first glimmerings of the great business expansion of the 1950s were appearing on the horizon—the Justice Department struck with its antitrust case against seventeen leading investment banks and their umbrella organization, the Investment Bankers Association. It was, said Attorney General Tom Clark, one of the biggest and most important cases ever brought under the Sherman Act of 1890; and it would, in due course, provide investment banking with its greatest triumph ever over the forces of government.

It was also a most peculiar case, not least in the choice of defendants. The seventeen indicted firms were not the seventeen leading syndicate heads of the time;

indeed, the top firm of all by this criterion for 1950, the year the trial began, was a nondefendant, Halsey Stuart—its headman, Harold Stuart, being a lead witness for the prosecution. (Partners of a few firms, such as Salomon Brothers, actually expressed chagrin that they had been slighted by being left out of the indictment.) Rather, the defendants seem to have been chosen not so much for their size and power as because they were the Old Guard and because they had been, and to a degree continued to be, leading opponents of competitive bidding. The arguments advanced by the government in its complaint sounded suspiciously like those advanced by Young, Eaton, and Stuart in their competitive-bidding campaign of 1937–41; and there was even some evidence that the government suit itself had been instigated by the veteran Wall Street hater Eaton—an allegation that the Justice Department prosecutors never flatly denied.

Whether or not it stemmed from an old vendetta, however, the government case raised various issues close to the heart of American investment banking—and, to all intents and purposes, settled them. In a legal sense, the case rested on three principles, which came to be called the *triple concept.* The first of these, the *traditional banker* concept, meant mutual recognition by the alleged conspirators that an investment bank's previous status as the lead underwriter of a given issuer's securities automatically entitled it to occupy the same position vis-à-vis that issuer in the future, for all time. The second, called *historical position,* meant that an unwritten code existed among the defendants as to who was and was not entitled to participate in their syndicates, and to what extent. The third, *reciprocity,* referred to an alleged agreement among the defendants to exchange participation, on a systematic basis, in syndicates managed by any of them.

In retrospect, it appears that there was at least some evidence to support the charge of reciprocity. The defendant underwriters *did* regularly participate in each other's syndicates, whether or not they did so systematically, and they *did* regularly exclude, or relegate to subordinate status, firms outside their circle. But the government case, like so many government antitrust cases, was ineptly handled, while the defendants were incisively—and expensively—represented, particularly by Arthur Dean of the law firm of Sullivan & Cromwell. As the case dragged on and on—pretrial proceedings alone lasted thirty-seven months—the government was forced to retreat step by step, modifying and reducing its charges; in November 1951, it withdrew them entirely against one defendant, the Investment Bankers Association. In particular, the "traditional banker" charge—the only part of the triple concept that, in and of itself, represented a potential violation of the Sherman Act—progressively appeared to be unsupported by evidence. Securities issuers, it became more and more clear, picked the same lead underwriter over and over again not because the investment-banking industry forced them to do so, but because they were satisfied with previous services and wanted to enjoy such services again. If "traditional banker" fell, the whole case fell; moreover, as Judge Medina saw the matter, the other two concepts would not stand the light of day, either.

As law, then, *U.S.* v. *Henry S. Morgan et al.* was a

one-sided case. Socially and philosophically, its core was the idea of courtesy as the enemy of competition. If the investment bankers treated each other in a civilized rather than a cutthroat way, the government seemed to be arguing, then by implication they were conspiring to violate the law. Much was made of Otto Kahn's statement to the Pecora committee more than a decade earlier that his famous firm "would not seek to take any client away from anybody." Now a new gloss was added to the subject when a veteran partner of Eastman Dillon said to Medina's court, "Courtesy generally requires that you conduct your business in a way so as not to make enemies, and if you think a man, firm, [or] friend of yours is engaged in doing a piece of business, it is not quite the polite thing to muscle in. . . ." But was such conduct, on its face, evidence of criminal conspiracy? Medina did not think so, and it was hard for even the most avid of Wall Street haters, in a time when courtesy on and off Wall Street was still far more respected by the public than it is now, to say so out loud. In focusing its attack on investment bankers' gentle manners toward each other, the government made a public-relations mistake of major dimensions.

At last, in October 1953, after more than three hundred courtroom days and a stenographic trial transcript of more than 5 million words, Judge Medina rendered his opinion. It was both caustic and decisive. "I have come to the settled opinion and accordingly find," wrote the judge, "that no such combination and agreement as is alleged in the complaint, nor any part thereof, was ever made, entered into, conceived, constructed, continued or participated in by these defendants, or any of them. . . . The complaint is dismissed as to each defendant on the merits and with prejudice."[10]

Perhaps Medina, a courteous man himself, was influenced by his personal overevaluation of that attribute into prejudice in favor of the investment bankers and against the government. In any event, with his decision, American investment banking emerged with colors flying, and with the affirmed sanction of federal law behind its customary methods. It did not begin to return to its turn-of-the-century power in relation to the corporations it served—rather, that power continued to be eroded as corporations prospered and grew—but, in the public view, its profits were legitimized and its honor vindicated. When Morgan Stanley led a syndicate that underwrote $325 million of General Motors stock in 1955, and Blyth & Company easily topped that record with a $642-million issue of Ford Motor Company stock the following year, there were few protests about the underwriters' profits. So long regarded by the public and many of its elected representatives as a member of a sort of illicit American peerage with a patent to rake off some of the profits of industry, the investment banker now came to be regarded—in the words of the historian Vincent Carosso—as "an accepted figure on the nation's economic landscape."

The clear sailing was to continue for about two decades—the final decades, as it now appears, of the old order. The issues of huge corporations with well-known names continued to be underwritten by syndicates headed by the handful of ancient and honored leaders of the industry—leaders who, however, remained relatively small in both personnel and capital and were relied upon for their prestige, experience, and expertise rather than for their financial clout. (In his opinion, Medina had noted the rather startling fact that, as of the end of 1947, only seven of the defendant firms had capital of $5 million or more—a rather modest fortune, even then, for a single individual of inherited wealth or corporate power. A decade later, these figures had not increased in any dramatic way.)

Beneath the giants and aristocrats of investment banking there was now a vast substructure. Some old and some new, the great bulk of securities firms were surprisingly small. Of the nearly four thousand registered broker-dealers in the United States in 1962, the median firm had capital of less than $50,000 and personnel of fewer than ten. Fifteen percent of them considered investment banking to be their principal activity, and the new issues they distributed were usually below $500,000 in size; in the first quarter of 1962, in the New York City area, underwriters with capital of less than $150,000 distributed more than half of such issues.

Investment banking, then, was becoming, if not more competitive or democratic, at least more populous. The many small firms were responding to a specific demand. In the United States in the 1960s, there existed for the first time a large public willing and eager to invest in common stock of a new enterprise that had a "story" but few or no resources. What was needed to sell stock to the public, and even to leading financial institutions, was not an actual company, but only an idea for a company. Early in the decade, the favored area of putative activity was electronics; a handful of young Ph.D.s, perhaps a patent or two, and a good promotion were the necessary and sufficient ingredients of a new "company" the sale of whose stock could bring in many millions. Later in the decade, in the "garbage market" of 1968–69, the field widened out to the point where almost any currently fashionable "story" could provide the nucleus of a new stock promotion: nursing homes, college students as consumers, leisure, weight-watching, pollution control. The giants and aristocrats would not touch such issues; the small firms would, and did with a will. (One transient firm of the time, Charles Plohn & Company, did so many initial offerings of new companies that its proprietor came to be called "Two-a-Week Charlie.") Insubstantial as the issuing companies were, their stock often went to a large premium immediately after the offering, and the underwriter, who almost always took a block of the stock in payment for his services, was able to turn a large profit, provided he was nimble enough to distribute his block in time. As for more respectable investors, Morgan Guaranty Trust Company, Bankers Trust Company, and Harvard and Cornell universities were among those who hastily invested in the initial offering of National Student Marketing Corporation in 1968, and later had occasion to repent at leisure.

Predictably, the garbage market ended in disaster; after the big market break of 1970, many of the new companies went bankrupt and their underwriters with them. In the aftermath, investment banking found itself under government attack again, the attack this time being focused not on the topside but rather on the underside. In 1972–73 the SEC held "Hot Issue Hearings" to try to determine what had gone wrong in 1968–69. In general, the conclusion reached was that, although participating underwriters had probably sometimes fallen short of the due-diligence requirements imposed on them by the Securities Act, lead underwriters had generally complied with their statutory responsibilities as to disclosure. Their prospectuses had stated very directly that the issuers had few or no resources, and had little chance ever to become profitable; the public had avidly bought the stocks anyhow. One witness at the hearings testified that in his experience, most buyers of hot new issuers, professionals included, never even read prospectuses about speculative new issues.

Obviously, this raised the question of whether disclosure was in practice protecting the investor. In 1973 some minor new rules regarding disclosure were adopted by the SEC. The same year, at the SEC's urging, the National Association of Securities Dealers proposed a set of reforms, tightening due diligence by requiring lead underwriters to conduct more active investigations of new issuers' plant capacity, management techniques, bank relationships, and the like. All of these proposals were withdrawn in 1975. A New York State study of the hot-issues market concluded ruefully that "the big winners were underwriters, invaders of the issuing companies, and those with contracts in these groups. The losers were those investors who purchased at inflated prices, and the economy itself."

But no reform measures ensued.

The garbage-market reform movement of the early 1970s collapsed under its own weight because the garbage market was already dead. It was a classic example of the weakness of reform in an area as technical and volatile as investment banking had come to be: the tendency of events to end old abuses and give rise to new ones, while the reformers are still debating. By 1973 burned investors, both institutional and individual, had learned their lesson, for the time being at least. They would no longer eagerly devour garbage, and therefore it was no longer presented to them. Market forces—inflation, competition, wildly rising overhead costs—not government intervention, shaped the vast changes in investment banking that were taking place during the seventies. The legacy of the garbage market, which came and went like a summer thunderstorm, was a lasting change toward short-term thinking on the part of investors, including the institutional ones who were fast taking charge of the markets.[11]

The changes of the 1970s are symbolized and epitomized in the person of André Meyer, at that time the autocratic head of Lazard Frères. The son of a Paris printing salesman, Meyer, in the best self-made-man tradition, had left school at sixteen and become a partner in the Paris office of Lazard before turning thirty. Having come to the United States as a refugee in 1940, in 1943 he took charge of Lazard Frères in New York, a conservative, well-regarded investment-banking firm that functioned independently of Paris and was known chiefly for bond underwriting. Over the following three decades he transformed it into the firm that led the way, for better or worse, into the era of the eighties.

As an investment banker, Meyer looked both backward into the past and forward into the future. In personal style, he came close to being an imitator of the Ur-figure of nineteenth-century investment banking, Pierpont Morgan. As his biographer, Cary Reich, points out, prestige and mystery—both personal and institutional—were of paramount importance to him; one of his first moves was to close Lazard's branches and fire its customers men, because he believed that conducting retail brokerage deprived the firm of cachet. He declined for a time to let Lazard participate in underwriting syndicates other than as a leading member, which it was seldom invited to be—a clear-cut sacrifice of profitable business on the altar of institutional prestige.

But Meyer had another motive for cutting back Lazard's underwriting business. Plainly put, he did not like underwriting. He considered it "silly," because the profit was so small in relation to the money committed. Bit by bit, he transformed Lazard into a deal-making firm, with underwriting as a sort of sideline mainly for advertising purposes. Under the inspired technical leadership of Felix Rohatyn, in the 1960s Lazard became known as "the merger house," presiding over the many conglomerate acquisitions of International Telephone & Telegraph, and between 1964 and 1968 bringing in some $10 million in mcrgcr-and-acquisition fees—an insignificant figure by later standards, but a significant one then. Still, arranging mergers for fees was not Meyer's heart's desire. What he really liked to do, and what he made his enormous reputation doing, was to arrange reorganizations, or to form new companies, in which Lazard took a large capital position, and thus to collect later in capital gains sums that make merger fees as well as underwriting concessions seem like trifles. For better or worse, Meyer, along with the trading firm of Salomon Brothers, showed America investment banking the way into its present "transactional" era.

An investment banker who considered securities underwriting "silly"? In the fifties and sixties, it sounded rather like a baseball team manager who considered the game of baseball silly. Yet some in Meyer's time (he died in 1979) took note of his eerie perception of what his industry was to become: David Rockefeller called him "the most creative financial genius in our time in the investment-banking field," and *Fortune* in 1968 called him "the most important investment banker in the Western world." His high-handed rule of his firm and his personal abrasiveness—characteristics, not incidentally, of many of the leaders of the era that followed him—alienated many of his subordinates, and the public scandals stirred up by some of his deals (particularly the 1970 merger of ITT and Hartford Insurance Company) put Lazard's reputation in temporary decline. By the time of his death, though, the change in investment banking that he had foreseen, and helped bring about, was an accomplished fact.[12]

We may end this scrapbook survey of the Old Investment Banking with a snapshot taken of it by Samuel Hayes in its last years—that is, at the beginning of the 1970s. After extensive research, Hayes found the traditional "club" of underwriters still functioning—a carpet or two frayed at the edges, perhaps, a brick or two loose or missing, but the structure standing and the members proud of its scars. The club's hierarchical structure—rigidly enforced from the top—was headed by what the underwriting business called the *special bracket.* Four firms—Morgan Stanley, First Boston, Dillon Read, and Kuhn Loeb—made up the special bracket's unchallenged cadre. Two upstarts, Merrill Lynch and Salomon Brothers, had recently been admitted provisionally, on the basis of their proven special ability in retail and wholesale distribution, respectively. (Goldman Sachs, a leader of the industry in the mideighties, was still hardly more than a glimmer on the horizon in 1971.) At the same time, two regular members— Dillon Read and Kuhn Loeb—had lost ground, largely because most of the securities they had traditionally specialized in, those of utilities and railroads, were now required to be sold by competitive bidding. Nevertheless, they clung to their positions in the special bracket on the strength of loyalty and tradition, just as once-powerful but now toothless old members of actual clubs continue to be heaped with honor within the clubrooms long after they have yielded their influence in the outside world. Just beneath the special bracket (metaphysically in industry prestige, physically as in listing in the tombstone ads for major underwritings) came a *major bracket* consisting of seventeen firms, among them Blyth, Goldman Sachs, Kidder Peabody, Lehman Brothers, Halsey Stuart, and Lazard Frères. Beneath the major bracket came as many as six separate subordinate brackets, the distinctions among them delicately but emphatically delineated in tombstone ads through separate alphabetical listings of each.

The admissions and discipline committee to govern this elaborate pecking order, Hayes found, consisted essentially of the two firms at the apex, Morgan Stanley and First Boston. The principals of those two firms had the last word on who stood where. Only six previously excluded firms had been admitted to the special or major brackets since 1954. Character and unique special capacity, rather than capital, were the chief qualifications for such advancement; Morgan Stanley itself was not even among the top one hundred securities firms in the country in capital holdings. Pushiness—as in the case of Lazard's unilateral demand for special-bracket standing—was discouraged as strongly as possible.

And so on. To be sure, some of the more insidious of the traditional social, educational, and ethnic distinctions were breaking down: for example, First Boston in 1970 could no longer very accurately be described as a Yale firm, nor Morgan Stanley a Princeton firm, and Jewish firms no longer found it helpful to have an Anglo-Saxon syndicate manager if they wanted to be in on the big action. (Moreover, they were no longer literally Jewish firms.) But members in good standing still respected the club's rules.

Did corporate clients mind dealing with a club when they needed to raise money? Apart from the few remaining diehard proponents of competitive bidding for all issues, apparently not. As regards the three-quarters of major underwriting still done by negotiation, ties between bankers and clients were still based principally on the two traditional factors: personal relationships and clients' satisfaction with services rendered. In the financial aspect that they were so fond of deprecating, the club members were doing fine. Gross underwriting spreads on negotiated issues averaged around 1 percent for debt and 6 percent for equity—far less than in the palmy days of 1900, but enough to pay the grocery bill with something to spare in an economy expanding so fast that the total of all kinds of underwritings had tripled in a decade, from $14.3 billion in 1960 to $43 billion in 1970.

"In the near term," Hayes wrote, "there is little chance of a dramatic upheaval in the patterns by which underwriters do business."[13] For the sake of his standing as a prophet, the percipient professor did well to use the imprecise term "near term"—rather than, for instance, "ten or fifteen years." For "dramatic upheaval" was, precisely, on its way—not just in underwriting techniques, but in the characteristic activities and basic assumptions of investment bankers.

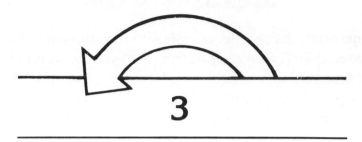

3

Names and Numbers
of the Players

On Wall Street, where giving things up-to-date names is a specialty, a firm's reputation is known as its *culture.* The usage offends the fastidious because of its suggestion that investment banking has some connection with culture in the sense of intellectual and artistic activity. However, it can be justified on grounds that the word also means "the totality of socially transmitted behavior patterns . . . characteristic of a community or population" *(American Heritage Dictionary).*

In some cases, an investment firm's culture is the product of its history, whereas in others it represents to one extent or another a reversal of that history. In all cases, it should be approached with a certain skepticism. A firm's perceived culture can be, to one extent or another, the product of the considerable public-relations effort that the firm must necessarily make to remain competitive. It is, after all, a key factor in the firm's degree of success, because when corporate clients choose among investment banks, the particular character of those banks, as they see it, goes a long way toward determining their choice. (The culture that a client seeks out may not be one that is "good" by traditional standards; for example, a reputation for unfettered aggressiveness may be preferred to one for experience and reliability.)

Thus, before tackling the specifics of the investment-banking game as played in the 1980s, and their implications for investors and the economy, we shall examine the well-projected cultures of the leading firms in that time, as an approach to learning the character of the leading players themselves.

The coming of the new order is dramatically illustrated in the recent rise of Salomon Brothers. In 1963, when William R. (Billy) Salomon, second generation of the founding family, took over as managing partner, the firm was a brash, brawling specialist in bond trading, far down in the underwriting hierarchy, and treated with condescension by the industry autocrats. Its record for 1984—when it was still brash and brawling; a Goldman Sachs partner said admiringly that year, "It's like a boiling cauldron over there, but it works"—speaks for itself. In lead management of underwritings of domestic taxable securities—

the traditional measure of rank among United States investment banks, and the field headed in most years over the past generation by Morgan Stanley—it finished first by a huge margin, its total of $21.3 billion amounting to more than twice that of its nearest competitor, and its share of the entire market coming to 26 percent. (Since then, it has been the perennial leader in domestic taxable securities underwriting.) In managing tax-exempt securities, it ranked second with $35.4 billion. Worldwide, it was the top lead underwriter of securities of all kinds, with over $150 billion. In the Eurodollar market, it placed fourth among lead underwriters of new issues. It was the U.S. leader in the private placements of debt and equity; and it was the top lead manager of the newborn giant market of mortgage-based obligations, having done $4.5 billion, representing 37 percent of the market and more than 50 percent more than the nearest competitor. Finally, its lead management that year of $1.5 billion of U.S. floating-rate notes for the Kingdom of Sweden—a deal largely engineered by a twenty-eight-year-old named Adam Lerrick— made it the author of the largest single taxable debt issue ever offered in the United States.

As usual, for 1984, Salomon was the leader in securities trading, turning over $3.4 trillion, including three of the year's four biggest block trades to cross the tape of the New York Stock Exchange. Its securities inventory averaged around $8 billion—typically hedged down to a much lower exposure, chiefly by the use of financial futures— and its securities inventory of almost $10 billion at the start of the year represented more than the inventories of Goldman Sachs and Merrill Lynch combined. In mergers and acquisitions, Salomon was involved in sixty transactions in 1984, including four of the six largest of the year, one of these the biggest of all time, the $13.2-billion merger of Gulf Oil and Chevron Corporation.

This astonishing record marked the culmination of a twenty-two-year period of breathtaking expansion and innovation, particularly in underwriting. Arthur Herbert and Percy Salomon—soon joined by Morton Hutzler, whose name was included in its title until 1970—founded the firm in 1910. In 1917 it became a primary dealer in U.S. government securities and established its still-maintained reputation for making a market in any security it sold. In 1961 it established its bond research department, which was joined the following year by the near-legendary Henry Kaufman, who in the early eighties could shake the national bond and stock markets—or, rather, could not avoid shaking them—with a simple declarative sentence. In 1963 it made its big move into underwriting by joining with Lehman, Blyth, and Merrill Lynch to form a utility-bond bidding group that became one of what was known as the Fearsome Foursome. In 1978—the same year that Salomon established Wall Street's first mortgage-securities department—John Gutfreund succeeded Billy Salomon as managing partner. Under Gutfreund the firm became, if anything, even more aggressive, although its risk-taking became more calculated and less gratuitous. In 1981 it greatly expanded its capital resources, and ended its partnership status, through merger with Phibro Corporation, a publicly held commodities trading firm; Gutfreund shared leadership of the merged firm with David Tendler of Phibro until 1984, when Gutfreund took it over by himself.

By that time, Salomon had in abundance the three

key strengths that, according to *The Economist,* are now requisite for global investment banks: a big capital base (Salomon's was $1.7 billion at the end of 1984 and $2.3 billion at the end of 1985); a broadly based and efficient distribution network (the firm insists that its vast trading operation, while highly profitable in itself, has as its principal *raison d'être* what it tells institutional investors about "what they can expect to accomplish for their clients"— which might perhaps be rephrased as "what it tells securities issuers about where they can find buyers for their securities"); and finally, a particular franchise in specialized areas—in Salomon's case, for example, mortgage-backed securities and zero-coupon bonds. As for Gutfreund, his style of leadership is paradoxical. He wants results and is not inclined to be fastidious about the methods he encourages to get them, yet he was an English and literature major at liberal-arts Oberlin College (class of 1951); he likes to talk in philosophical terms, and he insists that the point of his work is public service and not short-term profit. His merger-and-acquisition (M&A) team can be as tough and nasty as any, yet he has been known to tell his M&A men to "act like gentlemen," and he leans toward the more radical ideas for tender-offer reform.

Even though Salomon has been a leader in introducing highly profitable innovations like mortgage-backed securities, it is known, probably correctly, more for brute muscle than for subtlety. It has benefited from luck, in that it happened to be the industry leader in the trading of already-issued securities at the time when that activity replaced underwriting as the key to success. The firm's accomplishment in converting luck into achievement is measured by its current preeminence in many areas, underwriting among them.[1]

Goldman Sachs, another fairly recent recruit to the ranks of the very top firms, is the only remaining old-style private partnership among them. Compared to Salomon, it is generally known as being less aggressively innovative, more conservative in risk-taking, more nearly first-rate across the board, and far more harmonious internally, at least as far as an outsider's eye can discern. Despite its recent rapid rise, it does not lack for ancient provenance. It was founded in 1869 as a dealer in commercial paper by Marcus Goldman, an 1848 immigrant from Germany who had previously started and run a clothing store in Philadelphia; in 1882 Goldman was joined by his son-in-law Samuel Sachs. The firm's nineteenth-century reputation was for unusual probity; the American Rothschild agent August Belmont spoke of it as "one firm . . . nobody can say anything against." Early in the twentieth century it entered into an alliance with Lehman Brothers to underwrite stocks of retail goods manufacturers and distributors; in underwriting volume, however, it remained far below Morgan and Kuhn Loeb. In the early 1930s it ceased quite abruptly to be a firm beyond criticism. At the end of 1928, at the height of the speculative madness of the twenties, it had sponsored Goldman Sachs Trading Corporation, an investment trust with an original capitalization of $100 million, of which 90 percent was sold to the public and the rest kept by the partners. Subsequently, subsidiary trusts were formed, greatly increasing the leverage of the original one. In less than a month in mid-1929, the Trading Corporation issued more than a quarter of a billion dollars in securities. Thus exposed, it was exceptionally vulnerable to the 1929 crash; at the depth of the Depression the Trading Corporation's stock, which had originally been issued at 104 and then split two for one, was selling below 2, with the result that many investors were wiped out. On top of that, Goldman Sachs had had the particular misfortune to sell some of the Trading Corporation's stock to the celebrated comedian Eddie Cantor, who now made jokes at Goldman's expense a regular part of his repertoire.

In the public mind, the name Goldman Sachs became from coast to coast the occasion for a bitter laugh—and perhaps in the corporate mind, too. Between 1930 and 1935, the firm did not manage a single stock or bond issue, and seemed to be moribund. It recovered slowly under the leadership of Sidney J. Weinberg, the "Mr. Wall Street" of the early postwar years, who at his zenith sat on more than fifty corporate boards, and gained his greatest fame for masterminding the $650-million initial public stock offering of Ford Motor Company in 1956. Following Weinberg's death in 1969, Goldman was ably led for seven years by a wily trader and arbitrageur, Gustave L. Levy, who is also credited—at least at Goldman Sachs—with having invented the block trade (ten thousand or more shares at a time) in stock. The firm's reputation was tarnished a second time in 1970, when it was accused of selling large quantities of Penn Central commercial paper with knowledge of that firm's impending bankruptcy, and was forced to pay millions in settlement claims. Still, on his death in 1976, Levy left Goldman in good shape, as a specialist in commercial paper and in trading stock with institutions.

It was over the succeeding years, under the joint leadership of Sidney Weinberg's son John and John C. Whitehead (until Whitehead's departure to the State Department in 1985), that Goldman became the wonder firm that it now is. For 1983 it achieved record profits for the tenth consecutive year, earning an estimated $400 million. (Because of its private status, the firm need not publish earnings figures, and until now it has not done so.) For the same year, it was tops in corporate clients on the Fortune 500 list; tops in risk-arbitrage trading; tops in distributing stocks to institutional investors; tops in merger-and-acquisition fees earned; probably tops in handling Stock Exchange block trades; and, as usual, tops in commercial-paper dealings.

The methods by which Whitehead and Weinberg brought Goldman to its pinnacle were, by their own assertion, essentially those associated in the corporate world with IBM. Teamwork was emphasized; would-be prima donnas were discouraged. Department heads were promoted from within the firm rather than acquired through raids on others; conversely, professionals seldom left Goldman, and many of those at the top had spent their entire careers in a single department. The greatest rewards were reserved for low-key, almost anonymous excellence. The potential capital-base problem presented by adherence to the old partnership structure was dealt with by reinvestment of profits. With only a few exceptions, partners were required to put back in the firm all of their annual shares of profits, so long as they remained part of it. (Partners' compensation consisted of moderate sala-ries—less than $100,000 right up to the top—plus interest on their accumulated tranches of the firm's capital, a sum that, after a partner had been there a few years, usually ran into millions annually.) Reinvestment in 1983 raised Gold-man's total capital to $712 million—sixth in the ranking of all investment banks. It finished 1984 with $850 million, and 1985 with $1.2 billion. In 1986 it took Sumitomo Bank, Ltd., of Japan as a passive partner, adding $500 million to its capital.

An unexpected tribute to Goldman came in 1984 from one of its fiercest competitors, Drexel Burnham Lambert, when Frederick H. Joseph, soon to become that firm's chief executive, said, "One of the things I admire most about [Goldman] is that they do it nicely—they care about their people, they care about customers, they care about quality." Alone among the top firms, Goldman had never managed a hostile tender offer. Whitehead insisted that this was a practical matter rather than a moral one—"We don't believe that unfriendly tender offers work," he ex-plained—but there can be little question that the policy conferred moral stature on the firm among its peers, or that it was intended to.

Of course, a reputation for unusual rectitude always brings its possessor under scrutiny for flaws suggesting hypocrisy, and Goldman is no exception. For example, a top member of a top rival firm points out—anonymously, but not without glee—that Goldman sometimes profits from hostile tender offers that it *doesn't* manage. He points out that when Chicago Pacific tendered hostilely (and, in the end, unsuccessfully) for Textron in 1984,

Goldman "did all the numbers" for Chicago Pacific—only to pull out at the last minute and leave the actual offer to Lazard Frères. The implication is that Goldman's no-hostile-tender policy is partly sham.

The knives came out again the same year, when Goldman issued one of the "fairness opinions" that give rise to much mirth in Wall Street. Royal Dutch Petroleum was seeking to buy out the 30 percent of Shell Oil that it did not already own, and, as is customary in such cases, the investment bankers for both sides—Morgan Stanley for Royal Dutch, and Goldman Sachs for Shell—were asked to give their "objective" opinions of what the price should be. Morgan Stanley, for the prospective buyer, came up with $55 per share of Shell. Goldman, on the other hand, decided that $80 would be about right. A reasonable difference of opinion, perhaps, even though a startlingly large one. The trouble was that each of the "objective" appraisers had a contractual, monetary interest in the result: Morgan Stanley's fee arrangement with Royal Dutch called for it to be paid more if the deal went through, and Goldman's with Shell provided that the higher the price, the higher the fee. (Royal Dutch ended up paying $60 per share, suggesting that Morgan Stanley had been a good deal nearer the mark than Goldman.)

Perhaps the most disturbing aspect of the episode is that both investment banks involved were quick to assert that their fee arrangements had been "standard" for fairness opinions. Such opinions, they seemed to be saying, have little to do with fairness, and everything to do with bargaining for one's client. As for Goldman's fee arrangement, a Royal Dutch source—again anonymous—was quick to comment that it was *not* standard, but rather "highly unusual. . . . Other banks who bid for this business proposed flat fairness-opinion fees."

So bright was Goldman's escutcheon that a partner was able to murmur that "Goldman is widely known for giving objective opinions," and the criticism died out. Overall, Goldman Sachs—even after government accusations of insider-trading violations against two of its employees, in 1986 and 1987—may be again, as it was in August Belmont's day, the firm it is hardest to say anything against.[2]

In the public mind, Merrill Lynch has for years been "the Thundering Herd"—the giant of retail stock brokerage, with hundreds of offices and tens of thousands of salesmen spread-eagling the country. But in fact, from a historical standpoint this view is largely wrong; the firm has at intervals made dramatic changes in its activities, although not in its "culture," which has remained rather constant. Founded in 1910 by Charles E. Merrill, a former semi-pro baseball player originally from Florida, who was joined in 1914 by Edmund C. Lynch, it soon made its mark in retail brokerage and became widely known as the principal firm that "brought Wall Street to the nation." During the boom years of the 1920s it undertook an occasional underwriting, but concentrated on, and remained a leader in, retail brokerage—and meanwhile resisted most of the temptations that led so many firms at the time into scandal or disgrace. Foreseeing the Crash of 1929 and the subsequent Depression, Merrill took his firm out of brokerage at the end of the decade, turning his accounts over to

E. A. Pierce & Company. After concentrating on underwriting, primarily of retail-store stocks, during the thirties, Merrill Lynch returned to brokerage in 1940, merging that year and the next with E. A. Pierce and various other firms to form Merrill Lynch, Pierce, Fenner & Beane (the "Beane" became "Smith" in 1958), which came into being as the largest brokerage house in the world.

By the fifties, Merrill Lynch bestrode the U.S. brokerage scene, accounting for 12 percent of all sales on the New York Stock Exchange, and 20 percent of all odd-lot transactions. It seldom managed underwritings, but was in great demand as a participant in syndicates managed by others, because of its unique capability in retailing stocks. In 1958 it became the first top brokerage firm to incorporate. The firm's position remained relatively stable until the middle seventies, when—under the direction of Donald T. Regan, later Secretary of the Treasury and White House chief of staff in the Reagan administration—it moved decisively into investment banking. Motivated in large part by the progressive unfixing of Stock Exchange commission rates, which culminated in their complete freeing on May 1, 1975, this move was formalized in 1978 with the formation of the Merrill Lynch Capital Markets Group as the firm's investment-banking arm. It strengthened its foothold with two acquisitions of well-established investment-banking firms: in 1978, White Weld & Company, an old-line underwriter, and a member of the Club of Seventeen in the government antitrust case; and in 1984, Becker Paribas Inc., a firm that had suffered disastrous reverses, but that brought strong international connections and a strong commercial-paper business along with

$100 million in assets and another $100 million in tax-loss carry-forwards.

As an investment bank in the 1980s, Merrill Lynch is known more for its weight than its dexterity. Its capital, amounting to more than $3.1 billion in 1986, put it at the top of the list; its investment-banking income (almost $750 million for 1983) dwarfed that of such a mettlesome competitor as First Boston; its mergers-and-acquisitions income grew from virtually nothing in 1981 to second place (by its own reckoning) in 1983. But an air of bureaucracy tended to overhang the place. Growth of underwriting fees—from $30 million in 1979 to $40 million in 1984—was less than spectacular.

Merrill Lynch's much-advertised symbol, the bull, seems to have been all too well chosen. Among a pride of competitors who came across as cougars, pumas, and perhaps jackals, Merrill Lynch seemed to be an animal capable only of plowing straight ahead. Still, a bull cannot be ignored, especially when it is the biggest animal in the jungle; and neither can Merrill Lynch.[3]

In the 1980s, First Boston Corporation had the fanciest offices in the business (on plush, largely residential Park Avenue), the most aggressive advertising, and probably the most radically changed public image. As noted previously, it came into existence in 1934 as a result of the impact of the Glass-Steagall Act on the First National Bank of Boston and the Chase National Bank of New York, which joined together their securities affiliates to form the new investment bank as a publicly owned corporation. (Chase, wracked with scandal associated with the securities transactions of its former president, Albert H. Wiggin, had anticipated the effect of the act by terminating its securities business in May 1933.) First Boston flourished for a generation and more as a leading underwriter, particularly of public sealed-bidding utility bonds. (The firm opposed public sealed bids on principle, but, like some of its competitors, did not let that stop it from participating in them in a major way.) Meanwhile—even though its underwriters were inclined to be Ivy Leaguers who looked down on securities trading as an inferior activity for an investment bank—First Boston was a pioneer in developing a strong trading operation, and did much trading for its own account. By 1947, following a merger with Mellon Securities Corporation, its capital had risen to the then unusually high figure of $25 million. Over the subsequent years it enjoyed unquestioned membership in the select top bracket of underwriters, and membership in Judge Medina's Club of Seventeen in the antitrust case.

Ironically, when First Boston stumbled, it was in mergers and acquisitions, the activity that was later to bring it both fame and notoriety. In 1969, acting as merger adviser to the conglomerate Bangor Punta Corporation, it unintentionally allowed a misrepresentation of its client's financial position, and had a $36-million judgment entered against it. Even though the judgment was ultimately overturned, the firm was sufficiently chagrined that it all but dropped out of the M&A business for a time. During the seventies, First Boston underwent a general decline; for 1978 it showed its lowest profit since the Depression, and was no longer considered a major factor in the business. But at that very moment—under the new leadership of

George Shinn, a refugee from the presidency of Merrill Lynch—it was being reborn in a new skin. That year it entered into a joint overseas underwriting venture with Crédit Suisse, one of the three largest banks in Switzerland, called Financière Crédit Suisse–First Boston. This entity became the perennial leading issuer of Eurodollar securities, and early in 1985 First Boston overtook Salomon Brothers as manager of the largest volume of securities offerings in the world.

Meanwhile, First Boston was building an M&A department that would be the Wall Street sensation of the early eighties. "From nowhere, First Boston skyrocketed to the top ranks in M&A," wrote Lee Smith in *Fortune*. Among its clients were Du Pont in its almost $9-billion merger with Conoco in 1981, Marathon Oil in its $6.75-billion merger with U.S. Steel in 1981, Bendix in its $4-billion merger with Allied Corporation in 1982, and Texaco in its $10-billion merger with Getty Oil in 1984. Its merger fees came to $75 million for 1981, and $93 million for 1982. For 1983, it was involved in six of the ten biggest merger transactions, and was number one nationally in M&A (that is, by its own accounting; in determining M&A leadership, different results can usually be obtained by applying different criteria).

The M&A team that achieved these prodigies was probably the most publicized phenomenon of the new investment banking. Its leaders were Joseph Perella, born in 1941 to Italian immigrants in Newark, New Jersey, who joined First Boston in 1972 after graduation from Harvard Business School; Bruce Wasserstein, born in 1948, the son of a well-to-do New York City textile man (and brother of the well-known playwright Wendy Wasserstein), who had taken graduate degrees in both business and law, and done a stint as one of Nader's Raiders, before he was hired away from the Cravath law firm by Perella in 1977; and Bill G. Lambert, a former high school classmate of Wasserstein, who came to First Boston in 1982. Lambert, who carried a title perhaps unique in the annals of investment banking—"creative director"—specialized in dreaming up deals; Wasserstein—who, perhaps because of a quality defined by a rival as "motivated flamboyance," got by far the most publicity of the three—was the genius at structuring them; and Perella, at around forty the senior member of the group, put them into practice. Readers of popular magazines were informed breathlessly that for office wear the M&A men were inclined toward jeans and sneakers, and toward addressing each other as "Babe," to the outrage of First Boston's conservative element centered in its underwriting operation, who sometimes spoke of them as "the Manson gang." Undaunted, all three of them boasted racily about their aggressiveness and its results. Wasserstein said in 1984, "Look at the record. Other than the poison pill [see Chapter 6], what innovations [in merger and takeover tactics] didn't come out of this group?" Perella chimed in, "The path is littered with other firms who have tried to tangle with us."

But the ferocity of the First Boston M&A men's often-quoted public statements should not be taken at quite face value. Undoubtedly they were more aggressive in seeking business than were many of their counterparts at other leading firms, and undoubtedly their brash remarks genuinely irritated the more conservative underwriting cadre in their own firm, as well as practically everybody at competing firms. But in fact, most of the time they operated as low-key technicians, putting together complex, little-publicized friendly mergers, excelling in a nonpredatory form of expertise that happened to be very much in fashion. To one extent or another, the ferocious statements were bluff—a form of self-advertisement adapted to a time when old standards were reversed, and brashness combined with exceptional skill, rather than conservatism and good manners, was just what more and more corporate clients were looking for in an investment banker. This conclusion is strongly suggested, at any rate, by the fact that in 1985—by which time there was a discernible reaction against First Boston's M&A style not only among professional rivals but also among potential clients, some of whose executives were coming to resent Perella, Wasserstein, and company as glory-grabbers—the ferocious statements virtually ceased. The new, warlike—or, one might say, anticultural—M&A culture was hardly going out of style, but evidently those who were calling the shots at First Boston decided that a time had come to deemphasize it, especially since the firm was growing rapidly in other fields such as trading and underwriting mortgage-backed securities. Such was its overall success that total capital, which had stood at $424 million at the end of 1983, passed the billion-dollar mark in 1985, and reached $1.4 billion in 1986.

Unmistakably, the in-house conflict of cultures that for a time had served to keep First Boston in the public prints was also serving its overall commercial purposes. In June 1985 it was party to the coming of the merger game to a sort of apotheosis. When General Motors bought Hughes Aircraft Corporation for $5 billion in a friendly transaction, First Boston represented the seller, Hughes Medical Institute. The day the merger was announced, First Boston's *own* stock, traded on the New York Stock Exchange, reacted to the prospective fee (later estimated at $15 million) by jumping 3¾ points, or almost 5 percent. A time had come when one could do profitable arbitrage not only on the stocks of merger target companies, but also on those of the merger-making middlemen.[4]

To round out the top underwriting bracket, the ruling class of the industry, there was the traditional leader, Morgan Stanley, which we have already seen as linear successor to the pre–Glass-Steagall king of the industry, J. P. Morgan & Company, and as the perennial top choice of corporate America for investment-banking services from its founding in 1935 until very recently. In 1970 it was much as it had always been: still the king of corporate underwriting, which constituted all but a tiny fraction of its business, and still the firm most nearly able to decide which of its rivals ranked where.

Between 1970 and 1985, Morgan Stanley changed drastically, and yet in a sense did not change; more than First Boston, it went through an agonizing internal struggle between contrasting cultures. In the former year it gave up its partnership structure and incorporated, paving the way for large increases in its capital base—yet it remained a private firm, since almost all of the stock was held by its "managing directors," successors to its old partners. Over the fifteen-year period, its capital grew from $7.5 million to more than $300 million (still a small figure in relation to those of its industry-leader rivals), and its personnel expanded from around three hundred to over three thousand. It had opened its first overseas office in 1967; by 1984 it had more people in London alone than the whole company had contained in 1970. It remained the corporate-underwriting leader until long after the new era in investment banking had become established; from 1980 through 1982 it finished either first or second in volume of domestic lead underwritings of both stocks and bonds— only to drop to fifth in bonds in 1983, while remaining first in stocks. More recently, it has been well below the leaders in overall underwriting, and has yielded to Goldman Sachs its long-held status as banker to the greatest number of large corporations. Around 1980 it gave up its traditional haughty policy of refusing to participate in corporate offerings except as lead underwriter; by the middle of the decade—as a result partly of its new policy, and partly of its place in the alphabet—its renowned name was appearing in tombstone ads beneath those of such relative upstarts as Bear Stearns, Drexel Burnham Lambert, and E. F. Hutton.

Meanwhile—chiefly under the leadership of Robert H. B. Baldwin, president and chief of day-to-day operations from 1973 to 1983—Morgan Stanley was putting its toe, usually well behind the pioneers, into the waters of the new investment banking. It began trading securities (apart from stabilization operations in stock underwritings) in 1971 and 1972; it entered risk arbitrage in 1977; and, far behind the pack, it entered foreign currency and gold trading in 1982, and commercial paper, tax-exempt securities operations, leveraged buyouts, and trading in mortgage-backed securities in 1984. The one modern activity in which it got an early start, and became an early leader, was mergers and acquisitions, where the exceptionally aggressive Robert F. Greenhill was doing innovative deals as early as 1970 and, in 1974, changing the accepted practices of most of the industry by managing INCO's hostile takeover of ESB. Morgan Stanley's M&A men, like First Boston's, made no bones about going after merger business, even from nonclients; a group was established to spend its time studying every announced merger and trying to figure out how Morgan Stanley, by finding a better deal or a white knight, could muscle in on the deal, even by approaching a corporation with which it had no previous relationship.

In 1981, Morgan Stanley took a step that was widely interpreted as reflecting the internal cultural conflict attendant on modernizing itself. That February it merged its M&A department under Greenhill with its corporate finance department under Lewis W. Bernard, the merged entity to be headed by Richard B. Fisher, soon to become president and second-in-command. The move was seen to mean on the one hand that Greenhill's aggressiveness was thought within the firm to be violating Morgan Stanley's traditional culture and therefore to be in need of reining in; and, on the other, that the very same aggressiveness would now be useful in a wider context. In any case, Morgan Stanley did not then drop out of the ranks of hard-hitting M&A firms; a striking example of this is the way the firm in 1984—its M&A operations by that time under the direction of Joseph G. Fogg III—came in at the last minute to collect a quickly earned $20-million fee as adviser to Standard Oil of California in its purchase of Gulf Oil, the biggest merger in history.

Morgan Stanley obviously lost ground to its rivals during the eighties, partly because ingrained (although diminishing) old attitudes within the firm served as a drag on modernization, partly because relatively low capitalization was a handicap in the new game. (Even after a highly successful public stock sale in March 1986 brought in almost $300 million, the firm remained far below its chief rivals in total capital.) While understandably reluctant to own up to ingrained attitudes, Morgan Stanley cheerfully admits to errors of judgment; mortgage-backed securities, for example, were "one area where we clearly misjudged the trends," President Fisher said in 1984. On the other hand, those residual attitudes, along with the firm's age-old reputation, remain an asset with a minority of corporate clients who share the attitudes and value the reputation. The new Morgan Stanley stays near the top by trading on its honored old name and its newly acquired skills.[5]

Shearson Lehman Brothers, a firm on the edge of the magic circle at the top of investment banking, is a paradigm of a strange new creature in Wall Street, a leading investment bank that is just one sales counter in a huge financial supermarket. The mergers that went into its assemblage in 1984 are so numerous that a full recital of them would read like the biblical "begats." To compress drastically, the assemblage may be said to have begun in 1960 with the formation of an upstart, go-go firm first called Carter, Berlind, Patoma & Weill, and later Cogan,

Berlind, Weill & Levitt. Over its first twenty years this firm absorbed ten others, among them Hayden Stone & Company (founded 1892); Shearson Hamill & Company (founded 1904); and Loeb Rhoades Hornblower & Company, itself the product of a string of mergers, including one with old-line Hornblower & Weeks (founded 1880). In 1981 American Express, the huge financial-services company, bought Shearson Loeb Rhoades—product of the many mergers of the Weill firm—for $1 billion, thereby creating Shearson/American Express. In 1984, Shearson/American Express bought for $360 million what was then called Lehman Brothers Kuhn Loeb, to form the surviving firm, Shearson Lehman Brothers, a minority part of American Express.

Although many of the firms that went into this gigantic stew had long been important in brokerage, none but Lehman Brothers and Kuhn Loeb had ever been leaders in investment banking, and therefore—since Kuhn Loeb has vanished into the maw—our attention here focuses on Lehman Brothers. It arose in the dim past of the industry, around 1850, out of a cotton brokerage firm started in Montgomery, Alabama, by three recent German-Jewish immigrants, Henry, Emanuel, and Mayer Lehman. Moving to New York and expanding first into trading in other commodities, Lehman Brothers did its first securities underwriting in 1899. A few years later it formed a loose alliance with Goldman Sachs—based not on a contract but on an oral agreement between Philip Lehman, son of one of the founders, and Henry Goldman—to underwrite stocks, chiefly of retailing companies. The alliance lasted about two decades and provided key financing for the

Sears Roebuck, F. W. Woolworth, and B. F. Goodrich companies, among others. When it broke down in the 1920s, Lehman changed its character and became bitterly competitive for underwritings with its investment-banking rivals, including Goldman Sachs; it was a pioneer in competitive bidding for railroad and utility issues, well before such bidding became mandatory. Meanwhile, its partners and former partners developed a powerful reputation for gentlemanly cultural interests and statesmanship; to cite just two examples, Robert Lehman put together one of the greatest of all art collections (now housed at the Metropolitan Museum of Art in New York City), and Herbert H. Lehman served with distinction four terms as governor of New York State and one as a U.S. senator.

Lehman Brothers breezed through the 1950s as a leading manager of all kinds of underwritings, a leading commission broker, and a vintage member of Judge Medina's Club of Seventeen. In the late 1960s, however, it fell afoul of the dreadful back-office administrative problems that were endemic at that time; in August 1968 the SEC threatened to suspend the firm's registration as a broker-dealer. It avoided bankruptcy and oblivion only through two infusions of cash from outside—a $7-million investment by Banca Commerciale Italiana, and a $4.9-million merger with Abraham & Company—and effective new management headed by Peter G. Peterson, a former Nixon administration Secretary of Commerce, who became chairman in 1972. Its absorption of once-imperial Kuhn Loeb in 1977 was mainly a matter of saving the face of a firm that had lost its vitality: Lehman Brothers brought $60 million in capital to the transaction, Kuhn Loeb only $18 million.

From then until the sale to the much larger Shearson/American Express in 1984 was a period, for Lehman Brothers, of high profits and internal turmoil. It remained in the top ten in corporate underwriting, and was further up the list in other activities, among them securities trading and mergers and acquisitions. (For 1983, a year of record profits, Lehman publicly challenged First Boston's claim to M&A leadership.) Meanwhile, the tradition of fierce competitiveness for underwritings that it had maintained since the twenties appeared to turn inward, toward strife among members of the firm. What the Shearson Lehman chairman after the 1984 merger—Peter Cohen, who came out of the Weill firm—called "that Byzantine culture" reached its most destructive form in the much-publicized 1983 battle for leadership of Lehman between Peterson and Lewis L. Glucksman, a tough trader in the New Era mode. Glucksman won; but the scars of the battle, and the new boss's quick moves to increase the rewards of the firm's traders at the expense of its underwriters, were important causes of the partners' decision to sell out to American Express, ending the oldest continuously operating Wall Street partnership of them all.

It is ironic, and perhaps sad, that at the very moment and by the very act that Lehman Brothers, after more than a century and a quarter, arguably achieved membership in the top bracket of underwriters, it became a subsidiary of somebody else and fell into a degree of disgrace. The merger raised the firm's capital from $325 million to $1.7 billion ($2.8 billion in 1986), putting it in a position to compete in the new game with anyone. What remained was somehow to end internal strife, or somehow to make the strife work as well as it seemed to at Salomon Brothers.[6]

Drexel Burnham Lambert is a special case. Although its surface credentials for respectability are unmatched—the lead name in its title is among the oldest such names extant on Wall Street, and its principal area of expertise and source of profit is good old corporate bond under-writing—in the early 1980s it was the most scorned and reviled of industry leaders. The explanation of the anomaly lies in the *kind* of underwriting Drexel specialized in: the fountain of its new success was the underwriting of the high-yield, relatively low-rated kind of securities popularly called *junk bonds*. Drexel in the mid-eighties was the unchallenged king of junk bonds and, as a result, perhaps the Wall Street king of paradox.

Like Shearson Lehman Brothers, the firm is the outcome of many mergers, the keystone of the arch being Burnham & Company, an aggressive brokerage founded by I. W. Burnham in 1935. In 1973, Burnham merged with Drexel Firestone, Inc., which had in its own merger genealogy two members of the Medina Club of Seventeen, Harriman Ripley & Co. and Drexel & Company. (This was not the original Drexel dating from 1838, but rather its post–Glass-Steagall investment-banking successor, as Morgan Stanley is to J. P. Morgan.) In 1976, Drexel Burnham & Company merged with Lambert Brussels Witter, Inc., to form the present firm as Drexel Burnham Lambert.

Until the late 1970s, the Drexel firm was weak as a lead underwriter, and in general a minor-league presence on the investment-banking scene. At that time, a young man in the firm, Michael Milken—then about thirty, and acquired in the merger with Drexel Firestone—discerned a gaping opportunity in the fact that the price and yield differential between low-rated bonds and investment-rated bonds had become greater than the risk differential. Moreover, the underwriting spread available to an underwriter of junk bonds (technically defined as those rated BB or lower by Standard & Poor's, and Ba or lower by Moody's) was, and still is, substantially higher than that available to underwriters of top-rated bonds. Despite the profit opportunity, most of the leading underwriters were reluctant or unwilling to sponsor new issues of low-rated bonds. The bond business had a tradition-based differential of its own. Looking back toward the celebrated failures of low-rated bond issues in the past, with resulting disaster and disgrace to their underwriters, leading investment-banking firms reflexively shunned them. Under Milken's influence, it was Drexel, and Drexel alone, that saw a changed situation and set out to come as close as possible to cornering the low-rated bond market. In 1977 it allowed Milken to move his operation to Los Angeles—a more nourishing climate than New York City for junk-bond issuance, it was felt—and Drexel Burnham Lambert was on its way to becoming the junk-bond king.

Even before the move, Milken's desk at Drexel had been considered the only real secondary market for low-rated bonds. In California, his team's aggressive selling of them to investors, chiefly institutional ones, was so effective that Drexel began to rise rapidly up the list of U.S. lead underwriters of public securities issues of *all* kinds.

In 1973 it had ranked fifteenth; in 1983 it was up to seventh, largely on the strength of high-yield bonds. In 1984—by which time there were some $100 billion in such bonds outstanding in the market—Drexel lead-managed $9.5 billion in new ones, or about two-thirds of all that were issued that year; along with the $1 billion in investment-grade issues that it managed, its total for the year rocketed it to second place in overall domestic underwriting volume, second only to Salomon Brothers and ahead of First Boston, Merrill Lynch, Goldman Sachs, and everybody else. In short, Drexel's status as an underwriting leader, however suspect, had become apodictic.

Meanwhile, the firm's reputation as one willing to take on underwritings that its rivals would not, and thereby to subject investors to apparently high risk, was hardly diminished in a symbolic sense by the fact that it had become known as the principal issuer of the bonds of gambling casinos. Even more obloquy attached to the rise in the 1980s—largely stimulated by Drexel—of the junk-bond-financed hostile tender offer. (This subject will be treated in greater depth in Chapter 6.) It is enough to say here that junk-bond financing made it possible for the first time for raiders to mount hostile assaults on huge companies without putting up their own cash or borrowing it from banks, and that Drexel-arranged junk bonds were used in, among others, the raids of Saul P. Steinberg on Walt Disney Productions and of T. Boone Pickens on Gulf Oil, Phillips Petroleum, and Unocal Corporation.

In truth, Drexel in its high-yield bond issues (understandably, members of the firm avoided the pejorative term *junk bond*) was not acting as irresponsibly as that outline might imply. The firm's bond issues were rooted in massive and meticulous in-house research; moreover, of course, any underwriter's issuance of low-rated bonds is categorically regulated by the SEC under the due-diligence provisions of the Securities Acts. As a practical matter, Drexel could argue that its high-yield issues were not junk at all, but rather the true bargains that their buyers took them to be. In 1984 only a few Drexel issues had come to grief in the marketplace after issuance. (Over the decade preceding, the firm had been taken to court only three or four times on due-diligence accusations, and required to pay damages only once.)

By the mid-eighties, success was succeeding just as it is said to do; other firms were overcoming their fastidiousness and flocking to get in on the junk-bond bonanza, and Drexel was coming, for the moment, to be considered respectable. Whether traditional bond dealers liked it or not, Drexel and its junk bonds were almost certainly the most significant phenomenon of American corporate finance in the eighties. Perhaps, as the critics kept insisting, the junk-bond-financed takeover and corporate restructuring were setting the stage for general disaster in the next recession; meanwhile, beyond dispute they were entirely changing the conditions of life in major corporations by rendering all but a few of them vulnerable to takeover and at the same time providing an investment vehicle that brought financial institutions such as pension funds a higher return than would otherwise be available. The ordinarily judicious Samuel Hayes of the Harvard Business School said in 1986, "The only figure comparable to Milken who comes to mind is J. P. Morgan, Sr."

Whether or not that is an exaggeration, it seems certain that years from now, when the many bizarre details and vivid personalities of current investment banking are forgotten, Drexel and its junk bonds will be remembered.[7]

A handful of firms unarguably outside the top tier of underwriters deserve inclusion in this roster of the investment-banking leaders of the 1980s, and one of these is Lazard Frères, which we have already seen, under André Meyer's direction, blazing the industry's way into the new era. In the later 1970s, Lazard's fortunes declined along with its autocratic leader's health and the partial defection to public-service activities of its merger superstar, Felix Rohatyn. In 1978—the year Meyer was succeeded by French-born Michel David-Weill, a member of Lazard's original founding family—it was only marginally profitable, and considered even by some of its own people to be "dead in the water." But David-Weill succeeded in turning it around. By 1984, although well down the list of lead underwriters, and still small (thirty-seven partners and fewer than four hundred employees), it was again highly respected and highly profitable, chiefly as a result of well-conducted incursions into the newer areas such as securities trading, leveraged buyouts, and zero-coupon bonds.

As Lazard's tone-setter, David-Weill (who became head of the firm's New York, Paris, and London offices, something Meyer had never been) proved to be astute but less abrasive than his celebrated predecessor. He took on aggressive young talent from other firms, as Meyer had seldom done, but continued Meyer's policy of aversion to large risk; he followed in Meyer's steps regarding aggressive investment for the firm's own account, but avoided large short-term stock commitments. No longer "the merger house" as it had been in the sixties, Lazard continued strong in the M&A area, where, although it did not shrink from managing hostile tender offers, it became known for relative conservatism, in conformity with David-Weill's directive as outlined by one of his M&A men: "Don't seek publicity, don't make cold calls looking for deals, and consider whether something other than a deal is the client's best solution."

Primarily brokerage houses like Paine Webber and the Bache part of Prudential-Bache in 1984 occupied the lower rungs of the lead-underwriting top ten, and not far behind were such similar firms as Donaldson Lufkin & Jenrette and E. F. Hutton. Even so, these were probably lesser factors in investment banking in the 1980s than such firms as Bear Stearns, which made a splash as a merger adviser beginning in 1981, and L. F. Rothschild Unterberg Towbin, long a leader in small-company initial public offerings, which in the eighties became an across-the-board investment-banking leader. (Owned privately before 1986, Rothschild sold 37 percent of its stock to the public in that year.) Finally, two old-line American firms, Kidder Peabody and Dillon Read, apparently headed for desuetude a few years earlier, made strong comebacks based largely on exploitation of the merger craze. Under the leadership of Martin A. Siegel—who, as all the world now knows, would plead guilty to insider-trading violations in 1987—the Kidder merger operation made it the smallest firm to have a major role in that field. (Its takeover in 1986 by General Electric Financial Services made it a far larger firm in available capital.) In particular, Siegel had charge of Martin Marietta's celebrated "Pac-Man defense" in its battle with Bendix in 1982 (see Chapter 6). As for Dillon Read, its relatively low capital base and the perception of it as antiquated caused it to lose its special-bracket underwriting status in the seventies; but in the eighties—now no longer owned by the Dillon family that founded it, but by its managing directors, the Swedish bank Skandinaviska Enskilda Banken and the Californian Bechtel group—it became known as a specialist in defense against hostile takeover attempts and as such was chosen in 1984 by Unocal as one of its two investment bankers in its successful defense against T. Boone Pickens.

In 1986, Dillon Read was acquired in full by The Travelers Corporation for $157.5 million, making it— along with Morgan Stanley, Bear Stearns, Rothschild, and Kidder Peabody—the fifth major or formerly major firm to accommodate itself to the voracious capital needs of the new global investment banking by selling out either to public investors or to a corporation outside the investment-banking business.[8]

Such, then, were the individual characters of the leading firms in the 1980s, chiefly as projected in the bemused and avidly read financial press. As noted, the projections should be partially discounted to the extent that they may represent calculated self-projections in an environment of fierce competition. In any event, they may serve as an introduction to the principal players in the game—or, as Huizinga would prefer to say, the work—to be described in subsequent chapters.

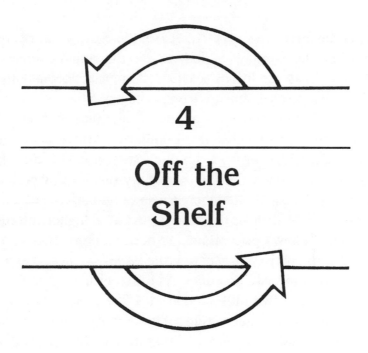

4

Off the Shelf

The underwriting "revolution" symbolized by the promulgation on a trial basis of SEC Rule 415 in March 1982 had actually been going on for some years before that. The precipitating factors were chiefly market conditions in the later 1970s. The basic law on the issuance of securities was (and still is) the Securities Acts of 1933 and 1934, which decree that underwriters shall conduct a "reasonable investigation" of the condition of the company being financed, and that a period of twenty days must pass between the filing of a registration statement and its effective date, when the securities may be issued. A 1940 amendment to the 1933 Act gave the SEC authority to shorten the waiting period at its discretion, when it thought that conditions warranted such action; but this authority was seldom used until the seventies.

With the rapid and accelerating inflation that followed the 1973–74 OPEC oil embargo, timing suddenly became a critical element for the issues of new securities, particularly bonds. During the twenty-day waiting period, bond yields would often increase and bond prices fall; new bonds would then have to be issued at a higher interest rate, and a lower price, than had been planned. In a word, the waiting period was costing the issuers money, and not necessarily in small amounts. As for stocks, in a common-stock issue of two million shares, a five-cent variation in price means a revenue variant of $100,000. (Paul Ferris has remarked that stock underwriting may be the last area in American life in which a nickel is worth anything much.)

The process, and the problem, escalated after October 1979, when the Federal Reserve, in its concern to contain inflation, decided to abandon its previous efforts to stabilize interest rates in order to concentrate, according to monetarist theory, on slow, stable growth of the money supply. This policy, although ultimately successful against inflation, had the immediate effect of bringing about unprecedented interest-rate volatility. Where previously a change of three basis points (that is, hundredths of a percentage point) in a couple of days had been considered a big move, in 1980–81 changes of fifty or more points in such a period came to be commonplace. The issuer of $200 million of bonds could now easily see $1 million or $2 million melt away over twenty days.

The SEC, complaisant to issuers and their underwriters, reacted by invoking the 1940 amendment to reduce the waiting period in appropriate cases. In 1978 it made available a short registration form for large primary issues, to substitute for the lengthy traditional forms and to cut the twenty-day period in half. Somewhat later it reduced the period for certain blue-chip issues to forty-eight hours. Sears Roebuck, Ford Motor, Philip Morris, and Du Pont were among the companies to take advantage of short-form registration. But meanwhile the enormous and fast-growing Eurodollar market, beyond the reach of the SEC and the Federal Reserve, was showing the way to a free-market solution to the problem of timing. In the Eurobond market—where U.S. assets were in strong demand, and intermediaries dominated by U.S. firms tended to control distribution more than in this country—there existed an aggressive mode of buying and selling debt. Distribution could be made immediately, with no waiting period, and the traditional syndicate tended, in more and more cases, to be replaced by the "bought deal," in which a single banking firm simply bought an entire new issue and distributed it as quickly as possible.[1]

Despite the SEC's rule-relaxing policies, the U.S. bond market was losing competitiveness, and the SEC decided to go further. In 1980, on the initiative of Lee B. Spencer, Jr., director of its division of corporate finance, it began planning a new rule that would allow large companies meeting certain financial standards—about 1,400 companies in all, as things turned out—to register a quantity of stocks or bonds and put them "on the shelf" for piecemeal issue at any time over a period of two years, with no waiting period at all between the decision to issue a portion of the registration and the act of doing so. (The new rule, so mysterious are the ways of bureaucracy, was referred to throughout the gestation period as Proposed Rule 269A; for the sake of simplicity, it will here be called by its ultimate designation, Rule 415.)

In considering the action, the commission by its own account intended not so much to accommodate issuers worried about volatile interest rates as to make the complex process of issuing new securities cheaper and more efficient. Rule 415, then, was to be part of the far-reaching deregulation program undertaken by the Reagan administration. For investment banks there appeared to be a couple of serious potential disadvantages in the proposed new system. For one thing, under shelf registration the underwriter or underwriters of an issue would not be decided until the very last minute, after all the bids were in; that is, it amounted to de facto competitive bidding. Therefore Rule 415 threatened to break down or end "traditional" relationships between corporations and investment bankers. Also, elimination of much of the massive technical paperwork that had attended securities issuance for nearly fifty years under the 1933 and 1934 acts might tempt corporations to market their securities themselves, without the help of an intermediary, thus leaving investment bankers out in the cold.

Nevertheless, even though the SEC periodically made its current plans known during 1980 and 1981, there was little outcry from investment bankers until shortly before the commission's announced date for voting on Rule 415. Apparently the complicated releases describing the commission's plans had become mired in the various firms' legal departments, and were being allowed to molder there. When a protest did come, it was led, appropriately enough, by Morgan Stanley, the firm with apparently the most to lose from any disintegration of traditional banker-client relationships. In December 1981, Thomas A. Saunders III, head of underwriting at Morgan Stanley, became concerned about the possible consequences of Rule 415 for capital formation in America. He put together an in-house task force to study the issue. He called various leading investment bankers—among them Gutfreund of Salomon and Whitehead of Goldman Sachs—to inquire whether they had thought seriously about the matter. Most replied that they hadn't, and when they did, they found that they were inclined to agree with Saunders. Indeed, among the top firms only Lehman Brothers Kuhn Loeb (as it then was) pronounced itself more or less behind the proposed rule.

Over the subsequent months, Morgan Stanley conducted what the SEC called an "intense lobbying campaign" against Rule 415. In 1985—three years and many successful shelf deals later—Saunders insisted that his firm had never opposed Rule 415 "in the sense of making a recommendation against its adoption." The record indicates, however, that it stopped just short of such a recommendation. At the beginning of February 1982, Morgan Stanley wrote to the commission stating that "implementation of the Rule as proposed may produce fundamental structural changes in the capital-raising process with undesirable consequences that have not been explored." Among the possible consequences identified by Morgan

Stanley were "internalization of the new issue distribution process"; concentration within the securities industry, resulting from a squeezing of smaller regional firms out of underwriting syndicates; the creation of a new and unhealthy adversary relationship between lead underwriters and corporate issuers; and a higher, rather than a lower, cost of raising capital in the American markets.

The most pervasive objection raised by Morgan Stanley and its chief rivals concerned potential compromise to the "due diligence" of underwriters, required by the 1933 Securities Act, in the matter of determining the soundness of the companies whose securities they issued. (In fact, although it has long since gained provenance in securities law through usage, the expression *due diligence* never appears in the 1933 Act; as previously noted, *reasonable investigation* is the term used.) Over the decades, due-diligence requirements in practice had been relatively lax or unclear. In 1968 came the case of *Bar Chris Construction Corporation* in the federal court for the Southern District of New York. The investment banking house of Drexel & Company had served as lead underwriter in an issue of Bar Chris stock, and eighteen months later the company had collapsed. The court found that Drexel had failed to see evident signs of impending disaster and had made no "effectual" attempt to verify the claims of management regarding the soundness of the company. (As usual, the other investment banks that had participated in the underwriting had relied on the due-diligence effort of their leader.) The *Bar Chris* case struck terror in investment bankers and their lawyers and accountants, and thereafter due-diligence standards were generally more stringent.

Under Rule 415, it appeared that this improvement in the quality of investor protection was to be emphatically reversed—not that due-diligence standards were to be theoretically relaxed, but rather that the practical ability to fulfill them was to be drastically compromised. In the short-form prospectus to be used under Rule 415, much of the detailed financial information about the issuer that had previously been included in long-form registrations and prospectuses was simply left out—or, rather, it was "incorporated by reference" to various documents regularly filed with the SEC by all large companies. A prospective investor, if he wanted this information, instead of finding it staring him in the face in the prospectus, would have to get it from the SEC on his own. (Such "incorporation by reference" was thought by the SEC to comply, at least technically, with existing law.) As for the lead underwriter, if it turned out to be a firm that had had little or no previous contact with the issuer, it could hardly be expected to know the ins and outs of the issuer's financial affairs, or to learn them in a matter of hours.

Concern bordering on alarm about the due-diligence problem under Rule 415 was suddenly widespread among leading investment banks—especially those that had many traditional-banker relationships and now apparently stood to lose them. In a pamphlet published in April 1982, Morgan Stanley said, relatively mildly, "In the context of a bidding for shelf securities . . . it may be more difficult for a potential underwriter which has no prior relationship with the issues to satisfy [the due-diligence] obligation." A bit later on, Whitehead of Goldman Sachs went much further, calling Rule 415 "a regression to the 1929 pre-regulation days," and Gutfreund of Salomon wondered aloud whether, under shelf-registration procedure, investors would have been warned of, say, the impending collapse of Penn Central in 1970. Even members of the SEC admitted that there would be a loss of due-diligence capability under the proposed rule—Chairman John Shad went so far as to say that such due diligence as would be available would be "of limited practical value"—but argued that the firms eligible for shelf registration were so strong, and their finances so well known, that any resulting danger to investors would be overbalanced by the advantages in efficiency and cost saving. To buttress its defense, the SEC invented a new concept, "differential due diligence," to suggest that in some cases it is less important to be diligent than in others.

At all events, in February 1982 the SEC voted to put Rule 415 into effect for a trial period beginning in March. And, whether ironically or not, the lead underwriter—or, rather, the sole buyer—of the first major stock issue sold off the shelf was none other than Morgan Stanley.[2]

Since its founding in 1935, Morgan Stanley had been American Telephone & Telegraph Company's "traditional banker," and the prospective severing of this lucrative tie by Rule 415—at a time when AT&T was heavily in need of new funds to finance its prospective divestiture of its operating companies under an antitrust consent decree—was the subject of considerable glee at less lordly firms. "Morgan Stanley's golden handcuff on its clients is broken," crowed a Merrill Lynch managing director in March.

But was it really? In the case of its most important client, AT&T, Morgan Stanley naturally went to work to show that it wasn't. In April, AT&T filed a shelf registration for 10 million common shares, which at then-current prices meant between $500 million and $600 million. "It was of course important for us to get it," Saunders says. "We had been AT&T's banker previously for all of their equity, as well as much of their debt, and we needed to show that we still were. We wanted to be at the cutting edge of risk-taking under the new rules—but so, of course, did our competitors." A Morgan Stanley internal memo dated April 28 reads in part, "The filing presents a clear profit opportunity and [a] reputational risk. . . . We don't *need* to be first, but it will help establish our role."

Meanwhile, the AT&T financial people (chiefly Vice-President and Treasurer Virginia Dwyer and Assistant Treasurer Larry Prendergast) found their telephones ringing off the hook. Some of the proposals flooding in were from institutional stock buyers who proposed to bypass investment bankers and deal directly with the company; but AT&T had already decided not to go that route, on the grounds that it needed the kind of advice and services that it was used to getting from an investment banker. Most of the calls were from investment bankers big and small, some of them proposing to take only a "small" block of, say, 100,000 shares. Saunders says, "We made new proposals to them every day, tailored to the market— AT&T stock was selling off a bit—and to the evolution of the company's thinking. AT&T's attitude was, 'Let's test the new mechanism.' They were interested in hearing the music, and they heard plenty. I don't think their financial people had time to do their regular business." Finally, early in May, Saunders sensed that AT&T had decided that "enough was enough," and was ready to close a deal. So Morgan Stanley made its big pitch: it would buy, and undertake to sell without a syndicate, 2 million of the 10 million shelf-registered shares at $55.40 per share—15 cents above the current market, or $300,000 above it for the 2 million shares—on certain conditions, including AT&T's agreement not to issue more shelf stock in the same month. Morgan Stanley's bid was marginally better than any other received by AT&T, thereby making it financially prudent for the company to stick with its traditional banker. Perhaps it would have done so even if Morgan Stanley's had *not* been the best bid. Whatever the case, the golden handcuff was not broken, and an important precedent for life under Rule 415 was set.

It remained to be seen how smoothly the machinery of the first great shelf issue—and the first great "bought deal" of this century, on this side of the Atlantic—would roll. On May 3, AT&T filed its shelf prospectus for the entire 10 million shares of shelf stock—a document only six pages long, in vivid contrast to the almost book-length prospectuses of old issues using the long form. Three days later—on the afternoon of May 6, after the market had closed for the day—AT&T filed a "prospectus supplement" stating that Morgan Stanley agreed to purchase 2 million shares of AT&T at $55.40, and then sell them for whatever price it could get. (Dwyer told Saunders that AT&T would prefer to have the stock sold by Morgan Stanley in relatively small pieces—in lots no bigger perhaps than 250,000 shares—to preserve the wide-distribution feature of the old syndicate system; but this stipulation was not part of the contract.)

Considering that its cost price was slightly above the market, and that it would have to sell at an even higher price to make a profit, Morgan Stanley seemed to face a sticky wicket on May 7 when it put its 2 million shares on the market. However, so efficient was the firm's distribution network—and so great the trading community's confidence in that network—that the sale went like lightning. At 3:12 P.M. on May 7, Morgan Stanley was able to announce through the Dow news tape that the 2 million shares had all been sold "at various prices."

Thus the books on the issue were closed, with the following results: AT&T, because of savings in paperwork and delay-related risk, had gotten more for its stock than it would have under the old system. Financial institutions, which comprised practically all of the buyers, had probably bought more cheaply than they could have if it had been a syndicated issue, with the traditional underwriters' spread added to the price. The investment banker had profited, although surely less per dollar risked than would have been possible with syndication. As for due diligence, such was the unassailability of the issuer's financial status, and the length and depth of its relationship with the investment banker, that the question had not been tested at all.[3]

The month following the successful AT&T bought deal, Morgan Stanley showed that its attitude toward Rule 415 was softening, perhaps under the impact of unexpectedly salutary experience. On June 7, Saunders wrote to SEC

Secretary George A. Fitzsimmons, noting with satisfaction that his firm had already been named as managing underwriter in thirteen registration statements covering $4.6 billion of debt and equity under Rule 415, and stating, "We would suggest that the Commission extend the Rule as a temporary rule for a reasonable period of time in order to explore its impact on the capital-raising process more fully." Meanwhile, there was new action on the AT&T shelf stock. During June and July, Saunders became convinced that the remaining 8 million AT&T shelf shares were overhanging the market and serving to impede the stock's performance, and that they ought to be sold as soon as possible to "clear the shelf." Over the course of many conversations (and with the help of a suddenly booming stock market), he says that he persuaded AT&T to his point of view—and apparently, not incidentally, to the point of view that negotiations with a traditional banker might still be preferable for a corporation under Rule 415 to bare-knuckles competitive bidding. The next question was would the new 8-million-share offering, amounting this time to around $450 million, be another bought deal by Morgan Stanley? Saunders says, "We could have done it, but it didn't make sense. It would have been a grandstand gesture." The main reason it didn't make sense, he thought, was that excluding everybody else from the transition would have set the hand of all of Wall Street, including the awesome traders at Salomon, Goldman Sachs, and elsewhere, against the hand of Morgan Stanley and AT&T. Knowing that Morgan Stanley was long, say, 5 million shares of AT&T, the typical desk trader would see a chance for a quick profit by selling his inventory of the stock—perhaps even in selling it short. Such a competitive environment might break down the deal; Morgan Stanley might lose a good deal of money and, in the process, drive down the AT&T stock price several points, thereby compromising AT&T's ancient reputation for showing extra concern for its shareholders. A year or so later, under very different circumstances, Morgan Stanley would in fact do a giant-size bought deal with $300 million of Eastman Kodak stock. For the AT&T issue, though, banker and client agreed that the prudent course was to co-opt the giants and, in Morgan Stanley's case, to share the risk, by including them in a traditional syndicate; thus would be tested for the first time on a huge scale the operation of the syndicate system under the new rules.

As co-managers for the new 8-million-share AT&T issue, Morgan Stanley naturally asked the other four top-bracket underwriters—First Boston, Goldman, Merrill, and Salomon. First Boston, Goldman, and Salomon quickly accepted. Saunders says—and Merrill Lynch flatly denies—that Merrill alone resisted, saying at first that Morgan Stanley was acting too aggressively, and expressing a wish to be left out—to the sharp dismay of Morgan Stanley and AT&T, who wanted the benefit of Merrill's celebrated retail-distribution capability. Moreover, Morgan Stanley and AT&T felt that it was of symbolic importance to have *all* of the top-bracket underwriters involved in such a bellwether issue. Saunders says—and again, Merrill denies—that he went back to Merrill and argued them into coming in. At all events, they came in. As the deal was structured in the prospectus supplement dated August 25, the five lead underwriters would each buy 1.6 million AT&T shares at $57.18 (as in the May issue, at slightly above the current market price); they agreed to sell 3.5 million shares to twenty-one firms who made up the rest of the syndicate; commissions and discounts to the underwriters would total $.795 per share, making the price to ultimate buyers of the stock $57.975. (Buyers had the option of taking their shares with or without a dividend of $1.35 per share due October 1, with a compensating price differential of that amount.)

It was unquestionably a daring and aggressive deal, the public offering price being more than a full point—$8 million in all—above the market price of $56.75 when the offer was made. Helped by a buoyant market, and by a stabilizing bid that resulted in Morgan Stanley's accumulating a massive temporary inventory of over 2 million shares,* the issue sold out even faster than the one three months earlier. It was announced on the Dow news tape at 4:20 P.M. on July 25, after the day's New York Stock Exchange closing. The same tape reported at 10:40 A.M. on July 26 that the offering was completed. Beyond a shadow of doubt, the first great syndication under Rule 415 was an outstanding success.[4]

But doubts remained.

On September 1, 1982, the SEC voted to continue Rule 415, still on a temporary basis, through 1983. The

---

*Price-stabilizing bids by lead underwriters during the offering period have always been allowed, and often used, in large stock underwritings. In 1940, the SEC admitted that they constituted manipulation, but ruled—probably correctly—that they may be necessary to the success of such issues.

margin of the vote was as narrow as it could be: two to one, with Commissioners John Evans and Bevis Long-streth in favor, Barbara Thomas against, and Chairman Shad abstaining on grounds of a personal conflict. (The fifth SEC seat was vacant at the time.) Then, in November 1983, the rule was made permanent, this time by a four-to-one vote, with Commissioner Thomas again dissenting.

By that time, Rule 415 had established a considerable track record, and the figures showed that it had brought about several fairly clear-cut changes in the nature of underwriting. The SEC calculated that between March 1982 and September 1983 there had been 369 delayed-offering shelf filings of debt, totaling about \$70 billion, or 53 percent in dollar volume of all debt filings of all kinds made during the period; and 195 such offerings of equity, adding up to \$12.5 billion, or 6 percent of all equity securities registered. Clearly enough, the new rule was having, and would continue to have, far more impact on the underwriting of bonds than on that of stocks. Indeed, shelf registration was on the way to becoming the dominant mode of bond issue by large companies, and by 1985 would account for more than 90 percent by volume of all public bond issues in the United States.

Just as the SEC had intended all along, issuing corporations were the group most clearly advantaged by shelf registration, and in consequence most pleased with it. With the tedious and expensive old procedures relating to disclosure and due diligence swept away, and with de facto competitive bidding for their securities now the rule, corporations could simply raise more money at less cost through their debt issues than formerly. Moreover, the

balance of power between corporate treasurers and investment bankers had shifted in the direction of the treasurers.
As one of them, ITT Financial Corporation's W. Gene
Gerard, put the matter in 1984, "We've done nothing but
benefit. . . . Bankers are aware that we're being inundated
with ideas from others, and that we are a lot more sophis-
ticated than we used to be. So their pencils are a little
sharper, and they work a little harder." On the other
hand, the benefit to corporations on shelf issues of stock
was less clear, because the price of shelf-registered stock
was showing a disconcerting tendency to perform significantly worse around the time of issue than that of nonshelf
stock. A study sponsored by the Securities Industry Association in 1984 concluded that although shelf offering of
stock had saved the issuers 28 percent on underwriting
spread and 25 percent on issuance cost, those savings had
been far more than wiped out by poor stock price performance resulting from the uncertainty of shelf stock offering—making shelf offering of stock, on average, apparently not an economical procedure for a corporation.[5]

As for investment bankers, the early results seemed
to show that they—or at least the giants among them—
had been overly alarmist in their prior concerns. Beyond
a doubt, the fierce competition of bidding on shelf issues
had reduced underwriting spreads still further, accelerating a trend that had been going on previously. By 1985,
gross spreads—the underwriting fee, the management fee,
and the selling concession—which had averaged 2.073
percent in 1981, were down on average to 1.692 percent,
including both shelf and nonshelf deals. Indeed, it appeared that underwriting no longer was, and probably

would never be again, the chief profit center for most investment banks, large or small. Underwriting did, however, retain its importance in terms of prestige and corporate contacts; a firm's name at the top of a tombstone ad for an important corporation's new issue was still the best advertisement available. And in their zeal to win issues away from their competitors at almost any price, investment banks were taking unusual risks. Goldman Sachs, for example, would report in 1984 that it was now bidding more aggressively for new issues than it had done before Rule 415. Late that year it bid so aggressively against Salomon for bond issues of Texaco and Sears Roebuck that it found itself sitting for two weeks with hundreds of millions of dollars of Texaco and Sears bonds unsold, and with millions of dollars in paper losses—until both issues were bailed out by a December bond rally.

On the positive side, for the top investment-banking firms, was the evident fact that, by and large, traditional banker-client relationships had survived, after all. Of the 204 shelf offerings in 1982, the first year of Rule 415, 74 percent were managed by the top five firms, and Morgan Stanley alone managed 24 percent. Lehman Brothers Kuhn Loeb calculated that of all shelf deals over the first eighteen months of Rule 415, the lead manager was the company's traditional banker on 77.6 percent of the deals. The golden handcuff seemed to have been loosened much less than had been expected.

The concentration within the industry that had been predicted had unmistakably taken place. With only large companies being eligible for shelf registration—until September 1983, 85 percent of debt filers were corporations with assets of more than $1 billion—and with the need for an investment bank to have large capital resources greatly increased by the more transactional character of shelf offerings, it was natural that the advantage of the top firms over their smaller rivals was increased. The Big Five firms all but monopolized shelf registration; their share of the management of all syndicated issues rose abruptly from 50 percent in 1981 to 70 percent in 1982, and their share of the underwriting of all new debt from about 25 percent before Rule 415 to nearly 50 percent afterward. The losers, of course, were the smaller firms, most of them based outside New York City; with bought deals now common and syndicates much smaller when they were formed at all, regional firms, used to small but usually profitable participations in large issues, often found themselves more or less squeezed out of the underwriting business. By 1985 syndicate managers at regional firms said that their underwriting participations had shrunk to less than half of what they had been before Rule 415. Regional broker-dealers began to find that when they were asked to join a shelf syndication, it usually turned out to be one with problems. Consequently they came to feel, somewhat like Groucho Marx about clubs, that any syndication they were asked to join was one that they didn't *want* to join. At the Securities Industry Association's convention at Boca Raton, Florida, in November 1984, a regional broker-dealer said that under shelf registration his firm now often lost money, especially after paying its share of stabilization costs, even on successful issues. "On small deals," he complained, "you have to say to the managing underwriter, 'Will you give us a little more money, so we have a chance to break even?' "

Yet the dire effects that many had expected to follow from such concentration had not materialized. Few regional firms had been forced by the loss of underwriting profits to close or merge; on the contrary, their profits were sustained by a flourishing brokerage business. As for competition, concentration had narrowed but not reduced it. While regional firms were being squeezed out, competition among the handful of New York–based giants had become so fierce that it was serving its economic purpose of minimizing costs to corporate issuers probably better than ever before.[6]

There remained, and still remains, the question, of paramount importance to the investor, of due diligence. Opinion was unanimous that the amount of due-diligence work done by lead underwriters and their lawyers had been sharply reduced under Rule 415. The rule, said John Whitehead of Goldman, "threatens to sweep away fifty years of investor protection and return the new-issues securities markets of the U.S. to the jungle environment of the twenties." In 1985, Whitehead agreed that nothing of the sort had happened until then—that, indeed, the efficiency of the capital markets had been improved by shelf registration. However, he pointed out, the SEC was created to protect investors, not to improve the capital markets; he still felt, as he had all along, that "a speedy reversal of [the SEC's] action is urgently called for." John Gutfreund of Salomon was more moderate—he merely said he had "some reservations" about shelf registration—but Peter T. Buchanan, chief executive of First Boston, said flatly, "It simply doesn't give the underwriter time to do his job in due diligence and disclosure." The Securities Industry Association (SIA), stopping short of asking for repeal of Rule 415, lobbied tirelessly, but in vain, for limiting shelf offerings to investment-grade debt and preferred stock, and for mandating a five-day cooling-off period between registration and issue. The academy and the press chimed in: Samuel Hayes and Joseph Auerbach of the Harvard Business School declared that Rule 415 "represents a subtle step away from the primacy of investor protection mandated by the framers of the Securities Act of 1933," and *Institutional Investor* declared that Rule 415 "makes a mockery of the whole concept of due diligence."

The facts, insofar as they were available, seemed to bear these commentators out. Among debt filings over the first year and a half of Rule 415, all but a handful were rated "investment grade" by Standard & Poor's. Where bonds of such quality are involved, due diligence is, by general consent, not much of a problem. In regard to equity filings over the same period, however, the case was somewhat different. Many more of the Rule 415 stock filers were relatively small companies, and many more were companies whose bonds were low-rated or unrated by S&P. In the bottom half of equity filers, as measured by their bond classification, more than half were unrated, while in the bottom quartile all were either unrated or else rated "single B," meaning that the issues contained "considerable speculative elements." So the assertion that all companies eligible for shelf registration were so unassailable as to make due diligence irrelevant was, it appeared, simply not true.*

Additionally, it should be realized that the investment prudence of investment-banking houses cannot rationally be counted on to restrain them from taking on shelf issues that they know to involve considerable risk to themselves. On the contrary, in the competitive context, investment banks have a strong incentive to bid for shelf issues that they realize may not turn out to be profitable for them. They may, for example—like Morgan Stanley in 1982—want above all to preserve a traditional relationship, and accordingly be willing to buy a shelf issue higher, and subsequently price it more aggressively, than they would do otherwise. Or they may want to establish new relationships that will subsequently lead to more profitable transactions: for example, by buying a shelf issue under conditions that involve a marked risk of loss, a firm may put itself in a position to get from the same issuer the management of its next merger or acquisition, for which it will collect a large fee without committing any capital. That is, with underwriting now no longer the chief profit center for investment banks, it could be used primarily as a means of advertisement and business-getting—with possibly increased risk on the underwriting deal to both the underwriter himself and the ultimate investor.

*To be eligible for shelf registration under the permanent rule, an issuer must meet one of three qualifications: (1) it must have voting stock held by nonaffiliates worth at least $150 million; (2) it must have similar stock worth at least $100 million and a trading volume of at least 3 million shares annually; or (3) it must be offering investment-grade debt securities or preferred stock. Initial public offerings of common stock, and other common stock of smaller companies, are thus excluded.

Finally, there was the vexed issue of whether or not in every case the winning bidder for a shelf issue could conceivably comply in a legal sense with the due-diligence provisions of the Securities Acts. Let it be recalled that the 1934 Act specifically applies to the underwriter's due-diligence responsibility the "prudent man" rule, originally intended for trustees, and established in 1830 in the case of *Harvard College* v. *Amory*. The famous language of that rule runs, in part,

> All that can be required of a Trustee [or, as applied here, a securities underwriter] is that he . . . observe how men of prudence, discretion, and intelligence manage their own affairs . . . considering the probable income, as well as the probable safety of the capital to be invested.

Could an investment firm that had no prior relationship with the prospective issuer, buying in competitive bidding its new issue of stocks or bonds for resale to the public, be expected, in a matter of hours, to acquire the amount of information about the issuer implied by the words "prudence, discretion, and intelligence"? Indeed, was it even theoretically possible for it to do so? Or had shelf registration created a situation where, in certain cases, for an underwriter to acquire and distribute an issue was automatically to violate the basic securities law? Obviously, the situation created the specter—so far, only a specter—of a deluge of lawsuits brought by the ultimate buyers of shelf issues, alleging that the underwriters had not performed due diligence—and citing as evidence merely the fact that on the face of the matter they *could* not have done so.

But the question was, so long as the customers were satisfied and did not sue, did it all matter much? Defending itself and its rule, the SEC majority insisted that the investor was still adequately protected—by continuing contacts between frequent issuers of securities and investment banks likely to purchase them, and by the fact that shelf registration was available only to companies of a certain size and soundness. And indeed, as a practical matter the SEC and its allies (who included, curiously enough, many free-market-oriented academics but few investment bankers) seemed to be right. Three years after the promulgation of Rule 415, no one on either side could point to a single shelf issue on which investors had been demonstrably hurt because of inadequate due diligence. Quite fortuitously, a great and long-lasting bull market had begun shortly after Rule 415 went into effect. So long as stocks and bonds are in strong demand, the buyers of them are not apt to sue the sellers. "The market bailed out 415," said Barbara Thomas, the lone dissenter among SEC commissioners in the commission's votes on the rule.

Her comment went to the heart of the matter: Could shelf registration withstand a *bear* market? Or would the institutional investors who ultimately bought almost all shelf securities then find themselves flummoxed by the pressure of instant issues, and the "incorporation by reference" of key information about issuing companies, and end up losing large sums earmarked to support payments to pensioners?

Leading investment bankers themselves, even while profiting regularly on shelf deals, said with virtually one voice that it might well happen that way. All-out backers of Rule 415, like Irwin Friend of the Wharton School of the University of Pennsylvania, said there was nothing to worry about because in the case of the huge companies eligible for shelf registration, disclosure and due diligence was simply not an important consideration. It is interesting to note that SEC Chairman Shad, the man who presided over the promulgation of Rule 415 as well as its first years of operation, was apparently not among its uncritical backers; in December 1983 he said to a convention of the SIA, "The true test of the shelf rule will come in the next bear market." Neither then nor over the next four years, however, did he or his fellow commissioners show evidence of giving serious consideration to the partial reversal of deregulation recommended by the SIA—or to the total reversal recommended by John Whitehead.[7]

Thus shelf registration charged forward under full sail across uncharted seas, toward a cloud no bigger than a man's hand.

5

The Trading
Game

The old investment-banking prejudice against securities
trading, as opposed to underwriting, was not all arbitrary
snobbery. It is true enough that, in general, underwriters
were and are more gently bred, well educated, gentlemanly of demeanor, and soft of speech, traders more
brash, overtly competitive, and loud. (Indeed, the very
physical conditions of trading often enforce loudness, just
to make oneself heard.) But the prejudice has a firm basis
in social utility. On the face of the matter, underwriting
is a more socially useful form of activity than securities
trading is. The immediate purpose of the former is, as

Judge Medina put it, to provide the lifeblood of the national economy; the immediate purpose of the latter, say what anyone will, is to provide profits to the trader.

Let it be noted that now that securities trading provides in some years something like half of all the revenues of the investment-banking industry, and now that it is heavily engaged in by even the most formerly aloof and snobbish of the leading firms, the prejudice, or at any rate the natural hostility between underwriters and traders, survives to a degree. It was, for example, the principal *casus belli* in the fratricidal strife at Lehman Brothers Kuhn Loeb in 1983, which ended with the once-proud firm's sale to American Express. For all its freely expressed greediness, Wall Street has always had, and retains, a sneaking, just-below-the-surface respect for work that has a social purpose—respect, one might say, for a certain lack of total greed. Just as the officers of the Federal Reserve Bank of New York, which makes money but has as its principal purpose the maintenance of an orderly economy, are still granted a certain edge in status over the leading purely commercial bankers, so in investment banking underwriters are widely granted a similar edge over traders.

Still, the fact is that, as sources of profit to their firms, traders have simply won out over underwriters. And the irony is that, in achieving their triumph, traders have gained a good claim to social utility—that is, that their activities are now the sine qua non of successful large-scale underwriting. In the old Wall Street, Morgan or Morgan Stanley or Kuhn Loeb needed little capital and no trading ability to form their huge syndicates and launch their huge corporate issues. In the new one, issuers insist that their lead underwriters have the delicate feel of the market and the access to the biggest investors that only massive trading can bring. Such a firm as Dillon Read, which has never emphasized trading, has lost its once-lordly place among underwriters (and such a firm as Kuhn Loeb has vanished from the scene). Among the heavy-trading firms that now rule the underwriting roost, traders are regularly consulted in the planning of underwritings, including Rule 415 deals. "Ten years ago we were consulted [on underwritings] infrequently," said (in 1984) Robert E. Rubin, co-head of trading and arbitrage at Goldman Sachs. "Now it's standard operating procedure." Indeed, underwritings are now sometimes initiated on the trading floor. Early in 1983, Salomon's equity trading desk sensed that metal stocks were poised for a runup. It told the corporate finance department, which advised several mining companies of a coming window of opportunity, and Salomon quickly, and successfully, managed several issues of mining-company stock.

Is trading now the key to investment banking, including even its socially useful component? The argument can be made, and is made, for example, by Salomon Brothers, the acknowledged king and forefather of securities trading in investment banking, which for nearly three-quarters of a century has committed itself to making a market in every security it sells. In its Annual Review for 1984, Salomon said flatly that trading is "central to the firm's operations." Peter T. Buchanan of First Boston says, "The opportunity for growth in revenues [in trading] has outstripped the opportunity in corporate finance." As for the crucial importance of trading capacity to underwriting, Salomon insists that, despite the huge profits it reaps from trading, "the greater significance" of its trading operation is the information it affords clients about the state of the markets. It seems beyond doubt that the principal reason Salomon has risen to the top in underwriting is that it stands, as it has long stood, at the top in trading.

The reason corporate issuers want their underwriters to be both wide and deep in securities trading is not difficult to see. It is the extreme volatility of the 1980s markets, which, as we have seen, arose out of market conditions in the 1970s, and is further fueled by the behavior of the institutional portfolio managers of the eighties. According to a Salomon estimate, institutions turned over less than 50 percent of their portfolios in 1980, and 100 percent in 1983. Driven by the fear of sudden losses, they tend, at the slightest sign of trouble, to unload first and figure out why afterward. Moreover, they are inclined to run in a pack; an unexpected earnings report, or even a collective whim, may induce them to act very quickly and in concert to buy—or, more spectacularly, to sell—vast quantities of a given issue, causing it to rise to the heights—or sink to the depths. Take the case of the common stock of Digital Equipment, the nation's second-largest computer manufacturer, in 1983. That October 15 it announced a quarterly earnings drop of 72 percent, whereupon its stock price proceeded to decline 22 percent in one day and 40 percent in two weeks. Did this mean, as it seemed to, that Digital as a company had suddenly fallen out of the sky, and was no longer a worthy institutional investment? Not necessarily; most leading companies suffer such temporary reverses at one time or another, for one reason or another. It meant, rather, that institutional investors knew that they themselves would cause the stock to take a nosedive on the bad news, and fulfilled their own prophecy by stampeding to be the first out. Indeed, three months later Digital came out with a favorable report; then the stampede was in the other direction, and the stock price rose 30 percent in three days.

Under such conditions, the institutional investors who for practical purposes *are* the market have put aside the old "buy and hold quality" theory. Some say that the "long-term holding" in institutional portfolios no longer exists. They have become traders, and chief among those with whom they trade are the great investment banks. (The corporate issuers hope that the liquidity provided by such trading will serve to stabilize the prices of their securities; obviously this didn't happen in the case of Digital in 1983.) In any case, one way or another, and for better or worse, trading has become king.

The characteristics of investment-bank securities trading are strikingly well defined. To begin with, it is mechanically expensive, and calls for large capital apart from that required to finance securities inventories. Just the basic communications equipment for a single trading desk—the CRT displays of prices and financial news, the high-speed telephones with built-in computer memories—in 1985 might have come to $30,000 to $50,000 before the first trade was made; in addition, there are the computers programmed to calculate net exposure of the bank to interest-rate and currency movements. The multibillion-dollar securities inventories carried by the giants are financed in part by *repos*—agreements under which the bank sells securities to a lender with a contract to buy the securities back after a short period at a price that amounts to an interest rate. Still, big-time trading is not a game for the capital-short; the traditional small-capital underwriter, a Morgan Stanley or a Kuhn Loeb of fifty or even twenty years ago, could not have dreamed of entering it.

Trading is, of course, backed by extensive in-house research. So it had always been in the case of equities; the big change in the 1980s was increased emphasis on research in bonds, an area where the traditional tendency, in a generally stable market, was to rely on the rating services for estimates of the issuers' creditworthiness. Now, with vastly increased volatility of bond prices, all of the top trading firms make huge investments in bond research. Salomon led the way in 1985 with seventy professionals doing bond portfolio research and thirty-five more doing bond market research. Meticulous in-house research is widely credited with accounting for Drexel's success in junk bonds. Bond analysts' average compensation as recently as 1981 came to hardly more than half that of stock analysts; by 1985, although there was still a differential, it had been drastically narrowed.

At most firms, a limit is set on the total exposure to which an individual trader may commit the firm at any given moment, after the mode of the limits set on loan officers at commercial banks. But not at Salomon, where, Salomon men say, each trader is free to commit as much as he thinks prudent. Restraint is applied from behind rather than from in front; that is, a trader who consistently loses doesn't last long.

The recent proliferation of new securities "products," the burgeoning "securitization" of assets that were formerly nontradable commercial loans—first real-estate mortgages, then automobile financing, computer leases, and so on—has contributed hugely to the increase in securities trading at investment banks by hugely increasing the supply of securities to be traded, by creating entirely new markets with great profit potential for those who understand them—as no one does better than their creators, the investment bankers. Finally, the scope of such trading has been and is now being broadened by its progressive internationalization, the result principally of communications advances that make the instant display of the price of a European or Japanese security on a New York trader's screen almost as simple as that of a domestic issue. Between 1980 and 1985, international bond turnover increased sevenfold, to $1.5 trillion per year. Early in 1985, Yves-André Istel of First Boston International estimated that $10–$12 billion in non-U.S. equities were owned by U.S. institutional investors—up from $1 billion to $2 billion a few years earlier.

In 1983, predictably enough, Wall Street firms began for the first time to go in heavily for foreign-securities research. Japan proved to be a particularly fruitful market for U.S. traders because it has a very high securities turnover; Europe was another, because Swiss bankers, masters of international deposit-taking and lending for a century or more, often lack the American aptitude, and perhaps the American taste, for in-and-out trading.*

*Hans Joerg Rudloff, deputy chairman of Crédit Suisse–First Boston, said in 1985, "Trading isn't a Swiss tradition. . . . Trading is where you make money on your brains, not your capital, and here the Anglo-Saxon culture is excel-

No wonder the New York Stock Exchange in 1985 was beginning to talk about staying open twenty-four hours a day. In one area, that of United States government debt securities, by the mid-eighties a gigantic, worldwide, around-the-clock market was already emphatically in place. By September 1986 the top investment and commercial banks of the world, each operating continuously by "passing the book" around the world from New York to Tokyo to London and then back to New York, were participating in a U.S. Treasury market that customarily traded around $100 billion a day—roughly twenty times the average dollar volume of trades on the New York Stock Exchange. Five years earlier, such a market had not existed in either London or Tokyo. Now the big new player, and the one that had been chiefly responsible for making the game a worldwide one, was Japan, which was pumping some $3 billion per month of its huge trade surplus into U.S. Treasury issues.

To get a whiff of the new atmosphere in domestic securities trading at New York investment banks, let us look briefly at one huge, yet not otherwise untypical, trading deal very much in the new style.

In October 1984, American Airlines had a $2-billion pension fund of which a substantial portion consisted of a bond portfolio that was *dedicated*—that is, it consisted of bonds selected so that their maturities exactly matched the company's future pension liabilities, thus avoiding the need for it to make further contributions to its pension

---

lent." Perhaps he might better have said "the American culture," because the British merchant banks have not traditionally been noted for trading skill.

fund to meet the obligations concerned. However, American's pension needs had recently been changed by an unexpected number of early retirements; consequently, its portfolio needed rededication in short order. Specifically, the company needed to sell $500 million in bonds that it already held and that were no longer appropriate, find an additional $100 million in cash from its other pension assets, and then buy $600 million in new bonds with maturities and interest rates that met the new specifications.

Like a good trader, American shopped around. Its assistant treasurer, William F. Quinn, set up a competition between Morgan Stanley and First Boston, two firms with which the company had had past dealings, to see which could offer it the best price on the bond swap. Both firms put their bond traders, their bond portfolio strategists, and their computers on the problem. When their bids were delivered, Quinn and his colleagues found that First Boston promised to deliver the deal for $500,000 less than Morgan Stanley.

So, after the close of trading on October 17, First Boston got the nod, with instructions to complete the transaction as quickly as possible. It turned out to involve one of those all-night sessions that now seem to be de rigueur in important investment-banking transactions. Through the evening of the seventeenth, First Boston's team put together buy-and-sell lists and sent them for approval to the American contingent and its investment advisers, who were holed up in a midtown hotel. According to the later account of Richard S. Davis, First Boston's chief trader on the deal, the evening was "both boring and nerve-racking, like waiting in a maternity ward." In the small hours of October 18, the First Boston traders began calling the European trading desks—not because they specifically intended to buy European bonds, but because, owing to time differentials, the European markets were open then while the rest of the world's markets weren't, and they wanted to get the feel of international bond trading at that particular moment.

Later, after the start of the American trading day, they began unloading American's old $500-million portfolio of bonds and buying its new $600-million one. The hard part was the buying; it turned out to be an up day for bond prices because of domestic economic developments in the United States, and First Boston, because it was doing the deal on a principal rather than a commission basis, would lose money if it paid more for the package than the price it had guaranteed to American. The trick was not, by word, inflection, or manner, to tip off the trader on the other end of the telephone line that this was part of a huge transaction. "If I could choose, I wouldn't have done the dedication that day," says Davis.

It worked. The heavy bond volume that day masked what First Boston was doing, and the $600 million for American had been bought before U.S. closing time. The new portfolio consisted of about 85 percent A-rated corporate issues, 8 percent zero-coupon U.S. Treasury securities, and 7 percent dollar-denominated foreign government issues. And the price allowed First Boston to fulfill its contract with American and take home on the transaction trading profits estimated at $2.5 million.

Thus a technical portfolio problem in the pension

fund of an American corporation had brought about a one-day securities transaction bigger—and more profitable to the investment banker—than all but the largest of underwritings.[1]

A specialized kind of securities trading that by the mid-1980s was both hugely profitable and ethically troubling is *risk arbitrage.* In contrast to *classic arbitrage*—buying in one market and selling in another, to take advantage of small inefficiencies brought about by such factors as imperfect communications or cultural differences—the activity called risk arbitrage is purely a by-product of merger-and-acquisition mania. It consists of trading on the prospect of mergers and corporate reorganizations that have not yet been consummated, with the objective of profiting on the premium above previous market price that is always paid for the stock of target companies by corporate acquirers, in both friendly and hostile transactions. That is, betting on mergers.

The fifty or so Wall Street entities that engaged full-time in risk arbitrage included departments of most major investment banks, and all of the top ones; they also included a number of independent "boutiques"—a few of them huge and powerful—with risk arbitrage as their sole or principal activity. The market power and explosive growth of arbitrageurs is suggested by the fact that in 1985 their *striking power*—the sum that they collectively had or could raise for risk-arbitrage investment—was estimated at more than $3 billion, while the following year it was estimated at more than three times that much. In a single instance, the 1984 takeover of Gulf Oil by Standard Oil of

California, arbitrageurs at one time or another held 20 million Gulf shares worth $1–$1.5 billion. Another reason for the power of arbitrageurs is the power of their natural allies. In a hostile merger attempt, the bankers and lawyers for the aggressor are rooting for the arbitrageurs because the categorical purpose of an arbitrageur in buying a stock is to sell it to the aggressor when the deal is completed. Therefore, arbitrageurs can be counted on as reliable friends.

There are essentially two ethical problems inherent in risk arbitrage. First, success at it is based on either superior analysis of the chances that a prospective merger will go through, or else superior information that it *will* go through; in the latter case, the arbitrageur's advantage over other investors is unfair, and may be illegal under SEC Rule 10b-5, which forbids any investor to trade on the basis of "material information" not available to others. Inherently, to be successful, arbitrage goes to the limits of legal conduct (of that, more later). The second problem is that the profits made by arbitrageurs come directly out of investors large and small, and often conservative investors in huge, long-established companies. If, for example, a company whose stock is selling at 20 becomes the subject of takeover rumors, and arbitrageurs begin accumulating it, holders of the stock—not knowing whether or not a merger will come about, or perhaps not even knowing about the rumors—may gladly sell their holdings to an arbitrageur at 23 or 25. If a merger subsequently goes through and most or all of the stock is bought by an acquiring company at, say, 38, the arbitrageur has made a profit of 13 to 15 points, the original investor a profit of

3 to 5. Advocates of mergers and acquisitions argue that they are advantageous to stockholders because of the premium, often very large, that is paid by the acquirer. But in practice, most of that profit almost always goes to arbitrageurs. Theirs is, pure and simple, a systematic skimming of the cream of profit to be made from takeovers.

To find out how an arbitrageur at the top of his profession actually operates, I talked late in 1984 with Robert Rubin, then head of Goldman Sachs's arbitrage department, one of the largest and most respected operations of its kind. The department consisted of only six professionals, apart from Rubin himself and one other partner, yet Goldman's arbitrage positions at any moment—it was involved in some two hundred situations per year—usually ranged between $250 million and $500 million. Although its profits were not made public, Rubin maintained that the department had made money every year for at least the previous eighteen.

Rubin told me that Goldman's arbitrage commitments were always made subsequent to a public announcement of a proposed merger, and that to his belief the other top investment banks followed the same rule. That is to say, the top firms did not "trade on rumors," as some of the boutiques were well known to do. (Insiders say that Goldman, for one, did not always follow this rule in the 1960s. It might be further remarked that price-affecting rumors are often afloat between the first public announcement and subsequent announcements.) Rubin said that Goldman's avoidance of rumor-trading was a practical matter rather than an ethical one; in his judgment, such trading just didn't work on average. Once an announcement had been made, Rubin said, the methods his department used were straightforward, not "mysterious or profound." "We get the files from the library," he said. "We take a yellow pad, or a mental yellow pad, and write down the issues—antitrust, business fit of the proposed merger partners, owners of the stock who might be opposed to a deal, and so on. The sole questions for us are: Will the deal go through or won't it? What will the stock be worth then? And how much will our firm lose if it fails? We come to a decision and act accordingly."

At Goldman as at other firms, Rubin said, a "Chinese wall"* was maintained between the arbitrage and the investment-banking parts of the firm, except in cases where the investment bankers consulted the arbitrageurs before undertaking an underwriting, private placement, or appointment as a merger adviser. In such cases, that firm's arbitrageurs do not take a position in the stock in question, to avoid a potential violation of Rule 10b-5. Indeed, anytime the underwriters and M&A people become involved with any corporation "in a way that causes them to believe we shouldn't trade in the stock," that stock goes on a "restricted" list, and may not be traded at Goldman until the investment-banking involvement is ended. (All of the major firms maintain similar systems of restriction.) The problem here is that such a "restriction," if knowledge of it leaks outside the firm, may in itself constitute inside information, perhaps "material" information in the eyes of the law. For example, another firm may ask to trade

*The term *Chinese wall* is taken from the designation long used to describe the division between commercial banking and trust activities at commercial banks.

with Goldman the stock of a company for which it is secretly structuring a merger at that very moment; if the Goldman trader replies, "Sorry, we can't trade that," then word of the restriction is out. (In September 1985, when word leaked out that First Boston had put General Foods on its restricted list, the stock of that company immediately jumped 2½ points.) Rubin said that the problem was not as bad as it seemed, because the *meaning* of a restriction was ambiguous to the point that it might actually constitute misleading information; for example, the restriction could be brought about not by a merger negotiation but by an underwriting, which would tend to depress the stock rather than cause it to rise, or the sale of a major division, which might move it either way.

Suppose Goldman's M&A department was approached by a company that wanted to be acquired, and turned down the deal? (Some firms, indeed, have turned down merger-advising opportunities precisely to allow their traders to be free to arbitrage the stock.) Rubin said, "In such a case, there would be no restriction unless Arbitrage accidentally learned of the approach and turndown, in which case Arbitrage would restrict itself." In other words, the Chinese wall was counted on. Was the Chinese wall perfect? "No," said Rubin. "Is life perfect?" An accusation that in one case the Chinese wall may have been a long way from perfect was made in February 1987, when the government brought insider-trading charges against three officers or former officers of Kidder Peabody; among them was Martin A. Siegel, head of the firm's celebrated M&A department until 1986, who was charged with having passed on inside information to Kidder's arbitrageurs during his tenure as M&A head. In a *Wall Street Journal* article that appeared a few days after the arrests, it was stated that not only had Siegel been in close touch with Kidder's arbitrage department but that he had been a secret member of it, and had actually helped create it. A Kidder spokesman called this account "a misstatement." If it was not, then Kidder's Chinese wall had not been merely imperfect; right from the start, it had been nonexistent.

Rubin, who had done arbitrage at Goldman since he joined the firm in 1966, and had headed the department since 1975, said that he enjoyed his work particularly because of the central position it afforded him in dramatic corporate events, and because it served a useful social purpose—that purpose being to help provide the liquidity needed in volatile markets by institutional investors. To him, that is, the skimming off of potential investor profits on mergers that arbitrage involves is redeemed by the smoothing-out of market movements, and the consequent reduction of investor risk, that it provides.[2]

To hear Rubin tell it, then, arbitrage, however profitable, is both respectable and necessary. (In February 1987, Robert M. Freeman, Rubin's successor as head arbitrageur at Goldman Sachs, was arrested by federal officials and charged with illegal insider-trading activities. He and his firm denied the charges and planned to fight them.) An arbitrageur in a somewhat different style was Ivan F. Boesky, proprietor, until his spectacular fall in 1986, of one of the most famous and powerful of the arbitrage boutiques. The son of a self-made Detroit restaurant man, Boesky first came to Wall Street in 1966 and gravitated straight to risk arbitrage, which was then generally looked on by investment bankers as a second-rate activity, and was engaged in by only a few firms. After working for several firms—among them Edwards & Hanley, where he set up an arbitrage unit in 1972—in 1975 he formed an arbitrage partnership of his own that lasted six years. It had its ups and downs, and in 1981—the year after the partnership had lost some $40 million on two deals that did not pan out—Boesky left the partnership and formed the Ivan F. Boesky Corporation, specifically to do arbitrage, with sidelines in merchant banking and investment management. As a private firm, it did not publish results, but figures obtained by *Fortune* indicated that the corporation earned $12.4 million for fiscal 1982; lost $11.2 million for 1983, entirely because of a loss estimated at between $18 and $14 million on Gulf Oil's planned takeover of Cities Service, from which Gulf abruptly withdrew; and earned over $76 million for 1984, giving it an average return on equity over three years of 22 percent. Its biggest and most successful plunges were in 1983–84 on Texaco-Getty, on which it is said to have made about $50 million, and Socal-Gulf, on which Boesky risked all his capital and the firm is said to have made $65 million.

Boesky defined risk arbitrage by saying, "The arbitrageur bids for announced takeover targets," but in what he called "special situations"—Socal-Gulf among them—he made his plunge before any announcement.*

*As do many other independent arbitrageurs. The effect of preannouncement buying, on the basis of rumors or information, by arbitrageurs or others, is beautifully illustrated by the takeover of Carnation Corporation by Nestlé, S.A., in 1984. In June, when Carnation stock was selling above 50, rumors began circulating that the company was a takeover target. On August 7, when the stock was around 66, a Carnation official said that there were "no corporate developments that would account for the stock action." Two weeks later,

Indeed, he was famous among arbitrageurs for often being the first one in. He vehemently denied ever using insider information.

Boesky was widely described as "a driven man," and he admitted readily to being obsessed with profit-making; his operation attracted from the press such epithets as "the money machine" and "Ivan's piggy bank." He was secretive about his methods, but it was well known that he used extensive in-house research done by a large staff, and that he sometimes called other arbitrageurs to tell them of positions he had taken. Since all arbitrage profits are short-term, he used various legal tax-avoidance systems extensively. All in all, he was to the stock market of the eighties roughly what Jesse Livermore had been to that of the twenties—an in-and-out investor so celebrated for his success that hordes of others, on learning of positions he has taken, blindly followed him. Indeed, announcement of a Boesky position automatically *created* takeover rumors—and almost certainly helped to bring about some takeovers by putting companies "in play."

In 1985, Boesky published a book titled *Merger Mania,* in which he blandly explained basic arbitrage techniques, described arbitrage as "Wall Street's best-kept

with the stock at 72, the company made another similar announcement. At last, on September 4, Nestlé announced an agreement to acquire Carnation for $83 per share—the biggest non-oil merger in history until then. The $17 premium over the price the day of Carnation's first denial came to almost $600 million, most of which presumably went to arbitrageurs. The profit left for postannouncement buyers was less than one-half as large.

More generally, a study conducted in 1984 by Dean Witter Reynolds showed that in eighty-nine large 1984 takeovers, stocks of the targets advanced 12 percent on average in the month *before* the announcement.

money-making secret," and seemed to urge the average investor to give it a try. (Indeed, some nonprofessional investors, working at home, did make substantial profits doing arbitrage in the early eighties.) He did—although less strongly than Robert Rubin—make the argument that arbitrage improves the market by increasing its liquidity; more to the point, he insisted that "undue profits are not made," and that arbitrage had by then definitively graduated from second-rate status: "Among market professionals, it is one of the most respected of crafts."[3]

Nevertheless, long before the revelations of 1986, at least one major-firm investment banker not involved in arbitrage called it (not for attribution) not a "respected craft" but rather "organized espionage." And there was considerable evidence that espionage had a role in large-scale arbitrage operations. Although in his book Boesky wrote nothing about his investigative methods, it was said that he assigned a staff member to tracking the movements of corporate jets around the country—to be sure, a relatively obvious and surely irreproachable form of "espionage." Hope Lampert, in her book about the 1982 Bendix–Martin Marietta–Allied Corporation affair, *Till Death Do Us Part,* recounts two cases of apparently serious espionage initiatives in connection with that transaction. According to Lampert, at a Martin Marietta board meeting at a New York City office, the company's general counsel spotted a photographer on the roof of a nearby building and closed the blinds. (The photographer's employer, of course, may not have been an arbitrageur.) A member of the board, former Secretary of Defense Melvin Laird, then said, "It's not really a photographer we ought to be worried about. It's someone with a directional microphone. Those things pick up the vibrations on the surface of glass. They can hear through windows and blinds." At another point in the same case, Lampert says that an unnamed arbitrageur telephoned Martin Weinstein of Salomon to say that for three nights running he had had a photographer posted in the lobby of Wachtell, Lipton, Rosen & Katz, the law firm for United Technologies, which was involved in the deal. The photographer had gotten enough to know that "something [was] cooking." Tim Metz reported in *The Wall Street Journal* in 1984 that a few arbitrageurs acknowledged—obviously not for publication—that they had bribed merger advisers for information, a process known in the trade as "wiring the deal."

The question remains: Apart from outright bribery, is such activity illegal, or should it be? In present securities law, the basic prohibition against trading on inside knowledge, Section 10b-5 of the 1934 Act, makes it unlawful for any person "to employ any device, scheme or artifice to defraud or engage in any act, practice, or course of business which operates as a fraud or deceit upon any person." Both civil and criminal penalties are available for breach of 10b-5. (In the Insider Trading Sanctions Act of 1984, Congress stiffened civil penalties against violators by making them liable for up to three times their illegal trading profits.) In the early eighties, the SEC broadened the scope of its activities against insider traders by developing a "misappropriation" theory; that is, someone who has stolen material inside information from someone else is prosecutable. (In the first few cases involving this theory, the courts showed reluctance to accept it.) Apart from actions against actual corporate insiders—officers, directors, and large stockholders—the SEC brought cases mostly against nominal outsiders: printers, typists, lawyers, taxi drivers and their girlfriends, a financial journalist.* In a 1980 criminal case against a financial printer who had decoded documents he was working on and bought stock in companies he thought were takeover targets, the Supreme Court eventually decided that there was no violation; however, in a related civil case the same defendant agreed to repay his trading profit of $30,000.

A 1980 proceeding brought by the SEC emphatically involved investment bankers, but only at the lower levels. The SEC charged that during the 1970s two young men of relatively insignificant rank in the corporate-finance department of Morgan Stanley (and one of them subsequently at Kuhn Loeb) had been systematically passing proprietary information about prospective mergers to a broker, who had traded on it for the benefit of all three. Eventually the broker was convicted and one of the investment bankers was found guilty. Not inciden-

*In 1983 R. Foster Winans, then writer of *The Wall Street Journal*'s "Heard on the Street" column, made an arrangement with a stockbroker under which he agreed to sell the broker advance notice of the contents of his columns, which were sometimes influential enough to move the market in mentioned stocks. That such action violated journalistic ethics seems clear; the principal issue at Winans's trial was the legal one of whether or not publicly available information collected by a reporter, or the fact that such information is to be published on a certain date, constitutes inside information under the law. The U.S. District Court in Manhattan decided that it did, and Winans was sentenced to eighteen months in prison. As this is written, the case is on appeal to the U.S. Supreme Court. According to trial testimony, Winans and an accomplice had together been paid only $31,000.

tally, their chief defense throughout the proceeding had been, as one of them put it, that "anyone familiar with the securities markets knows these circumstances are not uncommon."

Nevertheless, until 1986 the SEC had never brought an insider-trading case against an actual arbitrageur, or any employee working directly for an arbitrageur. Although this absence could, on its face, be taken to indicate that arbitrageurs' operations were blameless under present law, there is another, less reassuring, explanation, that is, existing surveillance facilities may have been inadequate. The stock exchanges maintain their own systems for detecting possible insider-trading activities, but ultimate responsibility rests with the SEC; and the SEC had far too few people to do the job. In 1985 its New York City regional office—the one chiefly responsible for monitoring stock trading—consisted of about 190 people, including 60 lawyers, 45 examiners, and 30 to 40 investigators; all of them were charged with many demanding responsibilities other than detecting and prosecuting insider trading, such as monitoring the net capital of securities firms, keeping an eye on back-office problems, and enforcing the rules applicable to investment advisers. Moreover, the 1985 staff size represented a cut of about 15 percent since the late sixties—when Stock Exchange trading volume was a small fraction of what it later became.

There is considerable evidence that investment-bank arbitrageurs in the mid-eighties operated more responsibly than some of them had in past years. Cary Reich, in his book *Financier,* states that in the sixties the arbitrageur at Lazard Frères repeatedly made profits on stocks of companies for which Lazard was negotiating mergers; Reich quotes the then-arbitrageur at Lazard, Justin Colin, as saying that the rule at the firm in those days was simply, "Don't get Lazard in trouble." That is, either there was no "restriction" rule in effect, or else it was honored in the breach. (In the eighties, Lazard had long since withdrawn entirely from risk arbitrage.)

The fact remains that at the very time when the police ranks were thinning, the temptations to abuse were greatly increasing. Only a handful of investment banks did both M&A and risk arbitrage in the sixties, but in the eighties virtually all did both. Ira L. Sorkin, director of the New York SEC office, pointed out in 1985 that the rise of the multidepartmental securities firm had in itself been a vast breeding ground for potential conflicts of interest, the M&A–risk-arbitrage connection being only one of them. Sorkin said that he had suspicions of irregularities and possible 10b-5 violations among investment-bank arbitrageurs, but that with the staff available to him he lacked the means to ferret them out. The most his office could do, he said, was "try to increase the risk" to potential violators. Meanwhile, SEC officials talked about investigations involving "some of the biggest names in Wall Street," including arbitrageurs. But, for the moment, nothing concrete happened.

And then, in 1986, several things did, in rapid succession. Early in May, the SEC charged no less a firm than First Boston with illegally trading on inside information obtained by the firm's corporate-finance department in the course of an advisory relationship with a client. First Boston had been retained by Cigna Corporation, a big insurer, to arrange a $1.2-billion writeoff to bolster the company's reserves. On January 30, according to the SEC charge, a First Boston corporate-finance man had told a First Boston research analyst about the writeoff, which carried obvious bearish implications for Cigna's stock. The corporate-finance man said that he had accompanied his revelation with a warning about the confidentiality of the information, but nevertheless, on the advice of his immediate boss, the research analyst had passed it along to the firm's head equity trader. The equity trader—apparently not knowing that First Boston had quite properly put Cigna on its "restricted" list because of the corporate-finance relationship—had caused First Boston to sell 21,000 Cigna shares and to buy *put* (that is, "sell") options on the stock. The firm profited on these transactions by about $132,000.

When the SEC made its accusation, First Boston quickly, and without either admitting or denying guilt, disgorged its profit and paid a fine of $264,276. Chief executive officer Peter Buchanan attributed the events to "extreme and extraordinary sloppiness," and surely his explanation could be believed: First Boston's traders, accustomed to dealing in millions and with a valuable reputation for integrity to maintain, would not have been likely to violate the law intentionally to reap such a small profit. Still, the case was an ominous cloud on the Wall Street horizon. Although it did not categorically involve risk arbitrage, it did represent a categorical, however inadvertent, failure of the Chinese wall. If the head of equity trading at a leading firm had been unaware of a trading restriction that had no purpose other than to restrict *him,* who *had* been aware of it—and of what use was the Chinese wall when it could be breached so casually?

On May 12, barely a week after announcement of the First Boston settlement, came that of another, far more disturbing case, involving principally Dennis B. Levine of Drexel Burnham Lambert. Thirty-three at the time, with a middle-class background in New York City's borough of Queens, Levine had worked as an investment banker since mid-1978, first at Smith Barney, then at Lehman Brothers Kuhn Loeb, and, since January 1985, at Drexel Burnham. Throughout that career Levine had worked in mergers and acquisitions, specializing in collecting rumors or information about mergers—chiefly through telephone conversations with investment bankers at other firms, among them arbitrageurs—that might be useful to his own firm in getting in on planned or pending deals. That is, he was known as a "rainmaker," and one of such skill that Drexel Burnham, in hiring him as a managing director, had guaranteed him annual compensation of at least one million dollars. The SEC, in by far the largest insider-trading action it had ever brought, now charged Levine with making more than rain. Over the previous five and a half years, it said, while working at the three different firms, he had amassed profits of at least $12.6 million by trading for his own account on impending mergers on which he allegedly had nonpublic information. To cover his tracks, he had traded through a Bahamian bank using two dummy Panamanian corporations, made his calls from public telephones, and resorted to other subterfuges. Among the fifty-four companies in whose stock he was accused of dealing illegally—only six of them companies in which he had been personally engaged in merger negotiations—were several that had been involved in some of the most publicized takeovers and takeover attempts of the eighties: Esmark, Crown Zellerbach, Textron, Nabisco Brands, Carter Hawley Hale, and Bendix.

On June 5, Levine pleaded guilty in federal court in Manhattan to four felony counts carrying maximum penalties of twenty years in prison and fines of $610,000; he agreed to settle the SEC's civil charges by giving up almost all of his estimated net worth of $11.5 million, and being permanently barred from the securities business. He also agreed to cooperate with the prosecution, and did so, in naming other offenders. In February 1987, Levine was sentenced to two years in prison and fined $362,000. In October, as the first fruits of Levine's informing, Ilan K. Reich, a former partner of the law firm of Wachtell Lipton, and David S. Brown, formerly of Goldman Sachs, agreed to pay civil penalties to the government totaling over $630,000 after they had admitted to passing on inside information intended for Levine. Reich was subsequently sentenced to a year and a day in prison.

Quite apart from the secret account and the huge illicit profits, the implications of the Levine case were highly disturbing in regard to the operations of arbitrageurs. What was a senior M&A man at Drexel doing talking regularly to arbitrageurs at other firms in the first place? And what were the arbitrageurs doing talking to him? Didn't the situation itself suggest that the purpose was to exchange nonpublic information, to be used on the one side by Levine in both the legal rainmaking for which he was paid and the illegal trading on which he profited so hugely, but also, on the other side, by arbitrageurs for acquisition of nonpublic information to be used in trading for their firms' accounts or their own? And weren't Levine's employers, by seeming to encourage such conversations, abetting potential abuse in the arbitrage community in exchange for tips useful to their M&A operation?

Another almost concurrent case, although it involved far smaller sums, appeared to confirm the pattern. On May 28, after an SEC–led investigation, a New York County federal grand jury indicted five young men, all between the ages of twenty-three and twenty-seven, and all relatively new to the securities business, on insider-trading charges. One of the young men, Michael N. David, was an associate at the law firm of Paul, Weiss, Rifkind, Wharton & Garrison. Of the others, two were analysts working in the arbitrage departments of invest-ment-banking firms—Andrew D. Solomon at Marcus Schloss & Company, and Robert Salsbury at Drexel; one, Morton Shapiro, was a stockbroker at Moseley Securities Corporation; and the fifth, Daniel J. Silverman, was a customer of the Moseley firm. According to the indict-ment, the information supplier to the group had been David, who did not himself work in M&A at Paul, Weiss, and had gathered the information by looking at papers in his colleagues' offices. The arbitrage analysts Solomon and Salsbury, having received the information from David, had passed it along to their firms, which—although they were not named in the indictment—had allegedly traded on it, even though, according to the two analysts, they had known it was nonpublic information. Meanwhile, the stockbroker Shapiro had also been given the information and had used it in trading on behalf of the personal accounts of three of the other defendants (although the resulting profits, according to the prosecutor, had been "not much"). Early in June, all of the defendants except David pleaded guilty; he did so in November.

The cases of the Yuppie Five, as they quickly came to be known on Wall Street, appeared in one perspective to be small potatoes—a group of inexperienced and misguided young men starting their careers on the wrong foot by collaborating on a not-very-subtle cheating scheme that was bound to be detected and punished. (In fact, the case had been initiated on the basis of a tip to the federal authorities from the compliance officer at Marcus Schloss.) In another perspective, however, it appeared important as part of an ominous black cloud rising on Wall Street's horizon. Fitted together with the careless Chinese-wall breach in First Boston and the implication of firm-sponsored trading of information in Levine, it seemed to show, however dimly, the lineaments of an investment-bank arbitrage industry conducted along lines very different from the austere ones described by Robert Rubin. Little wonder that the prosecutor, U.S. Attorney Rudolph W. Giuliani, found the cases of the Yuppie Five "very troubling in terms of the atmosphere they suggest."[4]

The dark cloud burst into violent storm, containing damaging and perhaps catastrophic lightning, on November 14, with the exposure and confession to massive illegal inside trading of Ivan Boesky, until that day the acknowledged king of risk arbitrage and one of the half-dozen key figures in the eighties merger scene. On the basis of information supplied by Levine, the SEC and the U.S. Attorney for the Southern District of New York revealed the following: that Boesky, in February 1985, had entered into an agreement with Levine under which Levine would supply him inside information on impending mergers in exchange for a percentage of Boesky's resulting profits; that, over the subsequent year, Levine had supplied and Boesky had used such information concerning Nabisco Brands, American Natural Resources, and other large companies, with profits to Boesky of at least $50 million (much more, according to outside estimates and calculations); and that Boesky, admitting to these charges, had paid the government $100 million in penalties and restitution of improper profits, had agreed to plead guilty to one criminal charge and to leave the securities business forever after a phaseout period of eighteen months, and had himself turned state's evidence. Boesky—whose estimated net worth *after* the forfeit and penalty was still apparently in the hundreds of millions of dollars—said, "The announcement . . . by the SEC and the U.S. Attorney justifiably holds me . . . responsible for my actions. I deeply regret my past mistakes. . . ."

A couple of days later, the investment world—and, indeed, the larger world of readers of newspaper front pages and magazine cover stories from coast to coast and around the world—learned of one of those dazzling ironies—funny or sad or infuriating, according to one's perspective—that so often accompany great criminal cases. The SEC, ostensibly to prevent panic in takeover-related securities, and perhaps also in consideration of Boesky's informing on others, had categorically authorized him to sell almost half a billion dollars worth of securities from his arbitrage portfolio *before* the public announcement of his crime and punishment, thereby avoiding huge losses that he would have suffered if the sales had been made afterward. Boesky's very accusers had thus been party to his last great insider trade, one based precisely on his privileged knowledge of his own impending exposure.

So Boesky became the first of the 1980s Wall Street pantheon to fall from the sky. (More would soon follow.) What with his eager cooperation with the authorities, which was reported to extend to having allowed his office conversations to be recorded on tape over some time before his public exposure, it appeared that others might follow, including perhaps some even more central to the structure of the takeover scene than he. A large question entirely unanswered in the first aftermath of the shock was why he had done it. By February 1985, the date he was accused of having made his deal with Levine, he had by the sheer force of enormous wealth (shortly before his exposure he had appeared among *Forbes*'s list of the four hundred richest Americans), combined with an active program of philanthropies and an absence of any show of wrongdoing, attained a marked degree of respectability. Why, then, put his public honor and his career in the hands of a much younger, very talkative, and not necessarily trustworthy Dennis Levine? Perhaps some sort of answer would emerge in time—a hidden self-destructive urge, or some other dark psychic flaw. Meanwhile, in the early postexposure days the immediate and possible consequences of the fall of Boesky seemed to be the following: a sharp and instantaneous decline in the public and official reputation of arbitrage, and a concomitant decrease in its practice; a related decline in the number of huge take-overs, and particularly those financed by junk bonds, in which Boesky had been particularly closely involved through close connections with Drexel Burnham; and a sharp decline in the public reputation of Wall Street as a whole, leading to a sharp turn in the regulatory climate in Washington toward activism.

Depending on what the sequel events might be, in the early going after November 14 it was unclear whether the matter at hand was only a symbolic moral event or part of a substantive economic one. Even as the former, it was the biggest Wall Street scandal since Richard Whitney's consignment to Sing Sing in 1938, and one certain to be long remembered.

Felix Rohatyn of Lazard is quoted by Reich as saying, "Risk arbitrage is a business that really doesn't belong within a firm that is active in mergers." In 1986, before the Boesky exposure, Rohatyn was calling it an "arguable proposition" that, by legislative fiat, M&A and arbitrage should be prevented from being conducted "under the same roof."

To argue on the opposite side, such a law would probably be unenforceable, and might be counterproductive. How would risk arbitrage be defined? If it were defined to include trading on merger rumors, how could those rumors be identified, and how could it be proved that stock purchases were made on the basis of them rather than for some other reason? If, on the other hand, arbitrage were defined as trading on the basis of merger *announcements,* the law's effect would be to prohibit the most acceptable form of risk arbitrage—that now practiced, at least according to their own assertion, by the big firms—while actually permitting the less acceptable form, trading on rumors. Indeed, it would probably drive large amounts of capital into rumor trading, and thus tend to increase market speculation.

The best hope for regulation of abuses in connection with risk arbitrage is still Rule 10b-5—probably strengthened by a more specific definition of what constitutes insider trading (which the SEC had under consideration beginning in 1985), and surely made more enforceable by a definitive reversal of the trend toward reducing SEC staff. Post-Boesky, both the popular and the professional view was obviously that risk arbitrage is among the most abuse-prone of the accepted practices of investment bankers. From an investor standpoint, its theoretical advantages—providing liquidity, and putting a large part of the risk into the hands of professionals—balances, and perhaps overbalances, the disadvantage that it enables those professionals to skim off most of the profits to be made on mergers. But to the extent that it involves unpunished or undetected cheating—legal or illegal—the balance is tipped toward the professional arbitrageurs and away from the investors.

Large-scale securities trading by investment-banking firms is here to stay. It has swept over the business like a tidal wave; no conceivable legislative or regulatory action, even if desirable and constitutional, could hold back or reverse the wave. A total or substantial prohibition of such trading would certainly cripple the industry, cause many firms to leave it, and hobble the nation's capital-raising capacity. Nevertheless, it will be instructive to consider trading's negative aspects from the standpoint of investors and of the economy as a whole.

Risk arbitrage aside, an investment firm that trades securities for its own account, like one that makes venture-capital investments for its own account, is competing with its customers.

Since most investment-bank securities trades are made with institutional investors, it ought to follow that when the investment bank "wins," the institutional investor loses. The latter's constituents, chiefly pensioners, are theoretically disadvantaged by buying slightly higher, or selling slightly lower, than they would presumably have done if the bank trader had been working on behalf of the investor rather than for his own account. Fortunately, however, the effect of investment-bank securities traders "taking money out of the game" in the form of profits to themselves has been only theoretical until now. The firms have net long positions more often than short positions; that is, they buy more securities than they sell, and thus the capital that they commit tends to drive prices up. What is worthy of concern is what the effect of investment-bank securities trading might be in a sustained bear market, when conditions would be reversed.

Meanwhile, it is to be noted that the bank trader "wins" with alarming consistency. Trading being a game of risk, in a purely theoretical model any trader should end up breaking even. Obviously this is not the case; an industry that now derives something like half its revenues from securities trading is not breaking even on securities trading. On the contrary, even while suffering frequent losses on individual trades, the top investment banks make huge profits on it year in and year out. First Boston, to take just one example, made slightly under $100 million from trading in 1980, slightly over $100 million in 1981, more than $200 million in 1982, and slightly less than $200 million in 1983 and 1984.

How, then, do investment-bank traders contrive thus to defeat logic? We must assume that it is because, in general, they are better, and better-equipped, traders than other investors are. Their communications equipment, their narrow but powerful skills, the sensitive feel of the market that comes from constant communication with other traders, all give the people at the trading desks a slight but crucial edge over the institutional investors who sit in their cloistered offices poring over earnings forecasts and economic projections.

Then there is the matter of research. Institutional investors have their own research, of course—but much of it is derived from who but their sometime trading antagonists, the investment banks? These banks vary in the amount of their research that they make public. Morgan Stanley, Merrill, and Donaldson Lufkin & Jenrette publish extensively—according to Robert Platt, head of fixed-income research at Morgan Stanley, his firm prides itself on taking a "buy-side perspective"—but Salomon's credit research, for one example, is kept for the firm's own use. When an investment bank profits by using information or expert opinion that it does not make public, it would appear to be disserving its customers.[5]

Investment traders can reply, with considerable justice, that their trading advantage is more than compensated for not only by the market liquidity that their trading unquestionably provides, but also by the fact that their advantage on any given trade is so small. Thought of as a commission earned for investment in skill and equipment, the advantage can be shown to be a smaller commission per individual trade than investment bankers earned from institutional investors in the old days of fixed stock exchange commission rates. The fact remains—and should be kept in mind in considering the relationship of investment banks to the public welfare—that the lion's share of the billions of dollars that investment banks earn annually on their trading operations comes directly out of the institutions that hold and invest the savings of the nation's small investors and pensioners.

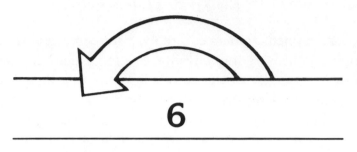

6

A Walk Through the Merger Battlefield

If the philosopher William James was right that one of the principal needs of modern society is to find a moral equivalent of war, then the corporate merger contests of the 1980s may be said, outside the economic realm, to serve a useful social purpose. In a whole constellation of ways, their maneuvers and countermaneuvers offer parallels to, when they do not actually mimic, many of the time-honored military and military-political moves of real war—the conventional rather than the nuclear kind, of course.

To begin with, the physical premises where corporate aggressors secretly plan their assaults, and those where target companies secretly plan their defenses either before or after an assault has begun, are inclined to be designated in a way that insists upon the parallel. Such places might be called "strategy rooms" or "planning rooms"; more often they are known as "war rooms." The custom of designating the target, in preliminary discussions within the aggressor company, by a code name in order to preserve secrecy, exactly matches a procedure that has since antiquity been used by the authorities in nations planning military aggression. The usual initial act of corporate aggression—acquiring, as secretly as possible, a minority stake in the stock of the target company—suggests the familiar process of infiltrating a "fifth column" of sympathizers with the aggressor inside what is soon to be the military target. The initial salvo of the assault proper—the tender offer for the target company's stock, in whole or in a majority part—represents the equivalent of a military ultimatum: the target must decide whether he will fight or lay down his arms and surrender his independence. The two-tier tender offer, in which some of the target company's stockholders are treated markedly better than others as a measure of dividing to conquer, calls to mind the similar policy of many military aggressor nations toward their victims. The practice of *greenmail*—allowing a target company to keep its independence by buying back the aggressor's stake in it at a premium price—is simply the corporate equivalent of the ancient custom of exacting tribute of one sort or another through the threat of military force, as, for example, did the Munich Pact of 1938. The role of arbitrageurs who profit on threatened takeovers may be likened, not totally unfairly, to that of war profiteers who enrich themselves by exploiting war or the threat of war. The junk-bond takeover, in which the corporate aggressor attempts to use the target's own resources to help bring about his submission, mimics a military practice that was routine through centuries of conventional warfare.

On the defensive side, the various methods that target companies use to protect themselves by damaging their own viability and thus reducing their attractiveness are spoken of in corporate circles as "scorched earth policy." As does "war room," the language itself makes the analogy. One particular corporate defense—the counter-tender offer by the target company for control of the aggressor, a move that in 1982 *The Wall Street Journal* christened "Pac-Man," after a popular video game— represents the military analogy pushed to a surrealistic extreme. If it succeeds, the result is as if two rival military powers, each succeeding on attack and failing on defense, have captured each others' capital cities and are proposing to run each others' governments, with resulting chaos and anarchy. In both cases, the only rational outcome is mutual withdrawal or submission of one or both parties to a third.

All the while—not to press the parallel too far—it must be remembered that the equivalency is only moral. The corporate wars, unlike the military ones, are fought in comfortable corporate headquarters, lawyers' and bankers' offices, aircraft, and courtrooms, and nobody dies in them. A whole body of economic thought, generally identified as the Chicago School, holds that any takeover, friendly or hostile, that works in the market is of eventual benefit to the economy and the majority of individual participants in it. Ultimately, law rather than brute force rules the takeover wars, and the guns are only pieces of paper. Even so, there are analogues, albeit paler ones, to the dead soldiers, sailors, airmen, and civilians of real war. When a corporate takeover results in the liquidation of a company or some of its parts, real jobs are lost, real communities disrupted or destroyed, and real production lost; when a company exists, as so many do, under the constant threat of a takeover, morale may be destroyed, the corporate polity disrupted, and employees at all levels made to live in a state of fear or hysteria.

Need things—for the sake of economic law, or for some other reason—be that way? As the Ninth Circuit Court of Appeals said in connection with a 1984 takeover case, "It is nowhere written in stone that the law of the jungle must be the exclusive doctrine governing sorties in the world of corporate mergers."[1]

To be sure, American corporate wars today are a good deal less like real war than they were at their outset. In the contest for control of the Erie Railroad in 1868, in which Cornelius Vanderbilt was the aggressor and Jay Gould, Jim Fisk, and Daniel Drew the defenders—the first great corporate takeover battle in our history—law did not rule except in name, because judges and legislators were controlled by the participants on both sides through the free use of bribery. The chief tactic of the defenders, despite its validation by corrupt public officials, was patently illegal; it consisted of issuing themselves, without authorization, huge quantities of new stock in their own company. (Vanderbilt himself had used comparable tactics the previous year, in seizing control of the New York Central.) Nor were the guns used in the Erie battle only pieces of paper. At one point Gould, Fisk, and Drew, fearing for their lives or their liberty if they remained in New York, fled under the protection of a gang of hired thugs to the New Jersey shore of the Hudson River, where they set up headquarters at Taylor's Hotel (which the press then renamed "Fort Taylor") and mounted on the waterfront three small cannon as protection against the Vanderbilt forces. The outcome of the battle was decided not by law or economics; Vanderbilt eventually conceded defeat only because he came to realize that his opponents were at least as adept at cheating, bribery, and *force majeure* as he was. Although, somewhat miraculously, no one died in the Erie contest, many did over the following years in a series of accidents caused by the grossly poor maintenance of Erie trains, and the railroad was left so financially crippled by the depredations of its owners that it was able to pay no dividends over the next sixty-nine years.

Such an event, and others more or less similar, raised justified fears that democratic capitalism in America was descending into barbarism, and a reform movement arose, sparked by the brilliant and responsible journalism of the patricians Charles Francis Adams, Jr., and Henry Adams. By the 1890s, law, however inadequate, was generally respected in corporate circles, and (as we have seen) the investment bankers who then controlled the destiny of corporations had developed a code of conduct that was proper and gentlemanly at least by their own lights. It was late in that decade that there began the first of the three great waves of corporate mergers that preceded that of the 1980s.

Exactly why mergers should come in waves is not well understood. What is clear is that they have done so, and that the years of the first three great waves were roughly 1897–1904, 1925–30, and 1967–69. The first wave consisted largely of horizontal combinations agreed to by the parties, and formed to obtain market dominance; it involved about 15 percent of all the nation's assets, it created more than seventy near-monopolies, and it was marked by the formation of such celebrated companies as U.S. Steel, Standard Oil, General Electric, United Fruit, Eastman Kodak, and American Can. It might be thought ironic that this first merger wave came on the heels of the passage of the Sherman Antitrust Act of 1890, but it probably is not. As at first interpreted, the Sherman Act was directed at a technical business structure common at the time, the *trust,* in which stockholders assigned their shares to a board of directors and received dividend-bearing trust certificates; it did not forbid monopolies as such. Indeed, a strong body of economic thought holds that the 1897–1904 merger wave came about in *reaction* to the Sherman Act—which, of course, was later interpreted more broadly to apply to attempts to attain monopoly by mergers of corporations.

The Nobel Prize–winning economist George Stigler has characterized the first wave as "merging for monopoly," and the second (1925–30) as "merging for oligopoly." In the interim, broader interpretation of the Sherman Act, along with passage of the Clayton Act of 1914, which categorically forbade acquisition of stock in another firm where the effect might be to lessen competition, had made merging to achieve monopoly more difficult. The 1920s mergers—involving some 12,000 firms, somewhat more than the turn-of-the-century wave, but a smaller percentage of the economy's assets, 10 percent as opposed to 15—was concentrated in the banking and public-utility sectors rather than in heavy manufacturing; in the manufacturing sector, it involved only modest increases in market share for the merged companies, and tended to emphasize vertical integration, between, say, a manufacturer and his suppliers. Its principal adverse economic effect was the creation of top-heavy pyramided public-utility holding companies, with control based on very small stockholdings, and even this effect was substantially reversed by the collapse of such companies in the 1930s, and their stringent regulation under the Public Utility Holding Companies Act of 1935.

Investment bankers and lawyers played an important role in both of the first two merger waves. In the first one, bankers often called the tune, as in Morgan's sponsorship of General Electric. Morgan's fee for reorganizing the Erie in 1895 was reputed to have been $500,000, and the promoters of the consolidation of International Silver a few years later collected 3 percent of a capitalization of $20 million, or $600,000, in common stock; as for lawyers, in 1891 John R. Dos Passos, father of the novelist, charged $500,000 for legal work in setting up H. O. Havemeyer's sugar trust. Again, in the 1920s, bankers were important; according to the economist Willard L. Thorp, writing in 1931, "A group of businessmen and financiers in the summer of 1928 agreed that nine out of ten mergers had the investment banker at [the] core." But it was not until the third merger wave—the "conglomerate" wave of 1967–69—that bankers and lawyers, led by Felix Rohatyn, Joseph Flom, and Martin Lipton, began to have the public visibility as merger-makers that they have now. An important piece of postwar legislation, the Celler-Kefauver Amendments of 1950, which strengthened the antimerger

provisions of the Clayton Act to the extent of making large horizontal or vertical mergers almost impossible when those laws were strictly enforced, prepared the way for the conglomerate wave by making mergers between companies in unrelated businesses—*conglomerate* mergers—for practical purposes the only type available. In Stigler's terminology, the 1967–69 wave consisted of "merging for growth."

Measured by sheer number of transactions, the conglomerate wave still stands as the biggest in our history. In the year 1969 alone, there were some 6,000 acquisitions, and over the decade of the sixties, almost 25,000 firms disappeared through merger. Meanwhile, because of the absence of horizontal and vertical integration there was virtually no effect on market concentration. Indeed, the usual goal was not market concentration, but rather stock promotion in a historic bull market. Characteristically, the conglomerate merger was a friendly, tax-free exchange of securities; because the market had bid the shares of conglomerates up to huge price-to-earnings multiples—100-to-1 or more, in some cases—the conglomerates were able to acquire companies with lower multiples and thereby increase earnings per share on a pure accounting basis, without any real growth at all. This phantom growth of earnings led to further stock appreciation, making further acquisitions attractive, and completing a self-sustaining spiral. Unlike the previous waves, this one was stock-market driven; and like any bubble it had to burst.

When it did, in 1970, there appeared to be a number of immediate causes. In 1968 the government for the first time turned away from antitrust toward securities regulation as a means of controlling merger activity. The Williams Act of that year (of which more in Chapter 9) attempted, through a set of rules for acquirers, to create a "level playing field" between aggressor and target in the unwanted takeover attempts that were just beginning to become common again, and at least temporarily slowed the pace of such attempts. A tightening in 1970 of the accounting industry's rules for takeover accounting made it harder for conglomerate acquirers to write up their earnings without achieving real growth. More to the point, a typical boom-and-bust stock market collapse in 1970, followed in 1973–74 by a deep recession related to the sudden skyrocketing of oil prices, turned the upward spiral of conglomerate stock prices, which had been crucial to the whole process, into a downward spiral. As Peter Drucker remarked, the conglomerates became "stranded giants"; to save themselves, many of them began the long, slow process of unraveling, through divestiture of their ill-considered acquisitions, the gossamer web of promoted profits that they had woven.[2]

Let us pause to look at the situation in 1980, at the starting point of the fourth great merger wave, that of the eighties.

A Walk Through the Merger Battlefield

It was a time of momentary lull—W. T. Grimm & Company reported that for the first half of the year merger-and-acquisition activity was at its lowest level in fourteen years—but the lull was the calm before a storm; indeed, over the previous five years there had been a comparatively minor merger boom, and it had shown a new set of characteristics that, as things turned out, faithfully presaged those of the major boom soon to come.

First, mergers were showing an incipient tendency to involve the very largest companies, as acquirer and also as acquired. Prior to 1980 there had been seven acquisitions involving $1 billion or more, while over the next three and a half years there would be thirty-seven. By the end of 1983, all but 11 percent of the biggest mergers of all time, measured in current dollars, had occurred after 1978. Bigness would be a primary characteristic of the eighties wave; in numbers of transactions it would consistently trail far behind the conglomerate wave at its height, but in gross sums involved it would dwarf all previous waves.

Second, the hostile tender offer was gaining ground at the expense of the typical conglomerate-era friendly exchange of securities. As early as 1967, Samuel Hayes and Russell A. Taussig had noted in the *Harvard Business Review* that the surprise cash takeover raid on an unwilling target was ceasing to be considered unethical and was achieving "a new respectability" (even though, in the decade preceding that date, only about one-third of such attempts had succeeded). As we have seen, however, it was not until the middle seventies that the hostile cash tender had become so generally accepted as to raise only a few eyebrows, and was poised to become the characteristic acquisition technique of the early eighties, accounting for almost one-third of all tender offers between 1980 and 1983.

Third, since 1975 there had been a large increase in the number of foreign acquirers of U.S. companies—a reflection of the internationalization of markets brought about principally by deregulation and new communications technology.

Fourth, the premiums over current stock price offered and paid by corporate acquirers were in a very sharp uptrend. In 1967–69, the typical premium had been 10–20 percent; in 1975–80 it was 40–50 percent, and occasionally reached 100 percent. By way of explanation, we need look no further than the market: during the former period stocks were priced high in relation to earnings and assets, while during the latter, a time of economic stagnation and rampant inflation, they were priced low. Obviously, the premium increases vastly enhanced the popularity of mergers with investors large and small.

Finally, a key characteristic of late-seventies mergers was that in about half of them, what to the buyer was an acquisition to the seller was a divestiture: that is, the purchase was of not an entire company but of a part of one that was unwanted by its owners. This tendency, too, would continue in the eighties, although then driven by different forces. In the seventies it most often represented the dismantling of troubled conglomerates, now become stranded giants; in the eighties, it would very often represent the breakup, sometimes preplanned, of prosperous and viable companies that had been acquired with borrowings that could be repaid only through partial dismemberment of the thing bought.

Already by 1980, the forces behind the new form of takeover contest—the nearest thing to jungle warfare in American corporate affairs in more than a century—were readily discernible. Most visibly, these forces were apparent market underevaluation of the assets of many companies, including very large ones; ready availability of huge quantities of cash, both from liquid corporate treasuries and from commercial banks, which tended to look on takeover loans as good credit risks involving premium interest rates; the federal tax code, which encouraged borrowing by allowing corporations to deduct interest payments in full from taxable income; and the rise of financial men, oriented toward transactions rather than operations, to the head of many key corporations. In a broader economic context, a 1980 Department of Commerce paper identified four forces behind the emerging new merger boom:

1. It was driven by conditions of low growth, low profitability, and high inflation.

2. It was an adaptive response to financial, economic, and geopolitical instability.

3. It was strongly supported by the development and application of new strategic planning and control tools.

4. It was furthered by a psychological and institutional climate that favored M&A transactions.

Robert H. Hayes and William J. Abernathy summed up the situation in the *Harvard Business Review* as follows:

Under [such] conditions it may well make good economic sense to buy rather than build new plants or
modernize existing ones. Mergers . . . produce fairly
quick and decisive results, and they offer a kind of
public recognition that helps careers along. Who can
doubt the appeal of the titles awarded by the financial
community: being called a . . . "white knight" or a
"raider" can quicken anyone's blood.[3]

All of these forces except high domestic inflation
would be operating, with increased strength, in the U.S.
merger wave of the eighties. And a new one would be
added: with the coming of the Reagan administration in
1981, federal antitrust enforcement would quickly assume
its most permissive stance since around the turn of the
century, paving the way for some of the largest horizontal
combinations ever, and the most economically significant
ones since the start of the century. Indeed, the wave may
fairly be said to have started with a spate of large oil-
industry mergers and near-mergers in 1981 and 1982: the
partial acquisition of Conoco by Dome Petroleum, leading
to the partial acquisition of Conoco by the Seagram Company, leading to a bidding war between Mobil Corporation and Du Pont for control of Conoco, with Du Pont the
winner at a price of just under $9 billion; the attempt of
Mobil to take over Marathon Oil, leading to U.S. Steel's
takeover of Marathon for $6.75 billion; and the intricate
affair of 1982 in which Mesa Petroleum and Cities Service
tendered for each other, but never went through with their
purchases because Gulf Oil made a higher bid for Cities
Service—only to withdraw before completing the transac-

tion, paving the way for Occidental Petroleum to acquire Cities Service for about $4 billion. Thus the merger games in the oil industry—a focus of attention because of its undervalued (and mostly underground) assets, real or perceived—were emphatically on; they would reach a crescendo beginning in 1984.

By selecting for brief description and analysis various mergers and merger attempts over 1982 through 1985—not for their size so much as their representativeness—we may trace in outline the evolution of the game over those years.[4]

Still considered among the most baroque of takeover plays, and still widely considered among those that redounded most to the discredit of American business, was the 1982 one involving Bendix, Martin Marietta, United Technologies, and Allied Corporation. Originally, Bendix, headed by the aggressive acquisitor William Agee, tendered for Martin Marietta, an important defense contractor. Martin Marietta, headed by Thomas Pownall, decided to defend itself by making a counter-tender offer for Bendix—the "Pac-Man" defense—even though that defense, tried twice over the previous months, had never been successful. In the Bendix-Marietta case, the issue, assuming both tenders were carried out, seemed to turn on state law. In Maryland, where Martin Marietta was incorporated, an aggressor who held a majority of Martin Marietta would have to wait ten days and then hold a special stockholders' meeting before it could take control. On the other hand, under the laws of Delaware, where Bendix was incorporated, a successful raider could take control immediately. Therefore, Martin Marietta had a technical edge based on timing. The issue was clouded, however, by the fact that both states had provisions forbidding a subsidiary to vote its shares against its parent; since successful tenders both ways would result in each firm being a subsidiary of the other, the possibility was raised that neither would be able to vote its acquired shares, and that neither could control the other.

After some soul-searching, each firm planned to buy a majority of the other in two-tier, front-loaded tenders, at terrible cost to its balance sheet. (In Martin Marietta's case, interest on the $900 million it needed to borrow to buy a majority of Bendix stood to eat up its entire profit for the next year, and perhaps ultimately to bankrupt it.) Before the cross-purchases had been consummated, a third firm, United Technologies, saw a chance to profit by buying control of Bendix and then selling some Bendix assets to Martin Marietta. When negotiations broke down, both Martin Marietta and United Technologies were ready to *lay down* (call off their tender offers by mutual agreement), but Agee for Bendix—against the advice of his investment bankers, Salomon and First Boston—insisted on going forward, whereupon Bendix and Martin Marietta bought control of each other and the standoff developed. The eventual solution (actually agreed to just before Marietta bought Bendix) was for Allied Corporation, as a Bendix white knight, to buy control of Bendix and then exchange a portion of Bendix's Marietta shares for Marietta's entire holding of Bendix. Allied came out with control of Bendix and 39 percent of Marietta. Soon afterward, Agee was forced out of Bendix, taking with him a $4.1-million *golden parachute*—a pension award specifically designed to protect him in case of loss of employment brought about by a change of corporate control.

The whole bizarre episode gave the corporate world, not to mention the public and its government representatives, the sinking feeling that corporate mergers were out of control and that predatory, injudicious top executives were making a shambles of corporate governance; more than any other single merger negotiation, it gave rise to the 1983–84 spate of regulatory and legislative concern about such matters. From a practical standpoint, the outcome was mixed. Martin Marietta, for reasons irrelevant to the takeover attempt, flourished so strongly that within a few months its stock price stood higher than Bendix had ever offered; moreover, it was able to buy back within two years the shares that Allied had acquired. Bendix became Allied's most profitable division—but at the cost of being stripped of some $850 million of its assets, most of that from the dismantling of company headquarters and sale or liquidation of several divisions, at the cost of hundreds of jobs.

As for investment bankers, at least on the Bendix side, this was a case of their relatively prudent advice being ignored repeatedly by a headstrong, ego-driven chief executive, backed by a complaisant board of directors, doing things his own way while protected from personal risk by pension arrangements. As Edward L. Hennessy, Jr., chairman of Allied, admitted afterward, "It was a pretty sorry spectacle. It gave American business a black eye."[5]

The big new development of 1983 in takeovers was the

appearance in their forefront of the leveraged buyout, or going-private transaction (which will be analyzed in more detail in Chapter 7). Indeed, 1983's most characteristic takeover event, or series of events, began with an attempted leveraged buyout. Early in June, an investor group headed by David J. Mahoney, chairman of Norton Simon, Inc., a "diversified company" (the term *conglomerate* being in disgrace) with interests in cosmetics, foods, liquor, and rental cars, among other things, announced an offer to buy all of the company's stock in a leveraged buyout. Since the price offered was a slim 10.5 percent above market price of Norton Simon stock—a virtually unheard-of premium in tender offers of any kind at that time—it was not taken seriously by Wall Street; analysts suspected that its real purpose was to announce that Norton Simon was for sale, and thereby attract a bidding war that would end with Mahoney and other stockholders selling out at a higher price. In any case, a bidding war did ensue. The first bidder was the leveraged-buyout firm of Kohlberg Kravis Roberts & Company; their bid, coming a week after that of the Mahoney group, was $33 per share, $4 higher than the previous one. Toward the end of the month came a third offer, again at $33, from Esmark, Inc., another large diversified company, successor to the old-line meat packer Swift & Company.

At this point the Mahoney group, apparently satisfied that its maneuver had achieved its purpose, dropped out. Norton Simon was emphatically "in play"—in a situation in which it had become all but inevitable that it would be taken over by somebody. The dynamic is as follows: with bids well above the market for all of its stock on the table, the directors of a target company—even though protected by the *business judgment rule,* which generally allows such directors to reject a tender offer on the basis of their belief that they are acting in the corporation's best interest—risk being sued by stockholders if they take that action. This dynamic led Francis M. Wheat, a former SEC commissioner, in 1984 to compare a company facing such a tender offer to a "trapped animal" that "cannot hope to escape." In the event, Norton Simon—which presumably did not *want* to escape, but only to sell at a high price—did not escape. After one more leveraged-buyout attempt involving the Kohlberg firm and a newly recruited partner, Esmark raised its bid to $35.50, and in September Norton Simon accepted, selling all of its stock to Esmark for slightly more than $1 billion.

But that was not the end of the action. As so often happens, the publicity attending Esmark's takeover made it that company's turn to be in play. In May 1984, Kohlberg came back with a $55-per-share leveraged-buyout offer for Esmark (for a total price of over $2.4 billion). Later that month, Beatrice Companies, Inc., the nation's largest food company, bid $56 per share for Esmark, and subsequently raised the price to $60. In August, Beatrice bought Esmark (along, of course, with the already engorged Norton Simon) for a total of $2.6738 billion. Then in 1985–86 came the capper. The persistent Kohlberg Kravis, which had twice bid unsuccessfully for firms that were later to be absorbed into Beatrice, bought out Beatrice itself for $50 a share, in by far the largest leveraged buyout ever. The $6.2 billion that the Kohlberg firm paid came from about $600 million of its own pooled funds, $4 billion from bank loans, and most of the rest from high-yield bonds arranged and sold by Drexel Burnham for a fee of $70 million.

The Norton Simon–Esmark–Beatrice–Kohlberg series of events, besides demonstrating the rising role of the leveraged buyout in the merger bidding process, represents an almost perfect example of the momentum generated by the "in play" process. In this case, as in many others, it swept aside all potential countervailing forces: antitrust considerations, the welfare of employees, the value of replaced managers, the theoretical rights of small stockholders. (In practice, of course, the target company stockholders large and small had little enough reason to complain. The premium above previous market price of the Esmark–Norton Simon takeover was 35 percent; of the Beatrice-Esmark takeover, 45.5 percent. David Mahoney, whose bid had started the whole thing, received some $25 million for his Norton Simon holdings in the Esmark takeover.) Clearly, by the end of 1983 the merger process had developed a self-sustaining momentum, and with the leverage, and consequent vulnerability, of the surviving companies leaping upward with every step.[6]

The year 1984 saw a number of developments in the evolution of mergers. One of them was their rise to unprecedented size; the ten largest for the year totaled $50.3 billion, as against $17.3 billion for the previous year. Indeed, the two largest of the year—Chevron's $13.4-billion acquisition of Gulf Oil and Texaco's $10.1-billion acquisition of Getty Oil—in themselves amounted to more than 1983's top ten. (Investment-banker fees: on Chevron-Gulf, about $17 million for Morgan Stanley, about $28 million for Salomon; on Texaco-Getty, $10.75 million for First Boston, $18.5 million for Goldman Sachs, $15.5 million for Kidder Peabody.) Both of these mammoth transactions were the outcome of wild bidding wars. During 1983, T. Boone Pickens, Jr., of Mesa Petroleum bought 13.2 percent of Gulf and conducted a proxy fight to change its structure drastically. Pickens narrowly lost that initiative, but Gulf, realizing it was emphatically in play, contacted half a dozen potential white knights, among them Atlantic Richfield. Eventually it accepted an $80-per-share offer from Chevron, then called Standard Oil of California—turning down a higher offer from the Kohlberg firm. In the Texaco-Getty case, in January 1984, after a series of moves and countermoves among members of the Getty family, Gordon Getty, who controlled 40 percent of Getty stock, and his board agreed by a handshake to a takeover by Pennzoil Company. In a two-day turnaround, Texaco, which needed a large acquisition because of a serious decline in its oil and gas reserves, outbid Pennzoil and took over Getty. (Pennzoil later sued Texaco, and was awarded around $11 billion in damages and penalties by a Texas jury. In April 1987, with the matter still unsettled after having gone through several appeals, Texaco, although solvent, applied for protection under Chapter 11 of the Bankruptcy Code to prevent Pennzoil from exacting bond while the case was still in the courts.)

The Chevron-Gulf and Texaco-Getty transactions—along with a third in March, Mobil Corporation's $5.8-billion takeover of Superior Oil, straight horizontal mergers among oil giants—showed that in the Reagan administration, antitrust action was scarcely a consideration, at least in regard to the oil industry. The Clayton Act and its amendments notwithstanding, huge consolidations that increased market share (although they did not provably reduce effective competition) seemed to be as permissible as they had been at the turn of the century. In the Gulf case, another tendency exemplified was the new increasingly frequent involvement of a *raider*—an initial investor who, since his resources were such that it seemed unlikely he could take control, could rationally be assumed to be playing for greenmail. The hard core of such raiders was, and for some time would continue to be, a handful of men, with or without existing corporate connections, whose personal resources, along with bank and other credit based largely on successful past deals, gave them the power to terrorize all but a few huge companies. Prominent among them, in addition to Pickens, were Carl Icahn, Irwin L. Jacobs, the Bass brothers of Texas, the Belzberg family of Canada, the Briton Sir James Goldsmith, the Australian Rupert Murdoch, and Saul P. Steinberg—the same Saul P. Steinberg who had tried to take over the Chemical Bank in 1969, and one of the few financiers to be prominent in both the go-go years of the sixties and the megamerger years of the eighties.

The profits from their forays into greenmail (more formally called "targeted repurchase," and euphemistically described by Icahn as "a kind of arbitrage") were nothing less than princely. As early as 1982–83, Icahn cleared $6.6 million on American Can, $9.7 million on Owens Illinois, $8.5 million on Dan River Mills, and $19 million on Gulf & Western. Later on, Jacobs made $20 million on Pabst Brewing, and $30 million on Kaiser Steel, among other large profits. The Bass brothers were said to have profited by $400 million on the Texaco-Getty deal, and Pickens's Mesa Petroleum by about $1 billion on all of its stock plays in 1984. The greenmail transaction that aroused the loudest public outcry, perhaps because of the high visibility of the target company, was Steinberg's 1984 play in Walt Disney, which left Steinberg many millions richer—and the company, nonetheless, under strong new management in the effective control of the Bass brothers.

In essence, as its slang name implies, greenmail is a form of blackmail—a payment well above market price by a corporation for a block of its stock to a holder who threatens an attempted takeover, in exchange for his promise to go away and not trouble the corporation further. As such, it is widely deplored, and many, including some greenmailers, feel (or profess to feel) that it should be outlawed. Nevertheless, there is an argument, made chiefly by Chicago School academics, that raiders and greenmailers are not business buccaneers but rather socially useful scavengers. Such raids, the argument goes, help stockholders of the target company by forcing the stock price upward, help the company itself by keeping management on its toes or forcing it to hire better management, and, in practice, seldom hurt the company by actually taking it over and then draining its assets through divestitures. Even *The New York Times* in March 1985 said of greenmailers that "their self-interest usually leads to a collective good." On the other side, opponents insist that raiders, besides taxing corporate treasuries by exacting enormous payments for their stock, hurt corporations by distracting management's attention from its regular duties and by forcing it to abandon long-term growth plans in favor of improving short-term profit performance. Moreover, so this argument runs, not even target-company stockholders are benefited, because greenmail repurchases constitute categorical discrimination against them in favor of the greenmailer, and because, after the payment has been made and the raider is out of the picture, the stock price almost always drops, often to a figure lower than what it was before the greenmail play began. (Indeed, in the leading cases in 1983 and 1984, the stock price of greenmailed companies dropped 20 to 40 percent after the repurchases had been made.) Not surprisingly, the strongest statements against the practice usually come from the heads of actual or potential greenmail targets. In 1985 William C. Norris, chairman of Control Data Corporation, roundly characterized greenmail as "a form of legalized banditry."

And greenmail has another disadvantage from the corporate perspective: unlike measles or chicken pox, an attack of it does not confer future immunity; on the contrary, the fact that a company has been willing to buy off one raider often attracts others. In what may well have been the paradigmatic takeover of 1984—that of St. Regis Corporation by Champion International—there were no fewer than three major greenmail attempts before the target's agony was ended by a relatively friendly merger. In March, after Sir James Goldsmith had announced that he held 8.6 percent of St. Regis stock and intended to attempt a takeover, the St. Regis board hastily voted to buy back the block for $161 million, giving Goldsmith a profit of $51 million. Only a few weeks later, Loews Corporation announced that it now held 8.5 percent of St. Regis, bought for $103 million. Again St. Regis decided to pay off; the $141 million it paid Loews for its stock left Loews a profit of $38 million. It must have been with a sickening sense of déjà vu that St. Regis learned on June 27 that yet another raider, Rupert Murdoch, now held 5.6 percent. St. Regis had paid all the greenmail its treasury could stand. A month later, Murdoch announced his intention to tender for a majority of St. Regis shares at $55 per share. A trapped animal if there ever was one, St. Regis chairman William Haselton went to his old friend Andrew Sigler, chairman of Champion International, with whom he had previously talked about the possibility of a friendly merger between the two companies as a last-ditch maneuver to save St. Regis from the raiders. The last ditch, Haselton said, had been reached. Having put together a six-bank, $1.05-billion credit line in less than twenty-four hours, Sigler for Champion offered to buy 60 percent of St. Regis for $55.50 and exchange the rest for its own shares. St. Regis accepted, and thus was formed the nation's largest producer of paper and second largest of plywood and lumber.

The outcome of the transaction for various parties at interest is instructive. Murdoch, the year's third successful St. Regis greenmailer, took down a profit of some $37 million. The arbitrageur Boesky, who had become involved early in the game, cleared an estimated $30 million. St. Regis stockholders, to the extent that they got into the proration pool for the cash part of the offer, made about $10 per share over the stock price before the Champion offer. Parts of St. Regis would subsequently be sold to help pay for the takeover, but top management of both companies remained in place. Morgan Stanley got a $6.4-million fee for representing St. Regis, Goldman Sachs $5 million for representing Champion. As for Andrew Sigler of Champion, the experience of being a white knight so shocked and disillusioned him about the economic consequences of the current takeover game that he soon thereafter became head of a Business Roundtable task force on hostile takeovers, and perhaps the corporate world's most militant crusader for legislation to curb them.[7]

In 1985, probably the principal new or evolving developments on the hostile-takeover scene were the following: an apotheosis (although perhaps not the final one) of the use of junk bonds as financing for such takeovers, along with the related tendency of successful bidders to pay off part of their enormous debt by partially liquidating their acquired companies; a growing tendency of threatened companies, or those who thought they might soon be threatened, to defend themselves by *leveraging up,* that is, retiring equity and increasing debt as a percentage of their capitalization; and a move of the final decision-making power in takeover contests from the marketplace toward the courts—in particular, the courts of Delaware, where so many of the largest companies have long been incorporated.

The ultimate step in the rise of junk bonds was occasioned by two factors: an increasing reluctance by commercial banks to finance huge takeovers in their entirety (as they had been eager to do in, for example, Champion–St. Regis), and the continuing, indeed increasing, willing-

ness of institutional investors—particularly savings institutions—to absorb such bonds in almost any quantity into
their portfolios. In the first case, the symbolic turning
point may have come in 1984, when Chicago Pacific,
poised for a takeover run on Textron, had to back down
when Citibank decided to withdraw as a lender. In the
second, junk bonds continued to lead a charmed life in the
markets, and thus, with their high yields, to look good to
short-term-oriented portfolio managers. If they represented sin, as some thought, it was sin without immediate
punishment. A study by the University of Pennsylvania's
Wharton School shows that between 1980 and mid-1984,
low-rated bonds had a total return of 13.5 percent, about
double that for AAA corporate bonds; meanwhile, according to Drexel Burnham Lambert (hardly a disinterested observer, it should be noted), the default rate for
such bonds of recent issue, the ones used to finance takeovers, was only .52 percent per year.* In sum, in the
mid-eighties junk bonds were outperforming blue-chip
bonds by substantial margins.

The magnitude of the increase of junk-bond use in
takeovers in 1985 was startling. Whereas the total of junk
bonds issued for that purpose from 1981 through 1984 had
been $200 million, for just the first half of 1985 the figure
came to $2 billion, and the figures were on the rapid rise.
The effect of such financing on the takeover scene was

*Further statistics available in September 1986, by which time roughly $100
billion in junk bonds (not all of them for takeovers) had been issued since the
start of 1980, showed that of the $86 billion issued over that period by the top
fifteen junk-bond underwriters, 3.4 percent were in default. However, the rate
for Drexel Burnham, by far the largest of junk-bond underwriters, was only
1.9 percent.

equally startling. For practical purposes, junk bonds all but eliminated corporate size as a takeover defense. If a raider could finance an attempt on a corporate giant largely with the giant's own resources, there was scarcely any limit to who could take on whom. Virtually all of the monster raids of 1985, starting with Pickens's on Phillips Petroleum and Unocal, had a huge junk-bond component in their proposed financing. Phillips and Unocal both escaped, but at the cost of restructurings that added $4.5 billion and about $4 billion, respectively, to their corporate debt, and would force them later to sell off assets to reduce that debt. The 1985 case that threatened to carry the junk-bond takeover attempt to absurdity, and thus ultimately to discredit it, was Turner Communications' attempt on CBS, Inc., in which the aggressor planned to put up no cash at all. However, despite the scorn heaped on this proposal by the financial community, CBS, in order to beat it off, found that it needed to buy in over one-fifth of all its shares, triple its debt, and make plans to sell off assets. As a result, CBS's own senior debt was downrated by the rating services, although not, to be sure, to junk-bond level.

The way to prevent a junk-bond takeover in 1985, it seemed, was to make something approaching junk of one's own company before the raider could do so.[8]

The rising importance of the courts in deciding takeover contests was another feature of the Pickens–Mesa versus Unocal encounter. The main issue before a court in such a situation is interpretation of the *business-judgment doctrine*—that is, the question of what a target company's directors may and may not do to foil a takeover attempt. In an important 1984 case, after The Limited, Inc., had tendered for over half the stock of Carter Hawley Hale Stores, the target had responded by buying in $18.5 million of its own shares and selling a large new issue of convertible preferred stock to General Cinema on condition that the block be voted according to the Carter board's wishes. The Limited, with support from the SEC, had sued on grounds that the Carter stock repurchase had violated the Williams Act rules for disclosure in tender offers, including self-tender offers. However, a federal court in Los Angeles had ruled that the repurchase was not a tender offer and therefore did not violate the Williams Act. Under the business-judgment doctrine, the court seemed to be saying, a target company's board has wide latitude indeed.

A key judicial finding in Mesa-Unocal tended to confirm that impression. As part of its defense, Unocal proposed to buy in roughly one-third of all its shares—specifically excluding from the offer the shares held by the prospective acquirer, Mesa. It appeared to be a case of greenmail in reverse: open discrimination between its own stockholders by a target corporation, this time *against* a would-be greenmailer rather than, in the more familiar scenario, in his favor. Mesa sued and the Delaware Supreme Court, rejecting the suit, ruled that corporate directors have leeway under the business-judgment doctrine to discriminate against one stockholder if they believe such action to be in the best interest of the company as a whole. So Socal stayed independent, although restructured Unocal crowed that Mesa had lost $100 million, but Pickens later insisted that his firm had cleared $83 million after taxes, through the use of an obscure tax provision.

Perhaps, although the Court didn't actually say so,

what appealed to it about the Socal buy-in was the poetic justice of the situation: a would-be greenmailer hoist on his own petard. In any event, the decision was a move toward tipping the balance in hostile takeover attempts toward the defender.

But the key legal battles of 1984–85 regarding tender offers concerned the so-called poison pill, and the key case was *Moran* v. *Household International.* First appearing on the scene in 1983—its technique, but not its racy name, generally credited to the inventive brain of the takeover-defense lawyer Martin Lipton—the *poison pill* is essentially a means of making a takeover more expensive, perhaps prohibitively so. In its early version, it consisted of the issuance to target-company stockholders of a dividend consisting of convertible preferred stock. In the event of a takeover, the successful raider would be forced to honor the convertible feature and in effect issue new voting common stock, thus diluting his holding; his only antidote to the pill was to buy all or nearly all of the convertible preferred issue himself, perhaps at prohibitive expense. However, some of the first poison pills were ineffective in practice. Lenox Inc., which adopted the defense in 1983 in an effort to fight off Brown-Forman Distillers, was taken over anyhow when the aggressor bought most of the issue and Lenox agreed to an accommodation, achieving, nevertheless, a somewhat higher takeover price than would have been possible otherwise. Also in 1983, Bell & Howell and others used poison pills successfully by putting them in place before any tender offer had been made; on the other hand, Superior Oil, threatened by Pickens, was forced to withdraw a planned poison-pill defense as a result of an outcry from the company's stockholders.

By the following year, Lipton and his colleagues had devised a much more lethal pill. Adopted by Household International to fight off a planned leveraged buyout by a group led by John A. Moran, a Household director, it had as its key feature a triggering mechanism, activated categorically by a takeover attempt, that would set off events unfavorable to the aggressor. Specifically, Household gave its existing stockholders rights to buy a $200-million issue of new stock with special qualities: if anyone should come to control 20 percent or more of Household stock, or announce a tender offer for 30 percent or more, owners of the Household shares would automatically get rights to buy shares of the *acquiring* company for half of market value. The prospect of this huge and entirely involuntary bargain-basement sale by an acquirer of his own stock would presumably deter anyone from assuming the role of acquirer. And so it did. Moran, head of the would-be buyout group, said later that the poison pill would have added $6 billion—three-quarters of Household's annual revenues—to the cost of buying the company, and that accordingly "it would take a company the size of IBM" to make a successful raid on Household.

Right from the start, the legality of the Household poison pill was in question. For one thing, although it had been adopted by the Household board with only one dissenting vote (that of John Whitehead of Goldman Sachs), it had not been approved by Household's stockholders, who as a result of it would presumably be deprived of the opportunity to sell their shares at the premium that a takeover would bring. For another, it could be accused of entrenching the company's management and thus freeing it from the discipline of the marketplace. (Joseph Flom, dean of acquirer-side takeover lawyers, commented that the Household poison pill, if affirmed by the courts, bid fair to end nearly all hostile takeovers.) Yet again, was it legal and proper for one company to issue rights in the stock of another?

The Moran group brought suit, and in January 1985, Judge Joseph T. Walsh of the Chancery Court of Delaware ruled that "the rights plan was properly adopted under Delaware law, was not intended primarily for the entrenchment of management, and serves a rational corporate purpose." He added, "There was ample cause for the concern of Household directors" on account of "the impact of partial tender offers deemed destructive of shareholder interests." The Moran group appealed to the Delaware Supreme Court, and in March the SEC took the unusual action (albeit by a narrow three-to-two vote) of siding with Moran in a friend-of-the-court brief. At last, in November, a three-judge panel of the Delaware Supreme Court affirmed the lower court's decision, and the takeover failed.

Thus the poison pill, which by this time had been adopted or was in the process of being adopted by dozens of companies concerned about being taken over—before the end of 1986, by about three hundred—was legal at least for the present, and the scales in the takeover game again tipped toward the defender. However, Flom to the contrary notwithstanding, takeovers did not end, or show signs of being about to end. Earlier in the year, Sir James

Goldsmith had successfully circumvented a poison-pill defense erected against him by Crown Zellerbach Corporation, and had taken over the company anyhow. (Indeed, the defense had actually worked *for* Goldsmith by deterring other suitors.) Again, in November an aggressive acquiring company named Pantry Pride, Inc. (later renamed Revlon Group, Inc.), completed a takeover of Revlon, Inc.—thereby bringing about "the demise of this enterprise, as we know it," commented former judge Simon H. Rifkind, a Revlon director—even though Revlon had a poison pill in place. The Delaware Supreme Court had cleared the way for a Pantry Pride victory by ruling that an option on some of Revlon's key assets that Revlon had granted to a white knight, Forstmann Little & Company, was not in the best interests of Revlon stockholders. The decision did not invalidate Revlon's poison-pill defense, but did cast doubt on the effectiveness of such defenses in the future; as Eric Gleacher of Morgan Stanley, who represented Pantry Pride in the transaction, commented later, the Revlon decision "makes a poison pill a risky instrument." It is interesting that, as in the Household-Moran case, the Delaware courts effectively decided the outcome of Pantry Pride–Revlon—but this time the opposite way. Further, it is interesting that the very judge who had decided the former case in favor of the target company—Joseph Walsh—made the ultimate ruling in the latter in favor of the aggressor.[9]

(In 1986, the poison pill was dealt several more direct judicial blows by federal judges, among them one in Indiana and one in New York.)

Thus the takeover wars seesawed through 1985, with

the huge and growing acceptability of junk bonds tending to favor aggressors, and court decisions, on balance, favoring defenders. A standoff seemed at hand—but one (as the next chapter will show) achieved at the cost of dubious benefit to stockholders, and enormous losses in terms of time, attention to business, and bankers' and lawyers' fees to corporations and the economy at large.

Two more or less new wrinkles emerged in 1986. One was a Byzantine technique of a raider to circumvent the Williams Act and thus make a takeover cheaper. It operated as follows: (1) the raider, in the usual way, announces a holding of 5 percent or more and makes a tender offer; (2) arbitrageurs, as usual, quickly accumulate a majority or near majority of the target stock; (3) the raider suddenly begins to act queasy about going ahead with the deal; (4) a single firm (customarily, the West Coast–based Jefferies & Company) buys out the now-nervous arbitrageurs, acquiring a controlling block of the target; (5) the raider abruptly terminates the tender offer, causing the stock price to drop; (6) soon or immediately after the termination, the raider, perhaps by prearrangement, buys the controlling block in the open market from the go-between firm, thus obtaining control for less than he could have through a tender offer. This technique was so fraught with overtones of manipulation and even conspiracy that it seemed unlikely to survive for long.

The other new wrinkle was a tendency of the biggest investment-banking firms to make short-term commitments of enormous sums of their own capital—$1.8 billion by First Boston in one deal, $1.9 billion by Merrill Lynch in another—to takeover deals, thereby in effect "buying" the deals from rival firms, and in particular from Drexel with its unrivaled junk-bond capability. The effect of this strategy was to raise greatly the stakes in the takeover game; bankers' fees in deals including such capital commitments were in the unprecedented $100–$200 million range, and, of course, the committed capital was at risk instead of *no* investment-bank capital being at risk as in a normal takeover. If the new practice continued, it bid fair to concentrate M&A business still further among the four or five most capital-rich firms, and presumably to make the incentive to those firms to foment takeovers that much greater.

We may round out this summary of the main tides of battle in the takeover wars through 1986 with a brief account of a kind of sport among mid-eighties takeovers. It was that of Trans World Airlines (TWA) in 1985 by Carl C. Icahn of New York. It began as a more or less routine junk-bond takeover threat apparently designed for greenmail. In May, Icahn—widely known, and feared, as a leading corporate raider and greenmailer—disclosed that he owned 20.5 percent of TWA and was tendering for the rest of the stock at $18 per share. After TWA had rejected this offer, Frank Lorenzo, chairman of Texas Air Corporation, bid $23 for TWA stock in a transaction, to be financed largely by Drexel high-coupon bonds, in which TWA would be acquired by two Texas Air subsidiaries. In June the TWA board accepted this offer, and the matter seemed concluded. However, all parties had reckoned without the intervention of TWA's unions and their leaders and advisers. Chief among the latter were John F.

Peterpaul, vice-president of the machinists' union, and Peterpaul's financial guru, Brian M. Freeman, a young man who had previously made his mark at the U.S. Department of the Treasury as a "bailout" expert, particularly in the matter of the government loan guarantee that saved Chrysler Corporation in 1980–83, and had subsequently advised the union employees of Conrail in their negotiations to buy that company from the government.

In the Conrail matter, Freeman had developed the new concept that labor, by making wage-and-benefit concessions in exchange for securities, could be a "capital provider" to industry. As Freeman summed up his credo: "Employees who are asked to provide a firm with concession capital should be treated like investors or creditors." At troubled TWA, where union wages were exceptionally high—pilots made $100,000–$150,000 per year—wage concessions appeared to be inevitable anyhow. The airline industry being exceptionally capital-intensive, wages and benefits generally accounting for 30–40 percent of costs, the TWA union leaders realized that they were in a position to be powerful "players" in the merger negotiation; through making concessions or not making them, they could significantly affect the value of the company, and perhaps the outcome of the takeover contest. Lorenzo of Texas Air, long reputed as a union-buster, had announced himself as disinclined to bargain with the TWA unions, and they were strongly disinclined to bargain with him; therefore Freeman—advising the machinists and subsequently, along with Lazard Frères, representing a coalition of TWA's pilots, machinists, and flight attendants—went to Icahn. He sought to persuade the New Yorker, who already stood to make many millions from TWA through his familiar technique of exacting greenmail, that he could make even more, and even turn the tide of the takeover contest in his favor, by dealing with the unions on concessions. Icahn was skeptical at first—"unions don't work together," he told Freeman—but eventually agreed to negotiations. From late May until August, such negotiations went on, without agreement being reached.

Meanwhile, the TWA unions were defying tradition by using to the hilt the familiar investment-banking bag of negotiating tricks. (Until the employees of the Wierton division of National Steel had engaged Lazard in their buyout from the parent company in 1983–84, a union had never used a leading investment bank as a financial adviser.) To put pressure on Icahn, the unions made overtures to other potential buyers of TWA, including Jay Pritzker of Chicago, Eastern Airlines, and Lorenzo himself. They raised the threat of labor unrest against any future owner of TWA who did *not* come to terms with them. ("Blue collar-mail," Freeman called it, vividly, if hardly felicitously.) Freeman even devised a way (not put into practice) that a labor contract might theoretically be designed for use as a poison pill to deter a corporate aggressor; and, resorting for a change to familiar union as opposed to investment-banking tactics, one day he arranged for TWA machinists and flight attendants to throw a picket line around Drexel's offices in New York and Los Angeles, to protest the fact that Drexel planned to finance Lorenzo. (Drexel's officials, utterly unaccustomed to being picketed, were at first amused and then outraged.)

At last, not long before a TWA board meeting scheduled for August 20, at which the board would decide among the various offers, Icahn and the TWA unions came to terms. Under their agreement, the pilots would make wage-and-benefit concessions of 26 percent, the machinists 15 percent, for an annual saving to the company of some $300 million, and the unions would guarantee labor peace for three years; in return, the company would grant employees up to 20 percent of TWA stock, up to 20 percent of corporate profits for three years, $300 million of liquidating preferred stock, and certain other benefits. Before the meeting, Lorenzo raised his bid to $26 per share, and Icahn, on the basis of the union concessions he had obtained, raised his from $18 to $24. The unions and Icahn hoped that the TWA board would feel that the slightly lower Icahn bid, with the union concessions tied into it, was better for the company than the higher Lorenzo bid, which involved no such guaranteed concessions. So it did: Icahn won control of TWA, and for the first time union action had determined the winner of a huge takeover contest.

Why had it never happened before, and was it likely to happen again? As to the first question, Freeman believes the answer lies largely in ingrained prejudices and labor's former lack of financial sophistication: for generations, labor and management-ownership had seldom even considered negotiations on anything but wage-and-benefit bargaining. Now labor had moved fully into investment banking at its most Byzantine. Did that mean that the takeover wars were now to become, as a regular routine, an opportunity for unions to play the competitors for ownership of companies against each other?

Not likely. For employees to be in a position to be such strong "capital providers" that they can force capitalists to treat them "like investors or creditors," certain prior conditions must exist: the industry must be one with such severe problems and such a labor-intensive structure that the alternatives appear to be wage concessions or disaster. TWA in 1985 met these criteria; few other companies in any industry did. A union-decided takeover contest could not occur in the case of a financially healthy and profitable company. Moreover, Icahn's experiences in the months after his takeover of TWA were not of a sort calculated to encourage other corporate raiders to emulate his example. Plagued by a strike of flight attendants (who had not joined in the original agreement), a sharp decline in overseas air travel attributed to the fear of terrorism, and other troubles, TWA became threatened with bankruptcy, and Icahn, with paper losses of many millions, seemed to suggest that he wished he had taken his greenmail and run. Still, the sudden and emphatic appearance of labor as a player in the takeover game stands as a landmark in investment banking's sloughing off of its traditional habits and set of mind.[10]

7

Buying Out
the Store

The sensation of the middle 1980s in corporate and invest-ment-banking circles was the leveraged buyout, a form of transaction that, by 1985, a Republican SEC Commis-sioner had spoken of as "little more than a charade," a leading class-action lawyer had called "intrinsically a scam," and the chief financial officer of Goodyear Tire and Rubber had called "an idea that was created in hell by the Devil himself."

In a *leveraged buyout* (or LBO), a publicly owned company is bought out in full—that is, taken private—by a small group that almost always includes members of the company's management, in a transaction financed largely by borrowing. Ultimately the debt is to be paid with money generated by the acquired company's operations or by sales of some of its assets. In a theoretical sense, it represents a kind of change generally thought to be healthy: a partial reuniting of corporate ownership with corporate management, reversing the broad twentieth-century trend toward their separation made part of economic canon law by Adolf A. Berle and Gardiner C. Means more than fifty years ago. In a more immediate financial sense, it is an offshoot of the merger craze—a variant of the highly leveraged takeover in which, so its critics insist, there is the additional problem that the managers who acquire part of the controlling equity from the public stockholders are acting as self-dealing fiduciaries.

By no means a new form of transaction, the LBO was formerly rather rare, and generally confined to comparatively small companies. Until 1979, most LBO deals involved less than $100,000. But things changed after 1980 with the rise of the concept that a firm's own strength, regardless of its size, could be used to take control of it. It is generally agreed that the deal that did most to popularize LBOs was the purchase in 1981 of Gibson Greeting Cards by a group headed by former Secretary of the Treasury William E. Simon. Eighteen months later, the Simon group took Gibson public again—a common objective of LBO organizers, suggesting that the permanent reuniting of management and ownership is scarcely their intention. The resulting proceeds to Simon and his partners amounted to some $200 on each $1.00 invested.

It was with such credentials that LBOs came into

vogue. Measured by total sales of companies going private, they increased tenfold between 1979 and 1983; in the latter year they accounted for almost 20 percent of all takeovers of public companies and almost as much of the market value of such takeovers. As of the end of 1985, the newly private companies for that year alone numbered ten industrial and eight service companies with revenues above $1 billion.

Meanwhile, investors in the huge pools of capital used to initiate LBOs were said to be making an average of something like 40 percent on their money. Those pools were sponsored principally but not exclusively by firms set up specifically to organize LBOs and invest in them. (The big investment banks, having previously shied away from LBOs, finally smelled blood in 1984, and entered the business one after another.) The largest of the "boutique" firms, Kohlberg Kravis Roberts & Company (KKR) was formed in 1976 by a group who broke away from Bear Stearns. Its biggest offer, $15.6 billion for Gulf Oil in 1984, was, as we have seen, unsuccessful; if it had gone through, many Gulf assets would have had to be liquidated to service the resulting debts. Its greatest accomplishment to date was, by a wide margin, the 1985 takeover of Beatrice. The second most prominent firm, Forstmann Little & Company, did its first deal in 1980. It formed its first investment pool of about $50 million in 1982, and the following year formed a new one of $250 million, most of the money coming from large U.S. corporations. Its most prominent transaction before 1987 was the $650-million LBO of Dr. Pepper Company in 1984, which, typically, led to large asset sales by the company. (Dr. Pepper was sold to Coca-Cola in 1986, at a 9.5-to-1 profit to Forstmann.) Its ambitious attempt to be Revlon's white knight against Pantry Pride in 1985 failed, as we have seen, because the courts disallowed a "lockup" option on Revlon assets that the company had been eager to grant.

Overall, Forstmann's record has been spectacular enough to make any investor's mouth water. Up to mid-1986, it had completed ten LBOs for purchase prices totaling about $2 billion, and six of the purchased companies had been taken public, at returns ranging from two to fifteen times investment, with no losers.

Under the conditions of the eighties, there are two great predisposing factors to LBOs. First, the Internal Revenue Code, principally by allowing interest but not dividends to be deducted from taxable income, provides them with a huge federal subsidy. (In the aborted Gulf deal, the saving on federal taxes alone would have been more than the $500 million that KKR proposed to invest.) Second in importance in causing their growth was the ready availability of commercial-bank credit in huge quantities and, more recently, the availability of credit through junk bonds. In mid-1984, Manufacturers Hanover had over $2 billion tied up in LBOs, and Citicorp about $1 billion. One banker summed up the reasoning of the banks by saying that LBOs "are much safer than loaning for petroleum exploration, or to the . . . government of Chad." In the typical LBO of 1983 or 1984, the participating executives of the company being taken private, having put up their own stock holdings but comparatively little or even no cash, would come out with perhaps 20 percent of the company's equity, and in a few cases much more.

The deal-making LBO firm did not assume management of the firm after the buyout—its sole concern was investment results—but always had a representative on its board. As to fees, the LBO firm would typically collect about 1 percent of the value of the deal plus 20 percent of subsequent capital gains to its outside investors.

So long—but just so long—as a recession did not come along to lower cash flow and perhaps force the leveraged firms into bankruptcy, LBOs seemed to be a case of everybody's winning. The bought-out stockholders got a premium over market price; the executive buyers got huge stakes in the enterprises they managed, and freedom from the quarter-to-quarter pressure for increased profits that being publicly owned implies; and the LBO firms got their fees plus a piece of the action. In one spectacular example, the more-than-$1-billion LBO of Metromedia, Inc., early in 1984, the stockholders got an 85-percent premium over market price; the holding of Harry Kluge, Metromedia's chairman, rose from 26 percent to over 75 percent with no cash investment; and the banks got the customary premiums over their normal lending fees. (The bank spread between cost of money and LBO fees was normally about twice the spread on ordinary financing.)

A magic money-making machine seemed to be in place—but one with certain limitations. It could not be universally used; to be relatively prudent, an LBO had to involve a company with certain characteristics: maturity, no big capital commitments, a low price-to-earnings ratio, stable earnings, predictable cash flow, and salable assets. Without these characteristics, the risk of inability to service debt after the buyout in the event of recession would be all but suicidal. Even with them, it was predictable that the company's profits would be depressed in the first years after the buyout, that its cash flow would be spoken for to pay off debt, and that in those years it would be extremely unlikely to undertake growth commitments—say, for new research and development. In mid-1984 the inherent risk in LBOs began to be widely noticed. "The more leveraged takeovers and buyouts now, the more bankruptcies tomorrow," said SEC Chairman John Shad in June (without, however, recommending specific steps to curb them). The big banks began to become more cautious about LBO lending. There was, however, an alternative source of money ready and eager to leap into the breach: the junk-bond market, which, as we have seen, was flourishing mightily. That December, Kluge was replacing more than $1 billion of Metromedia debt with Drexel high-yield bonds. And the nature of the LBO business was changing under the impact of junk bonds. Previously, LBOs had invariably been friendly transactions—and no wonder, because usually top-management board members were in effect dealing with themselves, as buying stockholders and selling directors. Now LBOs were coming into competition with hostile tender offers, achieving a "level playing field" with acquisitions of one corporation by another. Previously, management buyouts had been disadvantaged in competition with tender offers, because of the time factor: completing a buyout normally took more than twice as long as completing a tender offer, and when billions are at stake, time is not just money but big money. KKR in particular went into tender offers, partly junk-bond-financed. By spring 1985 there were about half a dozen two-tier tender LBO attempts pending, and that summer KKR was forming a $2-billion equity pool earmarked for white-knight bids in takeover battles. The 1985 KKR takeover of Beatrice epitomized, for the moment, another sort of merger—that of the LBO with the hostile or semihostile junk-bond-financed takeover.

The reason for the interest of investment banks in this new game, involving deals of such mind-boggling complexity as to make them almost immune to lay criticism, is not difficult to understand. In the KKR-Beatrice transaction, quite apart from the multimillion-dollar fees to Beatrice's advisers, Salomon and Lazard, KKR for its advice on the transaction took home $45 million, the largest advisory fee ever paid until then.

"All this frenzy," warned Felix Rohatyn—whose firm was glad enough to advise Beatrice in the KKR deal—"may be good for investment bankers now, but it's not good for the country, or for investment bankers in the long run." By the end of 1985, although no major firm taken private in an LBO had yet failed as a result, small cracks in the woodwork had begun to appear. Brentano's bookstore chain, taken private in 1982, had subsequently filed for Chapter II and been reorganized and broken up. Thatcher Glass Corporation, taken private in 1981, had filed for Chapter II in December 1984 because its cash flow was inadequate to meet payments on debt; by the middle of the following year, more than four thousand employees had been dismissed, and although Thatcher's large bank creditors were apparently all right on the strength of asset sales, second-line creditors appeared to be out in the cold. Even KKR, which had seemed to have the magic touch, admitted in 1984 that its American Forest Products deal was "not working out as hoped." Beyond that, there was the specter that future court decisions might hold that some LBOs that wound up as bankruptcies were fraudulent transfers under the Federal Bankruptcy Code, because they tended to reverse the basic bankruptcy-law principle that the interests of creditors are senior to that of stockholders. In the event of such a finding, the sellers of stock to an LBO group might be ordered to refund the money they had received.[1]

In its simplest outline, the LBO is a form of transaction with plenty of sound precedent. It may be compared in some ways to a plain citizen's purchase of real estate financed mostly or wholly with a mortgage—the mortgage to be paid off gradually with money from rents on the property itself, or by resale of part of it. The buyer assumes the risk that he may lose the property through failure to meet mortgage payments, but he is involved in no conflict of interest.

Consider in contrast, however, the situation of a corporate executive who becomes a party to an attempted leveraged buyout of his publicly owned company. As a corporate manager, it is his duty to stockholders to conduct the company in such a way that its stock price will be high. On the other hand, as a prospective buyer—not just of shares in the company, but, with his LBO group, of *all* its shares—he has a categorical and overwhelming personal interest in getting its share price temporarily as low as possible. There are, of course, many things that corporate managers can do to reduce their company's short-term reported earnings and therefore depress its interim stock price, without damaging it over the long term. Bevis Longstreth has given us an inventory of some of them: "The annual report can go from fifty pages of upbeat talk to one page of discouraging prognosis. . . . Assets . . . can be sold to book a loss; opportunities can be postponed or even foregone. Dividends can be cut, debts paid off, advertising budgets employed, all with . . . the interim purpose and effect of depressing the stock price." In sum, management, supposedly the stockholders' fiduciary, may have a powerful interest in damaging their investment over the short term as much as possible.

Along with being a self-dealing fiduciary, the executive in a management buyout is trading on information not available to the public stockholders he is dealing against. The company "numbers" used by LBO groups in applying for financing, which are not ordinarily disclosed to stockholders or the SEC, may present a far more sanguine picture of the company's prospects than do its published earnings and financial statements. Moreover, stockholders who are coerced into selling out in LBOs (their only recourse being to bring suit, as a few usually do) may thereby be coerced into missing a market move. Those who sold in 1981 or 1982 at price-earnings ratios of, say, eight to one were obviously deprived of profits that would have been theirs in 1983, when ratios for the same stocks were two or three times as high.

The theoretical arguments in favor of management LBOs center on two factors: the advantage to stockholders from the premium over market prices they receive, and the incentive to managers that allegedly comes from their increased equity in the company. With their enhanced personal stake, it is said, the managers achieve more efficient utilization of corporate assets; they achieve complete protection against hostile takeover attempts; they are freed from the burden of public disclosure under the federal securities laws; and they gain greater flexibility in management, including the freedom to take greater risks. Robert Greenhill of Morgan Stanley told a congressional hearing in 1984, "The organizers [of management LBOs] put their net worth into the business. . . . It is amazing how interested [they] get in the income of that business." Michael C. Jensen of Harvard Business School, often a spokesman for the laissez-faire view of takeovers of all kinds, has spoken of LBOs as a healthy development in the evolution of corporate ownership in general, calling them "an interesting experiment to watch. . . . For many areas of the economy, the broadly held corporation is a dodo."

The assault on LBOs addresses these points, and others as well. On economic effects, Andrew Sigler of Champion International points out that through management buyouts and leveraged takeovers "equity is being extracted [from the economy]. . . . The economy is being wounded." Louis Lowenstein of Columbia Law School, besides deploring the reduction of federal revenue brought about by the tax subsidy inherent in LBOs, argues that over the middle term they may actually decrease management incentive. He says, "If the managers, who have bought the stock at a very low price, succeed and after five years are very rich, it's going to be difficult to motivate them to keep slaving away at a normal salary." It is further pointed out that when LBOs are financed by employee stock ownership plans, as they increasingly were in 1984 and 1985, an additional tax subsidy comes into play: beginning in 1984, lending banks were allowed to exclude from taxable income half of the interest paid on loans that finance such plans. In 1984, Albert T. Sommer, chief economist of The Conference Board, expressed his belief that the funding of huge buyouts and buybacks was squeezing out short-term credit for other purposes. Even the most obvious public benefit of LBOs—the premium price paid to the selling stockholders—is widely challenged. Quite apart from the price advantage that may be gained by the buying managers through a less-than-arm's-length transaction in which they have superior information, when an LBO is accompanied by anti-takeover measures, it may be executed without competing takeover bids that would have brought the selling stockholders a higher price. Indeed, anti-takeover measures have sometimes been adopted by managements who have not, until later, disclosed that the purpose of the measures was to protect a planned future LBO offer from competition. When Dorchester Gas Corporation did exactly this in 1984–85, the SEC enjoined Dorchester from further violations of disclosure requirements—but let the deal stand. A banker commented, "As chairman, you have the trust of stockholders. And [in such a case] you're treading a little close to violating that trust."[2]

One of the most comprehensive critiques of management buyouts is contained in remarks delivered to the International Bar Association by Bevis Longstreth, then an SEC commissioner, in October 1983, just as the boom was approaching its peak. Longstreth's focus was on actual or potential abuses to the disadvantage of the bought-out public shareholders, the group that is most often described as the surest and quickest winner in LBOs. Longstreth begins with an analysis of the requirements in LBOs that are intended to guarantee fairness to bought-out shareholders. These are (1) a "fairness opinion" as to the buyout price, arrived at by the investment banker for the firm to be bought out; (2) the customary requirement of approval for the deal by "outside" directors who do not stand to profit from it; and (3) the stockholders' entitlement to exercise appraisal rights under state law. As to the first, without challenging the integrity of leading investment-banking firms, Longstreth calls attention to the fact that the investment banker's fee schedule is often arranged so that he receives much more if the deal goes through than if it doesn't, and that, furthermore, the management often ties the hands of its investment bankers by placing crucial restrictions on the scope of their review; for example, they may be told not to negotiate prices or terms with the buyout group, or to solicit bids from third parties as a market test of the price proposed by the buyout group. At all events, in one case (Stokely–Van Camp, 1983), the actual price eventually paid by a third party exceeded the "fair" price approved by the investment banker by 40 percent. Longstreth commented, "The range of fairness is too great to expect opinions to be a very good indicator of what a fair deal for shareholders might be." Concerning review by nonmanagement directors, "The relationship" [between them and management directors participating in the LBO] is "a powerful force in support of loyalty to management"; as for appeal to the courts, in addition to being expensive it is likely to be unsuccessful, because the courts have tended to rely precisely on the other two fairness tests—investment-bank fairness opinions and approval by outside directors.

On the problem of the granting of lockup options to the LBO group for the purpose of discouraging or eliminating third-party competition, Longstreth expresses the view that reliance on case-by-case court decisions is not sufficient, and that the SEC "should play a leadership role with the Congress and the states in fashioning a satisfactory solution through legislation" (until now, nothing of the sort has been done). On the problem of stock price manipulation by management for the purpose of lowering the LBO price, after describing how it can be done, Longstreth points out that such action would constitute fraud under the existing securities laws; however, he says, "To my knowledge, the Commission has never brought a case alleging this sort of conduct."*

Is it fair, Longstreth asks in conclusion, "for manage-

*The potential for management conflict of interest in management buyouts was illustrated in wildly exaggerated form in the course of the Revlon–Pantry Pride negotiations in 1985. As we have seen, at one point in those negotiations a white-knight buyout by Forstmann Little was under consideration; Michel C. Bergerac, Revlon's highly successful chairman, was to participate in the buyout and remain as chief executive, paying for his participation with part of the proceeds of a previously granted $21-million golden parachute. That is, the transaction triggering the benefits to Mr. Bergerac that were intended to protect him in case of a takeover would in fact *be* a takeover by, among others, Mr. Bergerac himself. The very money meant to solace him for loss of his job would buy him both the job and a big holding in the company. After much public criticism, he withdrew from the buyout group.

ment to put the company up for sale, so arrange things that it [is] the only bidder, and then bless its own offer, with the help of friendly outsiders?" The outside assurances of fairness—or "indicia of procedural due process"—in practice have become "boiler-plated passkeys to an advantageous buyout"; therefore "the rules that govern what appears to some as little more than a charade should be re-examined." Stopping short of proposing that management buyouts be prohibited, Longstreth proposes tentatively that management be permitted to buy out the shareholders only after it has afforded all potential bidders the opportunity to investigate the company and make alternative bids; that the granting of options or use of other devices for the purpose of freezing out third-party bidders be prohibited; and that, in cases where management already has a control block and is only buying out a minority, it be willing to match or top a third-party bid, or else sell out to the bidder. None of these steps has been explicitly taken to date.

It remains only to point out that Longstreth, during his term at the SEC, was a key proponent of the deregulatory Rule 415 and, more generally, of the view that the unimpeded marketplace is the best regulator.[3]

The defense of LBOs is eloquently made by Theodore J. Forstmann, the senior founding partner of Forstmann Little, a firm known in the field for its exceptional patience and self-discipline in waiting for the right deals, and for its avoidance of extreme financing methods. To begin with, he insists that self-dealing by management in LBOs is entirely theoretical.

I don't see it as a real subject for concern. It's theoretically possible for a manager to hold earnings down in order to get himself a bargain price, but in practice it doesn't happen. Analysts would quickly spot the company's bad performance and call the manager an idiot, thereby ruining his reputation. Moreover, the whole theory of a manager being so Machiavellian is alien to what happens in the real world. The market always knows.

Forstmann goes so far as to state flatly that "in our deals, the managers aren't trading against the stockholders," because Forstmann Little, not the managers, is the principal in the deal, with the managers in the role of minority partners.

What, then, about the fact that Forstmann Little's deals have so consistently resulted in huge profits to the LBO participants, managers included? Does not that very fact provide evidence that the original stockholders were induced or coerced into selling out too low? No, says Forstmann, because LBO investment is not a zero-sum game; the LBO group itself is able, by bringing about improved management performance, to add to the company's value and thus create the profit. (As for the Simon group's 200-to-1 profit on Gibson, Forstmann dismisses it by saying that it "was a long-shot gamble with his own money" by Simon that "doesn't prove anything any more than winning on Off-Track Betting proves anything.") He insists, against all contrary arguments, that the incentive to management provided by substantial equity ownership does work in practice, and has been a major factor in the success of Forstmann Little's deals.

Forstmann opposes LBOs in which "a security is created to get a deal done." Until 1987 his firm had used no junk bonds in any of its LBOs, and he opposes such use of them on principle: "If the sort of thing that Drexel Burnham has been doing is a leveraged buyout, then we need another name for what we do." The problem arises, he believes, when investment bankers put together LBO deals primarily or exclusively for fees; when they are not substantial principals, their interest is in making as many closings as possible, as quickly as possible, and thereby maximizing fees. By contrast, Forstmann Little, though it does collect fees, derives the bulk of its revenue from profits as an investment principal, and thus has a vested interest in avoiding shaky financing that courts later disaster.

Forstmann admits that lawyers for dissident stockholders in his firm's transactions routinely trot out various accusations, including that of management self-dealing, and this fact leads him to the unorthodox view that shareholder democracy may have gone too far, because in the present circumstances the stockholder at the time an LBO is being negotiated may have far less concern for the company's welfare than the buyout group has. He says, "The stockholder isn't Aunt Millie now. He's the toughest, meanest arbitrageur, and he cares only about short-term profit. I wish Aunt Millie owned more stock, and I wish institutional stockholders took a more active role in the affairs of companies they hold. But as things are, shareholder protection is not all that good for the economy."[4]

Judicial restraint of mergers that eliminate minority shareholders apparently began in 1977, when the Delaware Supreme Court ruled that such buyouts must meet the test of "entire fairness" and serve "a legitimate business purpose." In 1983, however, the same court reversed the "business purpose" requirement, finding that it did not provide any meaningful additional protection to shareholders. Such SEC regulation of LBOs as exists dates from 1979, and relates chiefly to disclosure. Rule 13e-3, promulgated that year, requires management to express its "reasonable belief" that a transaction is fair to stockholders, with detailed supporting evidence, and also requires disclosure of whether management has obtained a fairness opinion, approval of outside directors, and ratification by unaffiliated stockholders. However, the rule falls short of providing any federal forum for contesting fairness, and, in practice, Longstreth says, "may actually have served to put the Commission's imprimatur on management buyouts." (It is suggestive that the great surge in their number and size began precisely in 1979.) The same procedures asked for by the SEC are usually adequate to prevent a successful legal challenge to a management buyout under state laws. Ironically, the business-judgment rule—generally allowing corporate directors to take any action that they believe to serve the best interests of the corporation—fills the role of umbrella protection for management directors who are, at the same time, at least theoretically acting in their own interest against that of their stockholders. Such directors are in a position comparable to that of a Victorian parent whose unanswerable defense of any action involving his children was, "I think it is best." In the parent-child case, time and changing custom have effected substantive reform. The same cannot be said of the governance of management buyouts.

Buying Out the Store

The January 1986 Federal Reserve Board ruling, applying 50-percent margin requirements under the Securities Exchange Act of 1934 to certain hostile takeovers largely financed by junk bonds issued by a shell corporation, was not aimed primarily at LBOs and, as first promulgated, appeared to affect only a few of them.

Theodore Forstmann likes to speak of his firm as "old-fashioned," as if it were a demure, sensible, even straitlaced young woman. As, indeed, by the current standards of its field, it may be; the trouble is that those standards are, generally speaking, the opposite of "old-fashioned": they emphasize newness, brashness, fast action, extreme risk-taking, and flouting of tradition.

In retrospect from some future date, it seems likely that the LBO as typically practiced in the eighties will be looked upon as a temporary aberration that slipped through the legal, regulatory, and legislative net—like the stock-market pools of the twenties, or the fictitious write-ups of mutual-fund-held letter stock in the sixties, both of which were regarded as legal in their heydays. The reform measures proposed by Longstreth in 1983 might well be helpful for an interim period, but it seems likely that at some point—most likely during a recession accompanied by high interest rates, resulting in a huge spate of failures among overleveraged bought-out companies—social policy, whether enforced by the courts, by the SEC, by legislation, or by the bitter practical experience of investors, will so reduce the incidence of the LBO as to make it again a relatively minor and unimportant phenomenon. In mid-1986, Forstmann said that he expected LBO activity to decline as a result of the growing scarcity of companies appropriate to being taken private—that is to say, in response to market forces.

The strongest kind of LBOs, involving exceptionally sound companies with little debt, whose worth is for some reason not recognized by the market or even by their own stockholders, may continue to be effected, arguably to the advantage of all parties, the national economy included. But even in such cases, the basic economic problem, excessive corporate debt after the buyout, and the basic ethical problem, potential self-dealing by management insiders, will remain. It will still be hard to refute what the lawyer and economist Benjamin J. Stein wrote in 1985: "Managers and directors are, by law and custom, fiduciaries for their stockholders. Fiduciary care, as a matter of unvarying law from the Middle Ages to the present, requires that the fiduciary place the interests of the stockholder ahead of, prior to, and superior to his own interests at all times and in all cases."[5]

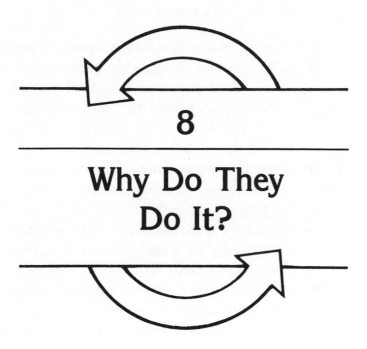

8

Why Do They Do It?

The arguments that mergers and takeovers are socially and economically useful, and should therefore be allowed to proceed without checks or with minimal checks, are made chiefly by two groups: active participants in take-overs on the acquirer side, such as T. Boone Pickens, and academics of the free-market persuasion, such as Frank H. Easterbrook of the University of Chicago Law School and Michael C. Jensen of the Harvard Business School and the University of Rochester Graduate School of Management. Chief among the arguments made by such persons are the following:

1. Target-company shareholders in takeovers benefit because they always get a premium over previous market price, often a very large one. (The Office of the Chief Economist of the SEC estimated that between January 1981 and May 1985 the stockholders of acquired firms in 260 tender offers profited by $40 billion.)

2. Takeovers and the threat of takeovers discipline management to better performance, or else result in its replacement by better management.

3. Takeovers on balance result in substantial economic gains to both acquiring and acquired companies.

4. The "reorganizations"—chiefly the exchange of equity for debt in corporate capital—that are brought about by takeovers or the threat of takeovers, were overdue anyhow, and represent a healthy rationalization of capital structure.

5. A high debt-to-equity ratio in corporate capitalization, the customary outcome of leveraged takeovers and management buyouts, tends to force management to operate more efficiently in order to achieve and maintain high cash flow.

6. Anti-takeover defensive measures adopted by actual or potential takeover targets tend, to the extent that they prevent takeovers, to harm both shareholders and their corporations.

It follows from the above that the activities of corporate raiders such as Pickens, Icahn, and Steinberg, quite apart from being profitable personally to the raiders, are useful to the economy in that they provide profits to other stockholders and force necessary reorganizations of corporations with outdated capital structures. Some free-market advocates go a good deal further. They categorically approve greenmail payments by corporations to raiders, insisting that the exacting of such repurchases is the only weapon available to the one attempting a beneficial takeover; they insist that the term *greenmail* itself, obviously pejorative in that it suggests blackmail, is used as a "Trojan horse" in the legal and political arenas by corporate managements seeking to entrench themselves by adopting anti-takeover measures. (Perhaps somewhat inconsistently, the same free-market advocates oppose self-tenders by threatened corporations when they exclude the would-be greenmailer—greenmail in reverse, as in Pickens-Unocal—and urge that such exclusionary offers be restrained by the courts.)

Even the practices most often deplored as excesses or abuses by the press, the public, and the more statesmanlike of investment professionals are defended by a segment of free-market commentators. For example, the practice of management directors voting themselves golden parachutes to ensure their personal futures in the event of their displacement as a result of a takeover is justified on the grounds that such arrangements free management, when it is deciding whether or not to accept a takeover offer, from a conflict between its own interest and that of shareholders. (The same conflict, as it inevitably occurs in management buyouts, is seldom addressed by these commentators.) The use of junk-bond financing in takeovers is praised as an ingenious new device for increasing healthy takeover activity by eliminating "mere size" of the target company as an effective defense. Even the market timing and disclosure requirements of the Williams Act—currently the principal takeover-regulation law on the federal books—are deplored because they discourage takeovers by diverting most of the profits in a takeover from the acquirer to "free-riding" third parties. These requirements, it is argued, should be repealed, thus increasing the incentive to corporate raiders and thereby the amount of takeover activity—in the view of Jensen, Easterbrook, and others, a consummation devoutly to be wished.

The academic tradition of playing devil's advocate, of taking the side more difficult to defend primarily as an intellectual exercise, may play some role in motivating these arguments. Nevertheless, they influence the policymakers' posture, which, in the political climate of the mid-eighties in the United States, tended to go along with them, in general if not in every detail. The all-out defense of merger and takeover activity contained in the Economic Report of the President for 1985 sounds almost like a carbon copy of the free-market academic arguments. Declaring that "the available evidence . . . is that mergers and acquisitions increase national wealth . . . improve efficiency, transfer scarce resources to higher valued uses, and stimulate effective corporate management," the report goes on to defend just about every familiar aggressor tactic, including two-tier tender offers and the threat of greenmail. Stopping short of calling for repeal of the Williams Act, the report states that golden parachutes "are not proper subjects for federal regulation." Nor, according to the report, are any of the other tactics used in the takeover wars: "Further federal regulation of the market for corporate control would be premature, unnecessary, and unwise." The only takeover practices characterized in the report as "abusive" are defensive tactics that tend to defeat or deter aggressors, and these, the report suggests, should be controlled by the courts rather than by regulation or legislation.[1]

Meanwhile, those who are more doubtful about the economic benefits of takeovers—apparently a majority in the press and on Wall Street throughout the takeover wave—have marshaled a mass of evidence that the key conclusions of the free-market school are questionable or false. Such critics point out, for example, that a 1984 study of corporate divestments showed that in a majority of cases, the acquirers themselves considered their targets already to be well managed: that is, their objective was not to discipline or replace poorly run companies but to own well-run ones. Warren Buffett of Berkshire Hathaway commented in his firm's 1981 Annual Report, "Many managements [of acquirer companies] were apparently exposed in impressionable childhood years to the story in which the imprisoned handsome prince is released from a toad's body by a kiss from a beautiful princess." Yet a multitude of academic studies of takeovers in the eighties show that the typical targets were well managed and profitable before the takeover. That is, those kissed in practice were usually not toads at all, but princes undisguised. Ironically, the characteristic weakness of takenover companies was the very worst one for the circumstances: they were already leveraged above average, making them particularly vulnerable to the greatly increased debt that the takeovers brought about. As far as results after the event are concerned, classic studies for the most part differ chiefly on only one question: whether the overall effect of mergers on acquirer profitability has been neutral or negative.*

To many academic economists, the most worrisome economic effect of takeover mania is its contribution—along with that of financial restructurings undertaken to *prevent* takeovers—to rising national corporate debt levels. Federal Reserve figures show that the debt-to-equity ratio of U.S. corporations, measured by the book value of assets less liabilities, stood at 57.1 percent for 1961, at 73 percent for 1983, and at 81.4 percent for 1984, making the increase for 1984 alone more than the total over the previous fifteen years.† Moreover—and particularly alarming—by early 1985 short-term debt stood at a record 52 percent of total debt, making companies more vulnerable than ever before to any increase in interest rates.

Such evidence led many—among them Edward S. Herman of the Wharton School and Louis Lowenstein of Columbia Law School—to conclude in 1985 that from an economic standpoint "there is nothing intrinsically useful about tender offers."

What, then, about the effect on stockholders of bidder and target?

The literature on returns to acquiring-firm stockhold-

*"A host of researchers, working at different points of time and utilizing different analytic techniques and data, have but one major difference: whether mergers have neutral or negative impact on profitability." From T. Hogarty, "Profits from Mergers: The Evidence of Fifty Years," *St. John's Law Review* 44 (1970). Cited by Herman and Lowenstein; see note 1 to this chapter.
†On the other hand, research done by Robert Toggart of Boston University indicates that debt-to-equity ratios at *market* value have not increased.

ers does not yield a consensus. Some studies find gains, some find losses. Indeed, if there is a consensus, it is that such stockholders break about even. (Michael Jensen, an extreme proponent of mergers, cites SEC estimates that between 1980 and 1985 bidders in tender offers earned zero returns on average, and grants that most acquisition benefits go to target stockholders.) Studies of mergers conducted before 1980, and dealing chiefly with conglomerate mergers, suggest that, in terms of profits and balance sheets, acquirer stockholders came out, at best, slightly better off or no better off. More recent studies that shift the focus to stock price performance suggest that acquiring-firm stockholders seem neither to profit nor to lose in any systematic way. The finding that acquirer stock performance was usually well above average for several years *before* the acquisition announcement suggests not that the acquisition helped their stock price, but rather that a high stock price may have contributed to their decision to make one or more acquisitions in the first place. Typically, according to the studies, the acquisition announcement itself has no large or systematic effect on the acquirer's share price, while in the postacquisition period the stock performance deteriorates relative to the pre-event performance—and also, some believe, relative to the performance that would have been achieved if there had been no merger or takeover. (These studies are summarized in Magenheim and Mueller's 1985 paper cited in note 1 to this chapter.)

All in all, then, the empirical evidence on the effect of acquisitions on acquirer stockholders is almost conclusively inconclusive. On average, nothing either very good or very bad happens to them. On the other hand, it is

indisputable, and undisputed, that target-company stockholders gain an immediate advantage, and often a large
one, by selling their shares to the acquirer at a price well
above the previous market. The premium always paid by
the acquirer guarantees that this will be so. Since mergers
and takeovers in general leave acquirer stockholders about
where they were, and bring windfall profits to target stockholders, they can be and often are justified, purely from
the standpoint of stockholder wealth, on that basis alone.
If one group breaks even and the other gets richer, why
not—leaving the question of broader economic effects
aside—get on with the party?

On closer examination, we find a number of factors
that compromise even the much-touted advantage of the
merger game to target-company stockholders:

1. The aggressor's bid, above the market though it be,
may not really be so advantageous as it seems. That bid,
made with the benefit of information almost certainly superior to that available to the target stockholders, is also
made of the aggressor's own free will. If he is assumed to
be rational, it is a bid on which he believes he will make
a profit—as he sometimes (though, as we have seen, not
consistently) does. Recall, for example, that Martin Marietta's price a few months after Bendix's tender offer
stood well above that offer.

2. The transaction is not made on equal terms; while
the bidder's hands are free, those of the stockholder are to
one extent or another tied. In a friendly merger for cash,
the stockholder, protected chiefly by a possibly tainted
fairness opinion obtained by his directors, must sell at a
price dictated to him, or else sue. (A very large stock-

holder may seek other bidders, but in practice this recourse is not available to small holders.) In the case of a
two-tier tender offer, the stockholder is coerced into tendering by the certain knowledge that to the extent that he
does not get in on the all-cash, front-end offer, he will
eventually have to sell his stock less advantageously on the
rear-end terms, which usually comprise a mixture of cash
and securities. The announced value of those securities
reflects the bidder's appraisal; often the market's appraisal
turns out to be lower, and the actual premium to stockholders is accordingly less than the announced one.

3. The empirical studies focus on mergers and takeovers that are consummated. What of those that are di-
verted by greenmail, or frustrated by defensive action
taken by management and directors? In the case of greenmail, all stockholders except the greenmailer sit helplessly
by while one fellow-stockholder receives a price not available to them. Having missed that chance, the stockholders
face a second indignity. Experience shows that following
payment of greenmail, the stock price usually falls below
where it stood before the raid. In the case of a successful
takeover defense, whatever its benefits to management and
even to the company, the defense in and of itself quite
naturally causes the stock to fall because it eliminates the
aggressor's premium-price offer. That is to say, the ordinary stockholder is subject to potential disadvantage *either way the deal goes*.

4. It may not be in a coerced stockholder's best interest to sell, even at a premium price, at a moment not of
his choosing. As a personal matter, emotional as well as
economic, he may not *want* to sell. He may be well sat-

isfied with his investment and its dividends, and suddenly—and involuntarily—face the loss of a long-term holding in a company he admires, and a large capital-gains tax. The tax problems of stockholders are not part of the calculations of takeover artists. Broadly speaking, the presumption of advantage to the stockholder presupposes that he functions as a trader rather than a holder; in a merger transaction he becomes a trader in spite of himself. Yet social policy theoretically encourages long-term investment.

5. Finally, there are the problems of those often-forgotten investors involved in merger transactions, the preexisting bondholders of the acquired company or of the company being reorganized as a defensive measure. Where junk-bond financing or exchange of equity for debt are heavily involved, as they so often were in the middle 1980s, the inevitable increase in the company's debt-to-equity ratio results in a weakening of its senior bonds—often reflected in a downgrading in their ratings by the leading rating services—and a loss to those who had invested previously in those bonds, presumably in total innocence of any approaching takeover attempt and consequent damage to the company's capital structure. Some examples from 1985: When R. J. Reynolds announced its acquisition of Nabisco, Nabisco stock quickly went from around 60 to over 80; meanwhile, the spread between yield on Reynolds's senior debt and that on comparable Treasury bonds increased over three weeks by 55 basis points. This translated into a 5-point decline in the price of the Reynolds bonds. Again, when CBS announced its billion-dollar restructuring to fend off Turner Communications,

the stock went from 80 to 120 while senior CBS bonds, downgraded by Moody's and Standard & Poor's, saw their market price drop so sharply that interest spreads against the Treasury-bond standard rose by more than a whole percentage point. As for Unocal, *its* restructuring—again accompanied by lowered bond ratings—led to a quintupling of Treasury spread, from 20 basis points to 100.

True enough, such reactions of the bond market to the sudden leveraging of companies are often largely transient; in cases where the leveraging causes no immediate disaster, the depressed bonds are apt to recover a good part of their loss over the next few months. (For example, four months after the Reynolds acquisition announcement, its bonds had recovered almost three-quarters of their peak Treasury-spread loss.) Nevertheless, the fact remains that, even in the absence of debt-caused economic disaster, in almost any heavily leveraged takeover or acquisition the target shareholders' short-term gain is, logically and inevitably, the acquirer and target bondholders' short-term loss.[2]

To sum up, then, the effect on target-company stockholders of being acquired: their immediate gains, while indisputable and often large, are not free gifts from philanthropic aggressors. They represent the trade-off for a whole constellation of advantages to the aggressor. The gains may be eliminated entirely if the firm's directors choose to pay greenmail; or, if the acquirer subsequently flourishes, they may in retrospect look not like gains but like losses. Above all, they are the outcome of unequal transactions in which one side has much freedom of action and the other little. They are bonbons forced down the

233

throats of not necessarily willing recipients. Their justification as beneficent contributions to stockholder wealth is somewhat analogous to the beneficence of a force-feeder who orders his victim to "shut up and eat."

What has been said herein about the more or less measurable economic effects of mergers ignores their far less measurable social and human effects. These appear to be largely negative. The net increase in unemployment brought about by merger-caused economies of scale—for example, combining the headquarters staffs of the merging companies into a single staff—is relatively small, and can be defended on economic grounds in that it represents increased efficiency. Not as much can be said for the disruption of communities that are built around a single company. The outcry from officials and citizens of Bartlesville, Oklahoma, when it appeared that Phillips Petroleum was about to be taken over by Mesa Petroleum, turned out to be, politically, a factor in the aborting of that takeover. Other, similarly structured communities, upon losing their status as the homes of important corporate headquarters as the result of mergers that did go through, have sometimes been seriously damaged and sometimes not, depending largely on the subsequent policies of the acquiring company.

Among the most serious adverse effects is on the morale of executives at all levels of companies taken over, and on those that fear being taken over. (As Peter Drucker has pointed out, in the mid-eighties the latter category included the overwhelming majority of all corporations.) Those at the very top of taken-over companies are often protected economically by their golden parachutes, which are theoretically intended to free them from personal pressures in deciding whether or not to support an attempted takeover, but in practice seem in many cases to imbue them with an intense wish to have the takeover go through, because that alone will activate their parachutes. Further down the hierarchy, there are no golden parachutes, and executives dismissed by the new management are on their own to find new jobs quickly. The psychological effect on such persons has been described by Dr. Bruce Ruddick, a New York City psychiatrist who has treated a number of them. According to Dr. Ruddick, they typically go through a form of depression clinically associated with the grieving that follows the loss of a loved one: rage against the injustice, including defiance, irrational guilt, and suicidal impulses, followed eventually, with luck or counseling or both, by gradual acceptance and recovery. The chief emotional problem particular to merger-related firings, in Ruddick's view, is that grieving thus caused is not mitigated by the time-honored social rituals that alleviate ordinary grieving.

It must be noted, however, that merger-related disruption of the lives of corporate executives is not confined to those who are fired, or those whose companies have fallen into the hands of hostile aggressors. Friendly mergers, too, particularly those that arise out of bidding contests, often result in a situation where the people of the acquired company are made, subtly or brutally, to feel like second-class citizens. Ten months after Gulf Oil had been taken over by Chevron as a white knight in a bidding contest, Gulf's general manager for marketing, John H.

Pronsky, quit because he felt that Gulf's management had betrayed him by breaking its "psychological contract" with him in making the sellout. Nor is the psychological damage all to the acquired firm. In the year after Champion International, as a white knight, took over St. Regis, various executives of Champion left because they felt that the Champion "corporate culture" had been changed by the merger so much that their former sense of loyalty was destroyed. Andrew Sigler, chairman of Champion before and after the merger, said in 1985, "The people trauma in this whole process almost guarantees [that] there won't be a productivity increase for a considerable period of time." In Sigler's view, that is, the "people trauma," disturbing enough in itself as a human problem, instantly translates into an economic loss. The psychological makeup of corporate acquirers, firmly oriented toward figures and deals, is seldom consistent with diligent attention to "people issues." Consultants and executive recruiters were saying in 1985 that they found merger mania to be a leading cause of a sharp drop in employee loyalty in general, and of a rising rate of management turnover at all levels.

Finally, acquisitions and management buyouts were at least threatening to inflict damage on what has traditionally been one of the most attractive aspects of American corporate life: corporate giving to nonprofit institutions. With many companies becoming so leveraged that virtually all cash flow had to be devoted to paying off debts, there often appeared to be little left over for corporate philanthropy. H. Martin Moore, president of the scholarship-fund-raising Independent College Fund of New York, said early in 1986, "We know that we will lose

$75,000 this year as a result of mergers, acquisitions, and buyouts since 1983."[3]

"Here, then," wrote former judge Simon H. Rifkind, a director of Revlon, following that company's takeover by Pantry Pride, "is a transaction which has absorbed countless hours of labor and many millions of dollars to accomplish something which is devoid of any redeeming virtue." Given the consensus that the clearest and largest benefits in mergers and takeovers go to the target-company shareholders, a great question arises: Apart from the prospect of collecting greenmail, which applies chiefly to lone raiders rather than to corporate acquirers, why do aggressors undertake transactions out of which the chief benefits stand to accrue to someone else? What, that is, is the motivation for corporate takeovers?

Among others, Richard Roll—a man with one foot in the academy and the other in Wall Street, as a professor of finance at the University of California and also a vice-president of Goldman Sachs—concedes that there is "a mystery" about the motives of bidding firms. A number of hypotheses, not mutually exclusive, to explain the motivation have been advanced by Roll. Among these are desire for increased market power; superior information, held by the aggressor but not by the market, that the target is undervalued and thus a plum ripe for picking; belief that the merger will result in *synergy* (that is, the combined whole will result in more than its separate parts); the replacement of inferior management at the target firm; financial motivations, such as tax advantages that will flow from a merger; management self-interest, based on the general rule that executives of larger firms, such as would be created by a merger, are better compensated than those of smaller firms; and, finally, emotional self-satisfaction on the part of the managers and directors of the aggressor firm, a force that need not imply any actual economic justification at all.

All of these motivation hypotheses can be defended, and all attacked; some appear to be more valid than others. Desire for increased market power—monopoly or near-monopoly—although it was originally what mergers were all about, does not appear to be a major factor in the eighties. Even when recent combinations have been among firms in the same industry or in closely related industries, and thus obviously resulted in some degree of market concentration, the outcome has not consistently been increased profits or gains for stockholders. Moreover, if intra-industry mergers were in fact causing disadvantage to other companies in the same industry, why has the market price of those firms not dropped when two of their rivals merged—as, generally speaking, it has not?

The superior-information theory—that the acquirer knows that the target is undervalued by the market, or at least *thinks* he knows it—is harder to dismiss. Surely all but a few bidders for corporations believe that their bidding price will sooner or later prove to have been a bargain. Moreover, there is an element of self-fulfilling prophecy; that is, the bid itself, especially when followed by competitive higher bids, increases the market value of the combination. But it obviously decreases the profit potential to the highest-bidding acquirer over lower bidders, and the evidence we have seen indicates that on average he ends up making little or no profit at all.

Why Do They Do It?

The synergy theory, a staple cliché of the go-go years of the sixties, has largely been discredited by the collapse and progressive dismantling of the conglomerates formed at that time. If two plus two really amounted to more than four in conglomerate mergers—as the chief economic justification for such mergers insisted that it did—why, then, in the seventies did so many conglomerates prove to be so unprofitable that they had to be dismantled? Nor, broadly speaking, does the synergy theory seem to have come into its own in the new merger wave of the eighties. Speaking in the context of commercial banking, Donald Flamson, chairman of Security Pacific, said in 1986, "Synergy is like an extra bit of chocolate on a chocolate sundae. If you rely on it to rationalize what you're doing, it's the quickest way in the world to deceive yourself about the profitability of what you're doing."

This is not to say that in the eighties there were not individual, industry-specific situations in which mergers were economically rational for reasons that might come under the rubric of synergy. Forces like technical innovation, foreign competition, and inflation had moved so fast that weaknesses were suddenly exposed in individual companies that had to be shored up quickly. We have already noted how in 1984 Tcxaco desperately needed to reverse a decline in its reserves, and did so by acquiring Getty. Michael Jensen has argued convincingly that radical changes in the energy market after 1973—a tenfold increase in the price of crude oil, reduced U.S. oil consumption, reduced expectations of future oil-price increases, increased exploration and development costs, and increased real-interest rates—had mandated a major restructuring of the American petroleum industry: "It had to shrink, and that means releasing resources to the economy at large through asset sales and returning capital to investors." The appropriate restructurings were usually forced, as in the cases of Phillips and Unocal, by threatened takeovers. In other industries prominent in the eighties merger wave, mergers and restructurings were similarly a rational response to new conditions—for example, the deregulation in the case of banking and finance, and increased output by low-cost foreign producers in the case of mining and minerals.

Nevertheless, the unfashionability of the very term *synergy* in the middle 1980s—one spoke instead of "reaching critical mass"—suggests the failure of the concept as a general explanation of mergers in that time. The substitution of a metaphor drawn from physics for one drawn from pharmacology does not alter the economic situation, which is that, empirically, the phenomenon is not observable in most cases.

The inefficient-management thesis must be regarded more seriously. Indeed, a prevalence of well-entrenched corporate management of inferior or mediocre quality during the 1970s was very probably the principal *original* cause of the current merger wave.

This prevalence had solid historical roots. "People's capitalism," much touted by the New York Stock Exchange during the fifties, had resulted in the dispersal of corporate ownership, particularly in the case of the largest firms, among millions of small holders, each and all of them powerless, as a practical matter, to influence the running of the corporation. The power vacuum was of course filled by corporate management, which in practice acquired the power to appoint itself, perpetuate itself, and be accountable only to itself. Such management enjoyed, in Peter Drucker's words, "unchallengeable security except in the event of a huge scandal or the firm's bankruptcy." (Sometimes, however, as in the case of the price-fixing scandal of the late fifties involving General Electric and other leading suppliers of heavy electrical equipment, top management essentially survived even scandal.) This unchecked use of power was made more or less legitimate in the public mind by a new cult of the "science" of management, which was encouraged by the leading business schools, and which led John Kenneth Galbraith to proclaim the coming of a "new industrial state" run by corporate managers.

The rise in the sixties and seventies of institutional investors, principally pension funds, as corporate owners—by the mid-eighties, pension funds owned one-third of the equity of publicly traded companies in the United States, and more like one-half in the case of the biggest firms—did not in itself increase management accountability to ownership. This was because the new owners hardly ever involved themselves in the management of the companies in which they invested, preferring to follow what came to be called "the Wall Street rule": If a company in which they were invested performed poorly because of poor management, they didn't tamper with the management, they simply sold the stock. Such sales naturally depressed the prices of the stocks involved. It was at this point that the corporate raider entered the picture as a friend of stockholders large and small. Seeing a company priced below its asset value because of poor management, he promised to take the company over, replace its management, and restore its stock price. Thus management accountability would be restored as a second-order effect of the rise of institutional investors as corporate owners.

It must be noted that almost from the start there was a flaw in this theoretically benign scenario. What, by definition, was "poor" management? Originally, it had been management that spent much of its time entrenched at the country club and feathered its nest with excessive bonuses and pension awards. But with the coming of the transactional era and the transformation of the institutional investor into an in-and-out trader, a manager who concentrated on short-term profits at the expense of long-term profits came to be regarded as "good," and one who, in conformity with traditional management practice, did the opposite to be regarded as "bad." This confusion of values was followed by another one: the loss by the corporate raider of his mantle of virtue as friend of the stockholder, and his assumption of a new mantle of vice as a self-interested greenmailer and destructor.

We have seen the 1984 finding that by that year, most corporate acquirers considered their targets to be well-managed before the takeover. A sea change had evidently taken place in acquirer motives since the beginning of the merger wave. Management entrenchment had essentially been routed; formerly a logical and beneficent motive for hostile takeovers, it no longer, on the face of the matter, filled that role.

To return to Roll's list: As to the tax-advantage hypothesis, while it is certain that some acquirers get such advantage through mergers, it does not seem to be the principal motive in very many; for example, it has been noted that the federal tax change in 1981 that allowed firms to sell depreciation and investment tax credits without merging actually decreased tax incentives to merge—yet was followed by a great surge of mergers.

Roll's last two theories—management economic self-interest, and purely psychic rather than economic advantage to management—doubtless help to explain the motivation for certain mergers; however, as Roll has pointed out, they founder as a general explanation of takeover bids. It does not follow from the fact that a merger takes place that a given manager at a certain level of the acquiring firm can handle the larger, and better-paid, comparable job at the larger merged firm—or that his directors will let him try. As for the "psychic reward" theory—that acquirer management acts uneconomically because of an emotional wish for the conqueror's crown, having convinced itself by way of justification that the target company is a better bargain than the objective evidence shows it to be—Roll concludes that if this were the motivation in every merger, every bid announcement would demonstrably harm the bidding firm and cause a decline in its stock price; since this is not the case, the theory "cannot be the sole explanation of the takeover phenomenon."[4]

So the mystery remains. But there is one more possible explanation—one that brings us back to our central concern, the investment-banking business. It is that many corporate takeovers originate in the minds of investment bankers, and are fomented by them for the purpose of collecting huge advisory fees—that is, the process is driven by the bankers (and lawyers) and their fees.

Little need be said about the size of those fees as incentive to investment banks. By 1985 they had for the largest transactions become disproportionately high—some, including some investment bankers, said they were obscenely high—essentially because, although always negotiable between banker and client, they continued to be based according to tradition on a percentage of the amount of the transaction involved, and the size of some transactions had become vastly greater than ever before. (By contrast, lawyer's fees in mergers, again in conformity with tradition, continued to be based mostly on the lawyers' time charges rather than on a percentage, and were therefore lower. They were high enough, though. The billing policies of Martin Lipton's firm for merger work in 1984 called ordinarily for time charges up to triple those charged in normal matters, and in cases where the law firm assumed responsibility for developing takeover strategy, "final charges [were] not based on time but on the responsibility assumed and the result achieved," with a resulting final charge frequently amounting to several million dollars on a single transaction.)

Morgan Stanley in early 1984, according to its proxy material, had a basic charge of 1 percent for a $100-million transaction, 0.5 percent for one of $500 million, 0.4 percent for one of $1 billion, and 0.23 percent for one of $4 billion. (The scale was later raised somewhat.) This meant that the $100-million deal cost the client $1 million, while the $4-billion deal cost him $9.2 million. At Morgan Stanley and its chief competitors, percentage fees went lower on even bigger transactions—but gross fees, of course, went higher. To give some examples from 1985, on the Philip Morris–General Foods merger First Boston collected $10.1 million from Philip Morris, and Goldman Sachs and Shearson Lehman $7.1 million each from General Foods; on General Motors–Hughes Aircraft, Salomon collected $8 million from GM and First Boston $15 million from Hughes; in Allied-Signal, First Boston and Lazard for the respective sides collected $10 million each. None of these fees amounted to more than 0.32 percent of the transaction size; yet their hugeness derived, at bottom, from the tradition-based percentage system.

The question that stockholders and the general public obviously ask is, What do the investment bankers actually do to earn so much money so fast? Typically, the investment banker's participation is brief—a few days to several weeks—but very intensive: dozens of highly trained people and their computers working virtually around the clock. Investment bankers themselves use various rationales to defend their charges. One is that their expertise is beyond price: "Would you question your brain surgeon's fee?" Another is purely economic; when the banker for a target company succeeds in getting a bid that substantially raises the acquisition price, the added value to that company's shareholders is often far more than the fee. (On the other hand, by the same logic the banker on the acquirer side in the same transaction has *cost* his client the same amount by allowing the client to pay the higher price—yet he, too, ends up getting something like the same fee!)

A more baroque defense of huge fees is that they

represent in part compensation for "opportunity lost"—the lost opportunity to the merger adviser being his firm's chance to make even more money by arbitraging the target company's stock, which, as we have seen, he cannot do after he becomes merger adviser. One can only comment that, to whatever extent such profit might be based on private information gained through being asked to be merger adviser, the "opportunity lost" is an opportunity to profit illegally.

There is evidence that one reason fees are so high is that some corporate executives in mergers either are indifferent to huge investment-banker fees or else are actually eager to pay them. This is a hypothesis that must be approached with caution. The directors and managers of large corporations are hardly naïfs in these matters; rather, they are people of great financial and legal skill and experience. It is hard to believe that they frequently fill the role of innocent dupes to the wiles of fee-hungry Wall Streeters.

Nevertheless, a mountain of opinion—coming, to be sure, mostly from investment bankers—holds that corporate executives often act irrationally and uneconomically in the matter of merger fees. William Benedetto of Dean Witter Reynolds said in 1984, "There's almost a cult of corporate executives who consider it a matter of pride to pay a multi-million-dollar merger fee." A high-ranking investment banker who did not want to be identified told me at about the same time,

> Corporations will pay the merger fees that are asked—are even eager to pay them. I think a lot of corporate heads are weak and self-serving, and will

do anything, including mistreat their stockholders, to save themselves. If a man heads a three-billion-dollar company, what does he care whether he pays ten million or fifteen million for a deal? But the investment banker cares.

Some corporate heads insist that they *do* care. Donald Kelly says that in his term as chief executive of Esmark (1977–84), during which he made over fifty acquisitions and divestitures, in the early days he regularly bargained hard with investment bankers over fees. Later, though, he came to feel that he had acquired "a gut feeling for what's fair," and tended to consciously overpay a firm on a given transaction if his "gut feeling" was that he had underpaid it on the last one. A corporate chief financial officer who claims to take a much harder line on merger fees is Kenneth A. Yarnell, Jr., of American Can Company. Yarnell came to American Can in 1975 to set up an acquisition-and-divestiture group; over the subsequent decade, while the company was progressively changing its principal business from containers to financial services, he represented American Can in about ninety deals—many of them small, to be sure, and the whole ninety adding up to only about $2 billion, but quite likely more separate M&A transactions than any other corporate executive has been at the center of.

Yarnell says that originally, before investment bankers understood American Can's guidelines for acquisitions, he got calls from them suggesting deals almost every day; later, when the investment bankers came to know the company strategy, the calls became fewer, although they were still frequent. When he first came to American Can, its sole investment banker was Morgan Stanley; early in his term, however, he asked that firm on one transaction to give a fairness opinion and do nothing else, and was told that Morgan Stanley wasn't interested—it would arrange the deal overall or nothing. ("On small deals, it's difficult to get their attention," Yarnell says.) Thereafter, he dealt at one time or another with virtually the whole pantheon of merger-advising giants, including, besides Morgan Stanley, Salomon Brothers, Goldman Sachs, First Boston, Merrill Lynch, Lazard Frères, Bear Stearns, and Drexel. In some cases American Can did deals on its own, without banker assistance; when such assistance was considered necessary, Yarnell says that he habitually bargained on fees, and paid a full 1 percent only once, "when a banker brought us the deal." In most cases, he says, he brought the deal to the banker, making his choice of banker first on the basis of a firm's experience in the industry involved (for example, Salomon and Lazard in insurance, Salomon and Goldman in retailing), and second on the basis of fee. Summing up his experience with deal-making and with the investment-banking industry, Yarnell says that "building through acquisitions is risky," and that a company doing it often unquestionably needs an investment banker; that the freedom to choose among them is important to the client company, and works much better for it than relying on a single "traditional banker"; that he admires and profits from investment bankers' creativity in "figuring neat deals"; and that they are, *if pressed,* usually willing to negotiate reasonably on fees.

In the end, high merger fees cannot be attacked on any conventional economic basis, because they are willingly paid by the customers in a market where trade is not unduly restrained. There are fee-cutters at large in that market—some of them large commercial banks, which are legally free to do corporate merger advice, and are naturally eager to get in on the giant deal-making business. The simple fact, though, is that those banks do not get much of the business, and none of the cream of it, because commercial banks have not been able to become recognized as capable of handling giant mergers as well as investment banks do. As Yarnell puts it succinctly, "Commercial banks are up against it when it comes to M&A. Even if you think the world of one of them, aren't you going to go to a Goldman or a Morgan Stanley? Of course you are." A handful of celebrated investment banks have a stranglehold on the giant merger business—a stranglehold based not on monopolistic practices and therefore vulnerable to attack under the antitrust laws, but rather one based on corporate perception of them as superior to all competition in prestige, skill, and experience.

We have still not directly faced the question of whether, or to what extent, the high fees paid merger advisers serve to create or drive mergers. It is not an easy question on which to obtain solid evidence, because neither investment bankers nor corporate chieftains are often eager to imply that, in making mergers, corporations are the mere cat's-paws of M&A wizards. An M&A man who did that would risk insulting his clients; a corporate chieftain would risk appearing a fool to his stockholders and the public. (Moreover, either or both might invite lawsuits.) We do know that some corporate financial officers, like Yarnell, are approached all the time by investment bankers proposing deals. Yet in the case of American Can, a company where the acquisition program was not merely opportunistic but was based on a well-articulated business plan, any suggestion that the mergers were "driven" by investment bankers seems far wide of the mark. Indeed, to hear Yarnell tell it, in American Can's case the M&A man was customarily treated as what he was originally supposed to be—a technically expert hireling of the corporation, a kind of super accountant.

Even in cases where a merger was indisputably suggested to a corporation by an investment banker, and when the corporation did not at first like the sound of the suggestion, we cannot too quickly conclude that the prospect of a high merger fee brought the deal about. To take one example, in 1985 Morgan Stanley's merger head, Eric Gleacher, called Robert Cizik, chief executive of Houston-based Cooper Industries, to suggest that Cooper buy McGraw Edison. Cizik said flatly that he wasn't interested. He did, however, agree to meet with Gleacher if Gleacher would come to Houston. Gleacher did so the very next day, and made an hour-long presentation, which, according to Gleacher, caused Cizik to change his mind and his company to go ahead with an acquisition that came to more than $1 billion. The prospective fee to Morgan Stanley (it turned out to be $4.25 million) certainly motivated Gleacher to take that plane to Houston, and to be at his most persuasive in the ensuing meeting. It cannot be said, though, that Cizik went ahead with the deal against his will—but only that, in the absence of such a juicy plum hanging on a tree that was itself still hypothetical, Gleacher might not have gone to Houston, and Cooper Industries might not have bought McGraw Edison.

Why Do They Do It?

Other recent huge transactions fall into a gray area regarding the degree of instigation by the investment banker, or else that degree cannot be determined. In the case of Texaco's takeover of Getty Oil—which led to the celebrated $10.5-billion-plus-interest Texas court judgment against Texaco for causing Getty to break a prior agreement to merge with Pennzoil—investment bankers were not among the litigants. Texaco's investment banker, Goldman Sachs (which collected a fee of $18.5 million), on the face of the matter had a large role in the two-day turnaround that ended in Getty's decision to change its merger partner. (Goldman's fee arrangement with Texaco called for it to get only $10 million if Getty decided to accept Pennzoil's bid; thus it gained $8.5 million more when Getty chose Texaco.) Yet Pennzoil, in suing Texaco for breach of agreement, did not sue Goldman at all, and for good reason: Goldman had an indemnity agreement, so common in such transactions that it is spoken of as "boiler plate," that was designed to insulate it against having to pay damages in any lawsuit. While its client, Texaco, faced actual and punitive damages for a deal in which Goldman had evidently been at the center, Goldman came out clean and whole.

First Boston's celebrated M&A department of the mid-eighties made no bones about devoting maximum effort to creating deals out of thin air.* The flamboyant

*According to two executive vice-presidents of Beatrice Companies, in August 1985, the day after Beatrice's stock had risen sharply amid takeover rumors, First Boston's M&A star Bruce Wasserstein said to them, "I put you in play. But it's not too late." The Beatrice executives interpreted this as a threat that if Beatrice didn't hire First Boston as its adviser, First Boston would find a raider to take it over. Wasserstein, though affirming that he had used the expression "in play," later denied that a threat had been intended;

statements to that effect by its merger stars were backed by systematic internal organization. Its M&A specialists, numbering well over one hundred, worked in squads, some fanning out to different parts of the country, some remaining in the home office and specializing in finding deal possibilities in particular industries. Of course they created mergers. In 1985, when American Hospital Supply (AHS) was planning a $2.5-billion merger with Hospital Corporation of America, First Boston saw a chance to torpedo that deal and replace it with another, larger one. Baxter Travenol Laboratories, which had independently decided that it wanted American Hospital Supply for itself—and had been turned down by one investment banker who warned the firm not to proceed because of the high risk—heard of First Boston's interest, and went to that firm. First Boston quickly arranged a higher offer for AHS; but AHS, anxious to save its Hospital Corporation deal, turned the offer down. Unwilling to give up, First Boston put a fifteen-man task force on the case, some of the members working one hundred hours a week, and one of them stationed for the duration in Baxter Travenol's offices. Meanwhile, arbitrageurs bid up AHS's stock price, and AHS postponed a stockholder vote, which would surely have favored the higher offer that management opposed. Eventually the AHS board concluded that it had no alternative but to accept the Baxter Travenol bid; it was accepted, and Hospital Corporation kept happy, or at

what he had meant, he said, was that Beatrice could have avoided becoming a takeover target if it had hired First Boston earlier in the year. What was implicit in both versions was that Wasserstein had been claiming the ability to put Beatrice "in play" at will. (See *The Wall Street Journal*, April 2, 1986.)

least prevented from suing, by a \$150-million settlement payment. Thus a friendly merger among equals was aborted, and replaced by an unwanted but unavoidable takeover orchestrated—to use the mildest appropriate term—by the First Boston M&A team. The transaction amounted to \$3.7 billion, and First Boston's fee was \$8 million.[5]

We arrive, then, at a new hypothesis to explain why corporate aggressors in the middle 1980s so frequently entered into huge transactions of a type that were sometimes, in Judge Rifkind's words, "devoid of any redeeming virtue." The hypothesis—that the executives who made such deals were sold on them by investment bankers (and lawyers) motivated by the prospect of high fees—does much to explain various other merger-motivation hypotheses that we have examined and found more or less wanting. In this perspective, those appear as the ingenious arguments used by merger promoters to persuade corporations to make deals, and thereby earn themselves fees— that is to say, as sales pitches.

Indeed, so long as merger mania goes on, there is always the possibility that the intrinsic-value arguments are actually irrelevant. After a merger has been effected, the same investment bankers who promoted it, using the same sales pitches, will be beating the bushes to find someone to take over the company surviving from the first merger. If they succeed, that surviving company's stockholders will profit from the premium paid. In such a chain-letter sequence, intrinsic value need play no real role at all; the mergers operate as pure stock-market plays designed to exploit a current market fad.

The evidence for such a thesis is circumstantial but persuasive. Consider the investment-banking industry's overall condition in the mid-eighties: underwriting profits, its historic staple, seriously reduced by the introduction of shelf registration and the series of events leading up to it; the newer methods of making money, particularly securities trading, inevitably tying up huge amounts of capital. There remains M&A—a golden window of opportunity that promises to bring in exotic sums without tying up any capital at all. By 1985 most of the big firms were bringing in $75 million or more per year in M&A fees, and a few of them more than $200 million; apart from a single-digit-million typical cost in salaries and overhead, that was all clear pretax profit. Merger-making was not just a quick way of bringing in huge sums, it was also a gloriously cheap way. No wonder investment banks were beating the bushes for deals, and making stars of their merger-makers!*

In the scenario just outlined, we immediately recognize the key element in the time-honored stock-market "bubble" phenomenon that is invariably followed by a stock-market bust—that is, transactions based on potential for paper profit rather than on underlying value. The merger adviser of 1985 appears as a Brobdingnagian coun-

*The astonishing tractability of corporate heads to investment-bank merger advisers in the eighties—to which William Agee of Bendix in the Bendix–Martin Marietta affair appears as an anomalous exception—would seem at first blush to be a reversal of the historic power shift between investment bankers and their corporate clients toward the clients. Note, however, that the basis of the merger adviser's power is more fragile, and presumably more transient, than was that of the late-nineteenth-century investment banker. The latter's power was based on the client's absolute need of him in the raising of new capital. The merger adviser's power is merely that of a persuasive and well-informed salesman.

terpart of the stockbroker of, say, 1928 or 1929, flogging whole companies for fees in the millions instead of mere stocks for commissions in the hundreds. If it were not for the fact that corporations do not and could not grant discretion to investment bankers to involve them in mergers, as investors often grant it to stockbrokers to buy or sell stocks, the merger advisers of 1985 could be accused of *churning*—making transactions intended chiefly or entirely to generate fees or commissions.

To whatever extent the fee-driven theory of mergers is true, the process is neutral or worse from a social and economic point of view, and ought to be changed. If fees are at the bottom of the merger phenomenon, things would be better if the fees were lower and therefore less enticing. The key, of course, is the corporate boss and his board. Legislative or regulatory setting of merger fees would be neither wise nor desirable; the appropriate check on their size is a greater reluctance of corporations to pay them. If corporate officers and directors would come to look upon paying excessive fees as socially irresponsible and potentially dangerous, the merger pace might be expected to slow to a more reasonable level. In the current frequent absence of such reluctance, what we see is a mindless speculative merger spiral that has many of the recognizable features of a boom before a bust.

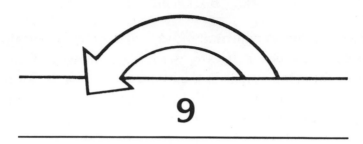

9

The Search for a
Level Playing Field

We have seen how, over the first two-thirds of this century, legislative restraint on corporate mergers was confined to the antitrust laws, which eventually became so stringent that the federal government had (and still has) the power to block virtually any vertical or horizontal merger. Even conglomerate mergers were challenged under those laws for a time around 1970, but this effort came to little and soon abated, as many conglomerates fell on bad times and public criticism of them waned. Then, in the eighties, the Reagan administration, eager to strengthen the international competitiveness of American industry and believing that mergers helped serve that goal, virtually allowed antitrust restraints on mergers to fall into disuse through nonenforcement. The principal exception was the steel industry, where in 1984 the federal authorities were instrumental in blocking planned mergers of U.S. Steel with National Intergroup, Inc., and LTV Corporation with Republic Steel. Even these restraining moves were attended by a sharp split within the Reagan administration, and by 1985 that administration was pressing for legislation that would relax the laws themselves to make them conform to its lenient policy.

Now we turn our attention to securities-law merger restraint, which effectively began in 1968. Previous to that year, federal disclosure and timing requirements for cash tender offers were so minimal that a company might find itself to all intents and purposes taken over before it knew who the raider was. The principal restraint on such offers was a regulation of the New York Stock Exchange that concerned chiefly the amount of time an offer should be open and the method of handling a partial bid when there were tenders for more shares than had been offered. All companies not listed on the exchange were, of course, unaffected. In 1965—a time when the number of cash tender offers had tripled in five years, and their annual aggregate dollar value had more than quintupled—Senator Harrison Williams of New Jersey introduced a series of amendments to the Securities Exchange Act of 1934, with the stated purpose of ending the secrecy made possible by a cash offer, and of creating a "level playing field" between offerer and target. The Williams bill was considered and passed by the Senate in 1967, and by both houses in July 1968; later that month, what came to be called the Williams Act was enacted.

The Williams Act, which, as later amended, was to constitute the principal federal regulation of merger activity in the merger boom of the eighties, has three key provisions. Administered by the SEC, it first required any individual or corporation that acquired 5 percent of a publicly held corporation to disclose that fact within ten days and, further, to disclose whether or not the purchaser's intention was to attempt a takeover. Second, it led to a requirement that, in order to give stockholders time to evaluate the merits of a tender offer, the offer must remain open for a minimum of twenty business days, thereby answering complaints about so-called *Saturday-night specials*—"shotgun" offers that had previously been open only a few days and therefore allowed the target little time to prepare a defense. Third, it required for the first time that in the case of partial offers that were oversubscribed, the offerer must purchase the shares on a pro rata rather than a first-come-first-served basis, thus preventing the squeezing out of distant or ill-informed stockholders.*

*A word should be said here about theories of regulation in general. There are basically two: the "idealistic" theory, since the 1930s deeply embedded in public and academic thought, which holds that the purpose and effect of regulation is to protect the public interest; and the "economic" or "capture" theory, which holds that "the history of [regulatory] commissions indicates that they have survived to the extent that they have served the interests of regulated groups" (Marver H. Bernstein), or even that "as a rule regulation is acquired by the industry and is designed and operated primarily for its benefit" (George J. Stigler), and is essentially "a product supplied to interest groups" (R. A. Posner). Bernstein notes that no other nation has attempted to control economic activities through government commissions on a comparable scale, but concludes that regulation "has not yet proved itself." Stigler espouses the economic theory, while Posner asserts that neither the public-

The Search for a Level Playing Field

The Williams Act was plainly intended to make hostile tender offers more difficult, and to slow their pace. For a few years it did both. But then came a turnaround, and as all the world knows, such offers climbed to record heights. According to the SEC and W. T. Grimm & Co., after there had been 113 tender offers commenced in 1967 and 115 in 1968, the totals dropped abruptly to 70 for 1969 and only 34 for 1970. Thereafter, the annual number rose in almost a straight line for a decade, from 43 in 1971 to 205 in 1981. Among the reasons for the turnaround appears to have been the discovery and exploitation of a huge loophole in the act—the ten-day "window" between the acquisition of 5 percent of a target's stock and the required disclosure of it. Offerers could, and did, use that period to acquire much more of the target's stock, still in nominal secrecy disturbed only by the intuitions of (or possibly leaks to) arbitrageurs. By the time the required 5-percent disclosure was made, the aggressor might, along with his allies the arbitrageurs, have the target, for all practical purposes, already in the bag. Because of this loophole, some feel that the principal impact of the Williams Act in practice has been merely to make takeovers more expensive to the acquirer, in that the twenty-day minimum

interest nor the economic theory "can be said to have, as yet, substantial empirical support." It is instructive to think of the SEC–administered Williams Act in this context. However, it is widely acknowledged that the SEC is generally among the most "idealistic" of the various regulatory commissions, and that, on balance over the years, it has served the interest of public stockholders at least as much as it has served that of the securities industry. See Bernstein, *Regulatory Business by Independent Commission* (Princeton, N.J., 1955); Stigler, "The Theory of Economic Regulation," *Bell Journal of Economics* 2, no. 1 (1971); and Posner, "The Theories of Economic Regulation," *Bell Journal of Economics* 5, no. 2 (1974).

offering period gives the target time to mount takeover defenses or find an alternate purchaser. (According to estimates cited in the Economic Report of the President for 1985, the Williams Act increased the average cash tender premium paid to target stockholders from 32 percent before its passage to 53 percent afterward. As the tender-offer boom of the eighties in itself makes obvious, that increase has not been enough to deter many aggressors.)

As for the "level playing field," knowledgeable critics insist that the Williams Act failed to bring it about. Francis M. Wheat, an SEC commissioner at the time the act was passed, said in 1984 that—chiefly because of the "in play" situation following the 5-percent announcement, and its tendency to convert the target into a "trapped animal"—"the notion . . . that the Williams Act established some sort of 'level playing field' for the bidder and the target is arrant nonsense." That is, disclosure, the SEC's principal weapon from its earliest days, proved in this case, according to Wheat, to be simply not enough to do the job.

Meanwhile, state legislatures were getting into the act, chiefly for the purpose of protecting companies based within their jurisdictions from hostile assaults from outside. (Senator Williams himself had originally become interested in the subject as a result of an assault on a New Jersey company.) In 1969, Ohio, without serious opposition, enacted a statute much stricter than the Williams Act, under which it was required that both the state and the target be given twenty days' advance notice of intention to make a tender offer; a state administrator was given power to hold hearings and to block the offer if his findings justified such action. Between then and 1982, thirty-eight states adopted more or less similar statutes. Finally, in the latter year, the Supreme Court, on constitutional grounds, struck down Illinois' statute and with it a number of others. Undeterred, the states went back to the drawing board to enact new anti-takeover statutes or to redraft their old ones to meet the constitutional test. By the end of 1985, ten more states, including New York, had adopted measures to frustrate tender offers, particularly two-tier ones, and several others had amended their older laws.

Again, in 1976 Congress adopted the Hart-Scott-Rodino Antitrust Improvements Act. Returning to the old antitrust approach to regulation of merger-and-take-over activity, this law requires parties to a proposed combination above a certain size to notify the federal antitrust authorities and then (unless the authorities chose to waive their powers) sit out a waiting period normally amounting to thirty days for a friendly merger or fifteen for a cash tender offer, while the question of antitrust compliance is studied. However, in view of the Reagan administration's highly accommodative antitrust policy on mergers, Hart-Scott-Rodino turned out in practice to have little effect on merger activity in the eighties.[1]

As is so often true, it took an instance involving apparent abuses that became a major media event—in this instance, the Bendix–Martin Marietta–United Technologies–Allied affair of 1982—to spur the federal government to action looking toward reform. Early in 1983 the SEC appointed an eighteen-member Advisory Committee on Tender

Offers to examine the question of what, if anything, should be done to supplement the Williams Act. In view of the facts that the committee was weighted toward people whose livings depended largely on advising offerers and targets on tender offers—among its members were the leading merger lawyers Joseph Flom and Martin Lipton, and the leading investment-bank M&A men Robert Greenhill of Morgan Stanley and Bruce Wasserstein of First Boston—and that the Senate Banking Committee stepped in to impose a four-month limit on the commit- tee's deliberations, many expected it to produce little in the way of suggested reform. In fact, starting from the premise that "there is insufficient basis for concluding that takeovers are either per se beneficial or detrimental to the economy or the securities markets in general," the com- mittee came up with no fewer than fifty recommendations and various pointed comments. Among these were the following:

- To close the "ten-day window" between acquisition of 5 percent of a company's stock and required disclosure of the acquisition by forbidding the acquirer to pass the 5-percent mark until forty-eight hours *after* public disclo- sure.
- To mandate, apart from exemptions in special cases, a tender offer when 20 percent of a company's vot- ing shares have been acquired.
- To prohibit a counter-tender offer by a target for an acquirer (the Pac-Man defense) when a cash offer has been made for all of the target's shares.
- To forbid a target company from issuing golden-

parachute separation agreements to its executives after a tender offer has commenced.

• To require approval of target-company shareholders before any repurchase of its own shares from the would-be acquirer (greenmail payments), or before issuing a substantial amount of new stock as a defensive measure.

• To continue to allow partial and two-tier offers, but only when all shareholders receive "the highest price per share price paid in the offer," and only when the length of the first-tier offer has been increased beyond the normal requirement.

• "Regulation of takeovers should not unduly restrict innovations in takeover techniques. These techniques should be able to evolve in relationship to changes in the market and the economy."

• "The Committee believes that certain misapprehensions concerning the takeover process have been created by a relatively few celebrated cases. . . . The Committee does not believe that they have provided an accurate view as to how the takeover process works in the vast number of unpublicized transactions."

The Advisory Committee's recommendations, contained in a report that it issued in July, represented a majority opinion, and were sharply dissented from by some committee members from polar points of view—those who felt they went too far, and those who felt they didn't go far enough. The post-report public debate on its recommendations was summarized and epitomized in the public comments of two committee members, the veteran and celebrated merger lawyers Flom and Lipton. Flom—

long known as the dean of takeover lawyers, although in fact his firm represented targets as often as aggressors—said that there was "almost nothing" in the committee report that he disagreed with; concerning the extent of his personal input in the committee deliberations, he commented, "Well, I'm not a shrinking violet." While admitting that the committee remedy for greenmail—requiring target-company stockholders to approve it in advance—was "a Band-Aid," he broadly asserted, "It's totally wrong to say [the report] is weighted toward the raider. If anything, it's the other way."

Lipton, who by his own assertion leaned philosophically toward restricting takeovers and giving the target broad leeway to fight them, took the opposite view. Stating that during the committee sessions he had been in a minority of one or two on most issues, he characterized the committee majority as being "essentially in favor of making tenders easier to accomplish." In particular, he asserted that the trigger point for a mandatory tender offer should be a holding of much less than the 20 percent that the committee had recommended—that is, it should be 10 percent or less. (Flom said that he would have settled for 15 percent, but hadn't been forced to.) Further, Lipton denounced the committee majority's failure to place a total ban on partial and two-tier offers that "stampede" shareholders into tendering lest they miss out on the all-cash, front-end offer. Let us note, in assessing the views of the protagonists in this joust, that as merger lawyers they were both self-evidently involved in conflicts between their philosophical views and their law practices. Lipton said afterward that in pressing for policies that would tend to reduce the amount of takeover activity, he was pressing for policies that would substantially reduce his own practice; he did it, he explained, because "I have always spoken out on public matters." As for Flom, ostensibly the champion of the tiger-toothed raider, he cheerfully invoked the traditional lawyer's pragmatic espousal of his client's point of view whoever the client, and admitted that in the matter of the rights and wrongs of takeovers, "I have many different moods depending whether I'm on offense or defense, and afterward I look out the window and laugh at myself."[2]

The Advisory Committee Report was followed by a flood of legislative and other proposals from many quarters. To begin with, the SEC commissioners were cautious about endorsing their committee's conclusions. In March 1984, after mulling over the matter for eight months, they went along with most of the proposals, but rejected on form the committee's proposed method of closing the "ten-day window" for disclosure of a 5-percent holding, and refused to endorse most of the committee's suggestions as to target companies' defense tactics, citing a reluctance to preempt state law. (The committee's judgment had been that federal enforcement *should* preempt all state law touching on takeovers, except in the case of purely local companies.) In May, two months later, the commission had changed its mind on this matter. Now its majority was plumping for federal enactment of the committee's key restrictions on the defensive actions of targets. Apparently the worry about conflict with state law had been forgotten somewhere along the line. In another switch, the committee's method of closing the ten-day window was now approved by the SEC—but by a split vote, with Chairman Shad dissenting on grounds that quick disclosure of a 5-percent holding "puts too much time pressure on the acquirer."

With such waffling at the SEC—surely to some extent a reflection of pro-merger views held elsewhere in the administration—the campaign for federal merger law reform seemed to suffer either from sabotage at the top or simply from confusion. But meanwhile others, mostly from Congress or from Wall Street itself, were generating a veritable blizzard of reform proposals. Between late March and late May 1984, Representative Timothy E. Wirth of Colorado held hearings on "Takeover Tactics and Public Policy" before his subcommittee of the House Committee on Energy and Commerce. Among those who testified were Shad of the SEC; Bevis Longstreth, formerly of the SEC; Lipton; Wasserstein of First Boston; Greenhill of Morgan Stanley; Felix Rohatyn of Lazard; and Carl Icahn. Lipton, Wasserstein, Rohatyn, and even Icahn wanted to go further than the committee recommendations in restraining acquirer tactics. (Rohatyn, for example, proposed a total ban on two-tier offers.) Following the hearings, Wirth introduced four fairly strong bills generally based on the SEC committee recommendations, two of them drafted by the SEC itself. Lipton sent Congress a bill of his own devising, proposing a law mandating a tender offer for all shares by any acquirer of 10 percent of a company's stock; such a law, he argued, would serve as a panacea by eliminating abuses on the acquirer side and making unnecessary those on the target side. In June the SEC threw cold water on this idea by issuing a study, conducted under the supervision of its chief economist, which concluded that two-tier offers are not disadvantageous to stockholders. In August, the Wirth Committee was giving generally favorable consideration to some of the measures that its chairman had introduced; but meanwhile the SEC, waffling again, withdrew its endorsement of the bills it had drafted. Legislatively speaking, nothing happened. In September, Lipton took a new tack, proposing that companies threatened by takeovers defend themselves by amending their own charters. The amendment he urged would prevent anyone who had acquired more than 5 percent but less than 90 percent of a company from exercising its stock voting power for a period of three years. This would impede greenmail and retard bust-up sales of corporate assets; but it would also violate New York Stock Exchange listing rules and might result in delisting unless the exchange was willing to change or bend those rules. (No listed companies immediately adopted such amendments.) In November, Lipton was back to attacking on the legislative front, sending Wirth and his Senate counterpart, Alfonse M. D'Amato of New York, a new proposed law considerably more draconian than his previous one, which had gone nowhere. This time he proposed that the disclosure trigger under the Williams Act be reduced from 5 percent to 3 percent; that the trigger for a mandatory tender offer be not 10 percent but 5 percent; and that all tender offers be required to be kept open for sixty calendar days, rather than the currently required twenty business days.

Thus, at the turn of 1985, the movement to reduce merger activity through legislation still had a good deal of momentum. Its history during 1985 is a study in changing Washington moods, and particularly in the effect of steady administration pressure on legislators and nominally independent regulators. Henry Kaufman, Salomon's celebrated chief economist, gave the movement a boost at the turn of the year when he issued an estimate that the effect of mergers, takeovers, LBOs, and defensive corporate restructurings during 1984 had been to take $80–$90 billion of corporate equity out of the national marketplace. But the administration kept throwing cold water, more boldly now. In February came the Economic Report of the President, with its unbridled endorsement of takeover activity at current levels and opposition to any new legislation; and in March a Cabinet council was reported to be quietly but forcefully reinforcing the Economic Report by spreading its view that raider tactics were not abusive and that restraint on defensive measures should be left to the various states.

Even so, the momentum continued for a time. In March, the widely respected Warren Buffett of Berkshire Hathaway zeroed in on the rapidly proliferating use of high-yield securities to raise takeover cash, saying, "Our industry should not be restructured by the people who can sell the most junk bonds." In April, the securities subcommittee of the Senate Banking Committee, chaired by D'Amato, began new hearings looking toward new legislation. By that time the congressional hopper contained a cluster of proposed laws reflecting a wide range of points of view. Chairman Peter Rodino of the House Judiciary Committee had proposed a two-year moratorium on takeovers that were opposed by a majority of the target's outside directors, and also a required disclosure of the social ramifications of a proposed takeover—a sort of securities-industry environmental-impact statement. Senator William Proxmire had proposed a law that would all but eliminate hostile takeovers. A delegation of Oklahoma legislators, reacting to the recent near-takeover of Phillips Petroleum, had urged a six-month ban on hostile oil-and-gas takeovers. Others focused on junk-bond financing: Chairman Pete Domenici of the Senate Budget Committee proposed a temporary ban on takeovers financed by junk bonds, and Representative James R. Jones introduced a bill that would end tax deductions of interest on debt used in hostile takeovers.

With such a legislative storm wind blowing, could the administration's wall of inaction stand? It could. In May the SEC voted, unanimously this time, not to seek new legislation, and withdrew all of its previous proposals for change (they were now "obsolete," Chairman Shad said) except for some unspecified sort of shortening or closing of the ten-day window. This probably marked the turning point. With the whole executive panoply of economic power arrayed against change, and with the SEC now solidly in the laissez-faire camp, Congress began to lose heart. In June there was a growing feeling among legislators that what was needed was not new laws but more vigorous enforcement of existing ones. Even Wirth, the man most visibly at the cutting edge of legislative reform, was saying, "The more I know about the issue, the less sure I am about what to do."

Over the rest of 1985—while mammoth junk-bond, two-tier, bust-up takeovers marched on, the courts decided this way or that on the legality of takeover defenses, and the banner of reform was carried chiefly by former SEC commissioners from Democratic administrations, corporate chieftains like Andrew Sigler of Champion International and William C. Norris of Control Data—nothing happened in Congress. In July the administration, sensing its advantage, went on the attack when James C. Miller, chairman of the Federal Trade Commission, called for a *reduction* of existing anti-takeover legislation. The SEC turned its attention to rule-making, requiring for the first time that companies whose stock was undergoing unusual market activity or were the subject of merger rumors, if asked directly for an explanation, in most cases must disclose any current merger negotiations rather than answering "no comment," as had been done so often in the past. The only new legislative proposal was a relatively mild compromise measure sponsored in November by Senators D'Amato of New York and Alan Cranston of California; it included some of the now-familiar antiraider measures such as closing of the ten-day window and lengthening of the minimum tender-offer period, but it also included some proraider features, such as forbidding Unocal-type targeted repurchases of stock by a target company as a defensive move. The administration, of course, opposed the measure, and the SEC withheld its endorsement.

By the end of the year—when Rohatyn was still stubbornly stating in press interviews what seemed to many laymen to be the obvious fact that things were "getting badly out of hand" concerning poorly financed takeovers, and that public confidence in financial institutions was thereby being eroded—not a single one of the many anti-takeover bills had come to a vote in either house of Congress. And in January 1986, the SEC, in its most extensive survey of the situation since early 1984, came out with a flat broadside against measures to restrict the practices most often called abusive, among them greenmail, golden parachutes, two-tier offers, poison-pill defenses, and junk-bond-financed takeovers. Wirth was now talking about "fixing potholes" rather than passing comprehensive legislation.[3]

Pretty clearly, then, broad reform through legislation was dead for the foreseeable future. A tide had risen, been contained by massive jetties and revetments, and then receded. The blocking jetties and revetments had not even been the usual "interest groups," since, as we have seen, the most vocal representatives of corporations and of Wall Street had *favored* reform of one sort or another. The blocking had been done almost singlehandedly by an ideologically inclined national administration.

In the circumstances, reform, if any, would apparently have to come from some quarter other than Congress. Some felt that such a quarter might be found in the stock exchanges themselves. The chief one of these, the New York Stock Exchange, had since 1926 maintained a rule that all common shares of listed companies must have equal voting rights.* The rule theoretically prevented listed companies threatened with takeovers from defend-

*Sometimes this rule has been compromised, as by the 1956 listing of Ford Motor Company stock despite the fact that the Ford family's Class B stock retained 40 percent of the voting power with only about 5 percent of the equity.

ing themselves by creating new classes of stock with inferior voting rights, or none. It was now suggested by
reformers disillusioned with the prospect of legislative action that the exchanges could become spearheads of takeover reform by adding new rules—for example, requiring
listed companies to get shareholder approval before making two-tier offers or, on the defensive side, before selling
off key assets, adopting supermajority provisions, or
granting executives golden parachutes.

The trouble was that meanwhile the key stock exchange rule, that involving equal voting rights, was being
enforced less rigidly than ever before. By the end of 1984
certain Big Board companies, among them Coastal Corporation and Dow Jones & Company, had created unequal
classes of stock without being delisted as a result. (Even
General Motors, after its 1984 merger with Electronic
Data Systems, created a new "Class E" stock with inferior
voting rights to represent holdings in that company; this
was acceptable, the exchange said, because Class E stock
was listed separately and traded independently, as if it
were a separate company. GM created yet another class
of stock with inferior rights after its 1985 merger with
Hughes Aircraft.)

Throughout 1984 and 1985, the exchange had a subcommittee deliberating the question of application of the
equal-voting rule; it adopted a policy of generally allowing
companies with unequal classes of stock to remain listed
while the deliberations went on. As a practical matter, the
reasons for such foot-dragging were fairly obvious. For
one thing, when a listed company agrees to a white-knight
takeover in preference to a hostile one, its existence as an
independent entity ends, along, of course, with its ex-

change listing; the threat of delisting becomes academic. Equally to the point, in the highly competitive market among the various exchanges for the listings of important companies, any exchange, even the imperial NYSE, is reluctant to adopt or enforce measures that will clearly harm its competitive position. In 1984 the NYSE sent out a letter to listed companies and others asking for opinions on whether its voting-rights standard, and other related standards intended to protect stockholder rights, should be rescinded or reexamined in view of the new climate— "a melancholy portent for the future of enlightened self-regulation," commented the former SEC Commissioner Francis Wheat.

Looking at the scene toward the end of 1985, while takeovers roared on and exchange-listed companies went on creating or thinking about creating unequal stock classes, Joel Seligman of the George Washington University National Law Center concluded that "security market self-regulatory organizations are improbable vehicles for reform," that, indeed, "it seems virtually inconceivable that the Exchanges . . . will adopt types of broad generic rules regulating takeover bidding or takeover defenses," and that "adoption of a generic approach to takeover transactions will either occur at the federal level or not at all." He appeared to be borne out when, in July 1986, the directors of the Big Board—"reluctantly," according to their chairman, John J. Phelan, Jr.—voted to abandon the one-share, one-vote principle, and allow listing of companies having classes of stock with unequal voting rights.[4]

Just when action at the federal level seemed most unlikely, action was taken—not by Congress or the SEC, but by the

Federal Reserve Board, which, of course, was designed and intended primarily to regulate not the securities markets but money and credit. On December 6, 1985, by a three-to-two margin, the Fed governors voted to propose that the use of debt in takeovers, in cases where the debt was issued by shell corporations that lacked major assets of their own, be limited to 50 percent of the purchase price of the target company.

The Fed's authority to enforce such a limitation was purely administrative and of long standing. It derived from Regulation G of the Securities Exchange Act of 1934, which gives the Fed power to set a percentage limit on credit used in the purchase of stocks. As applied to the loans of brokers to their customers, that authority had for a half-century been taken for granted on Wall Street. Indeed, it had come to be not only accepted, but generally welcomed there. It was widely credited (although not by the Fed itself) with having prevented any of the several postwar U.S. stock-market collapses from having turned into "another 1929," and for that reason was widely regarded in retrospect as the single most effective securities-market reform of the New Deal. However, applying it to takeover debt financing—the current forms of which were largely of postwar invention—was another matter. Was it appropriate for the Fed to set itself up as a sort of takeover review board? True enough, the proposed move was narrow in scope, aimed with gunsight accuracy at hostile junk-bond takeovers. The typical friendly merger or LBO would be exempt, because in such transactions, even when junk bonds were extensively used, those bonds were backed from the start by the assets of the target company or were guaranteed by the acquirer company. On the other hand, the proposed rule would have prevented, at least in the form in which they were executed, several of the mammoth and controversial successful hostile takeovers of 1985. Whether or not, had the proposed new Fed rule been in effect, it could have been circumvented in those cases by inventive investment bankers remained an open question.

The Fed asked for public comments, and it got them. The Fed majority's stated principal motive for its initiative was to slow down the progressive leveraging of the economy through leveraged takeovers, a process that Fed Chairman Paul A. Volcker had warned against repeatedly over the previous year or so. Opponents now argued that its effect would be to thwart the healthy operation of the free market, and also to bring about other unwanted side effects. Wall Street itself was sharply divided on the issue. Lipton and Rohatyn were predictably in favor of the move, Flom predictably against. (Lipton pointed out that Revlon and Unocal, in the course of their defensive campaigns a few months earlier, had both urged the Fed to take just such action.) Salomon and Shearson Lehman, firms possessing many ties with large companies concerned about takeovers, were in favor. Merrill Lynch and Prudential-Bache, having fewer such ties, were against. T. Boone Pickens and his fellow raiders were, of course, against. As for Drexel Burnham Lambert, the firm with a kind of patent on the issuance and distribution of junk bonds, apart from theoretical objections it was forthright about the presumed effect on its pocketbook. As Drexel's chief executive, Frederick H. Joseph, put the matter, "As

275

drafted, the rule could shut us down." The raider Irwin Jacobs was even more forthright: "If this was done to me five or ten years ago, I wouldn't be what I am today."

And the Reagan administration? On December 23, in a volley of criticism of an independent government agency all but unprecedented in its breadth and coordination of timing, the Departments of Justice, Treasury, Labor, and Commerce, the Office of Management and Budget, the Council of Economic Advisers, and the SEC—virtually every branch of government with even a remote interest in the matter—denounced the Fed's proposal, arguing, among other things, that it would cripple the free market, make useful takeovers more difficult and expensive, impose new regulatory burdens on government, and lead to more hostile takeovers of American companies by foreign ones operating outside the Fed's jurisdiction.

After some wavering—a week after the administration offensive, the Fed's own regional bank in Richmond, Virginia, stated that the proposed change was "probably unwise"—the Fed Board stood firm. On January 8, 1986, again by a three-to-two margin, its governors voted to adopt the proposed rule, with minor amendments that did little to alter the administration's opposition. Fed Vice-Chairman Preston Martin, a Reagan appointee, explained his negative vote by pointing out that the Fed already had a system under which its staff and regional banks could give their opinions case by case on whether or not Regulation G margin requirements were applicable in leveraged takeovers; Martin went on to say that the new institutionalization of the process indicated that the Fed was now on the "slippery slope" toward more heavy-handed and burdensome regulation.

What effect, then, did the new rule have in practice? The great junk-bond-financed takeovers of 1985 were unaffected, because they had been negotiated before it had been adopted, and it was not retroactive. No new huge takeovers with such financing were proposed in the months immediately following, suggesting that the rule was serving its purpose. By August 1986 it was being said that the rule had virtually no practical effect because it could be circumvented by the use of preferred stock—technically equity—rather than junk bonds, and because hostile takeovers were no longer being done by shell companies. Perhaps the effect was more psychological than substantive; the Fed, almost certainly the most publicly respected economic arm of government in 1986 because of its outstanding success in curbing inflation over the previous four years, had now served notice that it was concerned about the national economic consequences of leveraged takeovers, and was prepared—albeit by a paper-thin majority—to translate its concern into action. Volcker, evidently emboldened, pressed his advantage in February, urging the Senate Banking Committee to give serious consideration to including in the pending tax-reform bill provisions that would reduce the tax advantage of debt financing by corporations.*

Meanwhile, one of the bigger new takeover initiatives of early 1986—the $742.6-million offer, made in March, of Electrolux A.B. of Sweden for White Consolidated Industries of Cleveland, the United States' third largest producer of appliances—seemed to confirm the administra-

*The tax bill as enacted later in the year, to be effective in 1987, did in fact reduce the tax advantages of takeovers in various ways, leading to a spate of mergers at the end of 1986, just before the new law took effect.

tion's December prophecy that the Fed's action would lead to hostile acquisitions of American firms by foreign ones. The White board had previously rejected a $45-per-share Electrolux offer, taken the familiar legal steps to block a takeover, and authorized management to seek a higher offer from some other suitor. The fact that none had been forthcoming at least suggested that other aggressors were being inhibited by the Fed's credit limitation. But the sweetened $47-a-share Electrolux bid, which White's board accepted on March 10, did not seem to be a predatory one. Indeed, it seemed to represent a model acquisition bid from the standpoint of both White stockholders and White finances. For one thing, although it involved a lockup option on 18.5 percent of White stock, it was a one-tier offer in which all White stockholders would receive the same amount in cash. For another, since it did not involve junk-bond financing, or the issuance of any new debt securities by White, it would not cause a reduction of White's already tight cash flow, or change White's plans to spend $100 million a year over the next five years on plant modernization. All in all, if this was the kind of foreign takeover that Fed restrictions on junk-bond financing was going to encourage, then American companies and their stockholders seemed to have reason to say, "Bring on the foreign devils!"[5]

The Fed's move of January 1986 was a small crack in the government's wall of opposition to takeover reform. It did nothing to protect stockholders from the consequences of abusive techniques used on offense or defense. It affected only a small portion of merger-and-acquisition activity, and only a small percentage of total takeover debt. It certainly did not encourage the administration to keep the stubborn and independent Volcker in office any longer than necessary. Nevertheless, it struck, however weakly, at what most of those who took a broad economic view considered the worst danger of the takeover game as then played—the overleveraging of American companies. Not only was the administration wall still firmly in place, it was becoming firmer all the time. During 1986, Volcker lost his philosophical majority on the Federal Reserve Board. The Fed's move was a beginning that seemed unlikely to be followed by a middle and an end.

All the while, as the takeover wars and the legislative and regulatory skirmishes raged in the United States, reform-minded people on this side of the Atlantic were casting sidelong, sometimes envious glances at the British system, which seemed usually to have kept takeover action in that country within far better bounds. Dating from the late 1960s, the British system was essentially extralegal, a form of corporate and securities-industry self-regulation. Its standards were set by a written (and often-revised) Code on Takeovers and Mergers; its administration and such enforcement as was available were in the hands of a Panel on Takeovers and Mergers established by the Bank of England, the London Stock Exchange, and the private financial community, whose members were chiefly "players" in the merger game. Its stated goals were to ensure equal opportunity and information to all stockholders; to see that defensive action was not taken by target firms without their stockholders' approval; and, in general, to protect the reputation of the financial community. (Or, as Peter Frazer, Deputy Director-General of the panel, put the matter in 1985, to prescribe "how a decent chap behaves" in a takeover.) Its standard procedure was to hold hearings on individual cases and to make rulings. According to Frazer, after nearly two decades of operation, the rulings of the panel had been accepted in every case but one.

A key feature of the British code, from an American point of view, was that it made no substantive distinction between friendly and hostile mergers. (Indeed, the question was largely academic before the mid-eighties, because until then—the alleged British influence on Morgan Stanley in 1974 notwithstanding—there were few hostile takeover attempts, which were looked upon with distaste by the corporate and financial communities.) Its most important rules were that (1) any person or group holding 30 percent of a company's stock must bid for all the remaining shares at the bidder's highest previous price; (2) any substantial partial offer needs the approval of both the panel and a majority of the target's shareholders; and (3) any action designed to frustrate a takeover that is taken by a target company—adopting supermajority provisions, creating new shares, issuing options to third parties, or buying in existing shares, for example—must be approved by the target company's shareholders. (There were also restrictions on buying in shares written into British law.)

Clearly, the British rules were relatively permissive by the standards of the more enthusiastic American reformers. For example, the relatively high trigger point of

30 percent for a mandatory tender offer for all shares might permit an aggressor in some cases to gain effective control, while treating target shareholders unequally.* However, the requirements of panel approval and a target stockholder vote for a partial offer resulted, in practice, in enough deterrence to make partial bids rare. Concerning target-company defensive measures, the panel requirement of stockholder approval of them had the practical effect of making them more difficult for target-company management and directors to get adopted—and, to that extent, tipped the balance toward raiders.

The extralegal status of the British system was (and is) its most characteristic cultural feature. The chief sanction against takeover excesses or abuses on either attack or defense was, at bottom, community disapproval. One could theoretically flout the Takeover Panel and not go to jail or pay a fine; one didn't do so because, by community standards as represented by the panel, it wasn't done. Frazer in 1985 expressed the opinion that in practice, given the British ambiance, such sanction may work better than law: witness the general rationality and restraint of the British takeover scene until 1984–85 relative to the American one, and the fact that, as evidenced by the infrequency with which British companies erected defenses in advance of any actual takeover attempt, such companies were generally free of the American takeover paranoia.

Well, then, could the British system work here? The

*On the other hand, a British law, the Companies Act, required disclosure of a 5-percent holding within five business days, and was therefore more stringent than the Williams Act as in force in the mid-eighties. In February 1987, in reaction to a series of takeover-related scandals, the Takeover Panel lowered the disclosure trigger point to a 1-percent holding.

SEC's appointment of an Advisory Committee weighted toward "players" rather than regulators strongly suggested more than a sidelong glance across the Atlantic. In fact, as we know, the committee did not suggest the transatlantic importation of a Takeover Panel, although Flom allowed that, as a takeover lawyer, he could "live with" a British-style system here. But, as most commentators agreed, such an importation would involve enormous obstacles. For one thing, the British panel's reliance for enforcement on a gentlemanly consensus within the industry, along with its threat of informal sanctions, would immediately and clearly run afoul of the United States antitrust laws. (Of course, those laws might not be enforced; but in view of the Reagan administration's opposition to takeover restraints, this would seem to be an area where, if the British system were adopted, the administration would suddenly rediscover antitrust.) Beyond that, and perhaps more important, is the matter of cultural differences. This was noted by Frazer of the British panel in 1985, when he pointed out, with tactful restraint, that Britons are inclined to be less litigious than Americans and that they operate under a different constitutional system. To put the thing more bluntly, is it likely that American raiders, individual or corporate, would be much restrained by the decisions of a panel of their peers, which informed them, without legal backing, that they must cease because they were not acting like gentlemen?

One more factor: the absence in Britain (again, probably a cultural matter) of an arbitrage community anywhere near as active and powerful as that in the United States, made the economic pressure on extralegal sanctions less than it was here—even assuming that social pressure was equal, as it surely was not.

Finally, there is evidence that by 1985 the British system itself was showing signs of breaking down. During that year, hostile bids for British companies outpaced all previous years in both number and total value. Previous to 1985 there had never been a billion-dollar takeover bid for a British company; by early 1986 five were pending or under way.

The principal cause of this rising tide was not a new permissiveness on the part of the Takeover Panel; indeed, the panel's restraints on target defensive measures seemed to be serving as encouragement to raiders. Rather, it was a change in the attitude of British financial institutions, which held about 65 percent of all publicly traded British shares. Traditionally, these institutions had tended to be fiercely loyal to the major corporations whose shares they held, and to be reluctant to tender those shares to hostile raiders; now, under the impact of a wave of financial deregulation comparable to that in the United States, they were taking what a leading London merchant banker described as "an aggressive commercial attitude"—that is, tendering to raiders for short-term profit, and thus helping the raids succeed.

The barbarians, then—some of them British— seemed to be at the gates, and the British to be responding by acting more like barbarians themselves. The Takeover Panel notwithstanding, the British takeover scene was adopting something of the rougher ethical tone of its American counterpart. There were still ways in which it was far from American. For example, apart from the continuing smaller role of risk arbitrage, junk bonds had still not caught on. Commercial-bank financing, often led by American banks, was still the rule. The Takeover Panel and the press, rather than the courts, continued to be the principal arenas of battle. And there continued to be a general assumption that a hostile bid was bad unless proved otherwise, especially when the bid came from foreigners and could be looked upon as an assault on British culture. Still, it was clear enough that the gentlemanly ethic, embodied in the Takeover Panel and its headmasterly extralegal sanctions, was eroding under the pressure of social change and market conditions—much as a parallel ethic had eroded in this country a decade earlier, when Morgan Stanley had made hostile bids respectable.

Was it possible that a foreign system, at the very moment when it was weakening and perhaps collapsing through progressive Americanization, could be the solution for America? Many authorities on this side of the Atlantic thought not. "The British model could not be transported whole to this country," said former SEC Commissioner Albert Sommer in 1984, while allowing that a generally similar system, based on law rather than custom, might serve to bring "some restraint and respect" to U.S. takeover dealings. For his part, Frazer of the Takeover Panel has said, "It would probably not be possible to swap—that is, to ship the SEC to London and set up the Takeover Panel in the States."[6]

To sum up, then, the erratic and frustrating course of takeover reform efforts in the 1980s: They may be said to have begun in earnest with public reaction to the bizarre

Bendix–Martin Marietta affair of 1982, which gave rise the following year to formation of the SEC Advisory Committee. The committee's recommendations, variously attacked as too strong and too weak, in turn gave rise to a bewildering profusion of legislative bills and proposals. Most of these were themselves necessarily so technical that few but professionals were able to understand them, with the result that the general public never came to express strong opinions one way or the other. The measures were opposed, with progressively increased resolution, first by the Reagan administration and later by a majority within the SEC, the agency that had indirectly brought them about. Their high-water mark came in late 1984 and early 1985, when passage of some sort of federal reform measure or measures seemed quite likely; but in the course of 1985, even as some of the most potentially damaging transactions to date, both socially and economically, were being negotiated, the reformist wave rapidly receded— chiefly as an outcome of executive-branch pressure against it, but also because legislators themselves were becoming increasingly confused about exactly what should be done.

Meanwhile, alternatives to federal legislation were being explored, but none of them appeared to be very satisfactory. State legislation, because of the self-interest of state constituencies, was skewed sharply toward the defense of locally based companies, and thus did not even aim at producing the "level playing field" that the Williams Act had been intended to bring about; moreover, such laws ran into constitutional problems whenever interstate commerce was involved. Self-regulation by stock exchanges was hobbled by the competitive self-interest of the exchanges themselves; and adaptation of the British model, or for that matter any foreign model, came to seem improbable for both legal and cultural reasons.

One of the more interesting aspects of the whole movement was the evolving identity of its most enthusiastic proponents and opponents. The relatively mild nature of the industry-oriented SEC Advisory Committee's recommendations suggested the "economic" or "capture" theory of regulation in action—that is, the regulators bending to the will of the regulated industry, producing for it a "product," or at least a compromise "product." But then, over the subsequent two years, as the SEC moved progressively away from both the committee's recommendations and its own earlier ones and came more and more into conformity with the Reagan administration's do-nothing position, this interpretation became less and less valid; the SEC position came to look neither "idealistic" nor "economic" but simply noninterventionist. The hottest-eyed potential reformers by 1985 were representatives of takeover-threatened companies, like Andrew Sigler and the Business Roundtable, selected, but powerful, investment bankers and lawyers with aspirations to statesmanship, like Rohatyn and Lipton; and even a few raiders and greenmailers. (By 1985, Icahn had graduated from greenmail to attempting to run such a key company as TWA, and Pickens was reported to be looking toward running for public office. Rohatyn had already done a tour in public office as head of New York's Municipal Assistance Corporation, and Lipton had long wanted to be an SEC Commissioner.)*

*An interesting question is the view of Rohatyn and Lipton—the most outspoken merger reform advocates within the investment-banking world of the

The Search for a Level Playing Field

Leading industry players, then, became the principal public advocates of forcing an adamant administration, an almost-as-adamant SEC, and an increasingly fainthearted Congress to reform industry practices. Metaphorically put, assuming there were foxes in the henhouse, the chickens and even some of the key foxes were the ones pressing for stronger walls around the henhouse, while the farmer was doing nothing, on the grounds that making it harder for foxes to kill chickens represents unwarranted interference with the barnyard free market. Obviously, this was a formula for stalemate.

It was being said in early 1986 that merger-minded companies still had a three-year "window of opportunity" to make deals, before the complaisant Reagan administration would be replaced by a new one of unknown character; undoubtedly this argument was being pressed by deal-seeking investment bankers on potential merger clients.

The Boesky scandal in November, coming on the heels of the election of a Democratic Senate, suddenly and unexpectedly changed the public climate and reversed the legislative one. Latent popular hatred of Wall Street and its fat cats suddenly surfaced, and, among other legislators, Senator Proxmire, prospective new chairman of the Senate Banking Committee, promised to hold early hear-

middle eighties—by other investment bankers. Clearly, they were divided in their appraisals. The present writer's soundings indicated (off the record in every case) considerable grudging approval of their views, along with criticism of their alleged publicity seeking and failure to practice what they preached. On balance, the amoral, I'll-do-it-as-long-as-it's-legal philosophy appeared to predominate. Not surprisingly, members of firms having strong ties with many large corporations were more apt to favor restraints on aggressor tactics, and those with raiders as their clients to favor restraints on target tactics.

ings not just on risk arbitrage but on the whole scope of merger-related activities. Reformers had visions of a new version of the still-well-remembered Pecora hearings of 1933–34, resulting, as the Pecora hearings had done, in public outrage and broad legislation. As for the administration—which was preoccupied at the time with a larger problem, rising public denunciation of its disorderly Iran policy—it was silent on the Wall Street crisis, tacitly maintaining its stance of opposition to legislative reform.

The question, of course, was whether, while an industry played its games and Washington dithered, permanent damage had been done. The damage done by the Great Depression, sequel to the 1920s securities-industry spree, need not be commented on. The evidence of damage from the go-go years is less clear, but still convincing, especially in regard to investor losses and the creation of irrational conglomerates. In the present case, even apart from the huge investor losses that may eventuate and the lasting social disruptions that the merger craze may leave in its wake, the question of whether or not the unprecedented corporate debt that the craze brought into being will bring havoc to corporate America in the next recession remains an open one.

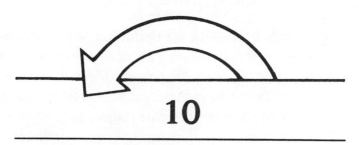

10

Commercial Banks in the Global Arena

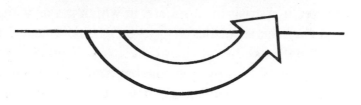

In the beginning, a bank was a bank and a banker was a banker. Great deposit-taking and loan-making institutions were freely allowed to underwrite corporate bonds and stocks—and they did so, some of the deposit-and-loan banks, such as Morgan, National City, and Chase, being among the leading investment-banking institutions in the nation. (In those days, of course, corporate bond underwriting was by a wide margin the principal investment-banking activity.) Then came the 2,300 bank failures of 1931; the virtual collapse of the national banking system in 1932; and, soon after the Roosevelt bank holiday of March

1933, the passage of the Glass-Steagall Act, which decreed that national commercial banks, as well as state-chartered ones belonging to the Federal Reserve System, were forbidden to underwrite securities except general-obligation bonds of the United States or of its states and municipalities. Thus was created a sharp split between commercial and investment banking in the United States, and the existence of a separate investment-banking industry. The split has lasted, with increasing recent erosions, for about half a century.

Passed in a crisis atmosphere, in which it was widely believed that the securities activities of banks had led to their downfall and that of their depositors, Glass-Steagall was under attack almost from the beginning. The attackers were the commercial banks, now deprived of business that they had formerly had, and the defenders were the investment bankers, seeking to protect their newly won exclusive turf. The first broadside attempt in Congress to repeal Glass-Steagall came in 1935, and was defeated. For many years thereafter, relative calm prevailed, as commercial banks—partly because it was a period of doldrums for underwriting—came more or less to accept the separation and their allotted territory. When they did resume the attack, in the 1960s, it was with a different tactic—chipping away at Glass-Steagall piece by piece rather than seeking its repeal in toto. The first attempt was to get permission to underwrite municipal and state revenue bonds—those backed by revenues from the projects being financed, as distinguished from those backed by the issuer's full faith and credit; this was briefly permitted to commercial banks by the Comptroller of the Currency, but in 1968 the Supreme Court, backed by the Federal Reserve, ruled that Glass-Steagall did not generally countenance such action. Again, in the mid-sixties Citibank (at that time First National City Bank of New York) moved to get indirectly into the business of selling equity mutual funds; again, after succeeding briefly, this initiative was struck down in 1971 by the Supreme Court. A few years later some commercial banks tested Glass-Steagall again with a system of "automatic investment services," under which checking-account customers could designate sums from their accounts to be invested periodically in stocks. This time the courts never had a chance to rule on the system, because it failed as a commercial venture.

Meanwhile, in the sixties and seventies major new developments in the world and national markets were bringing about an entirely new situation in the relationship between commercial and investment banks. The rapid rise of the Euromarkets created a huge arena where U.S. commercial banks could freely underwrite and trade in corporate securities, beyond Glass-Steagall's reach. (No country apart from the United States has a counterpart to the Glass-Steagall Act except Japan, which has one because the United States put it there during the postwar occupation.) In effect, the Euromarkets put U.S. commercial banks only an ocean away from being able to do everything that investment banks could do—a mixed blessing, to be sure, since Eurobond lead underwritings, the most competitive in the world, usually produced low profits and often produced losses.

At the same time, rapid inflation and interest-rate deregulation pressed even harder on commercial banks' profit margins. And their bread-and-butter business, that of making loans, became progressively riskier; in particular, first real-estate loans, then third-world loans, then oil-exploration loans, and finally agriculture loans went so sour that even some of the leading commercial banks faced failure or the need for government rescue. In the new environment, what was riskiest to depositors seemed to be not securities dealings but lending—not investment banking but traditional commercial banking. Thus the presumed previous usefulness of Glass-Steagall seemed to have been eliminated if not reversed.

Also at this time, investment banks were broadening their activities now to include massive head-to-head competition with their commercial counterparts in fields not forbidden to the latter by Glass-Steagall—for example, trading in U.S. government securities and foreign currencies. That is, while commercial banks were fighting to get back territory lost to them through Glass-Steagall, investment banks were flanking them to seize ground previously left mostly to commercial banks by default. Yet again, nonbank institutions like American Express, Merrill Lynch, and Sears Roebuck were moving in on commercial banks in the consumer area by setting up comprehensive services that included deposit-taking and lending along with insurance and investment brokerage.

All in all, by 1980 American money-center banks were feeling such a pinch that they insisted they urgently needed, for their health or even their survival, further access to a "world beyond lending." It was in this context that there arose a new and powerful legislative push for repeal or drastic reform of Glass-Steagall. The campaign culminated in a white paper issued by J. P. Morgan at the end of 1984. We have seen that a principal motive for Glass-Steagall had been the conviction that the securities activities of commercial banks improperly subjected their depositors to undue risk. Morgan now set out to prove that the premise had been wrong in the first place: the terrible bank failures of 1931–32, Morgan argued, had been caused not by securities activities but by national economic factors abetted by inadequate bank regulation, while "the establishment of federal deposit insurance and the strengthening of the Federal Reserve [had been] highly effective responses to the conditions that had led to the banking crisis," as "the Glass-Steagall Act was not."

In regard to the various conflicts of interest inherent in combining the loan-making and underwriting functions in a single institution, which were part of the original rationale for Glass-Steagall, Morgan argued that such conflicts had either been illegal all along, or were now adequately controlled by regulation imposed after the passage of Glass-Steagall, or were phantoms because they would be self-defeating for the banking institution. If, for example, a bank attempted to bail out a questionable loan by selling questionable securities of the borrowing corporation to its own trust accounts, it would thereby "ignore the clear legal duty of a trustee to refrain from self-dealing." If it tried to sell unsound securities of its borrowers to third parties for the same purpose, it would be subject to civil and possibly criminal liability under the Securities Acts of 1933 and 1934—both passed subsequent to Glass-Steagall. If it made imprudent new loans to its underwriting clients for the purpose of keeping their favor or encouraging the sale of the securities, the risk on the imprudent loans would far exceed the potential underwriting profit. Thus the bank would "jeopardize its assets" in a way that, as Morgan pointed out, the Federal Reserve Board had recently characterized as "not rational." In general, Morgan's position was that changed conditions, laws, and regulations since the passage of Glass-Steagall now "effectively control the potential conflicts that exist."

Concerning the profitability, and concomitant safety, of commercial banks in the new era, Morgan pointed to the wide edge of investment banks over commercial banks in recent and current profitability and argued that this suggested that if commercial banks were allowed to engage fully in investment banking, their depositors' money would be not at more risk, but rather at less. In sum, "Far from jeopardizing the safety and soundness of the banking system, permitting [commercial] bank affiliates to underwrite and deal in corporate securities would increase the system's stability."

Almost at the moment when the Morgan paper was released, Glass-Steagall was in the process of coming about as close as possible to being dismantled in Congress. In the summer of 1984, Jake Garn of the Senate Banking Committee introduced a bill that would have allowed commercial banks to underwrite and deal in revenue bonds, mortgage-backed securities, and commercial paper—a potentially huge bite out of Glass-Steagall that would have left virtually nothing but corporate stocks and bonds the exclusive preserve of investment bankers. In September the whole Senate approved the bill by 89 to 5, a margin so overwhelming as to indicate a consensus, and suggest that a new era for the structure of American banking—or rather, a return to an old era—was in the immediate offing. But Congress, being a creature of both moods and feuds, does not necessarily move in a straight line. Garn's House counterpart, Fernand St Germain—a man who leaned toward the investment-banking side of the matter, as Garn leaned toward the commercial-banking side—managed to prevent a House vote in 1984 by bottling up the Garn bill, and in 1985 disagreements between the two legislators prevented further votes in either house.[1]

So Glass-Steagall staggered on. But all the while, through the early eighties, the chipping away had proceeded, mainly through the work of deregulation-minded, Reagan-appointed bank regulators at the Federal Deposit Insurance Corporation (FDIC) and the office of the Comptroller of the Currency. In the absence of broad legislation, these agencies seemed bent on repealing Glass-Steagall piecemeal by administrative rulings. "There is more than the nose of the camel in the tent right now," complained an official of the Securities Industry Association, guardian of investment bankers' rights, in 1983. As indeed there was. Back in 1978, for example, Bankers Trust had begun operating a commercial-paper operation, on the theory that commercial paper—short-term loans between corporations, amounting by 1985 to well over $200 billion at any given time—did not constitute securities. The Federal Reserve agreed with this contention, but in 1981 and 1982 the federal courts reversed the Fed and declared that commercial paper *was* a security for purposes of Glass-Steagall. Bankers Trust had another string to its bow, however. It contended that its method of selling commercial paper consisted of serving as an agent for a fee, rather than as an underwriter, and was therefore acceptable under Glass-Steagall. Again the Fed agreed; but in February 1986, a federal district judge in Washington ruled that the Bankers Trust commercial-paper operation—which by that time amounted to $4.5 billion per year, making it the sixth largest among all institutions, including investment banks—was indeed illegal under Glass-Steagall. Pending appeal, Bankers Trust had to change its method of operation in ways that seriously inhibited its profits from commercial paper.*

Over the same period of years, the administrative chipping away was proceeding at a furious pace in other areas. With encouragement from the Comptroller of the Currency, commercial banks began, through affiliates, to move into discount brokerage of stocks, skirting Glass-Steagall by serving only as order-takers rather than as salesmen or advisers. Between 1981 and 1983 the number of commercial banks in discount brokerage went from virtually none to about 1,500. Then, in November 1984, the FDIC undertook the most breathtaking administrative flouting of Glass-Steagall until that time. Having "discovered" a loophole in the fifty-one-year-old law—it did not

*Whatever the legal situation, there was a logical, self-defensive justification for commercial banks in the eighties attempting to enter the commercial-paper market. During that time there was a tendency among their prime corporate customers, urged by investment banks, to defect from the short-term loan market to the commercial-paper market, thus depriving commercial banks of a part of their historic source of profit. Bankers Trust could argue that it was only trying to hold on to a form of business it had always had.

categorically forbid a state-chartered bank to acquire a securities company—it moved to authorize some 9,000 such banks to underwrite corporate securities through subsidiaries. The "carnival of deregulation," as it came to be called, went on to its next act in June and July 1985, when the Supreme Court ruled that banks were permitted to make interstate mergers within designated regions, in apparent defiance of the McFadden Act; although this move did not bear directly on Glass-Steagall, it served as a signal to encourage money-center banks to diversify further into investment banking. That November, retiring FDIC Chairman William M. Isaac, who for five years had served as ringmaster of the carnival, told a panel of senators that he was for flat repeal of the Glass-Steagall Act, the McFadden Act, and the Bank Holding Company Act—virtually the whole panoply of banking legislation of the 1920s and 1930s.

None of those laws was in fact repealed, and in 1986 the carnival seemed to be ending. Indeed, a reregulation trend, forced by a spate of bank liquidations and mergers under stress in 1985, caused this time mainly by bad farm loans, seemed to be in the making. Meanwhile, commercial banks had for several years been taking a new tack: that of inventing new products and new forms of transactions not dreamed of by Glass-Steagall's framers, and thus escaping its grasp to become progressively more competitive with the leading investment banks.[2]

How were they doing in that competition, and what prospect did they have of changing the character of the securities markets through their participation?

As things stood in the mid-1980s, the biggest commercial banks were highly successful in some fields that were by that time generally thought of as coming within the province of investment banking—and far less successful in others. They were, for example, among the leaders in trading government securities and foreign exchange, activities in which they had been heavily engaged all through the Glass-Steagall era and in which they therefore had the benefit of a long experience. Bankers Trust, for one, was in 1984 one of the five largest primary dealers in U.S. government securities; in the same year, maintaining a twenty-four-hour-a-day foreign-exchange trading capability with ten geographical locations around the world, its foreign-exchange transactions ran at a daily average of $3 billion. The handling of the huge foreign-exchange trading needs of multinational corporations was to a significant extent in U.S. commercial-bank hands. In another area of corporate finance—overseas underwriting of stocks and bonds of U.S. and foreign corporations—Morgan was near the top among all institutions of whatever character or nationality, and Bankers Trust not far behind. Citicorp, for its part, had made itself the largest investment bank in several Latin American countries, and in June 1985 it reorganized its London-based Citicorp International Bank into Citicorp Investment Bank, an entity of a size on the order of the top old-line London merchant banks, with plans to be a major player in European securities, venture capital, financial, brokerage, and bond underwriting. All in all, by 1984–85, activities generally classified as investment banking accounted for almost 20 percent of Citi's net income, with Morgan and Bankers Trust not far behind.

Domestic corporate finance, though, was another story, with no commercial bank even in a class with the investment-banking giants. Here Glass-Steagall was only one dimension of the problem. Even if the law were to be suddenly repealed, there was no prospect of any commercial bank suddenly appearing along with Salomon or Goldman among the leading domestic securities underwriters and traders. A half-century of legal exclusion from the securities markets had deprived them of the day-to-day participation in and feel for the markets that, especially under Rule 415, had become so necessary to pricing decisions and distribution capability. (Management of stock-and-bond portfolios for trust clients—which, of course, commercial banks had engaged in all through the Glass-Steagall era—carefully regulated as it is by the laws covering trusts and pension funds, is generally considered by investment bankers to be so different from wholesale securities trading at a huge investment bank as to provide only a limited amount of preparation for the latter activity.) Initial mistakes born of enforced inexperience might well give rise to underwriting disasters. In such circumstances, the chance of any leading corporation choosing a commercial bank (or banks) as its lead underwriter for a huge issue just because Glass-Steagall was off the books would be slim indeed. Although in time commercial banks would surely become as adept at securities trading as a Salomon or a Goldman, in the early stages they would almost certainly be risking their money in exactly the same way that a beginning poker player risks his when he sits down in a long-established game among experts.

In the matter of that much-discussed gold mine

for investment bankers, merger-and-acquisition advice, Glass-Steagall was no barrier. It put no restrictions on commercial-bank activity in that field; such banks have always engaged in it, and in recent years, hardly surprisingly, they had been casting envious eyes at the huge fees regularly collected by investment banks. The problem of commercial banks was that they were not collecting those fees; while the leading investment banks were bringing in $100 million or more per year in M&A fees, the figure for the top commercial banks was usually more like $10 million.

Formidable problems faced the commercial banks in their efforts to get a bigger share. First of all, as we have seen previously, trading and underwriting are to a marked extent prerequisites to effective M&A work; thus barriers to trading and underwriting, such as Glass-Steagall, are in themselves barriers to M&A. Second, any lending institution must deal with an inherent conflict when it ventures into the jungle world of M&A. Suppose the planned target of a hostile takeover attempt is a valued loan customer of the bank offered the chance to mastermind the takeover? The bank probably faces a choice of losing the loan customer, perhaps permanently, or giving up the merger fee. Investment banks, in the era of transactions, are considerably less apt to face comparable conflicts. Third, in trying to transform themselves into M&A sharks, the commercial banks are fighting not only inexperience but their own long-standing and deeply ingrained culture—one that emphasizes conservatism, respectability, and minimization of risk, qualities in direct contrast to those characteristic of the celebrated Wall Street merger-makers. Reversing such tendencies in a huge and long-established institution is not something that can be accomplished overnight. Finally, there is the matter of compensation, which traditionally has been lower and less performance-based at commercial banks than at investment banks. Consequently, it is the investment banks, rather than the commercial ones, on which newly fledged MBAs of exceptional talent most often set their sights. Even though commercial banks in recent years have moved aggressively to increase salaries and add incentive compensation in order to be more competitive in investment banking, in the mid-eighties it was a frequent occurrence for commercial banks to develop young talent in their offices, only to see that talent move to greener pastures at the very moment when it had become highly useful. As one commercial banker turned investment banker put the matter bluntly, and a bit brutally, in 1984, "We can make on one deal what a lending guy makes in a year."[3]

Regarding investment banking, then, commercial banks have powerful forces working for them and probably more powerful ones working against. On the plus side are their close contacts through loan dealings with many of the largest companies, their vast financial resources, and their frequent presence, in some cases long-established, in almost every corner of the world. On the minus side—quite apart from conflicts with loan operations—are, first, their inexperience in the transactional mode of doing business that is the essence of investment banking as now practiced; second, their possible residual distaste for that mode, along with the legal restrictions still imposed by Glass-Steagall; and, finally and most crucial of all, their tendency toward an imprisonment based on tradition in the mind-set still defined by the very word *banker.*

Nonetheless, as noted, money-center commercial banks—especially Citicorp, Morgan, and Bankers Trust, the three that in the mid-eighties were taken most seriously as potential rivals by the big investment banks—were making resolute efforts to break out of that mind-set and find a profitable "life beyond loans." Each of them set about staking out its own territory. Morgan, for example, apart from its well-established position in Eurobond lead underwriting, was making huge profits in trading foreign exchange and U.S. government securities. In the first quarter of 1986, Morgan's net profits on "other operating income"—a rough measure of investment-banking activities—reached a record $84.7 million, or roughly one-third of all earnings; at the same time, over half of a one-third increase in "noninterest" operating expenses had been related to incentive pay, indicating that Morgan was going to great lengths to get in the battle for investment-banking talent and stay in it. Citicorp, in addition to its emphasis on London and Latin America rather than Europe, was the recognized world leader in such fields as currency and interest-rate swaps.

Perhaps the institution making the strongest push in the new direction was Bankers Trust. Beginning in 1978, it progressively sold off its consumer banking network in order to concentrate on what it chose to call *merchant banking*, meaning a combination of wholesale deposit-and-loan business with investment banking. In addition to its bold and profitable plunge into commercial paper,

Bankers Trust went heavily, at home and abroad, into such fields as swaps, lease financing, private placements, and trading. It pioneered in the conversion of loans through selling them; the bank sold 30 percent of its loan portfolio in 1984 alone, and had plans eventually to sell 75 percent. (The selling of loans to institutional investors—a "new product" introduced into commercial banking by Bankers Trust in the early eighties—was in effect a way of increasing liquidity by converting a loan into a twilight entity that looked and acted like a security, but, for Glass-Steagall purposes, wasn't one. By the mid-eighties, all of the money-center commercial banks had followed Bankers Trust's lead in loan selling.)

Bankers Trust's incentive-compensation program, the most aggressive at any of the commercial banks, frequently met the investment-banking test that the top-performance stars should, with bonuses, be able to earn more than the chief executive. All the while, Bankers Trust went in heavily for what might be called investment banking by proclamation. A typical 1984 advertisement ran, "What do you get when you combine an investment bank with a commercial bank? Bankers Trust." But there was plenty of substance along with the sound. Between 1982 and 1985, according to its annual report for the latter year, Bankers Trust's total income from interest on loans declined slightly, while its total noninterest income almost doubled, and its net income increased by more than half. A life beyond loans, indeed![4]

The inescapable truth is that by 1985 investment banking had changed so much that Glass-Steagall was to a marked extent left as a rule without a game. Rather than marking off an industry, the law now marked off merely a corner of an industry; the postwar globalization of the investment business, and the new tendency everywhere to convert such assets as loans and mortgages into securities or quasi securities, had brought into being vast new markets in which commercial banks were allowed and equipped to compete. Their mass move toward investment banking would surely have taken place even without the initiative of a few forward-looking banks and bankers; having previously followed trade to every corner of the earth, the commercial banks, unlike the investment banks, found themselves already in place when a large and profitable investment-banking business sprang up where they already had their flags planted. In effect, the investment-banking water was rising everywhere. Global commercial banks were finding themselves deeper in it even if they simply stood still.

Indeed, globalization of the financial markets—the erosion of national economic boundaries and the tendency of the formerly discrete national capital markets to meld into one market—far beyond its effect on the importance of Glass-Steagall, was the major new trend in world finance in the 1980s, and one bound to bring about vast changes in American banking, both investment and commercial, in the future. It has been a leitmotif in the previous chapters of this essay, touching almost every form of activity discussed. Let us pause to look directly at it and its implications.

There is an element of paradox here. The United States had not gained market share in international banking during the seventies, and was not gaining it in the early eighties. The reverse was true. This was mainly a function of erosion of the United States' world economic position. In the post–World War II period the United States had become a huge capital exporter; its banks had followed their customers abroad, and for a time it had been by far the dominant force in world commerce. The huge, London-based Eurodollar market, which arose in the sixties chiefly as a result of American deficit financing, was at first dominated by American financial institutions. After 1965, however, the economies of leading European nations were growing faster than that of the United States, as was the power and wealth of those countries' banks; meanwhile a new economic colossus was emerging in Japan. At the same time, protective domestic regulation in most countries tended to restrict the entry of U.S. banks. By the beginning of the eighties, as Dwight B. Crane and Samuel L. Hayes III have pointed out, the United States' loss of position in international finance could be measured roughly by three criteria: the number of U.S. commercial banks ranking among the ten largest in the world had fallen from six in 1960 to three; among the twelve top Eurobond underwriters, only three were now U.S.-owned; and among the top twenty syndicated loan managers, the number of U.S. institutions had fallen from ten in 1973 to seven.

However, U.S. overseas banking was not declining in absolute terms; rather, it was poised for enormous expansion as it fought to maintain a smaller share of a much bigger pie. Various factors in the seventies, such as the end of the old fixed currency-exchange rates in 1973 and the huge oil-price rises beginning the same year, had greatly increased the profit stakes in international financial trans-actions. Now in the eighties came a historic move toward the creation of a single global financial market.

This change was driven chiefly by two forces. One, probably the most important, was the development of new communications technology that suddenly made the loca-tion of a transaction, no matter where in the world, almost irrelevant from a purely technical standpoint. The other was a wave of financial deregulation brought about in part by international political pressure and in part by a vogue for free-market economic policies, even in countries run by nominal socialists. Let us pick a few examples: In 1983, Australia for the first time allowed foreign banks to com-pete in its domestic markets, and in 1984 Norway, Sweden, and Portugal—the last holdouts among the twenty-four members of the Organization for Economic Cooperation and Development, comprising the leading European countries—followed suit. Also in 1984, Japan allowed for-eigners to raise yen outside Japan, giving rise to a huge Euroyen market that immediately became a competitor with the Eurodollar market. (In the first half of 1986, yen-denominated bonds were the international bond mar-ket's top performers because of the rise of the yen against other currencies.) The London Stock Exchange ended fixed commissions in November 1986, as the New York Stock Exchange had done in May 1975. The United States took a major step in the international deregulatory trend when in 1984 it lifted the 30-percent withholding tax to foreigners on U.S. bond interest, thereby bringing about increases for that year of 75 percent in foreign purchase of U.S. Treasury bonds and notes and of 72 percent in foreign purchase of U.S. corporate bonds.

By 1986, an integrated global market, particularly for debt instruments and to a lesser extent for equities, seemed to be in place. Corporations of any nationality could and did raise money in whatever place they chose, in whatever currency they chose, thereby tending to denationalize national currencies and make them into fluctuating international securities. On the international markets, securities that had once had entirely different characteristics were now regarded as comparable—for example, Eurodollar bonds and U.S. Treasury bonds and notes. Japanese investors had become a major factor, perhaps *the* major factor, in the U.S. Treasury market. Cross-listing of stocks on the world's stock exchanges was increasing rapidly, and leading American investment firms were at last granted access to the one in Tokyo, long the most xenophobic of major stock exchanges. Cross-national stock ownership had become a commonplace. When Morgan Stanley went public with a large stock offering in March 1986, one-third of the shares were reserved for buyers outside the United States and Canada, giving the firm truly international ownership. Even Wall Street's "new products," the trendiest of securities, had become tailored to a world marketplace; for example, Salomon's "mini-Max," introduced in July, was a short-term investment vehicle designed to allow favorable currency-rate-change exposure with minimal risk.

Thomas C. Theobald, vice-chairman of Citicorp in charge of investment banking, insists that with the new technology in operation it no longer matters very much where a transaction takes place—except, of course, to the enforcers of a law like Glass-Steagall, which was written in another area. For example, in the new marketplace

Citicorp found the domestic commercial-paper market, besides being of questionable legality for a U.S. commercial bank, largely sewed up by a few investment banks and one commercial one, Bankers Trust. Accordingly, Citi turned its attention to "Europaper"—a bigger market engaged in conducting exactly the same form of business in Europe, and one in which Citi quickly became a leader. "With the modern, computerized markets, sometimes it takes a lawyer to tell where a transaction did take place, anyhow," Theobald says, with a smile.

Theobald goes so far as to say that even the mammoth domestic investment-bank M&A operations, for all their pomp and glory, are under the global aspect mere "mom-and-pop operations." He cites some figures: the very biggest investment-bank M&A operations gross $100–$200 million per year, *before* expenses and taxes; while Citicorp, as stated in its annual report for 1985, derived from worldwide investment-banking activities gross revenues of about $1.6 billion and net income *after* taxes of $425 million. Even if Citi were able to spring instantly and magically into the ranks of the top domestic merger-makers—a prospect that Theobald does not look on as a practical possibility—its current annual net on investment banking would probably rise by less than 10 percent.

The tendency of world financial markets, once separate and inward-looking, to change into something approaching a single market has heartening political implications in that financial integration is often looked on as a harbinger of political integration. When the European Economic Community was launched in 1956, one of its explicit goals was the eventual replacement of the separate currencies of its members with one currency. Despite moves in that direction, the change has not yet actually taken place. But now, with technology and deregulation tending to reduce *all* major national currencies to the status of different-color chips in one poker game, it appears that the EEC's objective is being achieved de facto in a world rather than a European context.

However, the short-term implications of globalization for U.S. investors and the U.S. economy are unsettling. U.S. regulation is threatened with loss of part of its franchise. The more U.S. investment- and commercial-bank business is conducted abroad, the more is beyond the reach of U.S. regulation; conversely, of course, the same erosion of control affects regulators in all other countries. By general agreement of long standing, banking and securities trading need regulation; yet as things stand now, the new global marketplace is virtually unregulated. A first step was taken in November 1985, when an International Securities Regulatory Organization (ISRO) was formed in London to provide self-regulation for the London-based markets in Eurobonds and other internationally traded securities. The initial participation in ISRO comprised 187 world financial institutions, including the leading banks and securities firms of Britain, Europe, Japan, and the United States. In September 1986 the London Stock Exchange agreed to combine operations with it.

ISRO shows promise—no more than promise—of becoming a valid voluntary force for international cooperation, somewhat analogous to the group of central bankers who meet regularly at the Bank for International Settlements at Basel to deal with currency problems. But self-regulation, of course, can be no better than the enlightened self-interest of market participants. Formal, binding regulation of the global marketplace will have to wait much longer.

To return to Glass-Steagall: In a time when something like 75 or 80 percent of securities of all kinds issued in the United States, along with all securities issued abroad, are not proscribed to U.S. commercial banks, has not the law been repealed by events? Does it matter anymore? Many of the legislators who have wrangled over it in recent years now agree that no issue of public policy remains, but only the political issue of allocating territory to investment and commercial bankers, respectively. The lobbyists for the two industries still ritually plead their cases, but not all of them with as much conviction as they did before new markets and new products made the law irrelevant to a degree. In practice, its repeal might, certainly at first, be something of a nonevent: commercial banks might find themselves unable to capture significant positions in domestic securities underwriting even if they made great efforts (as they might not); meanwhile, the whole, ever-expanding, Glass-Steagall–free game, from foreign-exchange trading to swaps, from Eurobond underwriting to M&A, would go on as before.

Theobald of Citicorp, who feels, along with many other commercial-bank men, that Glass-Steagall was a mistake in the first place—that it was written "to cure imagined evils," as "a solution to some other problem"—believes that as things now are, it is "not exactly irrelevant" in that it now stands, after half a century in effect, as a sort of embarrassment on the national books, a law that is now demonstrably far wide of the mark it aims at. Its elimination would thus be in the nature of an overdue cleanup. The chief practical effect of repeal, he thinks, would be not on the profitability of either investment or commercial banks—neither of which group now finds a leading source of profit in domestic securities underwriting—but rather on competition in that field, which Theobald describes as "shockingly concentrated" in the era of shelf registration and the bought deal.

True enough, there are others among leading commercial bankers who take a different view. For example, George J. Vojta, executive vice-president in charge of strategic planning at Bankers Trust, insists that Glass-Steagall *does* matter in substantive ways, in that it "restricts a commercial bank's capacity to serve its most credit-worthy customers, and thus inhibits the bank's competitive ability." He says that its repeal, which was repeatedly urged by Bankers Trust in the mid-eighties, would have a significant impact both on the current concentration of the corporate underwriting business in the United States— "the new OPEC," Vojta likes to call the top investment-banking firms—and on the financial stability of commercial banks. The current problem, as he sees it, arises as a result of deregulation. Originally, Glass-Steagall was part of a trade-off: the investment banks got their protected preserve, while the commercial banks got low-cost funds through interest-rate regulation. Now, with interest rates set free, "the contract has been broken," with the result that commercial banks have been driven to make riskier loans, sometimes with fatal consequences.

Vojta and Bankers Trust apparently have no doubts

about the ability of a few commercial banks—probably no more than five or ten, Vojta believes, with Bankers Trust among them, of course—to muscle their way into leadership positions in domestic corporate underwriting. "Underwriting is a skill game," he points out, and insists, "We already have the skill, based on our present operations in federal, state, and municipal securities and our overseas operations in corporate ones." Concerning the economic effect, Vojta declares that, with Glass-Steagall out of the way, over a period of years the percentage contribution of nonloan income to Bankers Trust's annual profits could be expected to rise from the 1985–86 level of around one-third to more than one-half.

Summing up the Bankers Trust view of investment banking, Vojta says,

> It is a business heavily driven by innovation. You need one hundred and fifty to two hundred and fifty highly skilled people, daily in touch with clients and the market, providing a stream of new financial structures to meet clients' changing needs in changing market conditions. If one of your products scores a hit—as, say, mortgage-backed securities did—you build a business out of it; then after a while conditions change and you need a new product. In a way it's almost like the pharmaceuticals business—three-quarters of the products you sell may change over five years.
>
> The typical pattern is that a new product enjoys a wide margin at first, and then the margin is driven down by competition. If commercial banks are al-

lowed into the investment-banking game more fully, margins will be driven down, to the advantage of clients. The market for services—for example, corporate underwriting—will become more efficient, and the margins of the oligopoly now protected by Glass-Steagall will be reduced.[5]

Perhaps so; or perhaps not. Repeal or substantive liberalization of Glass-Steagall might bring about a healthy increase in underwriting competition, and a modest one in commercial-bank stability. Or it might bring about no significant changes at all. In either case, it is probably desirable. What surely need not be seriously feared any longer is what was most feared through most of the half-century life of the law: the specter of, say, a reconstituted J. P. Morgan–Morgan Stanley that would bestride the world of banking like the colossus that the firm once was. The fact that the 1980s spate of mergers among investment-banking firms did not reduce competition among the surviving giants would seem to provide ample evidence that, in the age of the global market and the securitization of practically everything, single-firm domination of the securities markets is not a practical possibility.

Glass-Steagall is a side issue now. Under existing law there is plenty of investment business available to both investment and commercial banks. Legislators and regulators have more important business before them in regard to securities—for example, adjusting to globalization, and curbing the various games now being played on the economy, and on investors in it, by securities dealers regardless of what name they give themselves.

313

11

The Insider Trading
Scandals

What exactly did Ivan F. Boesky do wrong? And why, in
the eyes of the law and of all but a few students of market
ethics, was it wrong? The evident initial bewilderment of
very many intelligent laymen, including stock investors,
concerning the answers to these questions, suggests that a
review of the agreed-on facts and a consideration of the
law and ethics of the matter in the context of history are
in order.

According, then, to the SEC complaint released on
November 14, 1986, and publicly acceded to by Boesky the
same day: Beginning in the spring of 1985 and continuing

until February 1986, Boesky had an agreement with Dennis Levine of Drexel Burnham—whose work in the mergers-and-acquisitions department there normally gave him access to advance information about pending mergers in which his own firm was involved as an adviser, and who, by his own subsequent admission, regularly received advance takeover information from informers at other investment-banking firms—which stipulated that Levine would pass along such information to Boesky in exchange for a cash fee. That fee was initially 5 percent of all profits realized by Boesky on investments based on Levine's information; later it was agreed between the two that the fee would be only 1 percent in cases where Boesky had already invested in a stock before Levine tipped him off about it, and Boesky decided to hold or increase his investment on the basis of Levine's tip. The amount due Levine from Boesky in fees by the contact's end was $2.4 million; however, the payment had apparently not yet been made at the time of Levine's exposure in May.

As to specific cases in which Levine had provided Boesky with nonpublic information regarding takeovers or other takeover-related information, the SEC mentioned Nabisco Brands, American Natural Resources, Union Carbide, and General Foods, among other stocks. Going on from there, the complaint described in some detail several of the cases. For example:

In May 1985, Nabisco, planning a merger with R. J. Reynolds, engaged Shearson Lehman as its investment banker. Ira B. Sokolow, Levine's contact at Shearson, learned of the pending deal and told Levine about it, whereupon Levine notified Boesky. Between May 22 and

29, Boesky bought 377,000 shares of Nabisco. On May 30, the SEC complaint went on, "Nabisco publicly announced that it [had] had exploratory talks with Reynolds, and the market price of Nabisco increased. On May 30 . . . [Boesky] caused certain of [his] affiliated entities to sell approximately 377,000 shares of common stock of Nabisco." Total profit: approximately $4 million. Elapsed time: eight days.

In April 1985, Houston Natural Gas Corporation asked Lazard Frères for advice in dealing with a possible takeover attempt by InterNorth, Inc. Robert M. Wilkins, Levine's man at Lazard, told Levine about it, and Levine told Boesky. On May 1, Boesky, through his affiliates, bought 301,800 shares of Houston Natural Gas. The next day, before the market opening, Houston and InterNorth announced an agreement to merge. On May 14 and 15, Boesky sold his Houston stake. Profit: $4.1 million. Elapsed time: fifteen days.

And so it went. The SEC complaint stated that Boesky's net profit on all of the transactions on which he had received nonpublic information from Levine amounted to "at least" $50 million. Ten days later, *The Wall Street Journal*—basing its calculations on the SEC data, and in particular on the fact that in April 1986 Levine and Boesky had agreed that the latter owed the former $2.4 million in fees—estimated Boesky's profits on Levine's tips not at $50 million but at over $200 million.[1]

Quite obviously, the rationale behind laws forbidding stock trading based on material, nonpublic information is that a trader using such information has an unfair advantage over other traders, and a stock exchange permitting such trading is conducting a game played with the equivalent of a stacked deck or a fixed wheel. The winnings of insiders come directly out of the pockets of the unwitting outsiders who trade with them. In the light of prevailing modern ethics, such a game is a scam; in the light of modern economics, it is a deterrent to outsiders to participate, and is therefore bad business. Considering these facts, it may seem astonishing that over the four centuries before the present one that stock exchanges existed here and there around the world, insider trading was scarcely challenged anywhere. In the general opinion, it was an accepted hazard of the game—indeed, it almost *was* the game. The very first stock exchange, opened in Amsterdam in 1602, was in some ways the most rigidly regulated that has ever existed; it functioned entirely by leave of the City of Amsterdam, and, along with enforcing many other rules, it tried to prevent all short selling and disciplined brokers who hung around the building after trading hours. The rules, however, did not so much as mention insider trading. For one thing, the ships of the two companies whose shares were first traded at Amsterdam, the Dutch East and West India companies, were usually so distant and so definitively out of touch that there was usually no firm inside information available anyhow. Price changes were based essentially on unverifiable rumors. Moreover, the unchallenged ethic of the time and place was that if any trader *did* by some chance possess firm inside information, so much the better for him and for anyone else deft enough to follow his lead.

Over the succeeding centuries, as stock exchanges

appeared one by one in England, various European countries, and the United States, possession of inside information continued to be looked on as a tribute to the enterprise of the possessor, and the presence of innocent others in the trading game an instructive demonstration of human gullibility. Legend holds that Nathan Rothschild's use of advance word of the outcome of the Battle of Waterloo was the chief basis of the English Rothschild fortune; in America, John Jacob Astor made a bundle on advance news of the Ghent treaty ending the War of 1812. It is probably fair to say that most nineteenth-century American fortunes were enlarged by, if not actually founded on, insider trading, much of it by officers and directors of the companies whose shares were being traded. At the turn of the twentieth century, Bernard Baruch made a fortune in the Northern Pacific panic on a tip from the son-in-law of James Keene, who had inside information—and Baruch did not scruple to boast about this exploit in his autobiography, published in 1957. As late as 1929, J. P. Morgan & Company in the Alleghany case defended itself (perhaps disingenuously) against the charge of having dispensed patronage in the form of common stock by insisting as a matter of principle that common stock was too risky for the ordinary investor (see Chapter 2); if so, the presumed reason was chiefly that the ordinary investor in common stock stood such a good chance of being victimized by insiders. (In Britain, meanwhile, sanctions against insider trading were social rather than legal; for example, at the time of World War I for a British Treasury official to use proprietary government information for his own benefit in the market was considered "dishonorable," but was not prohibited by law.)

So all but universal acceptance of a stock market as a stacked deck, or a fixed wheel, proceeded well into the present century, when it gradually ended. Probably its end in the United States was brought about chiefly because there were for the first time anywhere, beginning in the 1920s, enough innocent outsiders—potential victims of insider traders—in the market to make up a political constituency strong enough to claim its equitable rights. In any event, the Securities Exchange Act of 1934 contains the trailbreaking language providing, in general terms, that insider trading is subject to civil and criminal penalties.

Perhaps because of the sheer weight and duration of contrary tradition, this language was glacially slow to be implemented with a usable specific provision. Not until 1942 did the SEC promulgate Rule 10b-5, enabling prosecution against insider trading, and not until the 1960s did the SEC invoke the 1942 rule except in cases so flagrant as to be probably prosecutable without it, under common-law fraud. At last, in 1966, there was heard in the U.S. District Court in Foley Square, New York City, what still remains the classic insider-trading case from a legal point of view—that of Texas Gulf Sulphur Company and a group of its directors and employees.

The case concerned a major new zinc, copper, and silver mine discovered by Texas Gulf between November 1963 and April 1964 near Timmins, Ontario, some 350 miles northwest of Toronto. Almost immediately after the first promising drill samples appeared in November, Texas Gulf's executive vice-president, who had heard the good news from Timmins, bought some 1,700 shares of the company's stock for his own account, and a company vice-president and an engineer bought smaller amounts for theirs. Over the winter—when the drill site was closed down because of weather conditions, and it still was not known for sure that a huge mine had been found—other Texas Gulf employees, including the geologist who had actually examined the promising drill samples, and several people whom the geologist had subsequently tipped off, made substantial investments in Texas Gulf stock or in options on it. In April, soon after work at the drill site had resumed, the presence of a huge mine was confirmed. On the day before the Texas Gulf press conference in New York to announce the find formally, two company executives bought Texas Gulf stock for their own accounts; and either before or immediately after the end of the press conference itself, Francis Coates, a Texas Gulf director from Texas, who was on hand in New York for a company board meeting held the same day, bought 2,000 Texas Gulf shares for four family trusts of which he was a trustee, although not personally a beneficiary.

The trial judge, Dudley J. Bonsal, exonerated all those defendants who had bought stock before April 1964 on the grounds that until then no material information as to the existence of a mine had been in hand, but only "educated guesses"; he exonerated the director Coates on the grounds that the law as to the timing of investment *after* a public announcement was not clear; and he found that the only violations of Rule 10b-5 had been committed by the two Texas Gulf executives who had invested on the day before the public announcement, with the knowledge that it was coming up. However, the U.S. Court of Appeals for the Second Circuit, which reviewed the case in 1968, took a much sterner view. Finding that the November drill hole *had* provided material information about a valuable mine, it reversed Judge Bonsal on all of the accused wintertime investors and declared them to have violated the law; it confirmed Bonsal's judgment on the two investors on the day before the public announcement; and it reversed him on the director, Coates, on the grounds that Coates had improperly and illegally invested too soon after the public announcement. Since there was no further appeal, the outcome of the case was that virtually everyone accused by the SEC was found guilty of insider trading.[2]*

The effect of the Texas Gulf case was to establish that the SEC was serious about enforcing the insider-trading law and that the courts were receptive to such enforcement. It also clarified the law. The relevant rule does not actually talk about insider trading as such; its principal clauses state that in securities trading it is unlawful to "employ any device, scheme or artifice to defraud," or to "make any untrue statement of a material fact or to omit to state a material fact." When originally promulgated, it was chiefly intended to prevent fraudulent new issues of stock and deceptive practices by corporate officers and brokers, rather than to outlaw insider trading. In fact, before the Texas Gulf case it was widely thought that the rule applied only to securities firms and their personnel.

*The major exception was Thomas S. Lamont, a Texas Gulf director and an officer of the Morgan Guaranty Trust Company, who had indirectly advised the bank's trust department to buy Texas Gulf stock soon after the end of the press conference, and had bought for himself and members of his family about an hour and a half later. Lamont—who had died between the trial court proceedings and the appeals court hearing—was exonerated by both bodies. The charge against him attracted unusual attention because of his secure and prominent place in the Wall Street establishment.

Texas Gulf established as a general rule that private information affecting the prices of stocks may not legally be used by any person or firm in any market in the United States. It confirmed an end in this country to the centuries-old legal stacked-deck stock market.

Over the years since then, various cases, most of them involving relatively small sums of money, have led to various refinements of the law, but no basic changes in it. Meanwhile, a minority group usually identified with Henry G. Manne, dean of law at George Mason University in Fairfax, Virginia, has continued to insist that unrestricted insider trading is either harmless or actually beneficial, or both, and that it ought to be legal. Among the arguments presented are that unrestricted insider trading tends to make stock-market prices more efficient (that is, more clearly reflective of true values) more quickly; that the profits derived from it represent deserved compensation to useful entrepreneurs; that most of the losses resulting from it are suffered not by long-term investors but by in-and-out gamblers, who need not be the subject of social concern; and that enforcement of anti-insider trading laws necessarily involves surveillance methods more appropriate to a police state than to a democratic one. Whatever merit these arguments have, they are overbalanced by the single consideration of fairness to all investors—at least in the opinion of a vast majority of students of the subject, including, to judge from his penitent statement after his exposure, Ivan F. Boesky.[3]

Of course, the Texas Gulf case and the Levine and Boesky cases present many contrasts. It is a far cry from geologists

322

who are drilling in the Canadian muskeg dropping their ore-dripping drills and rushing to the nearest telephone to investment professionals buying, selling, and trading on corporate secrets that have come their way as a result of their advisory activities, or have been bought from others. It is a far cry from employees of a single company profiting from that company's isolated secret windfall to people in the business of merging and restructuring hundreds of huge companies forming conspiracies to profit systematically from what they know—conspiracies that, in the worst case, could heavily damage the national economy. It is also a far cry from profits of a few points on a few thousand shares of one stock to profits to one man of over $50 million (or was it $200 million?) on a whole range of stocks.

Yet the principle is the same. The Texas Gulf executives stole information belonging to their company and used it for their personal profit; Boesky improperly bought from Levine information that Levine himself had acquired improperly and used it for *his* personal profit. It is reasonable to infer that without the ground-breaking of the Texas Gulf case, the one against Boesky might never have been brought.

Now let us turn from matters of law to matters of ethics. How, for example, did Boesky himself feel about the ethics of his trade during the years when he was acquiring his vast fortune, and taking time out to write a book about how he did it? For four months after Boesky's first exposure in November 1986, the earliest publicly known date of his illegal activity was spring 1985, when he had entered into his agreement with Levine. Then in February 1987 came the admission of Martin A. Siegel of Kidder Peabody that he had made a comparable agreement with Boesky in mid-1982. As Boesky did not dispute Siegel's assertion, it may be assumed that Boesky was engaged in insider trading throughout the time when he was writing his book, *Merger Mania,* published during the summer of 1985. (The book was withdrawn from circulation by its publisher, Holt, Rinehart and Winston, late in 1986, following Boesky's exposure.)

Boesky's book, which its author describes, probably correctly, as "the first comprehensive presentation of the fundamental theory of merger arbitrage," purports to be a self-help guide to the investor, to show him how to do merger arbitrage on his own; and indeed it has no other obvious purpose unless it be self-advertisement, which one would not think was in Boesky's interest in 1985 because of the increased scrutiny of his operations that might ensue. Boesky begins by defining his business with the statement, "The arbitrageur bids for *announced* [italics added] takeover targets that he believes are undervalued in the marketplace"—that is, priced below the probable takeover price. The arbitrageur's job is to calculate the probability that the announced merger will be consummated, and to bid or not bid accordingly; as for the process of making that determination, "there are no esoteric tricks." However, Boesky goes on to say that in certain cases that he calls "special situations" the arbitrageur invests before any public announcement, and the first of his own operations that he describes—in the takeover of Getty Oil by Texaco in 1984—involved such a situation. According to his description, his decision (an exceptionally profitable one, as it turned out) to invest in Getty shares was based entirely on analysis of public facts, and the successful outcome entirely a triumph of his diligence, judgment, and audacity. He insists that risk arbitrage "is not gambling in any sense"; on the contrary, doing it properly is largely a matter of minimizing risk through careful advance analysis of all elements. Rather than gambling, it is "a craft that borders on an art." (Art or not, exactly how little it is gambling when one has an agreement with a Martin Siegel or a Dennis Levine to supply insider information is a subject that Boesky does not touch on.)

The bulk of the book is a sober factual account of the standard procedures of risk arbitrage: the various criteria by which the arbitrageur decides whether or not an announced merger will be consummated, such as the antitrust situation, management attitudes on both sides, tax considerations, and the question of whether or not the merger makes business sense; and the various techniques by which, having decided to invest, the arbitrageur does so (in Boesky's case, by buying the target's stock and simultaneously selling short the aggressor's to lock up his profit in case the merger goes through). The book goes on to present analyses of tender offers and the offensive and defensive tactics available for use in them. Its tone is entirely unemotional except as it refers to Boesky's own career, which he says he hopes may inspire others "to believe that confidence in one's self and determination can allow one to become whatever one may dream" and to "gain some understanding of the opportunity which exists uniquely in this great land." Perhaps it is too easy, in hindsight, to paraphrase an old saw by remarking that when a stock trader's talk turns to patriotism, it is time to guard your wallet.

But what shouts loudest at the retrospective reader of *Merger Mania* is what it does *not* contain: that is, any account, or mention, of the problem of insider trading in the practice of risk arbitrage. In a two-page section on the arbitrageur's sources of information, Boesky lists only published documents—proxy statements, prospectuses, annual reports, and the like. Not a word about rumors, or Rule 10b-5, or even what would seem to be de rigueur in such a book: a warning to honest arbitrageurs to be on their guard against inadvertent violations of the insider-trading law.

In the words of the law, Boesky in his book seems to have "omitted to state a material fact." Again in hindsight, this crashing, almost comical omission gives somewhat the effect that might be produced by a straight-faced account of the techniques required to achieve victory in professional wrestling.

Apart from its publicized role in the progressive and disheartening exposure of investment-banking wrongdoing in the eighties, the Boesky case calls attention to what a field of ethical mines Wall Street had become in that time—mines capable of destroying not only a Boesky but (as I have suggested previously) a person of merely normal susceptibility to temptation, or perhaps even one only a few degrees south of sainthood. To an extent, the minefield has always been there. The traditional kind of investment banker, the underwriter, regularly had (and has) inside information before new securities were (are) issued. The prospectus that he writes in collaboration with the issuing company may contain corporate information not then publicly available, and the fact of the not-yet-announced new issue itself may affect the company's stock or bond prices in a predictable way. Again, what the stock-exchange floor specialist—once the key figure in stock trading, and still an important one—knows from his order book (which he is not allowed to disclose to other traders) is inside information to which he is constantly exposed in the line of duty.

What is new in the eighties is a vast increase in the number and size of the ethical mines in the investment-banking meadow. In particular, the rise of the multi-department firm—with traditional underwriting, junk-bond underwriting, mergers and acquisitions, leveraged buyouts, new-products creation, venture-capital investing, securities trading, and arbitrage all operating under the same roof and with the same pool of capital—has, despite vaunted "Chinese walls" and diligent compliance officers, brought a quantum leap in the number of employees exposed routinely, whether they like it or not, to inside information and therefore to the temptation to use it. But it is in the merger business that the institutionalized distribution of such information and the huge potential profits available from using it have combined to create the most satanic temptations of all. In 1984 and 1985, as the chairman of Drexel Burnham later revealed, that firm several times circulated "sealed envelope" letters to its clients in which it gave secret details of prospective tender offers that it was managing, the announced purpose of the letters

.g to get the clients' advance commitment to buy junk
.ds to finance the tender offers. Included in the letters
; a warning to the recipients not to trade on the inside
ormation contained in them; however, that this estima-
e advice was not always followed is suggested by the fact
at the prices of the target stocks in some cases began to
se unaccountably after the letters had been received and
efore the tender offers had been announced. (During
1985, Drexel stopped sending out such letters.)

Quite apart from Drexel's clients, consider the number of persons and institutions who routinely know in
advance of any big takeover: investment bankers for both
sides, perhaps dozens of them in each firm; lawyers for
both sides; people in commercial banks, perhaps dozens of
them, who either finance the deal or are asked to; public
relations representatives for both sides; as well as secretar-
ies, printers, proofreaders, and perhaps a sharp-eared taxi
driver or two. In a morbid bit of nose-counting, lawyers
for the Continental Group figured out that in advance of
Continental's $2.75-billion merger with Kiewit-Murdock
Investment Corporation in 1984, no fewer than fifty individuals or firms were officially in on the secret.

An Eden, then—to change the metaphor—containing not just one forbidden apple, but an orchard of them.
In the mid-eighties it must have been a rare investment
banker who went a year, a month, or perhaps even a week
without having such a forbidden apple of bankable information dangled unasked in front of him. The Boesky case,
although not in itself morally equivocal—few can muster
sympathy for an undeniable cheat who is already so rich—
calls attention to the fact that one of the tasks ahead for

investment bankers and their regulators in the coming years is to devise ways of sharply limiting the intentional dissemination of inside information concerning mergers, and thus reducing the incidence of temptation that may be beyond endurance as well as detection.

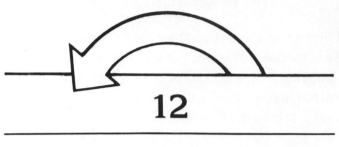

12

Toward Preventing Disaster

Ill fares the land, to hastening ills a prey
Where wealth accumulates, and men decay.

Deeply embedded in Anglo-Saxon thought is the notion
that moral obloquy attaches per se to the act of receiving
excessive compensation for work. Oliver Goldsmith in
1770 expressed it neatly and memorably in the famous
couplet quoted above from "The Deserted Village." In the
far more mobile climate of the New World, nineteenth-
century American rich men were hated, simply for being
rich, probably more and surely more vocally than they

had ever been hated in England—or than they would be in America in the twentieth century. Later, when it gradually became clear that many of the early American fortunes had been accumulated by means outside fairness, decency, and in some cases legality, the hatred was vindicated by rational cause. It became the common view that huge fortunes could be amassed in America *only* by such means, and that therefore the rich were automatically guilty. Acceding to the implication, the heirs to some of those fortunes sought to redeem their family reputations, and their own consciences, by establishing the giant philanthropies that became, and still are, among the ornaments of twentieth-century American culture. Thus was mitigated national animosity toward the rich simply *as* the rich.

Meanwhile, new fortunes were being made in new ways, and the arena where they were being made most conspicuously and quickly in the 1980s was that of investment banking and related activities. Thus it was to that arena that many of the brightest and most ambitious young graduates of that time gravitated, drawn by the well-publicized promises of reward beyond belief; it was to there that those who ended up in other fields looked, with envy and perhaps with self-protective scorn, at their colleagues who overnight were becoming not only very rich but also somewhat famous.

The old puritanical rich-is-wicked doctrine continued to hold a muted place in the back of the national mind. It was suppressed by such factors (in addition to philanthropy) as the decline of religion in general and of puritan morality in particular, and the relative legitimization of wealth-gathering brought about by the new existence of legal and governmental restraints on its methods. But it was still there. All through the early eighties there was suspicion abroad, inside and outside the investment-banking business, that if investment bankers were to some extent fiduciaries for the economy and the individual stockholder, they were somehow failing in their fiduciary duty merely because they collected for themselves millions or tens of millions in a few hours or a few days. And the suspicions focused, not unnaturally, on the activities with the most obvious potential for abuse, M&A advice and risk arbitrage—the making of mergers and the betting on them.

Then, beginning in 1986, came revelations suggesting that the suspicions had solid grounds (see Chapter 5). If a group of young men, some with access to secret merger information that provably had instant and massive market value, and some holding positions in arbitrage departments the sole purpose of which was to profit from merger-related market movements, had been for some time in systematic collusion to take improper advantage of other investors, might there not be many other such conspiratorial groups in existence? If a thirty-three-year-old Dennis B. Levine could be earning legitimately more than a million dollars per year and still think it necessary and appropriate to gain many millions more by illegally trading on inside information through a secret account in the Bahamas, did it not suggest that something was rotten on Wall Street?

It was still possible to argue that Levine et al., and even Ivan Boesky and Martin Siegel, were "isolated

332

cases," and that the personal integrity or, alternatively, fear of being caught out, on which public perception that securities trading is fair necessarily rests, was still the rule on Wall Street. The weakness of the argument was that the caught-out ones of 1986—Levine in particular—seemed to be such paradigms of the new Wall Street. When Richard Whitney, president of the New York Stock Exchange in the crisis years after 1929, and certainly a Wall Street paradigm in his time, was found in 1938 to have misappropriated funds entrusted him and was sent to Sing Sing, the event marked the start of a vast and permanent change: a gradual end of the exclusive "club" that had ruled the Stock Exchange, and to a great extent the national securities markets, since time immemorial, and the concomitant gradual rise of the open, meritocratic, relatively classless Wall Street that was so emphatically in place in the 1980s. If Whitney—fifty years old at the time of his exposure, a Harvard graduate and descendant of a prominent American family of three centuries' standing—was a characteristic type of Wall Street leader of the 1930s, perhaps Levine—a brilliant, achingly ambitious young man from Bayside, Queens, with an MBA from a principal spawning ground of business and financial strivers, the Baruch College of the City University of New York—might be considered a characteristic type of Wall Street success story of the 1980s.

Of course, such generalizations are treacherous and must be approached with caution. Surely neither man's actions could fairly be called typical of his type in his time; that is, the majority of Whitney's social and professional peers had not misappropriated trust funds, and surely the majority of Levine's did not profit illegally on inside information. But social change in the United States is apt to be driven by public and governmental attitudes arising out of dramatic events that are perceived as being symbolic; and it seems possible that, just as the Whitney case had done much to destroy public confidence in the probity of the patrician gentleman as a fiduciary of the financial markets, so the Levine case, along with the more or less similar other cases that surfaced at about the same time and soon afterward, might reasonably be expected to bring change in the Wall Street climate, and perhaps in the rules too, by drastically damaging public confidence in the new investment-banking hero and style-setter—the self-made young man of unlimited brilliance, diligence, and ambition.*

(Boesky, although the magnitude of his defalcation was far greater than that of Levine's and the publicity attending his exposure far greater, is in several ways less eligible than Levine to be compared to Whitney as the paradigmatic Wall Street criminal of his time. For one thing, Boesky was much older—indeed, about the same age as Whitney had been in 1938—whereas a key characteristic of Wall Street in the mid-eighties, as contrasted with 1938, was its focus on youth. Again, where the shock

*At any rate, the immediate effect of the first Levine revelations was dramatic enough. On June 20, just before May Department Stores announced a $66-per-share offer for Associated Dry Goods—the first big tender offer after the first Levine publicity broke—the price of the target's stock actually dropped slightly, to 46. Either no major arbitrageur knew in advance of the impending bid, or none dared act on his knowledge of it—a situation that one leading arbitrageur called "absolutely unheard-of." (*The Wall Street Journal,* June 24, 1986)

of Whitney's exposure was based on unexpected betrayal of trust—how could a member of a founding family and former stock exchange president conceivably do such a thing as embezzle trust funds?—Boesky, by contrast, had always cultivated [and traded on] a certain *louche* air, a sense that he might cheat but was probably too smart to be caught, and consequently the shock of his exposure was based on recognition that one had been righter than one knew. Even in the eighties, trust was still a key element in all securities dealings, and even Dennis Levine, partly because he was so young and so little known, was at least not generally *dis*trusted.)

A distinction must be made, though, between the symbolic significance of Whitney and that of Levine. Whereas Whitney's fall from grace had been almost pure classic tragedy, a collapse of character and morality brought about by a personal tragic flaw, those of Levine et al. had been more socially complicated. Insider trading, unlike misuse of trust funds by a trustee, is far from the most clearly defined of crimes. In the first place, a whole school of academic thought—the hard-core efficient-market school—considers that by rights it is not a crime at all, but rather a necessary and inevitable part of securities trading that serves the useful purpose of bringing market prices to their rational level sooner than they would reach that level without it.* Second, the line between violation

---

*The lengths to which free-market advocates will go to defend insider trading are illustrated by Daniel Seligman in *Fortune* (June 23, 1986, immediately after the revelations in the Levine case). Seligman, arguing that such trading is not unfair, cites Henry G. Manne's *Insider Trading and the Stock Market*, and states that Levine's insider trading "was in fact 'revenue neutral' for investors as a group"—that is, including Levine. So, of course, is burglary

and nonviolation of existing insider-trading law is an exquisitely fine one. When an M&A or arbitrage man from one investment-banking firm talks to a counterpart from another firm, for purposes of either covert information trading or simple social intercourse—as colleagues in all other businesses routinely exchange shoptalk—what is legal and what is not? Mere gossip or rumormongering is legal, as is stock-market investing by the recipient of such gossip. Trading on "material nonpublic information" is illegal. But such information, between people who know each other well, can be conveyed in a code that falls somewhere between a hint and an implication: gestures, shrugs, phone silences or hang-ups, potentially worth millions, yet probably beyond the law's reach. Thus it would appear that merger-makers and risk arbitrageurs in the eighties were subject to temptations to unethical behavior that must at times, for wildly ambitious young men recently risen from comparative poverty, have been all but beyond human strength to resist. An investment for his firm by an arbitrageur based on a veiled, cryptic phone conversation with a merger insider is one thing; Dennis Levine's secret overseas account in which he invested for himself is, of course, another. The former is morally and legally equivocal; the latter, at least in the majority view, is not. Still, Dennis Levine, and others like him having the reputation of being able to ferret out bankable information on the phone, were apparently hired (and rewarded in princely style) by their firms precisely because of that ability. That

---

"revenue neutral" for citizens as a group, assuming you include the burglars among the citizens.

336

is, sanction for treading the fine line came straight from higher authority.

In such a moral climate, did it not take a hero— or a loser—to be a thorough law-abider? And was not the game itself as much to blame for the mess as the gamesters?

Lawbreaking is not the core trouble with investment banking in the eighties. It is the visible lesion that betrays the presence of a pervasive disease, and that disease is the manipulation of money and paper for speculation rather than for the financing of production, and its concomitant, the uncontrolled creation of new debt.

Let us pause to reflect on what, under the aspect of eternity, is of overriding importance among the topics discussed in the preceding chapters, and what is merely corroborative detail. (To do this we must be bold or foolish enough to put on for a moment a prophet's mantle.) Excessive or outrageous compensation of very young and inexperienced persons, however demoralizing it may be for them and their seniors, is not in itself enough for a bill of indictment. Perhaps most of the young stars were earning their money in fees and profits, and even contributing to the economy. Moreover, such compensation is likely to prove to be an ephemeral phenomenon; when a time inevitably comes that the employer firms are no longer raking in millions by the bushel, paychecks will get smaller fast enough. Pervasive greed can be faulted in itself by a moralist but not by a social or economic analyst. Greed is a human constant; it is merely mobilized and unleashed by the possibilities that suddenly appear in times of high speculation. All of the engaging technical details that have loomed so large in our story—Rule 415, the partial tender, the lockup option, the Pac-Man defense, and so on—may be counted on to look quaint within a decade's time, like the stock-market pools of the 1920s. Even the ultimate weapons in the merger wars, the junk bond and the poison pill, will eventually come into perspective as details, albeit important ones, in a larger whole.

That whole is systematic, unbridled debt creation, the basis of all of Wall Street's great money-making machines of the eighties, from securitization of mortgages to leveraged buyouts and takeovers to debt-for-equity corporate reorganizations to the closed circle of seekers after short-term gains: pension-fund managers to corporate managements to merger-making investment bankers to arbitrageurs to junk-bond issuers and back to pension-fund managers. The debt-creating trend has historic roots in American finance, going back at least to the early sixties, when commercial banks learned how to buy new money at will through negotiable certificates of deposit—and perhaps, in a philosophical sense, beyond that to the influence of Keynes and his emphasis on deficit spending and mild inflation as the remedy for unemployment. Apparently the trend is so strong now that only a regulatory miracle can stop it short of wholesale default and disaster.

All of the iconic names of mid-eighties Wall Street— Pickens, Icahn, Boesky, Kohlberg Kravis, Drexel Burnham—ran operations based on debt, and were in the business of increasing debt day by day. Some have noted that this institutional disregard of the basic rule of household finance—that you do not borrow more than you will surely be able to pay back—has been accompanied in Wall Street by a corruption of the language used there, and have pointed out how often in the past the use of fudged language has proved to be a symptom of fudged thought. In Wall Street in the eighties there was "debt" that paid no interest, in violation of the basic principle of commercial debt. There were "bankruptcies" of solvent companies, entered into to evade liability claims. There were "fairness opinions," paid for by parties at interest, that were not fair. There were institutional "investors" who were really market gamblers. Even the term *junk bond* might come to look like a euphemism at a future time when such bonds have come to appear in retrospect to have some aspects of a Ponzi scheme.

As Michael M. Thomas has one of his saner characters say in *The Ropespinner Conspiracy* (1987), "We're living in a brave new world. Washington's running the country for the benefit of Wall Street, and Wall Street's become a gigantic video game."

The climate summed up in the sort of events just described is a thoroughly recognizable one, clearly associated with the times shortly before market crashes. (Every financial bubble in history has been associated with a pumping of new credit into the equity markets.) If in 1986 one wanted to look for parallels to the period before 1929, one could find them without trouble. In 1928–29, and again in 1985–86, the stock market boomed while the national economy stagnated. At the end of 1928, brokers' call loans at 12 percent financed stock investment on margins of 80 or 90 percent, leaving the investor subject to being wiped out by a mere blip in the market. In 1984–85, purchases of companies were being financed by junk bonds at 13 or 14 percent on margins sometimes as deep, making the companies similarly vulnerable. At the end of 1985, the national ratio of public and private debt to income stood at almost 1.7, a level usually associated with times of depression, war, or major inflation. In 1928–29, real-estate prices, having had their bubble in Florida in the middle of the decade, were falling precipitously coast to coast, with resulting bankruptcies of the holders and their banks. In the mid-eighties farm prices were collapsing again, and banks large and small were succumbing to defaulted and nonperforming loans. The stock market of 1928–29 was the plaything of insider technicians and the wealthy outside investors who profited from their manipulation of chosen stocks through investment pools. In the eighties, such stock manipulation was illegal, as it had not been before 1934; but what was it but a new form of manipulation when the price of a chosen company's stock could be reliably and predictably moved by a tender offer made with borrowed money—or even, in the case of offers made "subject to financing," without such money in hand? As for "new products," those of the twenties were leveraged investment trusts; those of the eighties, loans repackaged as securities, and junk bonds.

By way of comparison between professional stock-market techniques used before 1929 and those of the 1980s, let us look at some parallels between the notorious market "pools" of the former period and the typical greenmail operation of the latter:

On the other hand, there were marked differences. In the 1920s the national administration and the Federal Re-

1920s Pool	*1980s Greenmail*
Pool group, through pool manager and stock-market floor specialist, quietly accumulates large block of target stock.	Raider, through various brokers, quietly accumulates block of target stock.
Pool group, through sales and planted publicity, generates stock activity to draw public into the target stock.	Raider announces 5-percent-plus holding and intention to take over, causing arbitrageurs to rush into stock.
Stock price rises sharply.	Stock price rises sharply.
Pool group suddenly "pulls the plug," taking profits through open-market sales and leaving public holding the bag.	Raider negotiates sale of stock back to target company at above-market price, in exchange for promise to desist from takeover attempt.
Pool group dissolves with huge profit.	Greenmailer desists with huge profit.
Stock price collapses.	Stock price collapses.

serve, almost up to the time of the market crash, were working more or less in concert to encourage or at least to condone credit expansion. In the 1980s the Fed, most of the time, was standing against the administration on the matter; moreover, its authority under the Securities Exchange Act to regulate stock-market credit, along with the rise to market dominance of institutions that invested with all cash anyway, now made all but impossible the kind of chain-reaction crash, fueled by margin calls, that had occurred in 1929. The accomplishment of reform seemed to have been to make it unlikely that the stock market would again be, in Lester Thurow's words, "the hammer that shatters a fragile financial system." This time, if trouble were to come, it would apparently start with a national recession, triggered perhaps by an international financial crisis associated with defaulted international debt, and leading to major junk-bond defaults, bankruptcies of over-leveraged companies—and, sooner or later, a stock-market crash.

But the investment-banking excesses of the eighties did not need economic analysis to expose them. They were clearly visible to the intelligent layman's naked eye, to which they appeared as outrages to common sense. The nation had lost international competitiveness, and why? Surely in part because while Japan had been producing goods, the United States had been producing raiders, greenmailers, arbitrageurs, poison pills, and Pac-Man defenses. (In Japan there is still a whiff of disgrace for both firms in any merger, because of the implication that neither can go it alone.) Again, what of the notion, which we have seen to have been abroad in some parts of Wall Street in the eighties, that "total greed" is a virtue, indeed perhaps the key virtue for an individual or a firm in investment banking? One need not go along with the Catholic doctrine that covetousness is one of the seven deadly sins to accept the belief that in the context of financial transactions "total greed" represents a corruption of the Adam Smithian idea that self-interest promotes the public interest insofar as it promotes the beneficent functioning of the free market, but not when it serves to disrupt or obstruct that market. As a principle for investment bankers, it fails not only the theological test but also the most sympathetic economic test. It represents an idea—the social wisdom of the market—that, however controversial, has stood the

342

test of time, carried to the point of absurdity. As Peter Drucker wrote in 1986 of the takeover game as practiced in the United States in the eighties, it "deeply offends the sense of justice of a great many Americans."[1]

Such a pronouncement represents one of many indications that the state of public opinion on financial matters in the eighties enjoys at least one important, and cheering, advantage over that of the twenties. As is well known, excesses in the financial markets tend to self-correct—but only after vast damage has been done. Reform, which ideally should serve to prevent disaster and at best actually achieves that goal, tends to come at a time when the abuses addressed, having taken their toll and been fully exposed, are so thoroughly discredited that even without reform they would not reappear for a long time. So it was to a large extent with the financial reform associated with the 1929 crash. Before the crash, the voices of warning were few and muted. Stock-market pools, margin speculation, leveraged investment trusts, and pyramided holding companies caused some uneasiness, but the many who were profiting from them allowed themselves to believe that the party would go on forever. (As John Kenneth Galbraith put the matter in *The Great Crash,* in such circumstances "[government] inaction will be advocated in the present even though it means deep trouble in the future," because the alternative—immediate action—would mean "disturbance of orderly life and convenience in the present.") True enough, margin speculation and even market manipulation were still flourishing in 1933 and 1934, when the reform wave was at its peak; and, of course, some of the reforms lived to serve their punitive

343

and prophylactic role many years later. The fact remains that by 1933–34 the crash and its sequel, the Great Depression, had prostrated the nation as it had not been prostrated since the Civil War; and it is at least arguable that if all of the New Deal financial reforms had been put in place in 1928, there might have been, at the least, a far lesser crash and even a lesser depression.

In contrast, choruses of professional and public criticism greeted most of the securities-market excesses of the eighties all the while they were being committed. While the Reagan administration—following the path of the Coolidge administration—condoned the excesses, and sometimes seemed to root for them, and Congress after 1984 seemed for three years to lose heart in its efforts to achieve reform, the press and the securities industry itself kept up a drumbeat of criticism unmatched by anything before 1929.

Could it be, then, that the familiar pattern is broken, and that we have a national climate in which excesses might be corrected before rather than after the piper has been paid? On the hypothesis that such is the case, we now proceed to a summary of the principal investment-banking reform proposals that have been advanced until mid-1986 by government officials, legislators, academics, investment bankers, investment-banking lawyers, and other informed and concerned persons, along with a critical commentary on them by the present writer. Considerations of current political feasibility are ignored, partly because such feasibility is subject to changes as abrupt and unpredictable as those in the stock market itself—witness the sudden change in 1985–86 in the congressional climate regarding tax reform, and, again, the change regarding the securities markets following the Boesky scandal—and because the objective, in any case, is to present an ideal program rather than merely a possible one.

Underwriting. The long-held opinion of the highly regarded investment-banking leader John Whitehead to the contrary notwithstanding, it would appear that the SEC's two-year shelf-registration rule, or Rule 415, has earned the right to be continued in force for the present. On the record to date, its advantage to issuers stemming from more flexible timing, and to all parties to underwriting transactions stemming from reduction of the high administrative expenses that went with the old regulatory process, appear to outweigh the disadvantage of its clear tendency to bring about concentration among underwriters. In sum, this may be a case where drastically changed market conditions have made inappropriate regulatory rules that, when first promulgated, had been necessary and effective.

The great question that remains is whether a duly diligent and current investigation of the issuing company by the underwriters is now being conducted—or, indeed, *can* be—in the case of shelf-registered issues. No responsible observer has advocated a weakening of the relevant parts of the Securities Act to conform to the new situation, and surely such weakening would be an invitation to disaster. Samuel Hayes and Joseph Auerbach have suggested that Rule 415 is psychologically subversive in that it represents "a subtle step away from the primacy of investor protection." But does it actually represent such a step, rather than an accommodation of investor-protection technique to new conditions? The Securities Industry Association has gone further and suggested the exclusion of common stock from shelf registration. In the absence to date of demonstrable damage to investors, such action does not seem to be indicated.

The Rule 415 situation requires careful monitoring by the SEC and the securities industry. Rule changes, involving tightening of the eligibility rules for issuers, and perhaps the institution of a cooling-off period between registration and issue, should be carefully prepared by the SEC, and imposed at the first sign of trouble. Meanwhile, a calculated deregulatory risk has been taken that looks, as of this writing, like a sound one on balance.

Trading and arbitrage. Perfect enforcement of existing insider-trading rules would eliminate the abuses that now exist. In the absence of such enforcement—an absence readily admitted to by SEC officials—even spotty enforcement tends to induce investment firms to improve their internal compliance efforts, in the interest of protecting the fragile reputations that, along with equity capital, are their most important assets. SEC staff and financial resources should be heroically increased, especially as regards the key New York City office. The fact that in the mid-eighties the SEC, because of its income from such sources as registration fees, was actually showing an annual profit, suggests that the national commitment to securities-law enforcement in the interest of investor protection was grossly inadequate.

The 1986 insider-trading cases exposed the existence

346

of conspiracies within the investment-banking business to exchange inside information concerning prospective mergers and reorganizations. Congress should consider amending the securities laws to include a categorical prohibition of such information exchanges, with appropriate penalties, whether or not it can be proved that the individuals or firms involved profited from the information thus obtained.

Leveraged buyouts.   The two principal areas of concern relating to that great new market phenomenon of the eighties, the leveraged management buyout, are the price of the transaction in which a company's stockholders are bought out and the top-heavy debt with which the company is, by the nature of the transaction, burdened after the deal.

As to price, to the current checks on self-serving actions by management participants—that is, investment-bank fairness opinions, approval by financially disinterested outside directors, and state appraisal rights—should be added another: more intensive scrutiny of LBO proposals by the SEC in search of violations of the existing laws. A single SEC suit charging illegal stock manipulation by management participants in their own favor in an LBO would serve to put all managements on notice. Moreover, the SEC should use its basic disclosure powers to ensure that stockholders in companies being bought out by management have access to the same information, particularly regarding cash-flow projections, that is given to potential lenders.

New legislation is required to solve the problem of

the freezing out of competitive bidders who might otherwise stand ready to raise the purchase price. Such legislation should supplant case-by-case court decisions by prohibiting the granting of lockout options by managements planning LBOs, and permit LBOs to be executed only after all potential bidders have had an opportunity to investigate the company and bid for it if they choose to.

Concerning the potential harm in leveraging itself, the tax deductibility of debt used to finance LBOs should not be reduced or eliminated. Discriminatory tax policy should seldom if ever be used to influence public policy in areas remote from taxation. Rather, the Federal Reserve should extend, beyond its January 1986 restriction on junk-bond financing of takeovers, the use of its power to restrict debt for purchase of stock.

LBOs should not be outlawed across the board. A strong company managed and substantially owned by a family whose new generation has no interest in continuing the management—to take one example—may be well served by an LBO, as may once-strong companies whose quality of management has deteriorated. In such cases, a clear business purpose is served. A rough, though by no means invariable, rule of thumb in distinguishing between good and questionable or bad LBOs is whether the buying-out investors, at the time of the buyout, intend to hold the property for the long term or to sell it publicly or privately at a profit within a few years—that is, whether the buyers' objective is ownership-management for the long haul, or paper entrepreneurship. By that test, the major LBOs of the eighties, virtually all of them engineered by firms unabashedly involved purely as investors with categorical expectations of selling out, would fall into the questionable or bad category.

I have said earlier that the principal force in eventually curbing LBO excesses may be the market itself. Indeed, even as this is written, some would say that the supply of eligible companies has so contracted, and competition among LBO engineers has become so fierce, that the market, like the marines, has landed and the situation is in hand. But the market, for the interim and the future, needs some help from the federal government.

Mergers and acquisitions. The welter of federal legislative proposals and initiatives in 1983–85 reflected a growing national consensus that something had to be done about tender-offer rules—that Peter Drucker was right when he wrote, in 1986,

> There is a great deal of discussion about whether hostile takeovers are good or bad for the shareholders. There can be absolutely no doubt, however, that they are exceedingly bad for the economy. They force management into operating short-term. . . . But worse still, companies are being forced to do stupid things to prevent themselves from being raided. . . . The fear of the raider is undoubtedly the largest single cause for the increasing tendency of American companies to manage for the short term and let the future go hang.[2]

The 1983–85 proposals and initiatives came to nothing; yet in 1985 and 1986 the abuses and excesses addressed in them were as much in evidence as ever before, if not more so.

The simplest, most sweeping, and most drastic of the 1983–85 proposals—mandating a tender offer for all shares, with certain exceptions, when an acquirer's holding of a target company's shares reaches a stated low percentage, such as 5 percent—appears to be too drastic to be appropriate to the circumstances. Its advantages as a panacea—that it would theoretically make raider abuses impossible, and target-company defensive abuses unnecessary—are overbalanced by its excessive interference in the free-market process. Moreover, such a provision could probably be circumvented by a tender offer made at an intentionally inappropriate price.

What is still in order, as it was in 1983–85, is a legislative package carefully balanced between restraints on raiders and restraints on targets, aimed at fairness to stockholders, avoidance of damage to the aggressor and target companies, and, not least, making the unfriendly-takeover process more civilized. Such a package should include the following measures:

1. *Restraining the aggressor*
   • closing the ten-day disclosure window of the Williams Act
   • forbidding two-tier, front-loaded offers
   • forbidding tender offers made "subject to financing," which may distort markets and lead to takeovers without being financially viable themselves
   • forbidding the exacting of greenmail by the aggressor in exchange for abandoning his aggressive intentions

2. *Restraining the target*

• forbidding the issuance of golden-parachute separation agreements to executives after a tender offer has been made

• forbidding share repurchase programs that exclude the aggressor (reverse greenmail)

• forbidding counter-tender offers for the shares of the aggressor when they are "subject to financing"

• forbidding issuance of poison-pill securities that include contingent rights in the aggressor's stock

In addition to these measures, reconsideration might well be given to Representative Rodino's idea of requiring detailed disclosure by the aggressor of the likely social impact of the proposed merger.

As to merger and acquisition fees, if those currently paid to investment banks are unreasonably high, leading to excessive promotion of such transactions by investment bankers and damaging the public reputation of their industry, the fees ought to be lower. This, however, is not a matter for federal legislation or regulation. Price-fixing in the securities industry has not existed since the end of fixed commissions on stock-exchange transactions in 1975, and it should not be revived now. Nor should investment bankers—even though some of them have themselves said repeatedly and emphatically, either in public or in private, that fees are scandalously high—be urged on their own initiative to reduce those fees. The initiative should come from the client companies whose officials now agree to and pay the fees. If, as strong evidence suggests, some such officials either do not object to paying a merger adviser's asking price (which may be negotiable), or are actually eager to pay it, they should be called to account by directors and stockholders. Directors who fail to do this are neglecting their fiduciary duty to the company's stockholders. If large institutional stockholders would question managers and directors about announced fees that appeared to be excessive, and sell their stock if they did not receive a satisfactory answer, fees would presumably come down. And, at the least, there would be an improvement in the moral tone of Wall Street, where, as things stand now, every public announcement of a multimillion-dollar fee is a kind of boast, and a challenge to others to demonstrate their muscle and macho by getting more.

The other half of necessary takeover reform—reining in excessive use of credit—could theoretically, at least for the short term, be controlled by regulation rather than by legislation.

So long as aggressor companies can legally obtain virtually unlimited amounts of cash through bank borrowings or junk bonds, overleveraged takeovers will continue to take place. Under existing law, federal and state regulators of banks, insurance companies, and savings institutions have the power to set margin rules and capital requirements adequate to control excessive lending to finance takeovers. But in recent years such power has been laxly used. A start toward reversing the trend was made with the Federal Reserve's January 1986 imposition of margin requirements on junk bonds issued by shell corporations to finance takeovers. The Fed should extend the reach of these requirements, at least for a time, and the percentage margin requirement can be increased if conditions warrant. Bank and insurance company regulators have yet to act decisively or, apparently, to take seriously the dangers inherent in excessive takeover credit. Before they are likely to do so, there must be in office a federal administration that will appoint and encourage vigorous, skillful, aggressive regulators who are ready to intervene in the market as conditions demand.

Meanwhile, of course, the market's self-correcting tendency may be expected to operate, however late and painfully. The debt-raising restructurings, often negotiated under extreme duress, with which companies seeking to immunize themselves from takeovers by damaging their balance sheets and their economic viability, would decrease or cease if takeover fears were reduced or eliminated, either by new legislation and regulation or by the collapse of overleveraged aggressor companies. The viability of junk bonds would disappear if the appetite of institutional investors for them were to end, as a result either of regulatory discouragement of their use or of the default of a few major issues.

Looking beyond the merger market to the broader financial scene and beyond interim solutions to long-term ones, Henry Kaufman proposes a bold new federal move. Noting that "the distinctions among groups of financial institutions are rapidly diminishing" and that "their markets are not as segmented as they used to be," he urges Congress to establish a National Board of Overseers of Financial Institutions, consisting of members from the Federal Reserve System, federal supervisory agencies, and the private sector, with general responsibility to "provide an integrated overview of our major financial institutions" and to balance the use of credit to obtain profit against public responsibility. Such a board, Kaufman says, should be empowered to "promulgate uniform accounting standards and improved reporting procedures for balance sheets and income statements, and require fuller disclosure of information that would be helpful to directors and trustees of institutions and to the public." In Kaufman's dream, all credit-supervisory responsibilities should eventually come under its control, and "perhaps in time this board could take on greater importance than the Federal Reserve Board." Meanwhile, "a somewhat similar but looser board" would be formed to deal with multinational financial institutions.

All crises bring forth calls for superboards of "wise men" to take the situation in hand, and all such proposals, when first put forward, tend to sound like pie in the sky. Certainly Kaufman is right that recent rapid changes in financial institutions and their markets tend to make the current fragmented array of credit-controlling bodies look unwieldy and confused. On the other hand, a great deal of political infighting would certainly have to precede the virtual superseding of the existing bodies by such a national board; and certainly the multinational board's authority would be limited by the reluctance of nations to give up sovereignty over their affairs. Yet the Kaufman proposal deserves serious consideration and further study. After all, the now powerful SEC and the Commission of the European Economic Community looked visionary when first proposed.

Drucker, for one, fears that the takeover wave may

well end "with a whimper rather than a bang"—that is, with a single billion-dollar takeover–junk-bond default that would become a major scandal, destroy the market for junk bonds, and thus dry up the supply of money to finance hostile takeovers. In any case, Drucker feels optimistically that by one means or another—legal, judicial, or market-based—"we surely will find a way to protect the going concern against hostile takeovers which subordinate all other interests—employees, the enterprise's long-range growth and prosperity, and the country's competitive position in an increasingly competitive world economy—to short-term speculative gain."[3]

Even though it has sometimes seemed that what investment bankers do in the eighties is invent new games so that they can beat other people at them, it would be unjust to leave the subject of the American investment-banking industry in this decade with the impression that that industry has not generally served its clients, investors, and the national economy well. It has adapted to drastically changed conditions with astonishing agility. In the field of underwriting, its adaptation has been such as to put the market for new capital in perhaps as healthy a condition as it has ever enjoyed, to the advantage of corporate clients and, so far, of investors. Its traders have added vast amounts of liquidity to the securities markets. Its inventive minds have devised ingenious new instruments, such as currency and interest-rate swaps, that have served corporate clients without creating large new problems. In the merger field, it has provided the complicated carpentry to effect many mutually advantageous corporate fits. Even its instigation of mergers, to whatever extent such instigation has existed, has, along with less happy effects, been a leading factor in producing a stock-market boom that has enriched many investors. And its vast and well-advertised profitability and high compensation scale has attracted to it many of the brightest and best-motivated young Americans, creating a cadre that will surely be indispensable in dealing with further national and worldwide financial change in the immediate future.

In the midst of such innovation and turmoil, the appearance of new areas of abuse, and the reappearance of old ones, was probably inevitable. And we may finally note again that some investment bankers themselves have been among the first to call attention to those areas, and to call for reform.

Apart from abiding by the law, what may we reasonably expect of investment bankers in the area of social responsibility? Surely they cannot—and probably they should not—be expected to try to return to the old patrician style and live by a code of their own devising that they believe embodies a higher set of social standards than that held by others. In the present cultural and political environment, the signals that they get from society about where their duty lies are confusing indeed. The free-market school, as broadly embodied in the current national administration, would urge them to pursue their selfish interest to the utmost, in the faith that if they do so the public interest will take care of itself. Extreme reformers, on the other hand, would want them to be so hemmed in by laws and regulations that they could operate only as high-level technicians, with little room for creative innovation.

In achieving a civilized balance between these extremes, perhaps we may hope for a future change of moral fashion in Wall Street toward the prevalence of values other than money. For the one certain thing is that there will be changes. Whether the new investment banking of the eighties represents a permanent new mode of operation or a transient bubble is a complicated question. Structurally, the great trend toward internationalization of markets and of banking operations, with all its pessimistic implications of compromised regulation and its positive ones of closer international ties, appears irreversible; indeed, the trend seems bound to accelerate. On the other hand, the speculative frenzy—multiple mergers and buyouts, outrageous leveraging, rampant securitization of assets—has every historical earmark of a bubble that, like all bubbles, will be deflated or will burst. History tells us that when the bubble is gone, the ethical climate will be better. However, in the present climate, in which attempting to put other values above money in Wall Street appears to be an actual prescription for failure, we must rely on other sanctions to bring about salutary change.

One such sanction might be a disastrous economic and market crash. That would be the free-market solution. All historical evidence suggests that the Invisible Hand, if left unrestrained, turns eventually on the body it serves. Had we better not restrain its suicidal tendency while there is still time, by timely application of carefully chosen new legislative and regulatory rules, to supplement the restraining effect of court decisions and public opinion?

357

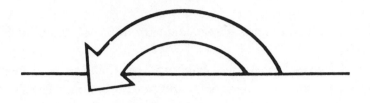

Notes

1: The Time of the Takeovers

1. Samuel L. Hayes III, "The Transformation of Investment Banking," *Harvard Business Review,* January–February 1979, p. 160; author's interview, Robert H. B. Baldwin; Paul Hoffman, *The Dealmakers* (New York, 1984), p. 142; *The New York Times,* July 19, July 20, August 17, 1974.

2. Jane Gross, "Against the Odds: A Woman's Ascent on Wall Street," *The New York Times Magazine,* January 6, 1985, p. 16ff. Samuel L. Hayes III, "Investment Banking: Power Structure in Flux," *Harvard Business Review* (March–April

1971). *The New York Times,* January 18, 1984, January 29, 1985.

3. Hayes, "Investment Banking," pp. 136ff.; author's interviews, Thomas A. Saunders III and Martin Lipton; "The Traders Take Charge," *Business Week,* February 20, 1984, p. 58ff; "Wall Street Puts Its Own Money on the Line," *Institutional Investor,* June 1984, p. 61ff.

4. In the District Court of the United States for the Southern District of New York, Civil Action No. 43-757, *U.S.A.* vs. *Henry S. Morgan et al.,* opinion of Harold S. Medina, C.J. (1953), p. 41 (hereinafter called "Medina Opinion"); author's interview, John H. Gutfreund; *Institutional Investor,* April 1984, p. 267.

5. Mortgage-backed securities: *The New York Times,* November 7, 1984, p. D1; *Institutional Investor,* February 1985, p. 55; Goldman, Sachs Annual Reports 1983, 1984. Stripped bonds: *The New York Times,* October 10, 1984, p. D23; October 16, 1984, p. D21; *Forbes,* February 11, 1985, p. 197; *Personal Investor,* November 1984, p. 52. Interest-rate swaps: *The New York Times,* February 7, 1985, p. D6; *The Wall Street Journal,* January 16, 1985, p. 1; *Institutional Investor,* November 1984, p. 71ff.

6. *The Wall Street Journal,* December 24, 1984, p. 9; *The New York Times,* January 13, 1985, sec. III, p. 4.

7. *The Wall Street Journal,* October 30, 1984, editorial page.

8. *Business Week,* December 31, 1984, p. 41; *The New York Times,* January 8, 1985, p. D5, and March 6, 1984, p. D4; *Forbes,* April 9, 1984, p. 41.

9. Johan Huizinga, *Homo Ludens: A Study of the Play Element in Culture* (Boston, 1955), pp. 197–98, 205.

10. Author's interview, John Gutfreund; *Business Week,* March 4, 1985, p. 80ff.; *Institutional Investor,* January 1985, p. 23; February 1985, p. 130.

11. *The Wall Street Journal,* May 18, 1984; J. M. Keynes, *The General Theory of Employment, Interest, and Money* (New York, 1964), p. 159.
12. *The New York Times,* August 19, 1984, sec. III, p. 12.

2: Dignity, Mystery, and Change

1. Irwin Friend et al., *Investment Banking and the New Issues Market* (Cleveland, 1967), p. 80.
2. Vincent P. Carosso, *Investment Banking in America* (Cambridge, Mass., 1970), pp. 1–3; 167. Fritz Redlich, *History of American Business Leaders* (New York, 1951), vol. 2, chapter 21, "Investment Banking," pp. 304ff.
3. Redlich, *History of American Business Leaders,* passim; Carosso, *Investment Banking in America,* pp. 14–20, 25, 33, 37, 73–74.
4. Redlich, *History of American Business Leaders;* Carosso, *Investment Banking in America,* pp. 5, 74–75, 77, 87, 89, 100–01; Garret Garrett, *Where the Money Grows* (New York, 1911), pp. 49–50. Thorstein Veblen, *The Engineers and the Price System* (New York, 1921).
5. Carosso, *Investment Banking in America,* pp. 128ff., 137, 159, 165ff., 194, 179.
6. Medina Opinion, pp. 2, 29ff.; Carosso, *Investment Banking in America,* pp. 204, 217, 224, 258, 261, 265–67; Friend et al., *Investment Banking and the New Issues Market,* pp. 94, 332.
7. Carosso, *Investment Banking in America,* pp. 282ff., 287, 290; Frederick Lewis Allen, *Only Yesterday* (New York, 1931); John Brooks, *Once in Golconda* (New York, 1985), p. 186ff.
8. "Public Policy Aspects of Bank Securities Activities," Department of the Treasury, November 1975; Rudolph L. Weissman, *The New Wall Street* (New York, 1939), pp. 198–247; Robert Sobel, *The Big Board* (New York, 1965), p. 293ff.;

Carosso, *Investment Banking in America*, pp. 356ff., 368ff., 375ff.

9. Medina Opinion, pp. 39, 44–45, 57, 260ff., 392, 397; Carosso, *Investment Banking in America*, 356ff., 368ff., 375ff., 395, 400, 406; Friend et al., *Investment Banking and the New Issues Market*, p. 385.

10. Medina Opinion, passim; Carosso, *Investment Banking in America*, p. 458ff.

11. John Brooks, *The Go-Go Years* (New York, 1984), p. 278ff.; Friend et al., *Investment Banking and the New Issues Market*, p. 18ff. *Abuse on Wall Street: A Twentieth Century Fund Report* (Westport, Conn., 1980), p. 365ff.

12. Cary Reich, *Financier: The Biography of André Meyer* (New York, 1983), pp. 15, 18, 19, 48, 158, 230–36, 345.

13. Samuel L. Hayes III, "Investment Banking: Power Structure in Flux," *Harvard Business Review*, March–April 1971.

3: Names and Numbers of the Players

1. Salomon Brothers, Inc., Annual Report, 1984; Paul Hoffman, *The Dealmakers* (New York, 1984), p. 38ff.; *Fortune*, September 7, 1981, p. 52ff.; January 10, 1983, p. 74ff.; December 24, 1984, p. 108ff.; *The Wall Street Journal*, September 17, 1984; *The New York Times*, October 10, 1984; *The Economist*, March 16, 1985, p. 28; author's interview, John Gutfreund, April 1984.

2. Hoffman, *The Dealmakers*, p. 44ff.; Paul Ferris, *The Master Bankers* (New York, 1984), p. 128ff.; *Institutional Investor*, January 1984, p. 53ff.; *Fortune*, July 9, 1984, p. 155ff.; J. K. Galbraith, *The Great Crash* (Cambridge, Mass., 1961), p. 48ff.; *Business Week*, November 12, 1984, p. 144; *The Economist*, December 17, 1983, p. 75; *The New York Times*, August

16, 1984; *Barron's*, July 2, 1984, p. 40; author's interviews, John C. Whitehead, John L. Weinberg.

3. Robert Sobel, *The Big Board* (New York, 1965), p. 334ff.; Hoffman, *The Dealmakers*, pp. 42–44; Ferris, *The Master Bankers*, p. 135ff.; *The New York Times*, January 29, April 7, June 4, 1985; author's interview, Thomas A. Saunders III.

4. Medina Opinion, p. 88ff.; Hoffman, *The Dealmakers*, p. 90ff.; Ferris, *The Master Bankers*, p. 106ff.; *Fortune*, September 6, 1982, p. 55ff.; *Institutional Investor*, January 1984, p. 56, and April 1984, p. 141ff.; *Esquire*, May 1984, p. 58ff.; *The New York Times*, April 1, June 6, 1985.

5. Medina Opinion, pp. 58–64; Ferris, *The Master Bankers*, p. 13ff.; *The Wall Street Journal*, February 17, 1981; *Institutional Investor*, June 1984, p. 86ff.; *The New York Times*, April 1, 1984; Morgan Stanley Annual Review, 1983, 1984; author's interviews, Robert H. B. Baldwin and Thomas A. Saunders III.

6. Medina Opinion, pp. 19ff., 51ff., 71ff., and 183ff.; Hoffman, *The Dealmakers*, pp. 51–53, 95–97; *Fortune*, April 16, 1984, p. 89, and May 14, 1984, p. 129; *Business Week*, May 6, 1985, p. 107; Ken Auletta, "The Fall of Lehman Brothers," *The New York Times Magazine*, February 17 and 24, 1985; *The Wall Street Journal*, April 4, 1984; *Institutional Investor*, August 1984, p. 79ff.

7. Medina Opinion, p. 87ff.; Hoffman, *The Dealmakers*, p. 62ff.; *Business Week*, December 24, 1984, April 22, 1985, and July 7, 1986; *Forbes*, November 19, 1984, p. 207ff.; *Institutional Investor*, October 1981, p. 217ff.; *Fortune*, September 3, 1984, pp. 89–92; Drexel Burnham Lambert, "On Corporate Control: The Takeover Threat to Middle Market Companies" (1983).

8. *The Wall Street Journal*, September 6, October 25, 1984; *Institutional Investor*, December 1984, p. 82ff., and June

1985, p. 199ff.; Ferris, *The Master Bankers,* p. 45; *The New York Times,* May 6, 1985.

4: Off the Shelf

1. Samuel L. Hayes III, "The Transformation of Investment Banking," *Harvard Business Review,* January–February 1979; Paul Ferris, *The Master Bankers* (New York, 1984), p. 27; author's interviews, Thomas A. Saunders III. See also Joseph Auerbach and Samuel L. Hayes III, *Investment Banking and Diligence* (Boston, 1986).

2. Author's interviews, Thomas A. Saunders III and Bevis Longstreth; Paul Hoffman, *The Dealmakers* (New York, 1984), p. 106ff.; letter, Morgan Stanley to SEC, February 2, 1982; *Abuse on Wall Street: A Twentieth Century Fund Report* (Westport, Conn., 1980), pp. 374–75; *The Wall Street Journal,* November 13, 1984.

3. Author's interviews, Thomas A. Saunders III; Morgan Stanley public and internal documents.

4. Letter, Thomas A. Saunders III to George A. Fitzsimmons, June 7, 1982; Ferris, *The Master Bankers,* p. 30; author's interviews, Thomas A. Saunders III.

5. *Institutional Investor,* April 1984, p. 86ff.; Gary Gray and J. Randall Woolridge, "S.E.C. Rule 415: Benefits and Costs for Equity Issuers," Securities Industry Association, *Securities Industry Trends,* vol. 10, no. 5 (1984).

6. Hoffman, *The Dealmakers,* p. 111; *The Wall Street Journal,* January 9, 1985; *Institutional Investor,* August 1985, p. 205ff.; author's interview, Bevis Longstreth.

7. *Financier,* April 1982, p. 59ff.; *Business Week,* March 5, 1984, p. 83; *The Wall Street Journal,* November 13, 1984, and March 13, 1985; *Institutional Investor,* February 1983; author's interviews, John Whitehead and Irwin Friend.

5: The Trading Game

1. Salomon Brothers Annual Review 1984; Paul Ferris, *The Master Bankers* (New York, 1984), p. 114ff.; *Institutional Investor,* May 1985, p. 197ff.; *Business Week,* February 20, 1984, p. 58ff.; *The Wall Street Journal,* August 7, 1985, and September 10, 1986; *The Economist,* March 16, 1985, p. 28ff.; *The New York Times,* September 11, 1985; *Institutional Investor,* January 1985, p. 247ff.; *Business Week,* November 26, 1984, pp. 163–64.

2. *The New York Times,* January 13, 27, April 10, 1985, and May 18, 1986; *Fortune,* July 9, 1985, p. 155ff.; author's interview, Robert E. Rubin.

3. *The New York Times,* June 24, 1984; *Fortune,* August 6, 1984, p. 102ff.; *Forbes,* August 27, 1984, p. 152ff.; *The Atlantic,* December 1984, p. 94ff.; *The New York Times,* January 25, 1985 and *Forbes,* October 8, 1984 (see note on pp. 147–48); *The New York Times,* March 7, 1984; Ivan F. Boesky, *Merger Mania* (New York, 1985).

4. *The Atlantic,* December 1984, p. 99; Hope Lampert, *Till Death Do Us Part* (New York, 1983), pp. 48, 87; *The Wall Street Journal,* March 2, 1984; author's interview, Ira L. Sorkin; Paul Hoffman, *The Dealmakers* (New York, 1984), p. 162ff. First Boston case: *The Wall Street Journal,* May 6, 1986. Levine case: *The New York Times,* May 13, 14, June 6, 1986; *The Wall Street Journal,* May 13, 15, 19, 21, 1986. "Yuppie Five" cases: *The New York Times,* March 28, May 29, June 2, 6, 1986.

5. *The Economist,* March 16, 1985, p. 28; *Institutional Investor,* May 1985, p. 165ff.; Cary Reich, *Financier: The Biography of André Meyer* (New York, 1983), pp. 243, 249; author's interview, Felix Rohatyn; *The New York Times* and *The Wall Street Journal,* November 15, 1986, *et seq.*

6: A Walk Through the Merger Battlefield

1. Ninth Circuit Court of Appeals, *Jewel Companies* v. *Payless Drug Stores Northwest,* 1984, quoted by Francis M. Wheat in a speech to the 16th Annual Institute on Securities Regulation, Los Angeles, November 1, 1984.

2. Charles Francis Adams, Jr., and Henry Adams, *Chapters of Erie* (1869–71; reprint, Ithaca, N.Y., 1956); Stewart H. Holbrook, *The Age of the Moguls* (New York, 1953); Vincent P. Carosso, *Investment Banking in America* (Cambridge, Mass., 1970); U.S. Department of Commerce, "Merger Trends and Prospects for the 1980s" (Washington, D.C., December 1980); Harvard Business School, "Notes on Corporate Mergers," paper no. 0-282-088 (1982); *Economic Report of the President* (Washington, D.C., 1985); David L. Babson & Co., "The Babson Staff Letter" (Boston, November 21, 1984).

3. U.S. Department of Commerce, "Merger Trends and Prospects"; Harvard Business School, "Notes on Corporate Mergers"; Samuel L. Hayes III and Russell A. Taussig, "Tactics of Cash Takeover Bids," *Harvard Business Review,* March–April 1967; Robert H. Hayes and William J. Abernathy, "Managing Our Way to Economic Decline," *Harvard Business Review,* July–August 1980.

4. For a chart summarizing the principal merger/tender transactions 1980–84, including those discussed in this chapter, I am indebted to Martin Lipton.

5. Hope Lampert, *Till Death Do Us Part* (New York, 1983); *Forbes,* March 11, 1985, p. 138.

6. Francis M. Wheat, speech, November 1, 1984.

7. Summaries of 1984 takeovers: *Fortune,* January 21, 1985; *Institutional Investor,* January 1985. See also *The New York Times,* March 10, 1984 (Gulf-Chevron); *The Wall Street Journal,* August 1, 1984 (Champion–St. Regis); *Fortune,* April

30, 1984; *Institutional Investor,* July 1985; and *Business Week,* March 4, April 30, May 27, 1985 (raiders).

8. *Business Week,* April 22, 1985, p. 66ff., *The New York Times,* July 4, 1985, *The Wall Street Journal,* September 10, 1985 (Turner-CBS); *The Wall Street Journal,* May 21, 1985, and September 29, 1986, *Business Week,* June 3, 1985 (Mesa-Unocal); *The New York Times,* June 20, 1986.

9. *The Economist,* December 3, 1983, pp. 89–90; *Institutional Investor,* January 1984, pp. 256–59; *Business Week,* October 1, 1985, p. 93ff.; Donald C. Clark, speech before the annual meeting of stockholders, Household International, May 14, 1985; *The New York Times,* November 20, 1985 (Household court decision); *The Wall Street Journal,* July 26 and October 31, 1985 (Crown Zellerbach); *The Wall Street Journal,* October 25 and November 4, 1985, and *The New York Times,* November 11, 20, 1985 (Revlon); author's interviews, Martin Lipton and Joseph Flom.

10. *The New York Times,* August 13, 1985; *Cornell Executive* (journal of the Graduate School of Management, Cornell University), Summer/Fall 1983; author's interview, Brian M. Freeman.

7: Buying Out the Store

1. Since 1983, the general and financial press has contained almost daily references to leveraged buyouts, in general or in particular, and not all sources used can be listed here. Among those of particular interest that have been drawn upon are *The Economist,* November 5, 1983, p. 83; *Newsweek,* March 19, 1984, p. 73; *Forbes,* April 9, 1984, p. 39ff., and April 23, 1984, p. 32ff.; *The New York Times,* May 14, June 9, 1984; *The Wall Street Journal,* June 19, December 6, 1984, and March 19, 1986; *Business Week,* July 2, 1984; *Institutional Investor,*

March 1985, p. 69ff. See also *Economic Report of the President* (Washington, D.C., 1985), p. 195.

2. *The New York Times,* April 4, November 23, 1985; *Institutional Investor,* July 1984, p. 136ff., and April 1984, pp. 183–85.

3. Bevis Longstreth, *Management Buyouts: Are Public Shareholders Getting a Fair Deal?* (Washington, D.C.: Securities and Exchange Commission, 1983).

4. Author's interview, Theodore J. Forstmann.

5. Longstreth, *Management Buyouts; Fortune,* November 11, 1985, p. 169.

8: Why Do They Do It?

1. This discussion of academic research is based largely on papers presented at the Conference on Takeovers and Contests for Corporate Control, Center for Law and Economic Studies, Columbia University School of Law, November 13–15, 1985. Of particular interest are Michael C. Jensen, "The Takeover Controversy: Analysis and Evidence"; Edward S. Herman and Louis Lowenstein, "The Efficiency Effects of Hostile Takeovers: An Empirical Study"; John C. Coffee, Jr., "Shareholders Versus Managers: The Strain in the Corporate Web"; Ellen B. Magenheim and Dennis C. Mueller, "On Measuring the Effect of Acquisitions on Acquiring Firm Shareholders." See also SEC, *Advisory Committee on Tender Offers: Report of Recommendations,* separate statement of Frank H. Easterbrook and Gregg A. Jarrell (Washington, D.C., 1983); *Economic Report of the President* (Washington, D.C., 1985).

2. Conference on Takeovers; *Forbes*, October 7, 1985, p. 173.

3. *The New York Times,* November 11, 1985 and January 21, 1986; author's interview, Bruce Ruddick.

Notes

4. Letter from Simon H. Rifkind to the author, December 5, 1985; Richard Roll, "Empirical Evidence on Takeover Activity and Shareholder Wealth," and Jensen, "The Takeover Controversy," presented at Conference on Takeovers; *The Economist*, March 22, 1986, p. 45; *The Wall Street Journal*, September 30, 1986.

5. *The New York Times*, September 30, 1984; *Fortune*, January 20, 1986, pp. 18ff. and 32ff., and February 17, 1986, p. 98ff.; *Forbes*, November 18, 1985, p. 122ff.; author's interview with Kenneth Yarnell; merger-fee schedule of Wachtell, Lipton, Rosen & Katz (1984).

9: The Search for a Level Playing Field

1. "Legislative History of the Williams Act, Public Law No. 90-439, as Enacted July 29, 1968": In the Supreme Court of the United States, October term 1975, *The First Boston Corporation, Petitioner,* v. *Chris-Craft Industries, Inc., Respondent* . . . Lodged with the clerk by the Petitioner, September 22, 1976. A. A. Sommer, Jr., "Untender Tender Offers: Time to Call a Halt?" George M. Ferris Lecture, Trinity College, Hartford, Conn., November 19, 1984; Francis M. Wheat, speech, November 1, 1984; SEC, *Advisory Committee on Tender Offers: Report of Recommendations* (Washington, 1983); *Economic Report of the President* (Washington, 1985); *Business Week*, February 11, 1985, p. 26.

2. SEC, *Advisory Committee on Tender Offers: Report of Recommendations;* author's interviews with Martin Lipton and Joseph Flom.

3. *The Wall Street Journal*, March 14 and May 10, 1984; *Fortune*, May 27, 1985, pp. 20ff. and 101ff.; author's interview, Martin Lipton. The 1984 chronology of congressional and other reform attempts is drawn substantially from the following: Hearings Before the Subcommittee on Telecommunications, Consumer Protection, and Finance, House Committee on Energy and Commerce, Timothy E. Wirth, Chairman, March 28–May 23, 1984; *Business Week,* June 11, 1984, p. 44ff.; *The Wall Street Journal,* June 22, 1984; *Business Week,* August 13, 1984, p. 58; *The New York Law Journal,* September 18, 1984; *The Wall Street Journal,* November 26, 1984, and January 2, 1985; *The Economist,* March 23, 1985, p. 163; *The New York Times,* May 20, 1985; *Business Week,* June 10, 1985, p. 54; *The New York Times,* July 1, 1985; *The Wall Street Journal,* July 9, 1985; *Business Week,* December 2, 1985, p. 41; *Time,* December 23, 1985, p. 51; *The New York Times,* January 9, 1986.

4. Wheat, speech, November 1, 1984; Joel Seligman, "Stock Exchange Rules Affecting Takeovers and Control Transactions," presented at Conference on Takeovers; *The Wall Street Journal,* December 28, 1984; *The New York Times,* July 4, 1986.

5. Chronology of Federal Reserve Board action: *The New York Times,* December 7, 9, 20, 24, 31, 1985; January 4, 9, and March 11, 1986; *The Wall Street Journal,* February 21, March 11, and August 18, 1986.

6. Deborah A. DeMott, Professor of Law, Duke University, "Antitakeover Rules," 1985; Peter Frazer, "The Regulation of Take-Overs in Great Britain," 1985; *Advisory Committee on Tender Offers: Report of Recommendations;* Sommer, "Untender Tender Offers"; *The New York Times,* November 25, 1985; *The Wall Street Journal,* April 4, 1986.

10: Commercial Banks in the Global Arena

1. Department of the Treasury, "Public Policy Aspects of Bank Securities Activities" (Washington, D.C., 1975); Securities Industry Association, "Erosion of Glass-Steagall Barriers," *Securities Industry Trends,* April 26, 1983; Samuel L. Hayes III, "Investment Banking: Commercial Banks' Inroads," *Economic Review,* Federal Reserve Bank of Atlanta, May 1984; J. P. Morgan & Co., Inc., "Rethinking Glass-Steagall," December 1984; *The New York Times,* September 14, 21, 1984.

2. Securities Industry Association, "Erosion"; *The New York Times,* December 4, 1984, June 5, July 9, 1985, February 6, 19, 1986; Hayes, "Investment Banking"; *The New York Times,* November 20, 1984, February 18, 1986.

3. *The Wall Street Journal,* September 19, 1984; *The New York Times,* July 9, 1985; *Fortune,* March 3, 1986, p. 54ff.; "Bankers Trust New York Corporation," Harvard Business School case study, 1985.

4. *The Wall Street Journal,* September 19, 1984; *Institutional Investor,* October 1984, p. 209ff.; *Fortune,* March 3, 1986, p. 54ff.; Harvard Business School, "Bankers Trust New York"; *The New York Times,* March 17, 1985, and April 10, 1986; Bankers Trust New York Corporation, Annual Report 1985.

5. Dwight B. Crane and Samuel L. Hayes III, "The New Competition in World Banking," *Harvard Business Review,* July–August, 1982; *The New York Times,* January 21, 1985, March 22, July 22, 1986; *The Wall Street Journal,* May 24, 1985, July 7, September 17, 1986; Citicorp Annual Report, 1985; author's interviews, Thomas C. Theobald and George J. Vojta.

11: The Insider Trading Scandals

1. *The New York Times,* November 15, 1986; *The Wall Street Journal,* November 24, 1986.

2. Bernard M. Baruch, *Baruch: My Own Story* (New York,

1957); Robert Skidelsky, *John Maynard Keynes* (New York, 1986); John Brooks, *Business Adventures* (New York, 1969), p. 118ff.

3. Henry G. Manne, *Insider Trading and the Stock Market* (New York, 1966).

4. Ivan F. Boesky, *Merger Mania* (New York, 1985).

5. *The Wall Street Journal,* December 9, 1986; *The New York Times,* January 15, 1987.

12: Toward Preventing Disaster

1. John Kenneth Galbraith, *The Great Crash* (New York, 1955); *The New York Times,* January 21, 1986; *The Wall Street Journal,* April 24, 1986; Peter F. Drucker, *The Frontiers of Management* (New York, 1986), chapter 28; Michael M. Thomas, *The Ropespinner Conspiracy* (New York, 1987).

2. Drucker, *Frontiers of Management.*

3. Drucker, *Frontiers of Management;* Felix G. Rohatyn, testimony before the Joint Economic Committee of Congress, quoted in *Financier,* March 1986; Henry Kaufman, *Interest Rates, the Markets, and the New Financial World* (New York, 1986), p. 59ff.

New-Era
Investment-Banking
Terms

Business-judgment rule   A legal doctrine generally allowing corporate directors wide latitude to take actions, including rejection of tender offers, that they believe to be in the best interests of their corporation.

Golden parachute   A special separation agreement that provides for a payment to a corporate executive only in the event that he loses his job as a result of a takeover of his company.

Greenmail   The repurchase by a corporation of the stockholdings of a raider, through an above-the-market offer not made to any other stockholders. In exchange, the raider agrees to desist from further takeover efforts.

"In play" Of a publicly held corporation: in such a situation that, as a result of one or more threatened takeovers and the resulting acquisition of a large portion of the corporation's stock by risk arbitrageurs, it is virtually certain that the corporation will ultimately be taken over by one entity or another.

Insider trading Broadly, stock trading based on "material," "nonpublic" information that has been misappropriated. Illegal under Rule 10b-5 of the SEC under the Securities Exchange Act of 1934.

Interest-rate swap A type of transaction of recent invention used by large corporations in managing their debt.

Junk bond A high-yield bond of less than investment grade. In corporate takeovers, such a bond is issued to help finance a transaction, and is so designed that the interest will be paid out of the resources of the target company after its takeover.

Leveraged buyout (LBO) A transaction in which the stock of a publicly owned company is bought out in full by a small group, usually including members of the company's management. The transaction is financed largely by borrowing, the debt to be paid ultimately out of the company's future operations or sales of some of its assets.

Pac-Man defense An attempt by a company for which a tender offer has been made to defend itself against takeover by making a counter-tender offer for the aggressor company.

Poison pill A right issued to stockholders of a company threatened by takeover, granting them privileges that are contingent on the possession by an aggressor of a stated percentäge of their company's stock. The rights are designed to make the completion of a takeover much more expensive, perhaps prohibitively so, for the aggressor.

Raider An individual or group that acquires a block of

stock in a target company with an eye to making a tender offer, forcing a proxy fight, or forcing a greenmail repurchase by the target company.

Risk arbitrage   Stock speculation by individuals or firms, based on whether or not announced or rumored mergers, or related transactions such as leveraged buyouts and corporate reorganizations, will in fact take place.

Rule 415   SEC rule, promulgated in 1982, drastically changing the nature of securities issuance by the largest companies, by allowing them to register a quantity of securities for a period of two years, and then put them on sale piecemeal, with no waiting period before each sale, over that period.

Stripped bonds   Bonds that are stripped of their interest and sold at a discount with no interest payable; the interest coupons formerly attached to them are sold separately.

Tender offer   An offer to buy all or part of the stock of a given firm, over a stated period, usually for the purpose of taking the firm over.

Two-tier tender offer   An offer to buy part of a target firm's stock at a stated price, often in cash, and the balance in a different transaction that may be less attractive to the target-company stockholders, such as in exchange for securities of the tenderer.

White knight   A third company solicited by a takeover target to outbid the original aggressor, because the white knight is more acceptable to the target than the original aggressor.

Acknowledgments

Among the many people who helped me in one way or another with this book, I want to thank the following in particular for information, ideas, and criticism: Karen Arenson, Geoffrey Bell, Stephen Berger, Warren Buffett, Ron Chernow, Joseph Flom, Brian Freeman, Irwin Friend, John Gutfreund, Samuel Hayes III, Erich Heinemann, Edward Herman, Thomas Huertas, Leon Levy, Martin Lipton, Bevis Longstreth, Louis Lowenstein, Morris Mendelson, Damon Mezzacappa, Willard Rappleye, Steven Rattner, Simon Rifkind, Felix Rohatyn, Bruce Ruddick, Cynthia Wainwright, John Whitehead, and Kenneth Yarnell, Jr.

Thanks are due The Twentieth Century Fund for its sponsorship of the project.

J. B.

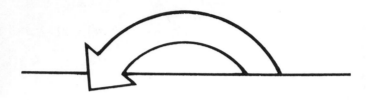

Index

Index

379

Index